THE PROPHETESS

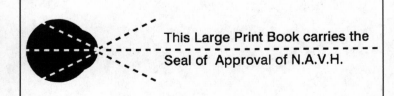

This Large Print Book carries the
Seal of Approval of N.A.V.H.

THE PROPHETESS

DEBORAH'S STORY

JILL EILEEN SMITH

THORNDIKE PRESS
A part of Gale, Cengage Learning

GALE
CENGAGE Learning·

Farmington Hills, Mich • San Francisco • New York • Waterville, Maine
Meriden, Conn • Mason, Ohio • Chicago

GALE
CENGAGE Learning®

LIBRARY OF CONGRESS CATALOGING-IN-PUBLICATION DATA

Names: Smith, Jill Eileen, 1958– author.
Title: The prophetess : Deborah's story / by Jill Eileen Smith.
Description: Large print edition. | Waterville, Maine : Thorndike Press, 2016. | © 2016 | Series: Daughters of the promised land ; #2 | Series: Thorndike Press large print Christian historical fiction
Identifiers: LCCN 2015051119| ISBN 9781410488428 (hardcover) | ISBN 141048842X (hardcover)
Subjects: LCSH: Deborah (Biblical judge)—Fiction. | Women in the Bible—Fiction. | Bible. Old Testament—History of Biblical events—Fiction. | Large type books. | GSAFD: Bible fiction.
Classification: LCC PS3619.M58838 P76 2016b | DDC 813/.6—dc23
LC record available at http://lccn.loc.gov/2015051119

Published in 2016 by arrangement with Revell Books, a division of Baker Publishing Group

Printed in Mexico
1 2 3 4 5 6 7 20 19 18 17 16

To Randy,
Who inspires every hero in every story.
Who instills hope in me with every
book I don't think I can write.
Who sees God's purpose and good
in every challenge.
And who bakes our Christmas
cookies every year.
Thank you.
I love you!

■ ■ ■ ■

Part 1

■ ■ ■ ■

When new gods were chosen, then war was in the gates.

Deborah,
poet, prophetess, and judge in Israel

And the people of Israel again did what was evil in the sight of the LORD after Ehud died. And the LORD sold them into the hand of Jabin king of Canaan, who reigned in Hazor. The commander of his army was Sisera, who lived in Harosheth-hagoyim. Then the people of Israel cried out to the LORD for help, for he had 900 chariots of iron and he oppressed the people of Israel cruelly for twenty years.

Now Deborah, a prophetess, the wife of Lappidoth, was judging Israel at that time. She used to sit under the palm of Deborah between Ramah and Bethel in the hill country of Ephraim, and the people of Israel came up to her for judgment.

Judges 4:1–5

PROLOGUE

1126 BC

Early morning dew tickled Deborah's sandaled feet on the path to the village well,
and palm trees waved their stout leaves as if
in greeting. She tugged the donkey's reins
closer to the well's open mouth and smiled
into the dawn's pink rays.

Today would be a good day.

She patted the donkey's neck, then undid
the ropes holding several goatskins. "You
wait right here for me now." The donkey
lifted its head, and she scratched its ears,
laughing. "I won't be long."

She hummed a soft tune and glanced back
at the beast once she reached the well. First
she would fill the trough to give it drink,
then fill the goatskins for her father's
journey to Shiloh the next morning.

"Oh, Adonai, I wish I could go with him."
The prayer came from a place deep within
her, one of longing to see the tabernacle of

the Lord again, to worship Him there. But she could not go, a virgin alone with just men, even if they were her family — not without her mother's agreement. "Why does she not see the beauty of Your holiness in that place, Adonai?"

The breeze kissed her face as if in answer, and Deborah closed her eyes, feeling the weight of the water filling the skin, while her mind sifted through memories of her past visits to that place where God had put His name. If only she had been born into a family of scribes who copied the pages of the law, or stood near enough to smell the incense and see the golden lampstand glowing through the curtained veil.

She released her longing in a heavy sigh. Perhaps next year she would be wed and could accompany her husband on the yearly journey. *Please, Adonai, let it be.* The face of her cousin Amichai flashed in her mind, accompanied by a quick flush to her cheeks. Surely he would speak to her father soon. At fifteen, Deborah should already have the promise of betrothal in hand, but still she waited. Why? Had not Amichai indicated he would call, that he wanted her to be his?

Deborah heaved the last of the water skins up the side of the well, the heaviness of change filling her heart. Perhaps she had misread his comments or had not listened with a discerning ear. But . . . was that possible? Surely his promise of "I am coming soon" meant exactly what his light kiss to her cheek indicated. She had not misread the ardent look in his eyes.

Then why? The fault could only lay with her, as her mother repeatedly said. "Save your opinions for after you are wed. Why do you argue with the young men who would speak with you? You tell them what to do! Ach! Is it any wonder they are not standing in line to speak to your father?"

Deborah's cheeks heated and her eyes stung with the memory. Her mother's sharp words were a slap to her face, and Deborah had tried to heed the rebuke. Truly she had. But advice just slipped past her tongue, and sometimes even her father had come to seek it when her mother was not within earshot. Did that not mean that her words held worth?

The breeze tugged her headscarf, and she yanked hard as the skin reached the well's lip. She quickly tied its leather strings, carried the heavy sacks to the donkey, and draped them over the sides. She glanced heavenward, fearful that her thoughts had taken more time than she had been given. But the pinks of dawn still shivered on the edges of the horizon, just now fading to the sun's yellow glow.

"We must hurry," she said, taking the donkey's reins, knowing the animal cared not a whit what she said to it. But she had chores she must attend to before her father left the next morn, and she dare not delay.

Still, the longing to linger remained, and the wind picked up, its breeze no longer gentle as it whipped the scarf behind her head, her hair blowing with it. She stilled, gripping the donkey's reins, fear curling in her middle. One glance about told her she was alone, but even the donkey's fur bristled and it did not move.

"Is someone there?" Deborah's bold call disappeared with the rush of wind. She braced herself in the face of its battering, her heart pounding strangely as she stared into the hills around her. She should run for cover. But her feet would not obey her sluggish thoughts. What was happening to her?

She placed both hands on her knees and sought to draw breath. *Please.* Fire heated her middle and she doubled over, sinking to her knees.

Do not turn to idols or make for yourselves any gods of cast metal: I am the Lord your God.

She gasped, the voice loud in her ear. *But I don't . . .* Her weak words fell away.

Consecrate yourselves! The command jolted her and she planted her face to the earth, her breath heaving.

Be holy, for I am the Lord your God. Keep My statutes and do them. I am the Lord who sanctifies you.

Her whole body trembled as the light of day suddenly blinded her already closed eyes.

I am the Lord your God. You shall not fear the gods of the Amorites in whose land you dwell.

Deborah's breath came in great gasps even after the light faded. She remained prostrate, waiting for more, but the air around her returned to its gentle breath, and her heart slowly found its normal rhythm.

I am the Lord your God, the voice had said. Had God Himself spoken to her?

The words were those she recognized from the Law of Moses, but clearly they had not come to her from mere memory.

What do You want from me, Lord? Even her thoughts carried the remnants of fear as they asked the silent question.

But she heard no more in response.

She placed both hands in the dirt and pushed her trembling body from the

13

ground, sweat tracing little beads down her back. She looked up at the waving palm fronds overhead and glanced about the area surrounding the well. Nothing seemed out of place, as though the day were like any other. She drew a breath, then another. But despite the normalcy of her surroundings, the sound of the voice in her ears still resonated.

The donkey nudged her hand, jolting her, reminding her of all that had yet to be done to prepare for her father's journey. *We will surely be late now.* The thought should have troubled her, for she hated to disappoint him when he counted on her for help, but home suddenly seemed like a distant country. And the memory of the words would not leave.

Lappidoth stretched his long legs from beneath the wooden stool and set his stylus on the table beside a length of parchment. Unable to sleep well, he'd started the tedious work by lamplight. He glanced at the copy of the law spread before him, written in his father's careful hand. The perfect lettering, an exact duplicate of one written by his grandfather before him, filled his gaze. This was his legacy, his calling as a Levite. A duty to continue the work of a

14

scribe that he had faithfully fulfilled since the day his father first taught him to read and write.

A familiar ache accompanied the memory, one of longing to again share this trade with the man he had so long admired. If his father and mother had lived, he would not be stuck in this small room on his uncle Yuval's vast estate. He would reside in the respected residence of his father in Kartah with a wife and sons by now.

He shook himself, the sudden urge to escape this musty room nearly choking him. He drew a breath, begging release from the pain of loss. If he had been older, stronger, wiser . . . Somehow he should have fought off the Canaanites and protected his family. But the attack on Kartah had reduced the city to smoldering embers.

Why did You let me live? He had asked the question of the Almighty more times than he could remember, but with every jot and tittle he copied from the law, he was reminded of a purpose. The God who made him was not the enemy. Canaan and their foreign gods and their evil ways — they were the enemy. Someday God would bring justice.

He swallowed, his throat feeling suddenly drier than the air in the stuffy room. He shoved his body from the chair, snatched the goatskin by the door, and headed to the well. Dawn had crested the horizon now, the time when the women would surround the well in their hurry to get water and head home to start the day's baking.

He blinked hard and breathed of the fresh air, realizing he should have tried longer to sleep than to work by lamplight. But if he had, he would have missed the women, and perhaps, if God were favorable to him, he would glimpse the beautiful Deborah there again.

He walked on, his step lighter at the thought, passing merchant stalls just beginning to open and mud-brick homes aligning the path in this village between Bethel and Ramah in Ephraim. Far from where Kartah once stood in Zebulun. But at least the place had been hidden from enemy forces thus far. His mother and father and sisters would have been safe here.

Anger, swift and dark, rushed in on him. The memories still clung too often to his thoughts like the sludge of a river to his feet. Seven years was time enough to move on with his life, as his uncle had frequently reminded him. "Take a wife," he had said at first weekly, now almost daily. "Raise children. Do you want to be alone the rest of

16

your life?"

Lappidoth had simply shrugged or found some way to put him off. The woman who had captured his imagination was too good for such as he. Beautiful, bold, fiery Deborah could have her pick of men in this town, and surely by now her father had secured her betrothal. Though Lappidoth's aunt would have spread such gossip to him quickly if his assumptions were true.

Perhaps spending his life alone was not such a bad prospect. At least then he would not feel the need to fear for his beloved's safety. He would not be guilty of helplessly watching her pain. He stopped several paces from the well, shoving the relentless thoughts aside. The past was past and there was nothing to be done about it. His uncle was right. He should find some nice woman and settle her in his home — a home he must begin to build if he expected to fill it with a wife and children.

He looked toward the well where the women had begun to gather. Surely there was an available virgin among the group. But then — there she stood, so close he could shorten the distance between them in a few easy strides. *Deborah.* His heart beat faster at the way her name sang in his thoughts. She stood tall and proud, a jar on her shoulder, beside a donkey heavy-laden with water skins. Her long dark hair blew like a wild thing, barely kept in place beneath a fiery golden-orange headscarf. Laughter spilled from her pink lips at something her friend or a cousin said, and when she turned toward him ever so slightly, he caught the shining brilliance of the rising sun reflected in her dark eyes.

His heart skipped its racing beat.

Ask for her. Ask Yuval to speak for you.

He couldn't. How could he possibly? He turned away, the sudden thought so unnerving he forgot all about the need for water until he was halfway home and had to turn back to the well once more. Foolish man to think such thoughts. She was Deborah. Favored only daughter of one of the village elders. Outspoken at times. He had heard her grand opinions at the wine treadings while she laughed with a male cousin she seemed to favor — and put often in his place. He had nearly smiled at the chagrined look on her cousin's face at that last gathering, until he recalled that at least that man could speak with her. Lappidoth had never been able to muster the courage to draw close, let alone say a word.

Had her cousin already asked for her hand? *You will not know if you do not ask.*

Then he would not know! He chided himself as he returned to the well to find it blessedly and yet disappointingly empty of the female chatter. He quickly filled his skin and hurried back along the path he had come.

Ask for her. The thought seemed different as he passed the merchant stalls once more, and it shouted in his head when he passed her house and caught another glimpse of her handing the reins of the donkey to her brother.

He paused but a moment lest she see him and think him odd.

"Deborah?"

Lappidoth startled at her mother's voice calling from inside the house, and then other voices of her father and more brothers came from behind, the men obviously preparing to take a trip. He fairly ran back toward his uncle's estate, slipped into his dim room, and sank onto his mat. He should continue his work until his aunt called him to the morning meal. The cool goatskin reminded him of his thirst, and he took a greedy drink. What kind of wife would Deborah be? A challenging one — of that he was certain.

Ask for her. Had God spoken to him? Or was the thought one borne of his silent

19

desperation after living alone in this place, far from home without the love of family, for too long? He sipped again, tied the string tight at the neck, and set the skin on the floor beside him.

He would never know if he didn't ask. He would be a fool to risk her rejection. But after sitting in darkness for too many breaths, he forced his weighted limbs to stand, opened the door once more, and strode to his uncle's house. He would give Yuval what he wanted — to seek a wife in Deborah and to silence the thoughts that begged him to ask.

Lappidoth folded his hands in front of him in a vain attempt to steady his nerves. How was it possible? And yet here he stood in Deborah's sitting room with his uncle and her father, who, though he carried a hint of anxiety to prepare to be off to Shiloh, had taken the time to hear them out and agreed to the match! The buzz of excited voices filled his ear as Deborah's mother and grandmother spoke in another room just off the sitting area, and Yuval reached into a pouch and pulled out a handful of gold to show Deborah's father he was quite willing to pay the bride-price.

"I am sure we can trust you to pay what is

required," her father said, brushing away the precious metal as if it was of no consequence. Yet Lappidoth caught the quick accounting gleam in his eye, the one that showed both men that her father was more astute than he let on. "We must at least let the girl give her approval before we accept," he said, smiling amiably.

"Of course she will accept." Deborah's mother stepped into the room, hands on her hips, her round mouth pulled taut in a grim line. She whirled about and muttered something about Deborah having few options, but Lappidoth decided he must have misunderstood the woman. Certainly Deborah had other choices. She was the most beautiful virgin in the entire village, probably in all of Israel. And those intelligent eyes! He could imagine getting lost in one look from her and, in quiet moments, holding deep conversations about the law he spent days copying letter by letter, carefully applying, leaving nothing out.

"She's coming now," her brother Shapur said, striding confidently from the courtyard into the house. "She filled the skins. We will be ready to leave tomorrow when you are, Father." He left again before anyone could speak.

The house grew suddenly still, and Lappidoth's palms moistened where he clenched them. He released both hands and rubbed them along the sides of his best robe. Deborah's mother came to stand in the arch between the two rooms, her grandmother's head poking behind, while her father strode to the house's main door.

Deborah's light footsteps seemed loud in his ear as she entered the court, and she stopped abruptly at the sight of her father. Her eyes, so expressive when he'd seen her laughing with her cousin, held an almost wild glow now.

"Is something wrong, Abba? I'm sorry I'm late. It is hard to avoid the gossips at the well." Her words were rushed, as though she had run the whole way. Her dark brows drew down, and a slight frown dipped the corners of her mouth. Lappidoth's breath caught and held, and he could not take his eyes from her. What would he do if she refused him? But a daughter would not refuse her father's choice.

Why are they giving her a choice? But he knew. The precedent had been set long ago by their matriarch Rebekah when her mother and brother allowed her to choose whether to go with a stranger to marry a cousin she had not seen.

The thought tightened his middle into a

hard knot. He stood rigid, barely glancing at Yuval, who seemed completely composed. But his uncle's outward peace did not ease Lappidoth's worry when he looked once more toward the door where Deborah stood staring at him.

"Nothing is wrong, my daughter," her father said, his voice gentle and cheerier than it had been moments before. "Everything is perfectly right." He touched Deborah's shoulder. She flinched, a strange reaction. Surely Lappidoth's presence had put her on edge. "We have an offer of marriage from this young man, Lappidoth, and his uncle Yuval. You remember Lappidoth, come to us from Zebulun when his family was killed in a Canaanite raid?"

Lappidoth studied Deborah's gaze, saw a myriad of questions replace the original wild look. Her mouth tightened, much like her mother's had done moments before, and he felt suddenly at a loss for breath.

"Yes, I remember, Abba." She looked at her father then, and her expression changed to one of uncertainty, even pleading.

"They have more than enough for the bride-price," her father said, as if to reassure her that he would be well compensated. "And they have promised you many gifts." As if she would be appeased with material

23

possessions. But wasn't that the way things were done?

And yet, Lappidoth wanted more. He wanted her to look at him the way he longed to gaze at her. He wanted her to smile into his eyes. Surely, once they were wed and she got to know him, he could coax these things from her.

"But what of Amichai?" Her voice had dropped in pitch, but Lappidoth did not miss the question.

Her father released a slow breath. "Lappidoth is here and his uncle and I have made the agreement, my daughter. You need say no more." He turned from her then and faced both Lappidoth and Yuval. "We agree," he said, louder than he had spoken moments before.

Lappidoth caught Deborah's sharp intake of breath. But she did not speak again, and after an awkward pause, her father and his uncle exchanged the kiss of greeting, Yuval paid the bride-price, and Deborah was quickly surrounded by her squealing womenfolk.

Lappidoth followed his uncle through the door. The wedding would take place in six months, as soon as Lappidoth could build a house and call for her.

But legally, she was his. Yuval slapped him

on the shoulder and made some disparaging comment about it being time he acted like a man, then walked ahead of Lappidoth, hurrying to make his own preparations to join some of the village men for the trip to Shiloh.

Deborah awoke three days later with a start, heart racing, beads of sweat dripping down her face. She sat up. Where was she? She looked about, frantic to see her surroundings in the predawn darkness. She never slept well when Abba was away, especially when her brothers accompanied him. Her mind whirled, searching for a place to land, until at last she recalled her recent rushed betrothal. Why had Abba thought it necessary to settle the matter so quickly? Why ask her opinion and then not allow her to give it?

A sick feeling settled within her. How could she possibly marry Lappidoth? He was tall and awkward, too quiet, and he lacked confidence and the qualities she respected in a man — though she could admit he was not without a few handsome traits in that straight nose and those vivid dark eyes. Still, she had wanted Amichai. A moan escaped and she curled onto her side, longing to sink again into blessed sleep.

A loud wail pierced the air, jolting her from her trek toward self-pity. What was that? She tilted her head, this time aware of distant screaming.

"Deborah!" The voices drew closer, snapping her attention, and moments later her mother rushed into the room. "Come at once! Get dressed. Hurry!" Her mother's normally high-pitched voice was louder than usual.

Deborah jumped up, snatched her tunic and robe, and ran barefoot as she tied the belt at her waist, completely forgetting her headscarf. "What is it?" The commotion was coming from the city gate. Women and children lined the streets, and the sounds of mourners filled the predawn air.

Her grandmother appeared at her side. "Come, child. I want to see, and I need your strength." The old woman clutched Deborah's arm, her grip tight, and the two hurried toward the gate. There they found her mother weeping and wailing, kneeling in the dirt over the prone body of . . .

"Abba?" Deborah tugged her grandmother forward and fell to her knees beside her father's broken body. Her throat clogged, and she found it difficult to swallow.

"Shapur!" Her sister-in-law's wail pierced

Deborah's ears, and she turned to see not only her father but her three brothers and several men from the village — all men who had taken the journey to Shiloh, including Lappidoth's uncle — dead.

Deborah felt the release of her grandmother's hand as the old woman sank to the dirt, her keening carrying with that of the other women. Deborah stilled at the sight, staring at her father's bloodied face. She stood slowly, like an aged woman, and walked down the row of men, counting and trying to recognize each face.

"Deborah?" Lappidoth's voice cut through her haze.

"There are twenty-three," she said. It was a normal thing to say, wasn't it? She moved among her brothers and stood over each one without answering Lappidoth or even looking his way.

He caught up with her and placed a gentle hand on her shoulder. "Come with me. Let the women prepare them for burial."

"We will never find enough biers or places to put them in the caves." Her voice matched the flat, lifeless feeling in her gut.

"We will find a way."

She looked at him then. "Why did you not go with them?" He was a scribe. Why had he stayed behind when so many men had gone up to worship?

"I could not leave my aunt, and my uncle did not allow it."

"But you are a man with a mind of your own. Surely you could have made the decision for yourself."

"Would you have preferred to find me here?" He pointed to the bodies even as he grasped her shoulder and turned her away.

"No." Her voice lowered and her cheeks heated. He was her husband. How strange that sounded in her mind. She could not wish him thus. But she could not look at him again. Better to have her father than him. For she had hoped to talk her father out of the agreement and still give her to Amichai.

There was no hope of such a thing now.

"There is no need to wait six months," she said without thinking. Surely he would think it himself. "That is why you are here with me, is it not?" How bold she was. Her mother was right. She was too outspoken for her own good.

"I came to help," he said, his tone holding neither rebuke nor censure. "But yes, it would seem prudent if we wed as soon as the time of mourning is over in order for me to care for you and your mother and grandmother. Unless you wish to wait."

How easily he changed his mind. Infuriating! But she nodded, for no words would come past the sudden lump in her throat.

This was not real. This carnage and wailing going on around her was just one of her many visions or dreams. She would awaken and find all was right with her world.

But a week later, after the bodies of her father and brothers lay buried in the cave, she quietly entered the bridal tent and married Lappidoth.

1

Ten Years Later
1116 BC

Deborah stood on the rise above the well, looking toward the forests that circled their village on three sides. A hill banked them on the fourth, neatly hemming them in. Except for the fields that stretched from their town walls to the edge of the trees, a man would have to walk a great length and to a great height to find them here. And yet, even here Deborah knew it was only by God's mercy that Canaan's forces and their commander, Sisera, had not discovered them.

How long, Adonai? The oppression of her people had been sporadic in the days when Lappidoth's family and her father and brothers had been killed. But the strength of Canaan had grown.

She glanced at her sons, Lavi and Elior, chasing each other in the grasses, battling

31

with sticks as though they were swords. The smile she showed at their innocent play vanished when she heard Lavi shout, "I'm going to kill you, Sisera!"

Elior, almost ten, stopped short. "I'm not Sisera. It's your turn to be him."

An argument ensued, one Deborah had heard far too often. She placed a hand over the growing babe within her. *Be a girl.* At least with a daughter she would not have to fear losing her to a battle against a force they could not defeat. Women did not go to war. A girl could stay safe in her home. *With me,* she thought, knowing how selfish that seemed. But the longing would not abate.

"Come, boys," she called to her bickering sons. "It is time to do your chores." She glanced behind her, lifted the water jug to her head, and strode down the hill toward the gate. Moans and complaints followed her, but both boys were quick to obey.

"Why can't we go to the fields with Abba? He's not far." Lavi's lower lip stuck out in a familiar pout. At seven he had a way of wrapping his desires into words she found hard to resist. But resist she did.

"No," she said in a tone that brooked no argument. To let them out of her sight . . . They were all she had. So she had taught them to obey her without question, something even their father seemed incapable of making them do. But she would not be manipulated, even for the sake of love.

The boys ran ahead of her and reached the gate before she could get there. Good. Time alone was a rare and blessed thing since her marriage. When had she grown so weary? Where had the spirit of the young girl gone, the one who had heard the voice of God and sang to Him as she walked along the way?

The babe moved beneath her hand, a familiar feeling from this active unborn child. "You are not going to give me a moment's peace, are you, little one?" But the feeling of coming birth did hold an appeal nothing else could equal. How was it possible to love her offspring more than the man who had given her the chance to be the mother every woman longed to be?

If Lappidoth would just stand up for himself now and then. Speak his mind. Stop always giving in to their children's every whim, even her every wish. Her cousins would laugh her out of the village if they could hear such thoughts. But what woman didn't want a man of solid strength?

She paused as the gate drew near, glancing up at the tower where her uncle and some of the older men sat debating and settling legal matters for those who needed them. The men were nearly ancient, and sometimes she wondered if they even heard half of what the people asked of them, but there was no one else in the village to take up such a task. Certainly not Lappidoth, despite his knowledge of the law. He was too busy farming their land and doing scribal work for those who could not read or write.

The sound of whistling came from behind her, and she turned. She had taken too much time at the well, for there strode Lappidoth, his thin frame making her feel as though she had failed to feed him well all these years.

"There you are," he said, smiling down at her as he approached.

"You are early." She glanced at the sky. "The meal won't be ready for some time. I did not expect you yet."

He shrugged. "It is of no consequence. I have a letter to craft for one of the elders."

She nodded, and he fell into step with her. Always the amiable one. Never complaining. Sometimes she wished he would complain just to give her a reason to argue with him!

"I was thinking," he said as they passed by the guards and the houses of their neighbors toward their home near the end of the main street. "Would you like me to teach you to read the law and to write the letters?"

She stopped so abruptly the water jar nearly slid from her head. She steadied it with a shaky hand and stared at him. "Why would you do that? I will have no time for such a thing when the baby comes." She barely had time now, but oh, how desire stirred within her breast at the very thought!

"I would teach you because I thought you would find pleasure in the knowledge." He gazed down at her, his dark eyes holding hers in that tender look he gave her when she knew she least deserved it. "You are an intelligent woman, Deborah. And God speaks to you in the dreams at night. I think He would be pleased to have you learn the law for yourself."

She swallowed, suddenly undone by such kindness. She had never told him of the vision she'd had the day her father sealed her betrothal. Yet he believed her dreams came from God. Why did he have such faith in her? Why was he so good to her when she sometimes barely tolerated him? "I will have no time," she said again.

"When the children are asleep, you can set aside other chores and I will teach you."

"Then who will spin the cloth for the clothes to put on our backs?"

"I will hire a maidservant for you."

She searched his kind face. Saw the hint of a smile tip the edges of his beard. "We can afford such a thing?"

He nodded and gave her shoulder a gentle squeeze. "We will make a way, beloved. Now say yes to my offer and let us go home."

Now suddenly he was bold? But the slightest hint of respect for him surfaced as she slowly nodded. "Yes," she whispered, afraid if she spoke too loudly she might risk revealing the sudden emotion filling her. "Thank you."

He slipped her hand in his and walked with her the rest of the way home.

A week later, Deborah heard the loud shouts of the men at the city gate, carrying to her on the way home from the well. If they didn't learn to hold their tongues, they would give away their village's hidden place. She glanced up, catching sight of her uncle Chayim standing toe to toe with one of his brothers. A sigh and swift surge of irritation filled her.

"Go and wait for me near the gate," she said to Elior and Lavi, "but do not go beyond the walls without me."

They ran off, fairly eager to play in the side room where unwanted visitors or those who would be questioned were held. Her sons loved to pretend they were prisoners when the room was empty, a choice of play that often left Deborah more worried than she should rightly feel.

The voices grew louder, interrupting her last glimpse of her sons entering the room. Her irritation mounted as she climbed the steps to the area where the men met above the gates. They abruptly quieted at the sight of her.

"Deborah, whatever are you doing here, and in your condition?" Her uncle's thin brows narrowed, his concern for her welfare comforting, though it did not ease her worries. Did the man have no sense?

"Uncle Chayim, you must keep your voice down," she said, her gaze stern. She glanced from this man who could have given his son Amichai to her to wed, to his younger brother who seemed ready to continue the argument. "God has graciously protected us from Sisera until now, but if you do not keep your speech to a normal tone, you will awaken the entire forest and anyone who might be spying within it."

Her uncle nodded, his smile too assuring. "Of course, my dear child. You are right, as always."

Deborah walked to the parapet and looked down on the fields and forest below. The babe kicked harder than usual, and sudden pain in her back caused her to grip the edge until her knuckles whitened. She drew a sharp breath.

"Are you all right, my child?" Uncle Chayim drew close and placed a hand on her arm. "Shall I send for Ilana to help you?" He spoke of Amichai's wife and distant cousin to Deborah, who had recently birthed a son, Shet, but who was also a woman trained in the art of midwifery. She had replaced Deborah's mother as the town's midwife soon after her mother rested in Sheol.

Deborah rubbed her back, longing in that moment for a sister or a different female cousin on which to rely. Ilana was not her favorite person, but there were few other choices.

"Yes, send for her." Deborah made her way slowly to the stairs, Uncle Chayim walking with her, unwilling to release his grip on her arm. "And send Elior and Lavi home." She stopped short as another pain ripped through her. This child would not wait long to make his or her entrance into the world. "And send for Lappidoth." He

38

should be near, just in case . . . She did not finish the thought. She would live through this. She would.

Hours later, much longer than Deborah first expected, the cry of a newborn filled the house. "A girl!" Ilana said, the gleam of triumph in her eyes. "With two sons already, how blessed you are, Deborah."

Deborah took the baby from the woman's arms and held her close while Ilana and another woman from the village brought in fresh bedding and settled Deborah among the soft cushions. She watched Ilana work, chiding herself for feeling curt and cross with this cousin. It was only right for Amichai to marry once she and Lappidoth had wed. What did she expect of him? To pine away after her or wait until some distant day when she may have become a widow?

A shudder swept through her, along with the familiar distant ache that seemed to come every time she thought of Amichai's inaction. Such thoughts were foolish and it did no good to think them.

The mewling sounds of her new daughter drew her attention to the perfect child in her arms. She guided the babe to her breast and closed her eyes. How familiar and sweet the joy of a nursing babe. And suddenly the ordeal of birth brought a wave of exhaustion over her.

"What will you name her?" Lappidoth's quiet words invaded her sleepy thoughts, but she looked at him and smiled just the same.

"Talya," she said, knowing he would not suggest any other name he might prefer. He had allowed her to name their sons without a single protest, as though he found such decisions impossible to make. Like all of the rest of the decisions they had faced in their marriage.

"It is a beautiful name." He lifted the blanket to peek at his daughter. "For a beautiful daughter." His smile brought out the handsome qualities in his face, and light twinkled in his eyes. He touched Deborah's cheek. "Thank you."

She nodded but said nothing.

"I will let you rest." He stood, his head nearly touching the ceiling in this room they normally shared. But he would sleep elsewhere until she could complete her sixty-six days of purification, a full twenty-six days more than when she had borne her boys. The thought did not displease her as she knew it should. What kind of a wife wanted time away from her husband? If she had married Amichai, would she have felt the same?

But the question held no worth, for what was done was done. God must have had a reason that she was forced to marry so quickly and to a man she barely knew. Even now, after ten years together, she did not really know him. He was elusive, wrapped in his work either in the fields or at the scribal table. His attempts to discuss the law had always ended in Deborah feeling like she had won an argument with him, which made her feel worse than before the discussion began. Shouldn't a wife respect and obey her husband? Why must she always feel the need to prove that her opinion had value to the one person who seemed to value her above all?

And still she resisted him. Did he know it? Surely he sensed her reticence.

At least he was kind to her. And if she judged honestly, she sensed he might actually love her. She kissed Talya's dark head, wishing with all of her heart that she felt the same.

Sixty-six days flew faster than Deborah expected they could, but between caring for Talya and her boys, and even with the help of the maid Lappidoth had provided, she'd had little time to sit with him to study the letters of the law or make more than a cursory attempt to read them. "I'm too tired tonight," she'd said on many occasions, and in truth, she was. She ached for something she could not define and missed something she could not see. Why was she not satisfied with her role as wife and mother? What more was a woman to do in Israel?

The road to Shiloh where they would normally be expected to offer a sacrifice for her purification was too dangerous to travel. "How then will we keep the law?" she asked Lappidoth one evening when the day had come when they should make the trip.

"I am a Levite. Though it isn't ideal, we will build an altar here and offer a lamb upon it. Pray that Adonai accepts us and forgives us for being unable to come to His tabernacle." Lappidoth looked at her, his smile serious. "I have already begun to search for the uncut stones for the altar."

"I am sure you will follow the law as best you can." Deborah sank onto one of the cushions in the sitting room, Talya in her arms. "So you yourself will pronounce me clean?"

"Does another priest or Levite reside within this village?" He raised a brow, but his question seemed sincere.

"No. Only the elders, but they are not Levites. Are you sure we cannot try to make it to Shiloh?" The desire to travel there had not been with her since that day her father and brothers and other men had gone up to a festival and been murdered by Canaanites, in what appeared to be a random violent act. But that was before Sisera took charge as their commander, before he had acquired iron chariots to terrorize her people. Still, shouldn't they obey the law despite the risk?

"We did not go up for Elior or Lavi. I do not think God has been displeased with us for that, do you?" He came and knelt beside her, placing his large but gentle hand on her knee. "Trust me, beloved. I am doing the best I can to keep you safe."

She gave a slight nod. "I know." She felt his eyes on her as she nursed Talya, and one glimpse told her his desire was for her.

"How beautiful you are, my sister, my bride," he said against her ear.

Her face grew warm, the words familiar, part of a song he used to sing to her.

"Thank you, my lord." She accepted his kiss above the baby's head. "When will we be ready for the sacrifice?" For she could not deny him, no matter how ambivalent her feelings might be.

"Tomorrow." He stood then. "I will go

43

now and finish building it. Elior and Lavi can help me."

She watched them go, a man and his sons. A surge of pride surfaced. This was her family. Whether the one she would have chosen or not, they were still hers. And she would do all in her power to protect them, and to respect the man who loved her in spite of herself.

Dawn broke through the latticed windows in her room, the room that Lappidoth would share with her again this night. She glanced about at the untidy conditions and called the maid. "While we are at the sacrifice, I want you to air out this room and put everything neatly in order."

"Yes, my lady," the woman said, quickly setting to work. That everyone obeyed her still seemed strange to Deborah. Her mother and grandmother had been the ones who commanded and gave orders, not her. No one had listened to her in her youth. But she was the mistress of the house now, and her mother and grandmother had not lived long after the loss of her father and brothers.

The thought still pained her, but Deborah shoved the memories aside as she hurried to dress and wrapped Talya in a blanket for

44

the walk to the altar in the clearing just outside the city gates. Her family, aunts, uncles, cousins, and their children joined in the solemn procession. Normally, she and Lappidoth would have traveled to Shiloh alone with their children, not half the town, but with the threat of terror on every side, the people needed distractions, and this sacrifice would remind them all of their need of a deliverer.

Forgive me, Adonai. She knew this sacrifice was meant to atone for any sin she had committed during her pregnancy and giving birth, any law she may have broken during the time of her outflowing. Why birth itself needed atonement, she did not quite understand, but perhaps it came from the father passing his sin through her on to their child. She did not hold the responsibility alone.

The gate drew near now, and she made her way up a slight incline to where a perfectly built altar stood. A lamb without blemish was tied to a nearby tree, bleating softly. Deborah handed Talya to Ilana and knelt at the lamb's side, burying her face into its neck, unable to stop the tears. *Why must it suffer on my account?*

Lappidoth knelt beside her and placed one hand on the lamb, the other on her shoulder. Neither spoke, and even the crowd waited in silence. At last Lappidoth stood, released her fingers from gripping the lamb's wool, untied the animal from the tree, and led it to the place of slaughter. In one swift motion, he slit its throat. Elior caught the blood in a basin, as he had been taught, while Deborah knelt in the grass, weeping.

Lappidoth heard his wife's cries, their soft sorrow gripping his heart. How small she seemed where he glimpsed her in the dirt. He hefted the lamb's broken body onto the altar and lit the fire, its smoke rising to the heavens.

Oh Adonai, send us a deliverer.

How often had they both prayed thus? Surely God had a plan for Deborah to fulfill in freeing Israel. Somehow he knew it deep in his heart where he discerned truth. Why could she not see it, despite his efforts to teach her? Despite her dreams?

The breeze blew the smoke upward, but moments later the fire flamed higher than the smoke, rising, rising, swirling above their heads until Lappidoth feared it would catch hold of the trees. He quickly glanced at his sons and then at the crowd, whose wide eyes told him they saw the same. He left the altar to join Deborah.

He found her on her knees, bewildered, looking about. Darkness fell around them except for the fire that burned bright from the altar.

"Is someone there?" Deborah called out.

Did she see something they could not?

"Who's there? Where is everyone? Lappidoth?"

The fire leapt from the altar and swirled about her, engulfing her.

A scream burst from within him. "Deborah!" The crowd fell to their knees, and a heavy fear forced him to do the same.

A bright light invaded the space around her, swirling, warm, strange . . . comforting. The light shone even beneath her closed eyes, and in a moment she was no longer kneeling in the grass before the altar but standing on a mountain surrounded by the men and women of Israel, all bowed with their faces to the earth.

Adonai Elohim, forgive us. Their cries pierced her, a blade to her soul, bringing the sting of shame, remorse. *Forgive me.* Her knees gave way and she sank to the earth again, tasting dirt. *Forgive us.* The words came from the tongues of the men and women of tribes from Dan to Beersheba. And in a blinding moment, she saw all the oppression of the Canaanites flash in her mind's eye. The people were weeping and crying out to God for relief, for deliverance.

Send us a deliverer, a redeemer, Lord God.

The prayer moved past the people and wedged itself like fire in her soul. And then the vision faded and the leaves waved above her head, and Lappidoth, the altar, and the people of her town on their knees came into view. Deborah stood, shaking, afraid to breathe, but did so for the air that had been sucked from her lungs in that fleeting moment.

What had she witnessed? Was she ill? Her heart pounded as she staggered toward Ilana, who knelt, shaking, as Deborah took Talya into her trembling arms.

"What did you see?" Lappidoth was suddenly at her side and grasped her elbow. The crowd of men and women rose and quickly surrounded her. "Tell me, beloved, for we know God has spoken to you."

His words brought the vision into clearer focus, and words grew heavy on Deborah's tongue. "We must pray," she said at last, addressing the crowd. "Each one of us must seek Adonai's help and cry out to Him to free us from Sisera, from Jabin, our tormentors."

48

Silence descended as though the darkness had returned. She caught the curious glances of her sons and the quizzical brow of Lappidoth.

"And with our praying, we must repent," she added. Could they not see the urgency? "All of us — our neighbors, our kinsmen — we will not find relief until we put away the foreign gods from among us."

The silence deepened as men and women exchanged guilty looks. She felt Lavi's touch on her arm, caught the awe in his gaze. She looked around at these familiar faces, her own face heating as though someone had scorched her. "You know I speak the truth." She set her jaw, her tone pleading. "Our men have taken Canaanite wives and given their daughters to Canaanite men. Is it any wonder that our God has sold us into such bondage to these people? We are no better off than we were in Egypt, for we have sinned against the Lord."

She released a deep sigh and held Talya closer, a shield against their disapproval. They must understand. She could not bear it if her family did not support the vision.

Throats cleared in the prevailing silence.

All eyes looked to her. Deborah swallowed the disquiet. "I saw a vision of our people today, every tribe from Dan to Beersheba

49

gathered on a mountain, begging God for a deliverer."

"If we are to pray, we must send messages to the rest of the villages to do the same," Lappidoth said.

Suddenly everyone began to speak at once, and Deborah could not take the noise, this onslaught of words. She slipped away with Talya, making the excuse of the need to nurse her, her heart thumping with fear.

Who am I that You should entrust me with such a vision? I am a simple woman, a mother of small children. What do You want of me?

Send us a deliverer, the people in the vision had said.

She entered her courtyard and sank onto a low stone bench, but one glance told her Lappidoth and her boys had followed. Thankfully, blissfully, they were alone. The boys went into the house as Lappidoth knelt beside her.

"God has called you to lead us, beloved. The men all agreed that the vision gives you the right to speak for us, to pray to God for us. You are a prophetess, Deborah."

"I am a wife and a mother. Nothing more."

He shook his head, his hand softly cupping her cheek. A stirring filled her at his touch, and suddenly she wanted to be

50

simply what she had said. A wife to him in a truer way than she had been all these years, and a mother to their three children.

"You are much more, beloved, though it almost pains me to share you. I dare not go against the will of our God." He took her hand in his and stroked Talya's head with the other. "The men will listen to you because you hear the voice of God, Deborah. You are called out for such a time as this, to help us during this awful oppression. God is going to use you, perhaps both of us, to bring about that deliverance."

She shook her head even as tears slipped down her cheeks. "I cannot. I am a simple woman with fanciful dreams."

"Who used to sing to the Lord songs that rivaled the trill of the birds, a woman who has lost too much joy since we wed." He traced a line along her jaw. "You lost much when you lost your family, beloved. But I am here to tell you that we saw the fire of God surround you. God gave you that vision because He takes delight in you, and you must heed it."

I cannot. But she did not say the words, for she could not look into those dark intelligent eyes and deny him what he believed to be true.

Forgive me, Elohim. Surely I am a woman

of unclean lips, a woman who speaks words without thought. I am not a man to lead my family, worse yet Your people.

She turned to face the bright sky, caught by the brilliance of the sun overhead. Music swirled in and around her, and a voice, soft as a whisper, filled her ear.

Hear My words: if there is a prophet among you, I the Lord make Myself known to him in a vision. I speak with him in a dream.

In a heartbeat, she knew Lappidoth was right. The vision had truly come to her from the Lord. "If I am to be God's prophet," she said softly, "I think it is time I let you teach me to read."

2

Fifteen Years Later
1101 BC

"No, you may not go to the fields with your father and brothers today," Deborah said, catching the flash of irritation in Talya's dark eyes. "I need you here to help with the children. With Libi due in a few months, she needs her rest, and Orel is handful enough for two women." She drew a breath and tempered her tone lest she start another battle with the girl. If her father would stand up to her just once . . .

"I'm old enough to marry, Mother. Surely I'm also old enough to watch out for bandits, who come nowhere near the fields where Abba works." Talya's tone, devoid of its occasional scorn, held a pleading edge. "You went alone to the well when you were younger than I, and Abba's fields are close — I am not asking to go far. Do you think I cannot defend myself?"

53

Deborah studied this beautiful, obstinate daughter and closed her eyes. "Of course you can defend yourself." How to make the girl see . . . "When I was your age, women were not kidnapped and ravaged in the streets. Times were much different then."

"But Canaanites killed my grandfather and uncles and Abba's whole family. How are times any different, Ima?" Talya fell into step with Deborah, her long dark hair swinging loosely beneath a thin veil. They moved from the sitting room where Deborah's daughters-in-law busily cleared away clay cups and dishes from the morning repast, to the courtyard where the men gathered their tools to head to the fields.

"Times were only beginning to change then," Deborah said, stopping long enough to kiss Lappidoth's cheek and hand him a pouch of dried fruits and nuts.

"Abba, please let me go with you." Talya stepped close, nearly coming between her parents. Deborah caught her elbow and leveled her husband with a stern glare.

"I already told her no." She was in no mood for an argument. "I need her here."

Lappidoth's mustache twitched as he gave Deborah a slight nod, but his attention turned quickly to their daughter — the girl who had his heart wrapped too tightly in her control.

"She is not the angel you think she is," Deborah had told him on more than one occasion, but the comments had gone unheeded.

"She is a young woman who is lonely and wants to see beyond our small settlement," he had said, giving her that lopsided grin of his, the one he knew could make her yield. "She is not so very different than you were at her age, if memory serves me well."

"Your memory is mistaken." The words had been a retort and untrue, but she couldn't fight them both. How was it that a daughter was more difficult to keep safe, to control, than her sons? She had such hopes that a daughter would be quiet and obedient and stay at home like a good woman in Israel.

Like you?

She crossed her arms, irritated with her own thoughts.

"Stay with your mother, Talya. Perhaps another time." Lappidoth touched their daughter's shoulder, then turned to join his sons.

"May I go with you tomorrow then?" Talya hurried to his side and tilted her head in that persuasive way she had.

Deborah felt her patience fraying as she

55

stepped closer. "You will continue to ask until he gives in to you. Then what? You will want to visit the neighboring villages? Perhaps you should walk alone in the middle of the road when Sisera's nine hundred chariots are drawing near." Deborah cringed. How like her own mother she sounded! She rolled her eyes at the whole mess she was making of this argument. Again. She turned away from them both.

She glanced at Lavi and Elior, two sons who obeyed both her and Lappidoth, who gave them no cause to fret — not like their willful sister. But they avoided her gaze. Huffing her frustration, she marched past them all and kept walking toward the center of town, toward her palm tree.

How could a man who watched his family perish at Canaan's hand even consider allowing their daughter to leave their village and risk her safety? Sisera had grown bolder in recent years, and word had come to them a few years earlier how Israel's commander Barak had lost his wife during a raid on a local well. Deborah blinked, seeing the image of the broken, bloodied young bride, feeling Barak's grief. Sisera raped and pillaged wherever he went, and Deborah could not risk a similar fate for Talya. No. Let the girl argue and plead. She would not win this argument even if Deborah had to outright defy Lappidoth to keep her from doing so.

Deborah sighed, a bone-weary weight she carried with her every moment she spent in Talya's presence, every moment she tried to find a solution to the mother-daughter struggle they could not seem to shake. The girl needed to settle in a home of her own, bear children. Perhaps then she would understand.

The thought troubled her. Shet, born a few years before Talya, had been one cousin Deborah considered. She had long since forgotten her feelings for his father Amichai and actually found Amichai's wife Ilana a woman to be trusted. Their children could have made a good match. But Shet had married an outsider the year before, and there were few men in the village who were eligible mates. With so many keeping to their own towns, and village life fairly ceasing for fear that a celebration would draw Sisera's attention, there was no joy of the bridegroom in the streets. People married in secret, celebrated in homes in private, worshiped alone. Few caravans traveled the land, and when they did, they kept to the hills, avoiding the main roads. Times were definitely not as they had been in her youth. They were worse. Much, much worse. And twenty years of oppression had taken a great toll on them all. Talya was simply expressing her frustration at all of the restrictions.

Deborah shook herself as the voices of her husband and sons carried to her while they made their way toward the city gate. She glanced in their direction, relieved to see that Talya was not with them. Tomorrow could be another argument, but at least today she could judge the people without that added worry.

"What word do you seek?" Deborah asked later that afternoon, after an already full day of judging the people. Ever since the vision she'd had at the purification sacrifice, the people of the village had begun to seek her advice. A few women at first, who came to her as she worked the grindstone. Then a woman and a man, then the men. Now even the elders sought her so often she had taken to holding court beneath the palm tree in the center of the town. Talya would play quietly at her feet in those early days, but soon she ran through the village with the other children, particularly Shet. Why had he not asked for her hand? *Just as Amichai did not ask for yours?*

A man wearing the colors of the tribe of Issachar approached, drawing her thoughts back to her duties. He removed his turban and bowed his head in deference. She nodded in response.

"A runaway slave from another tribe has sought refuge with me," the man said, rubbing a hand over his beard. His gaze showed uncertainty, but it held hers with a sense of acceptance, that he would abide by her ruling. "Should I return him to his master?"

Deborah lifted the scroll Lappidoth had copied for her and searched the words he had taught her to read. Most of the time she could recall the laws from memory, but now and then she was forced to consult Moses's Law.

"There it is," she said at last, careful of the parchment as her finger traced the words. " 'You shall not give up to his master a slave who has escaped from his master to you. He shall dwell with you, in your midst, in the place that he shall choose within one of your towns, wherever it suits him. You shall not wrong him.' " She looked up. "There is your answer."

The man nodded. "But what if he has committed a crime against his master? Should not his master have some say in the matter?"

Deborah took a moment to roll up the scroll and set it beside her on the bench.

"The slave has sought refuge with you for a reason. If he has killed a man, then the avenger of blood must seek justice. But if he has been mistreated by his master, then his master is the one who deserves to be brought to justice. It is impossible for you to know which one happened unless the avenger of blood comes looking for the man. In the meantime, treat him with kindness."

The man thanked her and stepped away, allowing the next person to approach. The questions had come in a continual stream. Some Deborah could answer, others made her feel at a loss for wisdom. Even her prayers did not always yield the words the person hoped to hear, and Deborah was forced to send people away the same way they had come.

The sun ebbed toward the west, and her men returned through the city gates. Deborah rose from her bench and began the slow walk to greet them. But as she took two steps away from the center patch of grass where the palm grew just tall enough to offer the comfort of shade, the air grew still and twilight flashed brilliant oranges and golds about her, swirling, blinding.

She stopped, bracing herself, unable to keep her eyes from closing against the light.

What do You want of me, Lord? She knew now the signs of a vision, but they usually came to her in dreams. She knelt in the dirt and removed her sandals, though no words came from the light. *Forgive me.* Her heart pounded, matching the rising dread she often felt at such times.

The words the ancient commander Joshua had spoken to Israel filled her mind. *Now therefore fear the Lord and serve Him in sincerity and in faithfulness. Put away the gods that your fathers served beyond the River and in Egypt, and serve the Lord.*

But, Lord, have we not done this? She had told the village to do so when Talya was but a babe. Lappidoth had sent clay tablets with the command from their new prophetess saying the same to every town in Israel.

Not all.

The soft words rocked her, even as the light faded and her breath slowed to its normal rhythm. So Sisera still possessed power because Israel still compromised and did not fully obey the Lord.

She rose slowly, pondering the vision as she returned home, consumed by it as her family spoke over a shared meal, her heart still beating with the feeling of awe and dread. Her hand shook as she dipped a piece of flatbread into the stew and gave it to her grandson Orel.

Her daughter-in-law Ahava drew her young daughter Tikva into her arms to nurse. Two chubby hands held her mother's cheeks and kissed them. Deborah warmed to see the affection of the child, despite the heavy feeling in her heart. Oh for the peace that once ruled the land, that her children's children could live in a world without the oppression of evil men. Talya should be free to roam as she wished, and joy should rule where fear now reigned.

But later as Deborah lay beside Lappidoth, listening to his even breathing, she could not rest. Not knowing that men and women, perhaps even in her own village, still worshiped other gods. If they did not root out the cause of their own faithlessness, they would never be free of Canaan's oppression.

3

Barak sat straight up. Sweat — cold, lifeless drops — beaded his brow, trickled down his back. Air escaped his lungs but would not return. Again he dragged for breath, clutched the neck of his tunic, ripped at its constraints. The forest taunted him, its deep shadows and willow branches mocking him now. His breath released at last, leaving him trembling. He shook himself, forcing his mind to grip what was. These surroundings, familiar yet so strange, were far from home. They could not, would not, pull him under as the house he had shared with Nessa did. The trees did not hold the strength, the waning warmth, of Nessa's arms.

It was only a dream. He blinked hard. The same dream, but only a dream. He rubbed the back of his neck, his fingers tangled in long, unkempt hair. He shook himself again. Not real.

His heart beat fast as he stood on shaky

legs. He glanced at his sleeping men. Dawn would come soon. He should attempt sleep again. But rest would not come. Not until he avenged her blood.

He picked his way out of the underbrush to the edge of their hideaway where the tree line rimmed a cliff that overlooked the road. Sisera took this road too often — from Bethshan to Shechem. Week after week. Month after month. For nearly twenty years.

The larger towns had been able to withstand the brazen attacks. But not by much. And only because their walls were tall and strong, and worship of Yahweh still resided there.

A knot, fist-like, gripped his middle. He held a trembling hand in front of him. The dream always had the same effect. He had to get hold of his emotions. If he didn't, his rage could drive his men away. Over half of the country already lived in terror. How many small towns had fallen to Sisera's sword? He *must* do something to stop the onslaught.

"Trouble sleeping again?"

He jumped. "You shouldn't sneak up on me like that." Though he instantly recognized Keshet, his silent shadow and right-hand man, his quiet approach still jarred him.

Keshet nodded an apology. "The dream again?" he asked.

Barak clenched both hands and looked away. How was it possible that a dream could reduce him to a weak-kneed woman? "Just once I would like it to end differently." He glanced at the few stars visible through the trees. "Maybe if she lived in the end, I would awaken and all would be well. This life" — he moved his hand to encompass the makeshift camp — "would be the dream. Nessa and I would still live in Kedesh-naphtali and be raising a quiver of children." He blinked, ashamed that after three years the emotion still stung.

"You cannot bring her back, Barak." Keshet's calm words, though true, did not soothe.

"They *destroyed* her." The words, a whisper, still twisted and burned within him. When Barak had found her, it had been too late to save her.

"And Adonai Elohim, blessed be He, will avenge her, my friend. Even now He is planning our enemy's demise." Keshet cupped Barak's tense shoulder.

Barak took a deep, cleansing breath. "If our God were with us, Nessa would not have died in the first place." He voiced the thought that had haunted him since that fateful day.

"Do not blame God for what men have done." Keshet spoke so softly Barak almost missed his words. Keshet had also lost a sister to Sisera's sword. How was it possible he did not hold God accountable for not protecting the righteous, the innocent?

"You have more faith than I," he said at last, surprised that to admit such a thing left him strangely bereft. "I am weary of living the life of a bandit. And yet we cannot go home until our women and children are safe." He paused, glancing once more into the trees where soft snores still met his ear. "How long until Adonai Elohim repays such evil? There is no good reason that Sisera still lives."

"Perhaps the next time you speak with the prophetess, she will know."

The very woman he took reports to of Sisera's movements when the news was worth telling.

"She might already know of Sisera's latest threat," Barak said, wondering just how much of a prophet Deborah was if she had to be told such news. Didn't prophets know everything before the rest of them did?

"She isn't God, my friend. She would only know what He tells her. And sometimes God uses men to do His bidding." Keshet smiled — Barak could hear it in his voice, though it was hard to see his features in the predawn darkness.

"I suppose you think God wants me to do His bidding and tell her?" It would mean traveling south, the exact opposite of home and away from Sisera's main haunts in northern Israel.

"She makes a good stew. And the last I noticed, she has a lovely virgin daughter." Keshet said the words to coax him, but suddenly the truth of them hit their mark.

"Deborah is a leader in Israel with a virgin daughter."

Keshet chuckled. "Yes, I think I just said that."

"Sisera is kidnapping the virgin daughters of leaders in every village and town where he can find them." That was the news Barak had managed to goad out of a captured soldier on his last raid. If the man was telling the truth. "Which means Deborah's daughter is at risk."

Keshet sobered at the reminder and ran a hand over his beard. "We should leave at first light," he said, voicing what Barak knew he must do.

"Yes." Suddenly his dream had become real all over again.

"Shema, Yisrael, Adonai eloheinu, Adonai echad." The Shema, "Hear, O Israel: The Lord our God, the Lord is one," spoken from Lappidoth's lips was as familiar as Deborah's breath. Did she take it for granted that God was one, was with them, heard their prayers? A soft sigh escaped as she lifted her gaze heavenward, listening.

"You shall love the Lord your God with all your heart and with all your soul and with all your might. And these words that I command you today shall be on your heart. You shall teach them diligently to your children, and shall talk of them when you sit in your house, and when you walk by the way, and when you lie down, and when you rise." Lappidoth's voice filled the courtyard where family members had gathered. Ever since the murder of her father and brothers years ago, few people ever traveled to Shiloh, but as a scribe who had copied the law, Lappidoth made sure that his family was not lacking in their knowledge of God.

And yet . . . did any of them truly take the Lord seriously?

She looked to her sons, her daughter and daughters-in-law, her grandchildren, her aunts and uncles and cousins. Were any of them among those who worshiped foreign gods in secret? *Please show me, Adonai.* Unless she caught them in the act, the only option she had was to send her husband and sons house to house to search for signs of idol worship. *Is this what You would have me do?*

She barely noticed when Lappidoth said the final prayer and dismissed the Sabbath meeting, until voices filled the yard and the women clustered together to bring the few items they could carry to share the Sabbath meal. There would be no time beneath the palm tree or hearing of cases today. There would be no work of any kind, only worship, joy in the Lord, and each other's company.

She rose from the stone at the sound of a commotion coming from the city gates. A young man with hair draped to his shoulders marched at the head of a band of twenty bedraggled men. He lifted a rugged, bearded face to look in her direction.

"It is Barak," she whispered to Lappidoth, who stood suddenly at her side.

At his approach, Deborah met Barak's gaze and saw a flash of anger in his dark eyes. Her stomach twisted. Something was wrong.

She shivered at the sudden memory of her father's and brothers' broken bodies, at the terrible keening of her mother and grandmother the day they were brought into their village, at the pain she had never quite been able to shake from her heart. They'd been beaten nearly beyond recognition.

She blinked, willing her heart to calm, searching Barak's face for some reassurance that did not come. "What is it?" She would hear the news no matter how bad it might be.

Barak ran a roughened hand over his beard. How long since he had bathed? Or slept?

"Your daughter is in great danger, Prophetess."

The men gathered around him in the courtyard at the central fire. Deborah's sons and Lappidoth sat with them. Deborah sank to a stone seat near her husband, her knees too weak to hold her. Where was Talya? One glance showed her standing in the arch of the door, wide-eyed, listening.

"Sisera has decided to try a new strategy," Barak said. "Apparently raping and pillaging our villages and towns and caravans and our innocent women drawing water for their families from our wells was not enough." He paused, the words charged with hatred.

"Now," he said, breaking the awkward silence, "he is seeking out the virgin daughters of every elder in Israel, in every town, from Dan to Beersheba."

Deborah heard Talya's soft gasp, which accompanied the sudden pounding of her head.

"He is planning to use your daughters to draw out the men to fight him in battle. He knows that we are few in number, that we sneak around and attack here and there but have no power to overthrow him. He would use your daughters as bait to draw fathers and brothers to war. With his nine hundred chariots and thousands more fighting men, he will squash Israel once and for all."

Barak's words hung in the air, and Deborah saw Talya slink farther against the wall, her face ashen. Deborah's heart beat an unsteady rhythm. Now for certain she could never let Talya out of her sight.

"What will we do?" Lavi spoke for the group, his question aimed first at Barak, then at her. "God speaks to you, Ima. Has He said what to do? Our women will never be safe as long as Sisera lives."

Deborah felt the heat of flames crawl up her neck at all of the attention they now cast her way, as if she should have every answer to their questions. She drew a

71

breath, placed both hands on her knees. "Not everyone in the land has obeyed Him," she said, her gaze taking in those who remained near. "Some among us, perhaps in this village, perhaps in other towns, worship foreign gods in secret. If we do not remove the idols from our hearts, we will never be rid of Sisera's oppression."

"What gods still remain among the towns?" Barak raised his voice, his anger clear. "If I must, I will travel to each one and search them out to destroy them and those who worship them." His dark eyes narrowed and his hands curled at his sides.

Arguments erupted, the men's words whipping all around her. They would go and fight each other this moment if she did not stop them.

"I do not think going house to house is necessary yet," she said carefully. "But God has clearly shown me that not all have returned to Him. If we do not humble ourselves and obey the Lord in what He has commanded us to do" — she met each man's steady gaze — "then our fight against Sisera will be in vain."

Lappidoth stood and faced the crowd. "Our prophetess has not commanded that our homes be searched, but I think we would all agree that we need to search them ourselves. Bring any foreign gods to the center of town and we will destroy them. I will send messages to the other towns to do the same."

Barak seemed satisfied with Lappidoth's words. "We will take the messages to the towns ourselves." He looked at Deborah. "If that is what is keeping us from defeating Sisera, Prophetess, I will make sure down to the last man that the word of the Lord is obeyed."

4

One blow. The metal tent peg sank deep into the earth, the hold firm. Jael sat back, pleased with her work, satisfied that the ropes would hold the tent taut and strong against the elements. The metal pegs her husband had fashioned in place of the older wooden ones pierced the ground with greater ease. She had often thanked Heber for making her life so much simpler in this way.

But her gratitude seemed a small thing compared to the blow she had dealt his pride on the day she had begged him to flee the Negev and his brother Alim's wrath. How fleeting the feeling of rightness now seemed in this foreign place. The oaks of Zaanannim near Kedesh were so far from Judah, so far from all they held dear.

One blow to her husband's pride, to his brother's authority, and everything had changed.

"Your son and daughter can find their spouses elsewhere," Alim had said the day they left. "I will give no more of my sons or daughters to a man who would save an unworthy Canaanite. What do you think Sisera will do to us when he discovers your true loyalties?"

If only Heber hadn't come between Alim and the Canaanite slave he was bent on beating to near death to exact information. The man had little to tell in the end anyway. So the beating was useless, and for what? All it did was cause a rift so deep between two headstrong men that Jael's persuasive words could not change them. So she had convinced Heber to leave.

She blew out a frustrated breath and moved into the dark interior of the tent. It was useless to fret over what was past, and yet she could not stop the ache, the deep longing for family, for aunts and uncles, for cousins to pair with her youngest son and only daughter in marriage. If they were both wed, they would be happily settled in their own tents with their spouses and babes on the way. Instead, they pined for what was lost.

As did she.

The thought pricked her already irritated spirit as she quickly unrolled the rugs and set her mat in one corner. Heber knew his family sided with the Hebrews over the Canaanites — as far back as the days when their leader Moses led them out of Egypt. He knew all Canaanites were looked on with suspicion. Still, Alim had gone too far in his treatment. The God of the Hebrews would not have wanted slaves treated as Alim insisted on doing. What choice did Heber have?

"Ima?" Her daughter, Daniyah, poked her head into the tent, her arms filled with baskets and colorful yarns for weaving. "Where do you want these?"

Jael motioned to a far corner where she intended to set up her loom. When the sides of the tent were rolled up, the light would illumine that corner better than the one on the north side. "How much is left to unpack? Where is your father?"

Daniyah set her burden on the ground and came to help Jael finish straightening a rug. "The donkeys are brushed and fed, and I just have my mat to bring along with the pottery. Ghalib said he would bring the rest."

"That is good." Jael wiped the sweat from her brow, looking in the direction of the donkeys for some sign of her son, the son whose gentle spirit had changed with the

76

move and the rift between his father and uncle.

"Abba is with Mahir. They are looking for the best spot to build the kiln to smelt the ore." Daniyah smiled, and Jael could not help but return it. If only Ghalib shared his sister's joyous innocence.

"They will be hungry." Jael walked with Daniyah to the area where the men had unloaded the pack animals and carts. She retrieved her three-pronged skillet and sent Daniyah to find large stones to circle a fire. "Don't wander," she warned. "We don't know this place yet. The trees can hide us, but they can as easily hide men who seek our harm."

"I won't go far, Ima." She skipped off like a child, but not out of Jael's sight.

Jael drew in a deep breath. The girl should marry soon, but what man would they find in this hidden forest? There was not another Kenite clan anywhere near them. Were they destined to intermarry their two remaining children to foreigners of Israel or Canaan?

Her jaw clenched, a habit that had become too frequent of late, causing a headache to form along her temple. She simply must stop fretting over the future and discuss the matter with Heber, make him see that they had no choice but to send a request to his brothers, with or without Alim's approval.

She gathered her cooking utensils and then dug a pit for a fire in front of her tent.

"Here is your loom, Ima." Ghalib carried the wooden structure into her tent and glanced back over his shoulder. "Put it in the south corner?"

"Yes." She paused in her digging to watch him. He should have married Parisa before they ever fled the Negev. A sigh escaped as she noted the tight lines along his brow. It did not take such concentration simply to carry a loom. He was not happy with the move either, if she knew him at all — and she was most certain she did. Surely she knew her own son.

Daniyah approached and set some large stones around the hole Jael had nearly finished digging, drawing her thoughts back to the present. As Daniyah ran off to find the dried dung to start the fire, Nadia and Raja, Jael's two daughters-in-law, came from setting up their own tents. One carried a large pot, the other a sieve and a sack of lentils.

Nadia sat crossed-legged beside Jael and sifted the lentils through the sieve, careful to remove the stones. Raja poured water into the stew pot while Daniyah returned and started a fire.

"Are you all right, Ima Jael?" Nadia's sweet voice broke through Jael's distant thoughts. Nadia was Alim's oldest daughter, wed three years to her oldest son Mahir. Surely a grandson would soon come of their union. But Nadia still waited, patiently waited. She was the exact opposite of her father. And Mahir had been kind enough to wait with her when he could have taken another wife by now. Or at least a concubine.

"I am fine, Nadia." She straightened her stiff back. "I will be glad to rest. I'm sure you all feel the same."

"It was a long journey. I thought it might never end," Nadia agreed. "I long to lay on my mat this night." She shook the sieve again and plucked a few more stones from the lentils. Now and then some of them made it into the stew regardless, but at least they sank to the bottom. No one had yet broken a tooth on one.

"I am just glad to be off the back of that donkey," Raja said, laughing. "Though at least I wasn't stuck on top of the camel as Fareed was. He didn't seem to mind the ride, but I was afraid if I had tried it, I would tumble off it to the ground."

Jael regarded her second son's wife with a smile, then a strange sound caught her ear, a slow churning rumble in the distance. She glanced at her girls, saw the curiosity and hint of fear in their gazes. "Go at once to your tents," she ordered, and each woman did as she was told. Daniyah hurried into the tent she shared with Jael. She would not have a tent of her own until she wed and lived in the village of her husband.

Jael stood and brushed the dirt from her hands. The rumbling grew, and a great roar like thunder shook the earth beneath her feet. The main road to Hazor was just beyond the tallest tree, the oak of Zaanannim. Their camp was secluded beyond the road, but not as well hidden as she would have liked. Her heart thudded, its slow rhythm making her sluggish, as though she were trying to awaken from a dream.

Running feet snapped her attention. A rush of air escaped her lungs as Heber and her sons ran toward her. "What is it?" Her words came out hoarse, a mere whisper.

Heber brandished a sword in his right hand. "I don't know. Sisera's chariots, I think." He moved past her without another word, her sons following close at his heels, each clutching one of the swords they had forged in their workshop back in the Negev.

They crept to the underbrush and crouched low. Jael moved behind them, snatched up her wooden hammer, and followed. She would not stand by and allow her daughter to be ravaged. She had heard tales on their journey northward. Sisera's iron chariots wrought terror in the hearts of all who heard them.

She winced and nearly choked on the dust at the sudden pounding of many horses' hooves and rush of wheels close by. She blinked against the blur, unable to count them. But she counted the breaths it took for them to become a memory, out of sight and hearing.

Heber stood at last, and they walked in silence back to the cooking area. The men sat on the ground in the familiar circle. Jael sank to the earth, her hands shaking. Nadia and Raja crept closer and joined them, and Daniyah came to sit at Heber's feet.

"What will we do about the Canaanites, Abba?" Fear laced Daniyah's tone, and Jael caught a glimpse of moisture in her bright eyes. This was not the first time they had encountered this threat.

"Why did we come here at all?" Nadia, normally quiet and cheerful, could not hide the tremor in her voice. "Were we not safer in Judah? Could not my father's wrath have been appeased?" Her boldness brought Mahir to kneel at her side.

He placed a hand on his wife's knee, but his gaze rested on Heber. "What will we do, Father? You have put off a decision these many weeks, and now we are camped in the very heart of the land Israel has claimed from Canaan. These trees will not save us from any man's cruelty if he is bent on harming us."

"Mahir is right," Fareed said, taking Raja's hand in his. "It is not too late to turn back. Even if we do not camp near Uncle Alim, we should not live so close to the Canaanite threat."

Jael searched her husband's stricken face. His pride rested in his sons' respect, yet here they were questioning his decisions. A decision she had begged him to make.

"Your father made the right choice," she said. She twisted the belt of her robe and had to remind herself to unclench her hands, to relax. Her children were not the enemy, they simply did not understand.

"We cannot go back. Not now." Heber's voice was strained.

"Then what will we do?" Ghalib's scowl troubled her, his eyes ablaze with barely contained fury. She sighed, wishing not for the first time that they could return to the days when her children were small and safely under her protective wing.

"We will make ourselves valuable to our enemy," Heber said, eyeing each son. His back stiffened, and he lifted his chin as if daring them to continue the argument. "The Canaanite we rescued from Alim assured me that this area was not troubled by Jabin's forces. And we have goods Jabin would find beneficial to his cause, should he or his men come calling."

"You would make peace with Israel's enemies?" She stared at him, her heart sinking with the realization that he would leave an ancient alliance to forge a new one with untamed men. "What are you saying, my husband?"

"I'm saying, dear wife," Heber said, taking in the entire group, "that to preserve our lives, we will do exactly that."

"Exactly how do you plan to make peace with Jabin and Sisera?" Jael asked the following evening as she rested beside Heber in his tent. He was nearly asleep, and she would leave him soon, but not until she received an answer to her question.

He rolled over and snorted. "I will offer my services. He needs weapons. I make them. A simple agreement should suffice."

Stunned, Jael stared at the man. "If you supply weapons to Sisera, you will surely guarantee Israel's demise."

"Sisera is not *my* enemy. And there is no reason I cannot also supply Israel with swords, if they but ask." He closed his eyes and put a hand to his forehead. "But I am tired, Jael. We can speak of this another time."

"Israel cannot afford to pay for weapons. The women at the well are poor. They've been plundered and pillaged, the land raped of its resources. What good are weapons when they need wheat?" Anger flared, and she knew she was pushing him past his breaking point.

He sighed, an insufferable sound. She should never have agreed to share his tent this night. But she knew if she did not give in to his needs, he would take a concubine who would. He could afford another wife, he had just never bothered to burden their household with one. But if she pushed him too far . . .

"Please, Heber, think about what I am saying. Do not sell us to an enemy that could destroy us in the end." She touched his arm, then leaned forward and kissed his cheek. He was a good man when he wasn't in the process of exasperating her so. She sat back on her heels. "Promise me?"

He grunted and shooed her away. "Be

gone with you, woman. I will promise nothing."

She held her tongue as she stood and
walked slowly to the door.

"But I will think on it." His words just
caught her ear as she slipped into the dark
camp and returned to her tent.

5

Three days after Barak's arrival, Lappidoth handed sacks of clay tablets to him and his men to take with them to the neighboring towns. "Where will you go once these are delivered?" He directed his question to Barak while Deborah's girls and maidservants served the men the evening meal. Barak and his men, who had taken to sleeping in the cave below their house or in various courtyards throughout the city, were clearly anxious to be off.

Barak's expression sobered as he glanced Deborah's way. "I would like to know we had a directive from the Lord. Once we know the idols are destroyed, how will we know the time is right?"

Deborah held Barak's look. "I cannot command the visions nor the dreams. When the Lord speaks to me, I will send for you."

Barak seemed slightly irritated by her comment, as though he would force the issue if he could. But he shrugged his shoulders instead. "We will head back to Kedesh-naphtali for a time then. You can send word there." He dipped flatbread into the stew pot and plopped the entire piece into his mouth.

Deborah glanced at Talya, who leaned down to refill Barak's clay cup with fresh goat's milk. Barak turned to thank her, and Deborah did not miss the soft smile in her daughter's eyes. Barak did not show the slightest interest.

Even when Talya stayed near her father the following morning to bid the men farewell, Barak did not acknowledge the girl with more than a brief nod and a parting, "Be safe. Do not travel without men to accompany you. You risk your life if you do."

Deborah pondered the slight frown between Talya's brows as she walked later that day to her palm tree. She had seen that look once too often on Talya's face, the one that chafed to prove another wrong.

The thought troubled her now as she approached the waiting crowd. Would Talya listen? A sigh caused Deborah's chest to lift in a sense of defeat she had grown accustomed to of late, a sigh borne of too much strife. She took time to settle herself on the bench and lifted her spindle and distaff to work as she listened. People flocked to her day after day, and one at a time she heard case after case until she nearly wearied of the mantle of judge she carried.

As the sun was beginning its descent to the west, two men approached, one holding the other by the collar of his cloak as though he had dragged him across the entire town.

Deborah set her spindle aside. "State your case." Her jaw tightened with the telltale ache that always accompanied such a look of malice in the eyes of one Israelite toward another, of a man against his fellow man. She faced the accuser. "Release him."

The accuser's eyes narrowed, his look distrustful, wary.

"Do not worry, he will not flee." Deborah focused on the one caught but spoke to the other. "Tell me why you accuse this man." The freed man stood, head bowed, and his rigid posture eased.

"I've caught this man" — the accuser pointed a bony finger, poking the man in the chest — "in my vineyard eating grapes every day for the past week. There will be nothing left to harvest if he does not stop. Tell him to find work in his own vineyard and leave mine be."

Deborah looked at the offender. "Does

this man speak the truth?"

The man nodded. "Yes," he said, his voice faltering, "but only because we have no vineyards. All we have is a garden that has not yet begun to produce enough food, for there has been such little rain this spring. I pass by his vineyards, which are overflowing and ripe for harvest." He ran a hand over his beard. "I do not take more than I can eat. Not even to share with my wife and small sons. I eat enough to take my fill so that they can eat the food we have."

Deborah waited a moment, but the man apparently had no more defense. "You do not fill a bag with the fruit?"

He shook his head. "No, Prophetess." He hung his head again as though to admit such poverty shamed him, which Deborah was most certain it did.

She faced the accuser once more. "Have you seen this man take bags of your fruit and carry them out of your vineyard?"

The man's right hand clenched then released. He rubbed the back of his neck. "Can't say that I've seen him carrying a sack, no. But he has stripped one of my vines of its bottom branches."

"Out of how many branches, would you say?"

The man looked suddenly uncomfortable.

"Does it matter how many?" His defiant tone caused Deborah to lift a brow.

"You have come to me for judgment to decide between you. Will you abide by that judgment?" She folded her hands and straightened, her gaze unflinching.

The man looked beyond her, then slowly nodded. "Yes, Prophetess. I will accept what you say, for I know you speak the words of God."

"I only speak what I know comes from the law that Moses gave to us, my lord. It is the law you must heed. And whether you have many vines or few, the law says this: 'If you go into your neighbor's vineyard, you may eat your fill of grapes, as many as you wish, but you shall not put any in your bag. If you go into your neighbor's standing grain, you may pluck the ears with your hand, but you shall not put a sickle to your neighbor's standing grain.' "

She motioned to the one accused, who had lifted his head in wonder at her words. "So you see this man has not broken any law of God. He has only filled his hunger by taking food that he could find." She looked once more at his accuser. "Perhaps you could find it in your heart to hire him to help you harvest your grapes and make your wine, and then he will have money to purchase food for his hungry family."

The man nodded grimly and seemed at least the slightest bit chagrined. He looked at his nemesis. "You could have told me you had no food. You could have asked for my help."

The other man glanced again at his feet. "I was ashamed. I thought we could live on the land. Except I did not expect my wife to become ill with the birth of our last child or the rains to be so slim. We are not near a brook where I can draw water as you can for your vines."

The accuser placed a hand on his neighbor's shoulder. "Come to work for me. I have more than I need, and I daresay I should have known this law long ago." He looked into Deborah's eyes, and she noticed the slightest sheen of regret in his. "Thank you, Prophetess. You are truly a woman of God."

They turned and walked off as comrades, and Deborah leaned against the tree, breathing a relieved sigh.

"That turned out well for you." Talya's voice interrupted her moment of respite. "You should come now and rest. It is almost time for the evening meal."

Deborah glanced heavenward. How had she missed the swirling orange and blues of the dusky sky? She gathered her spindle and distaff and rose stiffly from the bench. Talya came and draped the shawl more securely about her shoulders.

"That is kind of you, my daughter." She offered the girl a smile, but it was not returned. At least she had not been met with a scowl or a tone of bitter scorn.

They walked in silence toward the house when at last Talya spoke. "I have talked with Abba, and I wanted to make sure you agree."

By her daughter's unyielding posture Deborah knew that if she disagreed, Talya would make life more difficult than it already was.

"Tell me." Though she really was too weary to hear it now.

Talya seemed not to notice her exhaustion in the wake of her own enthusiasm. "Lavi has taught me to use the sling, and I have practiced in the cave below the house. But he said I need to practice in daylight in the fields so that I can gauge the angle of the sun as I aim. Abba said I could come to the fields with them tomorrow, if you will but agree." Talya touched Deborah's arm, her fingers warm and vibrant on Deborah's skin. "Please say yes, Ima." How rarely had the girl called her thus. It was always *Mother.* And with a tone of disdain. "I heard what

Barak said, and I promise not to stray. Consider this as helping me to prepare in case danger truly does arise as Barak has warned us."

Deborah stopped midstride to assess her daughter. The girl had inherited her father's full mouth and wide eyes but Deborah's own rounder face and high cheekbones, while she seemed to possess the determination of them both. The girl needed a husband more than ever.

"If you promise to stay close to your father and brothers, you may go." Though Deborah questioned her own sense in saying so.

Talya's smile lit her face, and she jumped like a young gazelle, nearly dancing in the middle of the dirt street. When she came to rest on both feet again, she bent to kiss Deborah's cheek. "Thank you, Ima. You will be proud of me. You'll see. And who knows? Perhaps one day, once I am as good as Lavi is with a sling, he will teach me the bow as well. Then just let Sisera try to come after us. If you can lead Israel's men in judgment, I can kill the enemy with one blow."

She skipped off, not waiting for Deborah to respond. A woman kill Sisera? Unheard of. She had long imaged Barak would be the one to deal that final fateful blow. She shook her head and walked slowly toward the courtyard where food awaited, trying not to think that her daughter was both obstinate and delusional.

Travel along the overgrown hillsides and through the dense forests was slow going past Shiloh toward the village of Arumah. Barak and his men took to moving in the open areas at night when the roads were clear, but even then one could not trust that Sisera's spies were not hiding in the bushes and caves that sometimes dotted the sides of the roads.

He stopped his small band of men a stone's throw from Arumah's broken walls and splintered bricks. The charred scent of a recent fire set his heart pounding. Surely Sisera had already been here — done exactly as Barak had feared. He stumbled a step forward, the weight of grief staggering.

Keshet caught his arm, his presence steadying. "How do you want to handle this?" he asked, his tone a fierce whisper.

Barak shook himself, blinking back the acrid, nauseating scent of death. He pushed one foot in front of the other. "We have to see if anyone is left alive. We will rescue those we can." He glimpsed the shaft of an arrow lodged into the side of the broken wall. "And bury their dead."

Sluggish and weary, he braced himself as the broken bricks and splintered doors of the gate drew closer. In the streets, men lay strewn like felled trees. No sign of the women or children.

"Check the houses for idols," Barak commanded, "and any living creature." But the search yielded neither life nor false god.

"Sisera has taken not only the daughters of the elders but their wives and livestock as well," he said after the last house was searched and the last man buried in a nearby cave.

"So it seems." Keshet's dark eyes flashed, his right hand keeping a tight grip on his bow. "Unless we find their bodies along the way."

"Some of them might still be alive." Barak's pulse quickened.

"More likely they have all been taken as slaves to Harosheth-hagoyim," Keshet said.

"We will search the brush along the road to Shechem. Perhaps we will find a few of the weaker ones." Or those so abused they would barely resemble a woman or child, as Barak had found Nessa those years ago. A sick knot tightened his gut. He turned away from the burial cave and started walking away from the city. Had Sisera taken idols they had hidden? Or were they simply victims of the whole nation's unfaithfulness?

Either way, this business of Sisera's treachery must stop.

How long, Adonai? When will You send us a deliverer?

"Do you think we can reach Shechem by nightfall?" Keshet's voice held a thin trace of worry.

Barak glanced at the sky. Doubtful they could make such a lengthy trek in their weary state, but he did not say so. "Of course," he said instead. Shechem meant refuge.

To Barak's relief, Shechem's walls were indeed intact, its people safe. But even here Barak could not rest. Urgency laced his words as he met with the elders and told them of Arumah and warned them of Sisera's latest threat. The elders in turn commanded every man to disclose any idols in their homes, eventually finding none.

Two days later Barak and his men headed north to Tirzah, then on to Beth-shan, near his hometown of Kedesh-naphtali along Kinneret's shores, each time meeting with the same reaction. No idol worship to be found, and every elder on edge. Barak's anger mounted.

"How can the prophetess say the land is

still filled with idol worship when we have found none?" he asked Keshet one night as they settled along Kinneret's banks.

"We have yet to search every town, my friend. Perhaps it takes only one as it did in the days of Achan and Joshua." Keshet whittled a piece of driftwood while the rest of Barak's men sat in a circle about the fire, talking quietly.

"I hadn't thought of that." Keshet's words were sobering. "What do you think of visiting that Kenite for weapons?" One of the elders of Beth-shan had informed them of a Kenite, a metalworker, living nearby in the sanctuary at the oak of Zaanannim.

"What makes you think the man will want to help us?" Keshet looked toward the south in the direction where the Kenite lived. "Just because he's a metalworker doesn't mean he makes swords. They make bowls, vases, cups, statues, and figures too. He could be making idols for all we know."

"Kenites have a history with Israel." Barak picked up a small branch and drew circles in the dirt. "Moses's brother-in-law was a Kenite."

"Family ties don't always bind together, you know." Keshet's words gave Barak pause. The man spoke from a life of broken promises, of not only a lost sister to Sisera

97

but a lost wife who returned to her father, considering Keshet too weak to protect her. Keshet had been forced to give the woman a writ of divorcement against his wishes. But her father had the power of the city on his side, and Keshet had nothing.

"Not everyone is like your family, my friend." Barak searched his mind for a good example of an intact, loving family. There were so few in the years of Canaanite oppression. Their land *had* become divided by worship of false gods — more so in the earlier years after Ehud died than today, but everyone still did what they thought right, whether the law agreed with them or not. "Deborah's family is one that has a tight bond." Funny that he didn't think of that earlier. With the memory, he recalled the daughter who seemed much too eager to please him or the men in her family but had less respect for the prophetess.

"Perhaps you are right. We won't know if we don't ask the man to help." Keshet's comment brought Barak's thoughts back to their goal.

"You and I will go alone," he said, "lest the man and his family think we have come to raid them."

Talya walked the winding path to the olive

grove that bordered her father's fields, her leather quiver hanging over her right shoulder and a small bow clutched in her left hand. She had taken to pulling her robe and tunic between her legs and tucking them into the belt that hung low on her hips to secure her ability to run at the first hint of danger. Keeping the belt lower allowed her to loosen the robe at the top, hiding her womanly curves, yet did not expose her legs to the point of indecency. Her father had accepted her actions, but if her mother knew the lengths she went to in order to move quickly, she would surely insist Talya's lessons in weaponry end.

A sigh escaped as she trudged along, her ear attuned to her surroundings. Her mother was far too protective. If not for Lavi's help in shaping the wood for the bow and teaching her to wax the linen for the string, and in whittling the long sticks into arrows and showing her how to grind the stones to sharp points to put at their heads, she would still be using a simple sling and stones, nothing more.

She tugged the strings of the sling still tied to her wrist, assured that they were secure. With two weapons, she would be a forceful warrior, even if she never got to use her skills for more than hunting birds in the trees. But in the weeks since Barak's visit, she had practiced, and she knew without doubt — she would not be taken captive by the Canaanites without a fair fight.

She approached the grove, taking in the familiar sight of the gnarled branches whose great arms spoke of long years in this place. Guilt nudged her as she rounded the bend in the grove, heading home. She should have waited for her father and brothers to accompany her through the main gates, but she feared her mother's greeting and another confrontation. She knew better. She also should have asked her mother's permission to follow the men today. But her family's fields had shown no evidence of Sisera's threat, and she was always within a stone's throw of her brothers. Better to slip away unnoticed by her mother than to face the constant strife.

She quickened her pace, eager to reach home before her mother's duties with the people came to an end. But a strange sound met her ear as she approached the next row of trees. She stopped. Was that a pagan chant?

Her pulse jumped. She edged closer, gauging the distance of the sound. The voice carried a familiar female lilt. She stepped warily over protruding roots and dry twigs until —

She stopped cold. In the clearing a tall idol sat stately atop a tree stump. Yiskah, her cousin Shet's wife, bent low before it, repeating guttural sounds and foreign words.

"What are you doing?" Talya spoke before she could think and headed straight for the idol. Asherah. She whirled about and faced Yiskah, whose wide eyes narrowed to slits, her expression moving from stricken to defiant.

"What do you think I'm doing?" Yiskah straightened, though she remained on her knees. "You are interrupting my worship."

Talya stared. Shet, her closest childhood friend, had chosen this woman in place of her? Her throat felt suddenly dry. She swallowed once, twice. "We are to worship the Lord our God and Him only." She repeated the words she had been taught all of her life, and suddenly she wondered why she had ever doubted them. Her mother was right — this foreign worship was hurting the whole nation and it had to stop.

"Your God does not listen to my prayers," Yiskah said, her voice slightly less defiant than it had been. "If He had, Shet and I would have a quiver of children by now."

"You have not been married long enough to hold a whole quiver." Talya knew the retort was unkind, but the girl was barely older than she was, by just a handful of years, and a child could still be forthcoming.

"I know that I cannot give Shet what he wants, and your God does not answer. Asherah gives life. She will hear my prayers." Yiskah lifted her chin and stood as if in challenge.

Talya took one lengthy look at this cousin she could not understand, then bent, picked up a heavy stone, and turned on the idol, smashing its head in.

Yiskah screamed. "What are you doing?" She rushed at Talya, who hurled her whole weight against Yiskah.

"Silence! Do you want all of Sisera's army to come down on us?" Did not Yiskah realize the danger?

"Asherah always protects me," the girl said through gritted teeth. She scrambled free of Talya's hold and ran into the trees.

Talya looked from the half-ruined idol to her fleeing cousin, trying to decide whether to finish the work of turning the idol to rubble or run after the foolish woman. Yiskah would surely get lost in the woods and Shet would be devastated. But Shet would be more devastated to learn that his wife secretly worshiped Asherah. Wouldn't he?

Decision made, she took off after Yiskah. She must find her even if it meant she would return to the village late and have to explain her actions to her mother.

6

Deborah's stomach twisted, the sick feeling all too familiar. *Oh Adonai, how long?* The prayer came as frequently as her breath, but despite the tears and the heart-wrenching yearnings that rose from the very depths of her soul, God had not spoken since that day weeks ago near the palm tree. Which meant idols must still have some hold over her people.

"Have mercy on us." The words were a whisper and a constant prayer. And how could she not pray? Her people were like children to her as they came each day for judgment. Even the warriors among them seemed so helpless, so lost, against this greater threat that was Canaan.

Should they search from house to house? Should they take the risk and sacrifice once more at Shiloh? But though the tabernacle resided there, Shiloh was home to corrupt priests, and if they traveled so far, the men in their villages would fear leaving their women unguarded.

Oh Adonai, what should we do?

Heart heavy, she gathered her spinning and headed home, her mind whirling with the speed of the distaff. When she reached the courtyard, her granddaughter Tikva raced toward her, arms outstretched, pushing aside Deborah's spinning and her worries.

"And how are my little ones this afternoon?" She scooped young Tikva into her arms and rubbed the top of Orel's head.

"We played and Ima helped us learn to draw letters in the dirt," Orel said proudly, a true grandson of a Levite. "But I missed Talya. She takes us for walks and lets us gather bugs."

Deborah smiled at the boy, but her gaze shifted to Libi, Orel's mother. "Why was Talya unable to care for them today?"

"She went with the men again." Libi brushed flour from her robe and blew the hair from her eyes. "She said you knew."

Deborah thought back through the conversation she'd had that morning with Talya and shook her head. "No. She did not tell me of her intent nor ask my permission." Irritation rose swift and harsh, causing her head to throb. She placed Tikva down, and

105

the two children ran into the house. "Are the men back yet?" They often returned before she finished her cases for the day, especially when the lines were long and people had come from a distance.

Ahava nodded. "They returned a short time ago. I sent them to clean up."

"And Talya was with them then?" Deborah's heart did a strange flip.

The girls exchanged glances. "I didn't see her. Did you?" Ahava's brow furrowed with the question, and Libi slowly shook her head as if the truth had suddenly dawned.

Deborah did not wait to hear more. She burst into the house in search of Lavi and Lappidoth. "Where is Talya?" Her tone was harsh, like her life felt in that moment.

The men looked at each other, then at Deborah. "She said she was coming home . . . hours ago." Lappidoth's face paled. Deborah's legs grew suddenly weak as a new kid's. She searched for something to hold on to when Lavi's arm came around her for support.

"She is not here." The words did not sound as though Deborah had spoken them. She searched her son's troubled gaze. "Did she tell you something, anything?"

Lavi's brows knit, a myriad of emotions filling his eyes. "She told me nothing, Ima. I

106

promise. I would not lie to you."

Elior entered the room at that moment. "Talya is missing?"

Lappidoth said something Deborah barely heard. She sagged against Lavi's strength, fighting to regain her own.

"We'll find her, Ima," Lavi spoke softly in her ear.

"But where would she have gone?" There had been no sign of Sisera's chariots on the road below. "Has someone checked the cave?"

"I'll do it now." Elior ran off before anyone else could speak.

"If you will be all right, Ima, I will check with the guards at the gate." Lavi squeezed her shoulders, and Deborah allowed him to lead her to one of the cushions where she sank down, drained of energy.

Deborah looked at Lappidoth, whose face mirrored her own sense of utter helplessness and loss. "Do you think Sisera . . . ?" She could not finish the thought.

"No." Lappidoth came and knelt at her side, taking both of her hands in his. His gentle touch brought back so many memories, so many times he had attempted to comfort her where this favorite of his children was concerned. And yet, too often he had made excuses for her. "You know how she is," he said, the familiar comment causing a sharp rift in her spirit. "She probably decided to explore something and got lost."

"She could die in the woods if she can't find her way out." How unsympathetic she sounded. Yet her anger simmered, and she could not seem to pull her mind from her helplessness and the reminder that where Talya and her father were concerned, she was a stranger, an outcast.

"She won't die." Lappidoth's voice rose, strong, insistent — defensive. "She's smart and capable and she knows how to survive."

Suddenly she did not want his comfort. She pulled her hands from his grasp, heart pounding. "You don't know that! You cannot possibly know what will happen."

He winced and she knew she should not take out her anger on him. And yet, if he had been a stronger man, disciplined their daughter more, said no now and then . . . She looked away from the hurt in his gaze.

"We must pray for her." He stood abruptly and walked to the window, no doubt hoping to see Talya even now hurrying up the street with some excuse for her delay.

"I have never stopped praying for her," she said. Yet the anger remained and her heart matched her bitter tone. His excuses, his assurances, even his prayers, did not comfort.

Talya turned slowly in a circle, fighting the fear that traced the edges of her thoughts. She couldn't be lost. Yiskah had come this direction. Surely she had. Talya had followed her steps, taken great care to pause now and then to read the footprints in the dirt, and even taken care to note the shape and color of the bushes she passed as she entered the dark forest.

But the sun had dipped so quickly — how had she missed the orange hues that warned of deepening shadows? She should have found her way back hours ago — had it been hours? She glanced heavenward but could not see the sky past the covering of trees.

Where was she? Her pulse jumped at the call of a night hawk and the answering squeal of captured prey. Barak's warning flashed in her heart.

Be safe. Do not travel without men to accompany you. You risk your life if you do.

Her hand clenched the bow so tight she thought it might snap. *Relax. You will find a way out.* But her self-assured words only tightened the sinking feeling in her gut with each passing moment.

She tilted her head at a sudden rush of wind. Leaves rustled the air in the trees above her head, and night creatures suddenly seemed to enter a celebration of mismatched song.

"Yiskah?" She called her cousin's name for the hundredth time, softly, lest someone besides the animals and insects hear.

Fear took up the melody of the night sounds and danced a strange rhythm in her chest. She slipped the bow into the quiver at her back and fitted a stone into the sling instead. Barak's men knew these woods — but Sisera's men did too, if Barak spoke truth.

Talya glanced again at the sky through the trees' thick tops, now seeing a small handful of distant stars. She squinted into the darkness ahead, her feet carrying her over broken branches that somehow crunched too loudly in her ear. Was she headed the right direction? How had she gotten so turned around?

Muscles tensed in every part of her body, and her senses rose to heightened alert. Birdcalls caused her heart to thump harder. Sometimes men mimicked birdsong. She paused beneath the limbs of a thick oak and pressed a hand against it for support. To chase Yiskah through the trees had been a foolish choice.

Surely her parents, her brothers, would be sick with worry by now and probably out combing the woods in search of her. But what if she had come too far east or south? Would Yiskah have returned, hidden the idol, and lied to Shet of her whereabouts? Would Yiskah care what happened to her, tell anyone where she had gone?

What a fool she was.

The dusk deepened further. No light broke through these surroundings, not in any direction. She turned slightly. Surely she had come from behind. All she need do was walk back that way. One step at a time, she felt her way through the darkness. But without the light, without even a torch to guide her, she would never find the markings now. She should stop and stay where she was until dawn broke. But with the loss of sun came the brisk threat of cold.

She shivered, though the chill air could not compare to her fear — that living thing crawling its way deep within her, as loud as the creatures that spoke all around her.

Deborah stood atop the city gate with both daughters-in-law, watching the torches carried by the men of the city move through the brush. Her heart beat with sluggish strokes, as though her body rebelled at the need to cling to hope. *Talya, where are you?*

An ache no words could comfort settled within her as she recalled the last words they had spoken. An argument. Always conflict with that girl, and always over Talya's need to prove herself capable of defending herself and anyone around her. Her boasts seemed so hollow now.

"They are returning," Libi said, pointing to the line of torches now drawing near the city gates. Guards pulled the leather straps, and the wooden boards squealed against their effort to open them. Deborah searched the stream of men for some sign of her daughter, but the darkness hid the outline of their faces.

"Do you see her?" She glanced from one daughter-in-law to the other. Both shook their heads.

"It's too dark to tell, Ima Deborah." Ahava touched her arm. "But do not fear. God is with her."

Was He? She nodded, unwilling to allow the thought to take hold, and flew down the steps with the strength of one young again. She hurried to Lappidoth's side. "Any sign of her?"

Lappidoth's shoulders sagged even as he reached for her outstretched hand. "I'm sorry, my love. There was no sign. It is too dark to see her footsteps."

Her strength drained as water from a broken cistern seeps into dust. The bitter taste of gall filled her throat, and she choked, nearly emptying her stomach in the center of the square. *Get hold of yourself.* She spoke to her heart, trying to wake it from its deadness, for her limbs refused to move until the men around her began the slow trek to their homes and the gate's hinges squealed once more, shutting out all who might seek entrance in the night.

Talya would not be coming home.

Where are you? Her heart cry echoed within her, seeking a place to settle, feeding the guilt, the anguish, she had feared since the moment she realized Talya had not returned with her men for the evening meal. Hours had passed. Stars now danced above them, and Deborah had the sudden urge to wish for clouds to hide their winking brightness. How dare they shine down on them to glimpse her pain.

She closed her eyes and sucked in a much-needed breath. Scents of earth and fire drifted to her. Footsteps receded into the distance as the men continued home. Silence filled the space around her now, broken only by the breathing of her husband, sons, and daughters-in-law.

"We should go home, Ima," Lavi said, coming to stand at her side. "There is nothing more to be done for Talya tonight but pray."

Deborah lifted blurred eyes to his and swiped errant tears from her face. She slowly nodded as one in a dream and allowed her son to guide her steps.

But a moment later the peace of the square shattered with the wails of a young woman. Deborah stopped, turning toward the sound. The woman's weeping grew louder. As she came into the torchlight, it was clear her husband had fairly dragged her out of their house and cast her toward Deborah's feet.

"Tell her what you just now told me." Her cousin Shet clenched both hands, and Deborah could see that he was using every bit of self-control he possessed not to lash out at his wife in front of them all.

Yiskah held her hands over her head as if waiting for a blow, her weeping carrying throughout the small village.

"Hush now," Deborah said, in no mood to put up with the exaggerated emotion. "Tell me what you know."

The girl's tears did not abate despite Deborah's command until her husband yanked her up by the arm and turned her to face Deborah. "I . . . that is . . . I saw Talya this afternoon." She gulped, and Deborah's body went rigid in a vain attempt to force herself to be patient.

"I was in the olive grove just north of our settlement . . . worshiping Asherah." The woman's words caused a look of near hatred to appear on Shet's face.

"Go on," Deborah said, trying to ignore the thought that Yiskah could be the cause of the nation's suffering and what she herself would do about it if she was.

"Talya caught me and confronted me, and . . . she picked up a rock and smashed it against the image. I feared she would use it on me or that the goddess would strike me dead for what Talya did." She turned suddenly defiant eyes on her husband. "Your own grandfather allows his wife to worship her."

Shet's hand connected with Yiskah's cheek so fast it left Deborah speechless. "My grandfather married a foolish woman after my grandmother died, as it appears I have done as well. My father and mother do not worship idols, *wife.* Nor do I." He was shouting now, and Deborah raised a hand to stop the outrage.

"We will surely deal with this, my son.

115

And you are right to be angry. We all have the right to be angry with this. But right now, we must find Talya before Sisera does." She looked at Yiskah, who seemed less defiant and not nearly as weepy now.

Yiskah held a hand to the cheek Shet had slapped. "I don't know where she went, Prophetess. I ran off and circled back to my home. I thought Talya would follow."

"Why did you not tell us this hours ago, before the men wasted precious time searching in what could very well have been the wrong direction?" Deborah curled her hands tight, forcing herself to calm. Beating the girl here and now would not give them the answers they desired. And stoning her would rile the men into a frenzy, and they would lose all strength to continue the search in the morning.

Oh Adonai, what do I do?

"It is too dark to look for Talya anymore this night," Lappidoth said, making the decision for her. "We will set out at first light. If she lost her way, she could have ended up in one of the forests that stretch between Bethel and Ramah. It could take days to search the area. In the meantime, go home. Sleep. And meet me at the gate at dawn." He dismissed the men who had

116

stayed while her sons half carried Deborah
to their house.

7

Jael stepped into the small clearing, a kind of simple courtyard she'd made in front of her tent, and lifted the clay urn atop her head. "Gather dung and twigs for the oven," she said to Daniyah as the girl emerged from Jael's tent, her hair disheveled and the look of sleep in her eyes. "I'm going to the well."

Nadia and Raja met her as she passed them, each woman carrying her own water jug.

"I trust you both slept well," Jael offered as they fell into a rhythmic step, the jugs balanced on their heads.

Nadia shrugged. "I fear I do not sleep as well as I did in the desert. The night sounds of the forest waken me."

"I hear them too," Raja said. "Fareed doesn't hear a thing. The man could sleep through a windstorm."

The girls laughed softly, but Jael held her

tongue as they approached the berm that they must cross to reach the road just above them — the road Sisera's chariots had traveled that first day and several times since.

Sisera had been to visit their camp, each time surrounded by hundreds of outfitted warriors, men who were too confident, too arrogant. Jael's heartbeat quickened at the memory of his first visit.

"Ah, Heber, such lovely women you have!" Sisera had turned from facing Heber and walked deliberately toward Jael's tent, where Daniyah stood beneath the awning, her hair draped in a thick veil that did not hide her face. He pushed past Jael before she could think to respond and stopped in front of Daniyah.

Fear rushed up Jael's spine, and Heber drew closer. But Sisera's men blocked his path. "And what do we have here?" His long fingers cupped Daniyah's cheek, stroking each side slowly, deliberately, his sneer evident. And then in one swift movement, he boldly undid the clasp of the veil that hid her flowing dark hair. Once, twice, he sifted the strands between his fingers.

Daniyah gasped but did not move, her pulse pounding in her throat.

If you dare touch her . . . But he *was* touching her right in front of them, and no

119

one moved for the fear he evoked.

"Someday you will come to me willingly, my sweet." He pulled back, his smile confident, then strutted like a peacock toward Heber once more. "I will be back for those weapons within two weeks. Do not disappoint me."

Jael closed her eyes, tamping down the rising panic that always accompanied the memory. The well was just over the rise, not far from the city of Kedesh-naphtali where she had met some of their women. She stopped abruptly at the sight of two men walking toward them.

"Stop," she hissed, extending a restraining hand toward the girls. "Go back."

The men drew closer, and the girls turned quickly and obeyed without question. But the men had spotted Jael, so she waited for them to approach, wishing now that she carried one of those daggers Heber made.

"Who are you and why have you come?" she asked, her tone strong, bold. She would not let them see her fear. By the look of them, they were Israelites, not of Canaan. Nonetheless, she took a cautious step backward.

The one who appeared to be the leader, with long scraggly hair and beard, held up both hands to show he carried no weapon.

"We come in peace. Is this the camp of Heber the Kenite?"

"Tell me who you are and perhaps I will answer your question." She did not have to trust them just because they were Hebrew, ancestral history between them or not.

The man gave a slight bow. "Forgive me, mistress. I am Barak, son of Abinoam of Kedesh-naphtali." He extended a hand toward his companion. "And this is my friend Keshet, son of Meshech, also of Kedesh-naphtali. We wish to speak to Heber the Kenite."

Jael studied the men for a lengthy moment, assessing the man's words. "Heber is my husband," she said at last. "Follow me." She turned and made her way back down the embankment, leading them toward Heber's tent, which was larger than the rest. She had even woven a striped banner to place along its awning to show visitors that his was the tent where they could seek welcome or refuge. A protection for the women, whose tents were off-limits to any visiting men, though Sisera had not cared one whit for the rules of hospitality.

"If you wait here, I will send for him." Jael motioned to a circle of large stones that acted as a courtyard in front of the tent's opening, then turned to her tent, where she met Daniyah just returning with dung and twigs. "Go and fetch your father."

Daniyah lifted a curious brow but did not question her mother's direction. Jael watched her run off toward the altar where Heber prayed each morning. These men were certainly early risers, the timing of their visit almost unseemly. She needed water if she was to prepare food for them, should Heber invite them to stay. But she couldn't leave until Heber returned.

She walked to the tents of her daughters-in-law and sent them to the well, snagging her son Ghalib to go with them in her place. Heber returned moments later while Jael sat at the grindstone in front of her tent, straining to hear what the men had come to say. When it became evident that the scraping and grinding would drown out their voices, she commissioned Daniyah to do the work and slipped behind Heber's tent to listen.

"We come in peace, my lord," Barak said, holding his hands out once more in that defenseless gesture. Both men had stood at Heber's approach, and all three remained standing. "We are neighbors to you, and we seek your help."

"And how can I help you, my son?" Heber folded his arms, clearly not opening his home to them yet.

"We are men of Israel of the tribe of Naphtali. As you may have heard, our land has been cruelly oppressed by the Canaanites for these past nineteen, nearly twenty years. King Jabin's commander, Sisera, has nine hundred iron chariots and thousands of men. They have brutally abused our women and children and killed many of our men. We are few in number, and we have few weapons at our disposal." Barak cleared his throat, but his bold gaze did not leave Heber's face. "We have heard that you are a Kenite, a worker of metal, and we would ask you to help us, to make us weapons to fight our enemies."

Heber stood silent so long that Jael wondered if he would speak at all.

"We had planned to come a few weeks ago, but we've been delayed by Sisera's raids on our people," Barak added.

Barak's question clearly posed a dilemma for Heber, since he would need additional supplies of ore to meet the demands of both Canaan and Israel. At last Heber sat on one of the large stones and motioned for them to do the same. He called Jael to bring the men water and food, and she hurried to gather both. When she returned, she released a frustrated breath. They had clearly spoken while she had left to do Heber's bidding.

"So Sisera brings you copper ore and tin, and you make them into swords and spears and shields for him?" Barak's tone held the slightest hint of anger, but his smooth features did not reveal what was surely in his heart. How could he not be angry with the man who was helping their enemy? Yet he accepted Jael's food with a grateful smile and did not say the cutting words she expected.

"I know it sounds harsh to you," Heber said as they ate. "But I do so to protect my family. If I had realized Sisera would act as he did . . ." He paused, swallowed hard, and Jael knew he shared the memory of helplessness they had felt when Sisera nearly defiled Daniyah right in their presence. Had the man no shame? "I would never have left the Negev."

"Do you plan to move back?" Barak sipped from the clay water jar.

"I have reasons that I cannot. But my daughter is not safe here." Heber did not meet Barak's gaze and seemed to find the flatbread and cheese most interesting.

"Forgive me, my lord, but none of your women are safe with Sisera." Barak wiped his mouth with his sleeve. "If I supply you with copper ore and tin, will you do for us as you are doing for Sisera? I cannot pay you. We have little gold or silver or even food to offer. But I can find a way to supply you with the materials you need if you will consent to make us daggers and swords." Barak touched the flatbread but did not eat, waiting for Heber's reply.

Jael studied her husband, her emotions so conflicted. She understood him. He thought he had no choice with Sisera. He had to protect them until they could find a way to flee. But why so hesitant to help Israel? Surely he could get the copper and tin as easily as this man could — a man who knew nothing of the trade.

"You can find the tin and copper ore near Succoth, across the Jordan. You can also find them near Gerar and farther south near Punon and the Arabah. But I warn you, Sisera frequents these same locations, along with plundering the trade caravans that bring the ores from the south. If you can find a caravan brave enough and careful enough to withstand Sisera's bands of outlaws, you will find what you need." Heber extended a piece of flatbread to Barak, a sign of acceptance.

Barak took it and ate. His smile made Jael realize that beneath his gruff exterior was a rather young and handsome man. Perhaps someone for Daniyah — to keep her safe? She would tuck the idea in her mind for now.

The men left soon, claiming the need to hurry. Sisera's men had grown bolder, kidnapping the virgin daughters of their Israelite leaders, they'd said, and in some cases killing whole towns of men.

Jael's heart skipped several beats at the news. Daniyah was not safe here. Why oh why had she ever thought it a good idea to move them away from their family?

Barak led his men south toward a trade center not far from Shechem, hoping to avoid crossing the Jordan at its high point near Succoth. He didn't like the odds of meeting Sisera on the roads during the day, so they kept to the forests and hills of Ephraim heading toward the Philistine territory of Gerar. Surely they would find the spot where Heber had directed them. Surely the ore they sought could be found.

The thought troubled him as it did every waking moment since his meeting with Heber, since the caravans they'd stopped had already been stripped of ore by Sisera. What made him think the Philistines would offer their ore to help their enemies? If they had long memories, they would recall Shamgar, son of Anath, helping Israel to the Philistines' detriment. The idea that they should sell ore to help Israel was the hope of a desperate man.

But he had no choice.

Dusk cast long shadows over the forested path, yet he hurried onward, trying to out walk the thoughts that were taking him to places he did not wish to go. A whistle, the familiar call of Keshet, caused him to make an abrupt stop and turn. Keshet strode closer and motioned him to a clearing not far from the main road to Bethel.

"You do realize that your pace would match the flight of a fleeing gazelle, my friend." Keshet touched Barak's shoulder, coaxing him to still. "The men are exhausted." He waved a hand heavenward where dark had descended. "We need rest."

Barak glanced at the purpling sky, then steadied a look at his men. They stood huddled some distance behind him. How had he not noticed the loss of their company, the lack of hearing their banter or murmurs?

"You are right, of course." He clapped Keshet on the back and flicked his gaze over the area. Keshet made the sound of a hoot owl, and some of the men bent low to strike a fire in a hearth they had apparently already built. "I see you decided to stop with or without me." He leveled Keshet with a look and raised a curious brow.

Keshet chuckled. "Just keeping the men happy, Captain."

Barak sobered despite his friend's attempt at humor. They had no assurance of finding the ore they sought. He couldn't even predict that his men would remain loyal and continue to fight Canaan. They had their slings and bows, but no swords, no chariots, no shields, nothing to sustain them in face-to-face combat. And they were so few in number. Sisera's men were like the grains of sand along the shore.

A defeated sigh he could not contain filled his chest. He ran a hand over the back of his neck. He needed to dip in the river. He needed a warm mat and his wife at his side. But life didn't always give a man what he wanted.

He looked at Keshet a moment, then nodded. "A wise choice." He moved toward the trees. "I need a few moments alone. Wait with the men."

"Don't get lost in there." Keshet said the words in jest, but Barak knew he meant them.

"I'll be careful." He walked off without a backward glance.

8

Talya shivered as her second night alone in the woods descended. She had walked on and on but after a while was certain she had seen the same trees, the same bushes, even the same bugs. Orel would find that amusing, and right now the thought of seeing her nephew sent a deep ache to her heart. *Oh Adonai, please let them find me. Or show me the way out.*

Another involuntary shiver worked through her. She didn't want to wander around here until she died of starvation or thirst. Or Sisera found her.

Her foot accidentally connected too hard with a stone and sent it flying. It landed with a thud. At least it hadn't hit a jackal or some other wild animal. She hugged her arms about her, more careful with her footfalls this time.

Light from the sky had turned from blue to gray long ago, but she could not will herself to sit on the damp ground and tremble through another night. She reached a thick oak and braced her hands against the rough bark, then tucked her head to her knees, praying again.

"I should never have left the village," she said aloud, hoping her voice would keep the creatures at bay. "I'm sorry, Adonai. Is this punishment for how I treat my mother? Wasn't it good that I broke that idol? Is getting lost like this really helping me?"

Tears threatened. She was hungry, tired, and terribly thirsty. Her prayers had gone from bargaining to begging to accusing to pleading again. She sank to her knees. What more did she have to say that would cause the Almighty to change His mind and rescue her? It was too late for any man to find her in the dark. And though her mother might see visions and dreams, *she* never did. There would be no angel like her ancestors had met to guide her way.

Weariness overtook her, and she wasn't sure she still possessed the ability to weep. She must have slept, for when she startled awake, the forest had come to life with its chatter of insects and the distant howl of jackals.

The crunch of leaves and twigs heightened every one of her senses, and she gripped the oak's bark, slowly rising to stand. Was it an animal? Or a man? Her heart beat fast at the sudden brush of fear filling her. The crunches stopped and started. She tilted her head. Were those whispers?

She strained to hear and caught the faint sound of men's voices in accents so thick that she found it hard to understand them. "Told you not to come this way. How we going to find our way out now?"

"Shh. Stop your shouting, you fool. That Israelite inhabits these places. You don't want him to find us, do you?"

The whispers ceased, and Talya fought to draw breath. The thick accent was Canaanite, and she clearly understood one word — Israelite. Had they seen her? What Israelite?

She stood still, praying the darkness would hide her from view, but the footsteps drew closer. She felt for the sling at her side. Little use it would be in the middle of so many trees. The stone could bounce off one and come back to injure her.

But as a man stepped into the clearing, another on his heels, she decided that she risked either a stone's misguidance or much worse at their hands. She slowly reached into the pouch and felt for the smoothest stone, slipped it into the sling, and began the rhythmic practiced motion. Round and round she twirled. The men stopped. One looked straight into her eyes. Without thinking, she let the stone fly toward the first man.

"Hey! What — ?" The other man staggered and took several moments to glance at his fallen friend, while Talya fit another stone into her sling and began twirling. The man jumped up and charged toward her.

She let the stone fly and screamed as he pounced on her. Her head slammed into the tree trunk, and the man's hand came down on her arm, dislodging the sling from her grasp. "What have we got here?" She did not miss the sneer in his tone, nor the leer in his eyes.

His face came close, his pungent breath foul to her senses. He covered her mouth with one strong hand while she kicked and fought him with both arms and legs. He uttered a guttural word, probably some curse. Her jaw worked, and when he moved his hand the slightest, she bit down hard on his fingers.

He cried out and she screamed long and loud. His palm connected with her mouth, stunning her. "Let me go!" She shouted and kicked, but his grip was strong. Her second stone had obviously missed its mark, and she had no ability to reach the sling again.

She felt around for a rock, a stick, something.

He grabbed both of her hands and held them down. His look carried such menace, such hate, it took her breath.

"Help me, please!" He had no way to tie her up, and she realized her best defense was to continue to fight him until one of them lost their grip or grew too tired to keep going. She would die here. She would die before she would let them take her to Sisera.

She kicked again, this time using her knees to shove him from her, as her brothers had taught her. He writhed in pain, his grip loosening on her arms. She scrambled free and ran. Branches whipped her face, and she stumbled among the brush, but she pushed up from the ground and did not look back.

His heavy footfalls sounded behind her, and she was certain he was following. Her heart kicked over and pounded like a thousand galloping horses in her chest. She dragged breaths as she ran. *Please, Adonai, show me the way out.* But the darkness shrouded all glimpses of light, and the trees grew thicker. Despair threatened as she weakened. Lack of food and water for the past two days had stolen the strength she once prided herself in. She could not keep this pace.

She slowed the slightest bit, straining to hear the man, glancing behind her, but the darkness obscured her vision. Had he stayed with his fallen comrade? Had he lightened his steps to creep up on her in silence?

She looked through suddenly blurred vision toward a large oak standing tall ahead of her. Perhaps she could hide behind it and wait to see if he truly followed. She listened a moment, carefully planting her feet the next. Forest sounds met her ear, and her eyes adjusted to this new location, catching glimpses of light. Was that a fire in the distance?

But a fire meant more men. Probably the group those men had parted from. Sisera's hounds. She reached the oak and looked from left to right, even above her to the branches that stirred only slightly in the night breezes. They were too high to climb or she would have found a way to scale the trunk and reach them. Instead, she sank to the earth, her heart still pumping too fast, her breathing staggered. *Calm down.* She repeated the words to herself over and over again even as she sought to hear, every nerve on edge. Perhaps she had escaped him.

Had she escaped him? The thought slowly moved through her, as the only sounds she heard were normal forest insects and the flight of bats' wings.

She drew a jagged breath, then another. Just a few moments to rest. Then she would follow the light to the campfire just to see. Perhaps she could steal a water skin while they were sleeping. In the meantime, she told herself, daring to believe it, she would be safe here for a time. If she wasn't, let them kill her. Just please, God, don't let them enslave her.

Barak moved into the familiar trees. They had taken this route to visit the prophetess so often he could find the way in his sleep. But that didn't make his guard lessen. He cocked his head, listening for any strange sound or cry of an animal that could prove trouble. Ever since Nessa's loss, his senses stayed taut as a bowstring. The tension wasn't good for him, as Keshet so often pointed out, but he dare not risk the chance that Sisera might figure out his moves, find his haunts in the forests and caves. Yet even the forests were suspect. He wished he could have convinced his men to keep going until they were within sight of the prophetess's hidden village.

He ran a hand over his beard, then felt the fine leather of the sling at his side. Moving stealthily, he took the narrow path where the largest oak trees stood sentinel, as if they could bar anyone who dared enter from coming too close.

His fingers touched the bark of one in a reassuring gesture, but he shook his head, questioning his own sanity to think of the oak as a welcome friend. On silent feet, he continued on, avoiding the sides of the path where the twigs would crunch and announce his presence to any intruder. He stopped again, listening for the sound of voices.

But the voices were only his men making too much noise for their own good. A sigh escaped, though he muffled the sound, holding even his breath in check. He moved farther into the trees, keeping his bearings on previous markings he'd set in his mind.

He came at last to a small clearing where another large oak stood tall and proud. His private place, one where Keshet could find him but no one came to trouble him. He could pray more easily here, though at the moment he could not seem to find words to form a decent prayer to the Almighty One. What more could he say that hadn't already been said? They needed deliverance. They needed Sisera and Jabin dead, but Barak had found Sisera a formidable foe, one who continually eluded his grasp. And no one stood a chance of infiltrating the walls of Hazor to the palace of King Jabin. If God intended to deliver them, then they needed more than prayer to accomplish the task.

But what? He could not possibly go throughout every home, question every man and woman in Israel to see whether they were true worshipers of Yahweh.

He neared the tree's giant trunk and stepped over several protruding roots to the spot he had smoothed of such intrusions, about to kneel in the dirt, but his foot found unstable ground. He caught his balance, startled at the shriek that met his ears. The soft uneven ground moved. And stood. A moment passed. He stared, pulse kicking up a pace.

"What? Who are you?" By the outline of her frame, she was obviously a young woman, but what on earth was she doing out here alone — in his forest?

"Who's there?" She responded with his very question.

"I believe I asked you first." He watched her step away from him, and in that moment, with the light from the moon that peeked through the tree line, he saw the whites of her wide eyes. "There now. You don't need to fear me. I won't hurt you."

She stepped back again, feeling around the edge of the tree, then turned and broke into a run.

"What — ?" He sprinted after her and caught her in several lengthy strides. She was quick, he'd give her that. And more frightened than a wild doe.

"Let me go!" She writhed and kicked his shin, nearly breaking his hold, but in one swift movement he secured both arms behind her back and forced her against his chest.

"Calm down!" he commanded, his voice low. "If you scream again, you will bring Sisera's army down on us. Is that what you want?"

She stilled for the briefest moment, but then struggled to free herself once more. "How do I know you are not one of them?" she whispered. "Sisera's men, that is. How do I know you will not take me to him?" She stomped on his foot and he uttered a bitter curse. Fool woman!

"Stop your kicking, you little wildcat. I am Barak, son of Abinoam, of Naphtali. Tell me at once who you are before I toss you over my shoulder and carry you to the prophetess. Let her decide what to do with you!" His breath grew heavy with the strain of keeping her arms from flailing.

She stilled once more and drew in a startled breath. He waited for her to respond or to try kicking him again, but she did not move. At last she turned her head, trying to see him, which was impossible to do with her back pressed against his chest.

"I am the daughter of the prophetess. It is I, Talya." Her voice choked, and he could not tell if she was going to laugh or weep.

"Talya? What are you doing out here?" He longed in that moment to turn her to face him, but he wasn't entirely sure he trusted her. "If I let you go, are you going to run or kick me again?" His shin still ached, and his foot throbbed from the places where hers had landed.

She shook her head. "No. I promise. I thought you were that man again, coming to take me to Sisera."

He dropped his hold on her and this time did turn her to face him, his hands gently gripping her shoulders. "What man?" He searched her face, seeing the hint of terror still visible in her dark eyes. "Someone attacked you?" He dared a glance at her clothing, but nothing appeared unduly torn.

She nodded, then tilted her head as if still listening for the man.

"Is he here now? In this woods?" Barak turned them both in the direction that led deeper into the forest. He searched as far as his eyes could see, but saw no movement nor form of a man.

"I got lost two days ago," Talya said quietly. "It's a long story."

"Which you will tell me on our journey to take you home." He wanted to throttle her here and now. And after he had warned them of the danger . . . He tamped down his anger. Perhaps she had a good reason, though not one possible good reason entered his mind.

He took her arm and began walking back to the camp where his men waited. "Where were you attacked?"

She shook her arm as if trying to free herself from his hold, but he would not release her.

"You're hurting me."

He relaxed his hold. "Sorry, but I'm not letting go of you."

She shuddered, and he wondered briefly if she were cold. The shock of all she had been through might cause such a malady. Nessa's teeth had chattered when he had found her, and her whole body shook as though it had no control to stop.

He halted his step and pulled her closer.

The action felt strange. This was Talya, La-vi's little sister. But just the same, he stroked her back in an awkward but hopefully comforting gesture. "Don't be afraid," he said, close to her ear. "I need you to tell me everything you remember about your attack, where you were, when it happened. Perhaps my men can track them down."

"I hit one of them with a stone from my sling . . ."

"Did you?" He could not hide the admira-tion seeping into his tone.

"He dropped hard, so he might still lie on the forest floor." She spoke softly, and he could feel her calming against him. How exhausted she must be. "The other man at-tacked me when I tried another stone. He held me and we fought, but I kicked him hard in a sensitive place and got away. I could not tell you how far I've come."

Barak nearly choked on his tongue at her comments. He held her at arm's length. "For a slight of a girl, you're stronger than you look." He cupped the side of her head. "But come. We will join my men and you will tell me the direction you came from. Then you will rest."

She nodded against his hand, and as he turned her to walk her toward camp once more, he felt strangely bereft of the feeling of holding her, of keeping her safe. But as he soon settled her before the fire with his cloak wrapped around her and Keshet standing guard over her, it was Nessa's face that appeared in his mind's eye. Nessa's broken body . . . which Talya's could have been if she had not been so strong and fast. He shoved thoughts of both women aside as he led six of his men into the forest to complete his mission.

9

Deborah leaned against the parapet of the tower at the city gate, knuckles white in their grip on the rough stones. Her heart beat with sluggish strokes, as though the life she lived in this moment was not her own. Her mind swirled with every imaginable thought, and as the hours waned and she took up the spindle and distaff for something to occupy her shaking hands, the thoughts spun faster, as though trying to keep up with her whirling fingers.

"They will find her, Ima Deborah," Libi said as she handed her son Orel a basket of tangled wool and set him to winding it into a ball. Her voice, always so calm, remained infuriatingly so now. Could she not see the danger? Was she simply oblivious to the reality of Sisera's threat?

"I know they will," Deborah said despite her true feelings, denying the guilt she felt for the lie. She had no word from the Lord that Talya would be safe. She did not know. She only hoped. Hope was such a fragile thread, like the thin strands Orel wound around his ball of wool.

A bead of sweat formed along her brow, and she quickly swiped it with her sleeve. She looked at Orel, whose toothy grin could not help but pull a responding smile from her despite the anxious pounding of her heart. *Please, Adonai, keep all of them safe.* Even children were targets in Sisera's war, often killed in front of their weeping parents. The thought brought the sting of tears, and she walked quickly away lest the girls see her misery, own her fear. Better to let them remain oblivious. What sense was there in breeding deeper fear in them?

She glanced at Tikva asleep beneath the bench in the shade, the image of complete peace. How Deborah longed for them to know such peace always. Why did the All-Knowing One send only visions of darkness and war? *I need hope.* But no vision of peace or hope filled the place where her fear lived.

Why was she finding it so difficult to trust?

She glanced heavenward, but even the sky had filled with clouds too numerous, blocking the sun. How far had the men gotten? Why would Talya run off when Barak had specifically told them the threat had grown too severe? If Yiskah spoke the truth, the girl had simply acted without thinking. So typical of her.

Irritation seeped into the place where worry rested, and she turned away from watching the road, from trying to see into the trees beyond where nothing moved but the leaves and branches. Birds flitted from the trees to the skies, and a lone dove came to rest on the parapet. Deborah studied it, and it seemed to gaze at her for the briefest moment before taking flight to another location out of sight.

Oh, to be like a bird and fly away and be at rest. But as long as her daughter remained lost, there would be no rest. *Did You not call me to lead Your people?* Her prayer held the slightest tinge of anger, for she could not shake the feeling that somehow by her very purpose, by her obedience, her family should be protected.

Shadows blocked the sun's filtered rays even more, and the call of a runner caught her attention. She leaned over the parapet.

"Who are you and why have you come?" she called when he was within earshot.

The man shaded his eyes as he glanced toward her. "I am come from the city of Shechem. The men sent me to tell the prophetess that Sisera has breached the city and kidnapped the daughters of the elders there."

Deborah stared, finding it suddenly difficult to breathe. So it was true. Barak's prediction had now reached Shechem. Had Talya been caught in that same web?

Hours passed and night fell quickly. Only the barest hint of light still clung to the edges of the horizon. Deborah's hands cramped from gripping the parapet so tightly during this final hour. But as the men straggled toward the village gates with no sign of Talya, Libi and Ahava grabbed her arms and held her steady.

"It's all right, Ima Deborah. They will find her. We must believe." Libi leaned her dark head against Deborah's shoulder and patted her arm for comfort.

"Libi is right," Ahava agreed, squeezing Deborah's hand. "Look, there is Lavi, leading a group. Surely he has news." She seemed eager to go to him yet reluctant to leave Deborah's side.

"Take me to him," Deborah said. She leaned on their strength as they maneuvered the steps. She staggered when they reached the last one, her heart skipping a beat, then another, in hope . . . always hope. Ahava,

147

with Tikva on one hip, left her side and raced toward her husband, grabbed his hand, and pulled him toward Deborah.

Lappidoth emerged from behind their son, and Elior stepped forward, catching Libi and Orel in his arms. The men circled Deborah and the girls and children, and Deborah stood stoic, reading the news in each defeated face.

"You did not find her." It was a foolish and obvious thing to say, but she found herself saying it nonetheless for something to fill the awful silence.

"We did not get as far as we might have," Lappidoth said, his tone carrying his telltale attempt to reassure. "The forests are many and thick in the area. She could have traveled a day's journey in any direction. The winds have blown the branches and leaves, hiding her footprints."

Deborah simply nodded, the news adding to the numb feeling she had courted throughout the day. She glanced toward the gate and glimpsed the guard she had put in charge of the man from Shechem, realizing in that moment that she had completely forgotten about him.

"There is news from Shechem," she said dully, looking to each son and her husband in turn. "Sisera has infiltrated the city and taken the daughters of the elders. He is trying to ignite war." She drew a heavy breath and smoothed her robe in a nervous gesture. "I have kept the messenger guarded until we can send a group to Shechem to confirm his story."

Lappidoth stepped near and pulled her close. "You are cold," he whispered against her cheek. "Come. You must not fret, beloved. We will find her."

"In what condition?" Talya's broken body beside a dry wadi filled her imagination. Was it a vision of the future? But it did not feel like a vision from above.

"In good health," Lappidoth insisted. "Come. You must rest."

"I have done nothing but rest all day." She lifted her hands to show him their lack of flax or wool dust, though in the dimness he could not tell to what she alluded. She had stopped her spinning long ago, feeling too restless to continue the task.

Lappidoth seemed to sense her disquiet and wrapped a patient arm around her shoulders. She walked slowly, her thoughts whirling, her feet sluggish. *Talya. Why do you not come home?*

Behind her the sound of the heavy wooden beam being dragged to bar the doors sounded like the high-pitched scream of

149

mourners. Deborah shook her head, angry now. She must stop thinking the worst had come. Hadn't Lappidoth assured her they had not searched every forest? Surely . . . surely . . .

She sagged against her husband's hold, too aware of the eerie silence of her children surrounding her. As though they all walked behind a bier, waiting for that final moment to bury their dead.

Crickets chirped, the sound grating, and high above in the treetops bats awoke, their wings like whispers on the wind. Deborah trudged onward. Their courtyard appeared like a foreign thing, and servants came with food and drink, but Deborah merely shook her head and allowed Lappidoth to lead her to her mat.

"Try to rest, Deborah." Lappidoth knelt at her side and pulled the scarf from her head. He brushed stray strands of hair from her forehead and wiped errant tears from her cheeks, where they could not seem to keep from falling. "We will pray God's protection over her." He bent to kiss her cheek.

"What if God says no?" She looked at him then, the question tasting like bitter herbs on her tongue. "He did not protect the daughters of the elders of Shechem. He has not stopped the slaughter and capture of our innocent women and children throughout all of Israel." She paused, swallowed hard. "He did not protect my father, my brothers." She rolled away from him, forcing back the urge to weep.

He touched her arm, but she shrugged aside his attempt to comfort. "God does not have to answer my prayers, Lappidoth. He will do what He pleases, for His glory." She could not keep the bitterness from shrouding her words.

Lappidoth sat silently beside her for the space of too many breaths. "You are right, beloved. God has no reason to hear our prayers, nor to answer them as we want Him to. But that does not mean we should not pray. Would you tell those who come to you for advice to forget the law, to do as they please?" He turned her gently to face him, his penetrating gaze holding her fast.

She shook her head, her heart feeling as though an arrow had pierced it.

"Did not Moses tell us that God is near when we pray to Him?"

She heard the kindness in his tone. She nodded but could not speak.

He grasped her hand and held it between both of his own. "Deborah." He stroked her palm. "My heart is breaking every moment

I do not hear our daughter's voice. But I cannot blame God for her absence. I can only blame myself for failing to protect her."

"It is not your fault." She spoke from some unimaginable need to comfort him, yet the slightest niggling of doubt accompanied the declaration. She did blame him for not standing up to Talya more often, for leaving Deborah to deal with their constant struggling. "Talya is strong willed. She would have run off whether you allowed her to or not."

The words were unfair and she knew it. Talya was obedient, even if she did beg to get her way. She had simply made a foolish choice, if Yiskah spoke truth. Or . . . Sisera had found her before she got her bearings.

"Talya is strong willed," Lappidoth agreed. "But she is good, and we will find her." He squeezed her hand and bent down to kiss her cheek. "Pray, beloved. And do not fret. We cannot know what tomorrow will bring. But we can trust the One who holds it already in His hand."

Talya glanced at Barak out of the corner of her eye. There had been a firm set to his jaw ever since he returned with the news that they had found no sign of the man who attacked her, though they recovered and buried the body of the one she had killed with her sling.

"How much longer?" she asked, feeling the need for something to fill the quiet.

"Not far now." He tapped the earth with his large staff, like the kind a shepherd carried. A weapon, she knew, to add to the bow and sling he already wore like ornaments across his back and side. He tilted his head to look at her, and she didn't miss his slight smile despite his intense sense of purpose. "Anxious to put your mother's mind at ease?"

"Anxious to sleep on my own mat and not share space with forest creatures." Talya's heart grew light at the full smile he gave her now. "Though Orel will be disappointed that I did not bring him any bugs."

His laugh was low, throaty, as though he would not allow himself to laugh loud and long, as she wished him to. "I could find a few for him." Barak stopped abruptly and moved the earth with his sandaled foot. He lifted a leaf and they both watched a beetle scurry from the intrusion.

She leaned closer. "I think he will be fine with no for an answer this time."

He straightened, his smile unnerving. "Unlike his aunt, who has a hard time hearing that word, especially from her mother?"

Barak's dark eyes probed hers.

"How did you . . . ?" She looked away. "That is not the same thing."

They continued walking, and Talya felt the heat of his gaze even from behind. "Somehow I'm not so sure," he said softly as they rounded a tree line, keeping well away from the road.

Silence fell between them. To argue with him here would cause their voices to carry, and she did not need his men hearing them sparring over something so personal, something she was not willing to admit to him.

She was spared the awkward moment when the gates to her village appeared in the distance moments later. Talya nearly broke into a run to reach them. But Barak stayed her with his hand.

"We go together," he said, his tone commanding. "There is no sense in scaring the guards and having them shoot at us from the wall."

"But it is nearly daylight. Surely they will be able to tell who we are." Talya looked over her rumpled robe — what she could see in the predawn light — and the dust clinging to the headscarf she wore. She couldn't possibly look as bad as her clothes did, but one glance at her hands told her it was still too dark to tell. "Perhaps you have a point. But my mother will soon be watching from the wall, and my father and brothers will be out looking for me." They would look for her. Of course they would.

"They will wait until dawn," Barak said, his pace continuing without a hitch. "Be patient, young one. We will be there soon."

Young one? So that was what he thought of her.

Talya picked up her pace despite his warning, tired of his older-brother patronizing.

He hurried to join her. "What are you doing?"

The gates weren't far now. She would take her chances with the guard on the wall. "I'm going home."

He gripped her hand, and she could not stop the shock that spread up her arm. She nearly stumbled, suddenly too aware of him.

"Talya." He spoke her name more gently now, but she pulled away. She would not be treated as a child.

"What?" She continued walking, not slowing her gait.

"Talya. Wait." This time his voice held a command again, and she stopped midstride. "What is wrong with you?"

She rolled her eyes at him. Such naivety. "I am not a 'young one.' In case you hadn't noticed, I am a fully capable woman who can take care of herself." She crossed her arms and stared him down.

His mouth twitched as though she amused him. She wanted to slap the smirk from his face.

"I can see that. And you are also a woman who can get lost in the woods barely an arrow's shot from her home. But a capable woman, one who can take care of herself." He crossed his arms, mimicking her pose, the staff still clutched in one hand.

"You mock me." The heat in her face intensified.

"So I do." He uncrossed his arms and stepped closer. "Talya. Please don't confuse my comments with insults. It is good to be young, and you are a young maiden."

Her gaze dropped to her feet.

"When you are old, you will wish to be young again. Trust me in this." She looked up to search his gaze, trying to read his age in the lines along his brow.

"You are young," she said at last. "Just because you command men does not mean you are old."

His chest lifted in a sigh, the sound weighty to her ears. "Sometimes a person's life is longer than their years." He looked away from her, his feet slowly moving toward the gate.

"You speak of your first wife." Talya kept his pace.

He looked at her. "My only wife." The bitterness in his tone felt like a barb. The interest and hope she had placed in him vanished. His heart was still wed to a woman who rested in Sheol.

10

"Ima!"

Deborah's heart twisted in an almost physical pain at the voice. She turned from handing her grandson a cup of water to see Talya running down the village street, headed straight for their courtyard.

"Talya!" Deborah couldn't run fast enough, and then Talya was there, flesh of her flesh, clinging, sobbing. "There, there. You're safe now." Deborah's heart pounded despite the assuring words, despite the feel of her daughter's arms around her, their tears mingling.

"Oh, Ima!" Talya hiccuped and leaned back, swiping errant tears. "I got lost in the woods, and the farther I walked trying to get out, the worse it became. If Barak hadn't found me, I would still be wandering among the trees."

A great weight lifted from Deborah's chest as she cupped her hands about her daughter's tear-stained cheeks. "You are safe." *Praise be to You forever, Adonai! Thank You for hearing the prayer of Your humble servant.*

Talya's breath came in short spurts, as though she had too many words to say all at once. "I found Yiskah worshiping in the olive grove, but then she ran off, and when I chased after her I could not find her."

Deborah pulled her close once more. "Hush now. Yiskah has returned and told us everything." She patted Talya's back. "You did well," she whispered against her ear.

Talya drew back as male voices grew closer, but a small smile ghosted her lips. Deborah turned to see Barak and Keshet leading a contingent of men. Talya stepped away from Deborah at their approach.

Barak stood before her, his appearance disheveled and dusty, as though he had not slept well in days. Deborah lifted a hand in greeting, and Lappidoth came from the house to wrap Talya in his arms. Deborah heard the soft weeping and the reassuring words of her husband to their daughter. She turned, thinking to join them, but Lappidoth's eyes were closed, Talya huddled in his arms as though she were a small child. Deborah faced Barak alone. Talya needed her father, and Barak seemed in no mood

159

to wait on them.

"Thank you for rescuing her," Deborah said, looking into Barak's haggard gaze. "Please, come and stay with us. There is much to tell you."

Several hours later, after Talya had relayed the story of her entire ordeal while the women and servants prepared a meal for the men, Deborah called the man from Shechem to stand before Barak and give every detail of the kidnapping of the virgins of his city.

"We don't know how they got beyond our walls," the man told Barak, repeating what he had told Deborah. "But the mothers are dead, the virgins are gone, and the elders have lost all hope. Please, help us."

"Sisera's tactics change from city to city," Barak said, running a hand along his jaw. "In Arumah, they broke through the gates and killed the men. There was no sign of the women or children."

"Why would Sisera not do the same to Shechem as he did to Arumah?" Lavi's question mirrored Deborah's own thoughts.

"Sisera does not want us to get used to his plans, lest we figure out a way to stop him." He looked at the messenger. "Did this all happen on a single day?"

The man nodded. "When the men and their sons left for the fields or merchant stalls, they returned later to find their women murdered and their virgin daughters missing. Only the children were left crying and alone."

Barak glanced at Keshet, then looked at Deborah. "Has our God given you any word?" His eyes flashed, his anger barely kept in check beneath the frustrated lift of a brow.

Deborah shook her head. "The only word I have received from Him of late is to pray. To remove the foreign gods from among us, repent, and pray." She glanced at Lappidoth, recalling Yiskah's so recent behavior. "I fear we are as guilty as the next village," she said as her thoughts sought some solution. "One of our own was caught worshiping a goddess of Canaan in the olive grove." She turned her palms up, her heart defeated. "I have yet to deal with the girl."

Barak's look said he had already heard the story. "This is the woman Talya came upon." It was not a question, but Deborah nodded regardless.

"When new gods are chosen, war comes to our gates." Deborah's words were a mere whisper, the source coming from a place she knew was beyond her.

"Shechem does not worship false gods, Prophetess," the messenger said, his voice nearly breaking. "Why would God allow our women . . . ?" A sob escaped and he sank to his knees. "We are faithful to Him."

Deborah watched the man weeping, her heart aching for answers she could not give. At last she spoke softly. "Only God knows the heart of any man, whether it is true and right."

Silence fell like the dread before a storm.

Finally Barak cleared his throat. "If I am going to rescue Shechem's daughters," he said, his voice low, uncertain, "I will need weapons and more men." He glanced at Keshet again. "We will leave at first light."

"What is your plan?" Lappidoth asked, hands clasped in his lap.

"We have secured the willingness of a Kenite near Kedesh-naphtali to make weapons for us if we can supply the ore. I intend to find the ore he requires, and perhaps recruit more soldiers to join us along the way."

"I will join you now," Lavi said before Deborah could respond. "If there is to be a battle, I will not back away."

Deborah looked into the eyes of her youngest son, her emotions a mixture of pride and fear. Dare she tell him not to fight if they were ever to stop Sisera's men? And yet . . . she had no word from the Lord. Nothing to indicate that Israel was ready for such a war.

"I will gladly accept your help when we are ready," Barak said, looking from Lavi to Deborah. "When our God tells the prophetess it is time, then we will go." His gaze shifted to the door of the house, where Talya stood. Deborah saw something pass between them, but she could not read the man's expression.

"In the meantime," Barak said, setting his clay cup on the floor at his feet, "we should leave your family in peace and plan how to execute our next move." He nodded to the Shechemite messenger. "I want to know every possible entrance to your city, and the name of every man."

The man's gaze held a fresh hint of hope, and Deborah prayed Barak would be successful in finding the virgin daughters of the men who had lost so much. She stood and waved an arm over the large court. "You and your men are welcome to stay with us as long as you need. You may sleep in the courtyard, or the cave beneath our house is spacious and you will have privacy there."

Barak stood along with the rest of his men. "Thank you, Prophetess. We bid you farewell then until morning."

Deborah set the oil lamp in the niche in the wall of her bedchamber and sank down among the cushions, every muscle tense. The voices of her sons and husband drifted to her from the sitting room, but Deborah's strength needed reviving, away from the opinions of men.

She stretched out on the bed she shared with Lappidoth, for the house was not large enough to afford separate rooms, and released a heavy sigh. Talya was safe. Relief seeped through her, and she slowly felt herself relax. Sleep flitted at the edges of her mind, stopping short at the sound of soft footsteps.

"Ima?" Talya's voice broke through the fog. Deborah sat up and beckoned the girl closer.

She came without comment, and Deborah's arms wrapped around her. She breathed deeply and sensed that Talya did too. "What is it, my daughter?" She patted the girl's back as she had when Talya was a child, before conflict had arisen between them.

Talya straightened and pulled away from Deborah's embrace, her dark hair falling gently over one shoulder, no longer bound up as it often was during the day. "I want to marry," she said softly. "If I marry, I will not be vulnerable as one of Sisera's victims. I could not be captured as a virgin and sent off to be one of his slaves." Her conviction seemed to grow in strength as she spoke.

Deborah studied her, fighting the exhaustion of the day. "I'm not sure tonight is a good time to discuss this, Talya." She touched her arm and smiled. "Perhaps after we both get a good night's sleep in our own beds." Hadn't Talya complained earlier about missing her bed on the nights she slept on the forest floor? But by the look in her eyes, Deborah sensed she was not ready for sleep.

"I only thought," Talya said, glancing at the door, then back at Deborah, "that perhaps a husband could be found among Barak's men. There is no one in town whom you have found suitable, and Barak will leave again in the morning. At least if we could secure a betrothal . . ." Her voice trailed off, her look uncertain.

"Is there a man you have in mind?" Deborah eyed her daughter, her gaze probing, trying to read her thoughts. "I do not know Barak's men, Talya. They may all have wives and children waiting for them. This is not a decision to make lightly, even to protect you."

Talya looked away from Deborah's scrutiny and kneaded the belt of her robe with both hands. Talya never acted nervous like this. Surely her encounter with Sisera's men had rattled her confidence.

"Barak is not married, Ima." Her voice barely rose above a whisper. "I know he may think he does not need a wife again, but I would be good to him."

Deborah shifted to better face her daughter and reached for her hand. Talya met her gaze and did not pull away. "Barak is a fine man," she said, touching Talya's cheek. "And we are most grateful to him for finding you, for keeping you safe." She paused, waiting for Talya to insist that she had also protected herself, but the argument did not come. "But Barak is not interested in another wife yet. He still grieves his Nessa."

"I know that." Talya glanced away. "He told me as much."

Heavy footfalls drew her attention. Deborah looked toward the door, surprised that Talya did not do the same as Lappidoth entered the room. He met Deborah's gaze.

"Should I wait?" He took in the scene, his expression softening at sight of their daughter.

"We were just discussing something," Deborah said, not sure whether to be grateful for or irritated with the interruption.

"I want to marry, Abba." Talya pulled her hand from Deborah's grasp and went to her father. "I have asked Ima to give me to Barak."

Lappidoth looked startled, but a moment later he seemed to recover his composure. He pulled Talya close. "You have had a difficult ordeal, my daughter. There is still plenty of time to find you a proper husband."

"But Barak is here now, and I don't want just any man. I want him." She lifted her chin in that defiant way that Deborah found hard to fight, especially tonight when all she longed for was a chance to rest, to forget the past few days. "What if that man who tried to capture me returns? Barak could keep me safe."

Lappidoth's eyes narrowed.

"Your father will keep you just as safe," Deborah said, catching Talya's barb before it sank into his thoughts to cause him shame.

"Barak is not looking to marry anyone so quickly." Lappidoth held Talya at arm's length.

Good. Don't give in to her. Deborah willed

167

Lappidoth to look her way, but he kept his eyes focused on Talya.

"Did he say something to you on the way home? Has he given you some indication of his interest?" Lappidoth asked. Why was he pursuing this? Talya was delusional, as she had been when she thought herself strong enough to kill Sisera. Had her near death at the hands of one of Sisera's men taught her nothing?

"He did not say so exactly. But I was alone with him, Abba. Is that not reason enough?" Talya lifted her head and gave her father her most coaxing, pleading expression, the one that had always gotten her what she wanted from him.

"Was Barak ever unseemly toward you?" Deborah interrupted, certain now that a marriage between the two was the last thing she wanted to see happen. Talya was not ready to wed if she thought she could coax her own way without a valid reason.

"He did not act unseemly, Ima." Talya turned to face her once more, her gaze moving from mother to father. "But Abba, I am not safe as a virgin alone. Did not Barak say so? You saw how they nearly caught me. If I marry, I will not be as easy a prey for Sisera."

"Marriage cannot protect you, Talya,"

Lappidoth said softly. "Did you not hear how Sisera killed the wives of the men of Shechem? He also killed Barak's wife Nessa. Virgin or married — it matters little to him — no woman is safe as long as Sisera lives." He drew a hand along his brow. "Barak is not ready for another marriage, Talya."

Deborah stood, relieved that Lappidoth had not given in to Talya's pleading, and walked toward her daughter. "It is late," she said, taking the girl's arm. "You must go to your bed and sleep."

Talya dragged her feet even as Deborah guided her toward the door. "But you will ask him?" She aimed the question at Lappidoth.

"Tomorrow your father and I will discuss it again," Deborah said, gently nudging Talya out of the room.

Talya glanced back at her father, but for once in his life, Lappidoth stuck to his word and did not give her the answer she wished to hear.

After a lengthy discussion in the recesses of the cave, Barak returned to Deborah's courtyard, feeling a sense of need to protect the prophetess and her family. He did not explore what prompted such a thought and slept fitfully in his cloak on the hard stones.

Dreams of Nessa mingled with the sight of Talya's wild-eyed fear in the forest until he could not distinguish one from the other. He awoke with a start, sweat coating his skin.

He rolled over again, trying to block the memories, but sleep would not come. At last he stood and moved silently toward the court's open gate to gaze at the stars. Would they find the copper and tin they needed? Worse, would he be able to gather enough men, even if he had the weapons, to take on Sisera and his chariots? There were not even enough horses in Israel, let alone chariots.

The crunch of stones set his heart pounding. He looked around, hand on his dagger, but it was just one of his men leaving the cave to walk the streets. Sometimes sleep eluded them too, and Barak relaxed, recognizing the man's need for space. He turned slightly toward the house as the man passed out of view and glimpsed a woman standing at the window of her room, her gaze lifted heavenward. Talya. She did not glance his way. Did she sense his presence? Had she seen him? He held his breath, not daring to move. With her hair down and combed and the swath of moonlight bathing her face, she was beautiful. His stomach twisted as he was gripped with a feeling of unfaithfulness. Nessa was beautiful. Talya was a child.

He breathed a sigh when she turned away from the window and took a step farther into the shadows, out of his line of sight. He had no time for such foolishness. He found a different spot against the court's half wall and laid beside it, his back to the house, blocking his memories as well as his wayward thoughts.

Movement caught Talya's eye, and she looked from the heavens to the courtyard. An animal? No. The outline of a man. Talya's heart skipped a beat, the memories of the man from the forest still vivid in her mind's eye. The only time the vision of that man left her in peace was in Barak's presence. Even her father had not been able to erase the image from her heart. Nor the fear.

She smoothed the linen night tunic that draped softly over her body and squinted, trying to see in the moonlight. The man moved to the edge of the courtyard and lay down along the bricked half wall. Barak often slept in the courtyard on his visits. But wasn't he in the cave with his men?

Curious, she donned her robe and padded on bare feet to the sitting room, then to the outer court. Her heart thumped in an excited rhythm as a new thought turned in her head. If she slept at Barak's side and he found her there in the morning, Ima would insist he marry her. He would not be able to refuse her. She drew a breath, steadying herself. Her feet moved forward of their own accord.

Whispers of night breezes tickled her legs beneath her tunic as she stood over the man. How he intrigued her! How commanding his voice, and how strong his arms. Memories of the way he'd held her to keep her from fleeing, then the gentle way he held her once he realized all that had happened to her, quickened the beat of her heart. She ached with sudden longing for that feeling again, for that sense of protective warmth, something her father, for all of his love, could not supply.

Would Barak accept her? Surely he would. Despite his feelings for his first wife — *only wife,* her thoughts corrected — he would not reject her. He was too brave and kind to do such a thing.

And besides, she needed him.

If she waited until dawn, it would be too late to discuss anything. Barak would leave and they would be forced to wait until he decided to come their way again. But if she could get him to betroth himself to her now . . .

She knelt beside him, holding her breath lest he awaken to the sound of it. His even breathing did not change. Talya's heart thumped harder, her mind warring with the decision. Her mother would be furious. Her father would eventually smile and promise all would be well.

She drew nearer and laid close enough to touch him without actually doing so. Eyes open, she waited, but she did not sleep.

11

Deborah lay awake, unable to sleep despite her body's cry for rest. Talya had managed to stir her emotions to the point of complete exasperation once more, and she fought the urge to awaken Lappidoth and complain profusely to him. Complaining did no good, for he always sided with their daughter.

But she could complain in her prayers, though she wondered whether Adonai ever grew tired of hearing from her. She grew weary of herself, so why shouldn't the Almighty feel the same way? If He could grow angry with Moses, He could most certainly grow angry or frustrated with her. Much as she did with Talya.

The thought was sobering, but the need to pray intensified. She rose quietly, careful not to awaken her husband, snatched her robe, and walked softly toward the court-yard. She needed no lamp with the moon's glow so bright, and with few trees to block the path from here to the center of town, she might even visit the palm tree. Then again, perhaps it would be better if she waited until dawn. Even in a village as close-knit as theirs, a woman alone . . . She refused to finish the thought.

She stopped at the entrance to the court, looking over the village, and lifted her face to accept the kiss of the night breeze, feeling as though God was surely aware of her angst, her heartache. *Why is my daughter so difficult, Adonai? I teach her, try to mold her to see things the way she should, and yet she battles me at every turn.*

Memories of her own past and her compliance to her parents' wishes caused another wash of anger to rush over her. She had been obedient all of her life. Why could her children not be the same?

She moved slowly over the cobbled stones of the large courtyard, past the open hearth and toward the open gate, when her eye caught the outline of someone sleeping on the stones. She squinted, drawing closer. Not one person, but two.

Her heartbeat slowed. Talya's bare feet came into view, her body nearly touching that of a man. Of Barak. Deborah closed her eyes, certain they had betrayed her, but when she opened them, Talya's form lay still beside Barak's. Barak's even breathing drifted toward her, but as she moved carefully closer, she did not hear Talya's steady breath, which she had so often listened to as the girl slept.

She bent and touched her daughter's arm. Talya did not move, but Deborah sensed she only feigned sleep. Deborah tightened her grip and nudged her with her knee. Still Talya remained still. Exasperation rose so swift she had to force herself to remain calm. Talya was too good at these silly games she played. Was she so foolish to think she could force a man to marry her by staying beside him while he slept?

Deborah winced, imagining Barak's response if he found the girl still at his side come dawn. All thoughts of offering her hand to him in marriage fled. Talya was a good girl, had a good heart — surely she did. But she simply could not be allowed to defy her mother and force her way in life. Her father might be caught in her games, but Deborah could not allow Talya's future husband to feel so obligated. Talya needed a man who was able to refuse her.

A sigh she could no longer hold escaped. *Adonai, what do I do with this girl?*

She released her grip on Talya's arm and slowly stood. Perhaps Barak should be the one to decide Talya's fate. If he wanted her, good. Deborah would no longer have to worry or wonder what to do with her. He would be the one responsible for his wife's decisions. If he refused her . . . then Talya would learn a valuable lesson.

But she could not wait for dawn to give the man the choice.

She glanced heavenward, silently praying for strength. Emotion rose close to the surface. Sleep would heal so much of the pain now piercing her heart. Talya, too, needed rest. She was not thinking clearly and would surely regret her actions come dawn. But if the girl would not move now and come with Deborah, then there was nothing to do but "wake" them both.

She knelt again, this time closer to Barak, and touched his shoulder. He startled, as she expected he would. Warriors did not sleep deeply, though somehow he had managed to stay thus even with Talya beside him. Was he part of this?

Doubt filled her. Surely she could trust him.

"Who's there?" Barak's hushed voice filled her ear.

"It is I, Deborah," she said. "And I think, my lord, that you should arise."

He scrambled to his knees, jolting again

when he looked down at Talya, who quickly moved away from him, her wide eyes still carrying a frightened doe expression. Was she acting on his account, or did she truly fear?

"What is going on here?" Barak's commanding whisper brought Deborah's thoughts up short, and she knelt in the darkness beside her daughter, who to her surprise said nothing.

"I believe my daughter has had trouble sleeping, my lord, and somehow ended up beside you here in the court. I tried to get her to move, but she did not stir." She glanced at Talya, whose gaze had moved to study her clasped hands. "I felt it best to wake you before others caught you like this at dawn."

Barak ran a hand along his jaw, his gaze clearly troubled. "Talya?" His voice gentled as one who speaks to a child. "What were you thinking to come out here?" He touched her chin, coaxing her gaze to meet his. "Tell me the truth." There was a set to his jaw that told Deborah he was not a man so easily manipulated.

"I . . ." Talya could not hold his gaze. "I felt safer with you," she said.

"We are not in the fields, and this is not appropriate for a capable woman." The last words were said with emphasis, and Deborah wondered at his meaning.

Talya shifted and faced him. "I want . . . that is . . ." She seemed suddenly at a loss for words. "It doesn't matter now." She pulled away from his grasp, and he crossed his arms, studying her.

"You put me in a position that some would find disturbing," he said, his dark eyes suddenly flashing fire. "Do not pretend I do not know your intent."

She placed both hands beside her, glanced at Deborah, then leaned closer to him. "Think what you want," she whispered. "It was a foolish thought. Forgive me." She rose, and he did not stop her. She did not look back as she hurried into the house.

Barak looked at Deborah, one dark brow lifted. "Your daughter put me at great risk, Prophetess. A man alone with a virgin . . ." His voice trailed off.

"She wants to become your wife." The admission seemed right, though Deborah could not read the expression in Barak's suddenly masked gaze.

He looked away and shifted uncomfortably. At last he stood and offered Deborah a hand. They faced each other in silence. "Is this your wish as well, or is it entirely her doing?"

Deborah met his gaze. "I will admit," she said, "I have considered seeking a match between the two of you. But not yet. And not this way. And now I don't know what to do with her. I am certain her ordeal and the lack of sleep has caused this rash act. But you know yourself that Talya is a strong woman who wants her way. She saw her chance to wed . . . and she wants that man to be you."

Barak studied her in silence.

"Say the word and I will seek a different man for her, my lord. No one need know of tonight's incident."

He looked down at her, his expression softening. "She is nothing like Nessa."

"No, she is not." Deborah searched his gaze until Barak looked away.

"I will not be forced into such a decision, Prophetess." He took a step back from her, toward the court's entrance. "I think it is best if I return to my men."

She nodded, her heart sinking. Had she just ruined Talya's best chances for marriage? And yet . . . what else was a mother to do? This was not the time to think of marriages. It was nearly time for war, and Barak had too much on his mind to add the worry of an immature girl to his thoughts.

Deborah sighed, glancing back at her

home where everyone still slept, where peace awaited. If only that were the truth.

■ ■ ■ ■

PART 2

■ ■ ■ ■

[Deborah] sent and summoned Barak the son of Abinoam from Kedesh-naphtali and said to him, "Has not the LORD, the God of Israel, commanded you, 'Go, gather your men at Mount Tabor, taking 10,000 from the people of Naphtali and the people of Zebulun. And I will draw out Sisera, the general of Jabin's army, to meet you by the river Kishon with his chariots and his troops, and I will give him into your hand'?" Barak said to her, "If you will go with me, I will go, but if you will not go with me, I will not go."

Judges 4:6–8

12

Deborah's heart burned like fire, a flame seized yet not quenched. Sweat dampened her hair, and she could not take a breath. She dragged air and thrashed about.

Lappidoth touched her shoulder. "What is it, beloved?"

She jerked free of him, still seeing the vision in her mind's eye.

"You are safe, Deborah. It is all right." His soft voice brushed her ear.

She stilled, slowly facing him. "I'm sorry. I did not mean to waken you." She sat up, heart still pounding, rubbing her eyes, wishing she could rub away the memories along with the sleep.

"Tell me what you dreamed." He stroked her hair, and she felt a sense of gratitude for him, despite the continual feeling that he could never be all that she wished he would be.

"I saw Shamgar killing the Philistines with

an oxgoad." She drew a breath. The dream mirrored the memory of what she had witnessed as a child. "And I saw your village the day your family was killed by the Canaanites."

Lappidoth pulled her close and kissed the top of her head. "They are dreams of terror and not worth remembering." He stroked her back as though she were a frightened child.

Deborah listened to the silence of the room, wondering why Adonai had reminded her of these things now. Though Shamgar had killed six hundred Philistines that day, he had not stayed to save Israel from the hated Canaanites. Only Philistia remained subdued.

"Shall I fetch you some milk?" Lappidoth asked, holding her at arm's length, his head tilted, his eyes half glazed with sleep.

She touched his arm. "No. Go back to sleep. I can get it myself."

His look held uncertainty, and she knew his sense of helpfulness urged him to please her, but she could not allow herself to be so selfish when he had a full day ahead of him in the fields.

"I am fine," she assured him.

He looked at her again but at last gave in and lay down, his even breathing soon filling the room. She rose, her heart a tight fist within her, no longer able to bear the trauma her mind battled in sleep.

What do You want of me? The prayer filled her mind as she moved to the sitting room, past the place where Talya slept. Were the dreams a result of her worries? She stopped to listen for the girl's even breathing through the curtained door. She must stop fearing that Talya might slip away unnoticed and unprotected.

But as she moved into the courtyard and faced the heavens, willing her racing heart to still, it was not Talya's face she imagined but Barak's. Months had passed since she had seen him, yet Barak remained one of the few men left in Israel who could lead a host of warriors against the enemy. Barak was not Shamgar. But he was strong and he feared Adonai.

Shall I send for him? How often had she prayed thus?

But still God remained silent.

Jael heard the chariots long before their dust filled the air. "Go to Nadia's tent and hide behind the stacks of wool. Hurry, Daniyah!"

The chariots were fewer in number this time, but they stopped in the road just opposite the camp. Jael looked to make sure the girls were in their tents, then ducked into hers behind the curtain. She glanced at Ghalib, who had just finished mending her loom, and nodded. He stood and came to her side, and they both waited, one ear pressed to the fabric, listening.

Sisera's men laughed and jostled each other as they stomped over the berm and crunched the underbrush in the trees. "They are a reckless lot," Ghalib whispered in her ear.

"They are beasts." Fear slithered down her spine at the memory of Sisera's bold arrogance with Daniyah. "Let us pray they leave quickly."

Ghalib placed a reassuring hand on her shoulder. One of the guards near Heber's tent spoke loud enough for them to hear.

"What do you seek, my lord? How can I help you today?"

"I seek Heber the Kenite. Or his wife and daughter will suffice." Sisera's words sent Ghalib from Jael's tent before she could stop him.

"I will send for Heber, my lord," the guard said.

Jael watched Ghalib, wanting to yell for him to stop, but she held her tongue, relieved to see him slip around the back of Heber's tent. He would find his father and brothers. Pray God they would return before Sisera began to search the tents of the women.

She leaned closer to the fabric opening, carefully pulling the flap aside to see. The impatient Canaanite soldiers tapped girded feet and talked among themselves. She took a step back into the tent. She should have kept Daniyah with her.

Voices grew louder outside her tent. Fear rose, along with a sick feeling in her gut.

"Please, my lord, those tents belong to our women." Their guard's voice held alarm. What was taking Heber so long? These men would not be kept waiting, and her girls were not safe.

Jael straightened her shoulders, forcing courage into her heart. She covered her head with a scarf and wrapped it about her face, then grabbed the staff she took with her when she tended their few goats and stepped from the tent. "What seems to be the problem, Musa?" She addressed the harried guard, who looked half afraid, half relieved to see her.

Footsteps drew closer, and she caught Sisera's scent as he stopped near, assessing her. "Ah, Jael. We meet again." He stepped closer. Too close, and before she could stop

189

him, he rested a possessive hand on her waist.

She gasped, her face aflame as his hand moved higher, probing, as though he had full rights to do as he pleased. She jerked, trying to free herself, but his other hand snapped like a snake, wrapping around her neck. "Ah, my sweet Jael. Did you think my threats held no weight?" He bent forward, his breath fanning her face, his meaning much too clear.

Jael's heart hammered, and she nearly choked on his stench. Where was her husband? Ghalib? Fareed? Mahir? Why did the guard not step forward to defend Heber's women? But one glance told her Musa was surrounded by Sisera's laughing men.

"Shall we take this inside your tent while we await your husband?" By his tone and the way he pulled her possessively closer, Jael did not think his words were meant in jest.

Her stomach revolted in the wake of the fear seizing her. His eyes roved over her body, his lust a living fire.

"If you do such a thing, my lord," she finally said past a suddenly dry throat, "how will my husband possibly continue to work with you? For you would have broken his trust. Unless, of course, you have found another metalworker who does finer work?" The words were a risk and she knew it. She could tell by the grip he had on her neck that he was too strong for her and could snap the bones in her wrist or neck with little effort.

"A woman that would bargain for her purity is all the more desirable, my sweet." His lips brushed hers then. She fought the urge to spit in his face.

At that moment Heber and her sons emerged from behind Heber's tent, their arms loaded with heavy baskets of weapons, swords, daggers, spears, and shields.

Sisera released her and whirled about.

"Your order is complete, my lord." Heber motioned to the baskets their sons set on the ground at Sisera's feet.

Sisera pointed to several of his men, who dragged the baskets away. Jael's limbs began to tremble as she watched them count the articles, no doubt to make sure Heber had kept his end of the bargain.

"It's all here," one of the men called out when the last weapon was counted.

Sisera pulled a pouch from his belt and dumped gold coins into Heber's hand. "I will bring more ore for you in a few days. I will need the order by week's end."

Heber did not show the slightest surprise,

nor did he say a word to Sisera for what he had surely seen, with Sisera standing so close to her. But Heber feared Sisera with good reason, and Jael realized in that moment that even her husband and sons could not protect her or her daughters from these men.

13

Barak stood on the ridge looking down on his city, Kedesh-naphtali. He had spent the night in the home of his parents, not far from the one he had built a short distance away, the home he once shared with Nessa. But fitful memories filled his dreams until he had flung the covers from him, donned his clothes, and snuck past his sleeping parents and his men to escape the stifling reminders. Even here, her presence still lingered in every corner of the house she had often visited to be with his mother, though her scent of wild roses had long since dissipated.

Grief gnawed at him in the pit of his very being. Shouldn't he be past these feelings by now? But coming home always brought them back.

"You're up early." Keshet climbed the hill and met Barak at the ridge, his face too cheery for such a morn.

"Couldn't sleep. At least not well."

Keshet nodded. "I expected as much. Perhaps it is time to bid your parents and the town farewell again and be off to Hazor."

Barak stared into the distance. Hazor was north of Lake Kinneret, about two days' walk if they took their time getting there. They had already delivered what little ore they could come by to Heber, and except to keep trying to anticipate Sisera's next move, they needed to spy out the capital of Canaan, where the king lived.

"I'm not sure how we think our small band will slip past the guards at the gates of such a fortified city. Hazor is nearly as defensible as Jericho was." Keshet blew on his hands in the cool dawn air.

"And look what God did to Jericho." Barak glanced at his friend. "What's the point of your question?"

"Only that we don't have a directive from Adonai to fight Hazor as Joshua had with Jericho." Keshet's tanned face carried the lines of a frown along his brow.

Barak dug his toe into the packed earth. "We won't be attacking. We are simply going to circle the city, and perhaps one or two of us will slip in and mingle with the people. If the time ever comes to destroy

King Jabin, I want to at least know how to access the palace and where the prominent buildings are located." Surely it was a wise strategy, though Barak wondered if in their current state the people of Israel would ever follow him into such a battle.

"Then let's get going," Keshet said, his normal smile suddenly replacing the frown. "If our God is for us, who can be against us?"

Barak nodded, his thoughts distant. Was God for them? Or had they gone too far this time? Would God forsake His own people?

Hazor sat in the hills of Upper Galilee near Lake Huleh. A mountain range bordered its west and south sides, making it hard to reach without notice. But Barak and his men managed to keep to the caves and skirted the edges of the mountains, sometimes walking single file or crouching low to keep from being seen by the guards that kept watch along the city walls.

On the morning of the third day, Barak called his one hundred men together. "Two of you must join a merchant caravan and scout out the city." He looked into each face, choosing two of them quickly. "Go and bring me word. I want a full report by nightfall." He itched to go with them, but his face would be recognized.

"Shall we try to enter the palace itself, my lord?" asked one of the men.

Barak glanced at Keshet. "If you can pull it off without getting caught. Yes."

He watched as the men scurried down the hill into the valley out of sight. How he longed to go with them, to get a look at Jabin's overfed face and do as the judge Ehud had done that long-ago day when his two-edged sword had killed King Eglon of Moab, freeing Israel of their oppressors. But Ehud's eighty years of peace had long since passed. Barak faced a different threat. A mightier, terrifying foe in Sisera.

A man who not only had every advantage but also had no conscience.

"The city is well fortified," Keshet said as they circled Hazor and rounded the bend from the front gates to the back. "At least this part is."

"There has to be a weakness somewhere." Barak motioned for Keshet to follow him north toward the spring that came from Lake Huleh. "Cities need water, and this one must be fed by the lake's runoff."

They moved in silence, weaving their way behind outcroppings of rocks and heavy brush. Barak glanced at the wall. "There are fewer guards at this end." He raised a brow at Keshet. "Curious."

Keshet nodded, then slid down the embankment toward the edge of the spring where it entered the city. "The way is blocked." He indicated the large boulders ahead. "But water can easily run beneath." He looked up, pointing. A lone guard stood halfway down the wall toward the main city gates. "They put too much faith in these rocks," Keshet said. He leaned close to Barak's ear. "It will take more than rocks to keep our God and some strong men from entering this city."

"Surely the guards would hear our grunts and the scraping of stone on stone, even if we do manage to lift them with ease." He cast a wary look at the wall. The guard turned, heading their way. "We should go." He scrambled up the bank, Keshet on his heels, and landed with a soft thud behind a copse of trees.

"We could distract them," Keshet prodded. "Perhaps start a skirmish from the opposite way. It is worth considering." He gave Barak his most convincing grin. "If God is in it, we cannot fail."

"Is God in it?" He met Keshet's gaze.

"The prophetess would know." But Keshet's look now held a hint of uncertainty.

"If she knows, she has not said so." Months had passed since he had heard from Deborah, nor had he returned to visit her. He had not been able to bring himself to look into her eyes, knowing what he knew about her daughter's wishes, which seemed to match her own. He could not give Talya or Deborah what they wanted. So he stayed away.

"I am sure she will summon us when she does," Keshet said, moving away from him to continue the trek around the city.

"I'm sure she will." But the fact that there had been no word troubled him more than he cared to ponder.

"Tell me what you learned," Barak said hours later when his men joined him in a cave outside the city. The two men who had infiltrated Hazor sat nearest the fire.

"The palace is in the center of the city, surrounded by temples, city buildings, and rows of small rooms that house servants and prisoners. The areas are well guarded," the first man said.

"The king rotates prisoners that he puts on display at the four corners of the city square." The second man drew a likeness of the prisoners in the dirt of the cave floor.

Two men and two women, each indiscreetly exposed for all to see.

"Israelites?" Barak already knew the answer, but when both men nodded, his heartbeat quickened and the blood rushed thicker through his veins. "How are they displayed? Is there no way to secretly release them and take them away?" The question held an imploring tone, and he knew it was pointless to ask or they would have done just that.

The first man shook his head. "No, my lord. They are lifted onto a round platform, their hands tied behind them. They remain there, pleading to be released." He paused. "It was hard to watch, my lord."

Barak stood abruptly, anger fueling his footsteps. He paced to the back of the cave and returned. "How often do they change the prisoners?"

"One of the guards said every few hours a new batch takes their place. But they are there at Jabin's pleasure, and he often delights in making a spectacle of them, even worse than we were able to see. Some are sent to the ring, where they lose their life." The man averted his eyes as he spoke. These men were not squeamish or easily rattled, but whatever they had heard and seen had shaken them.

"When we destroy Hazor, we will save the prisoners. That will be our first obligation." Barak spoke with conviction, though his heart felt hollow even with his strong words. How could any man of the earth treat his fellow man or woman so atrociously?

He strode off again, clenching and unclenching his fists, digging his nails deeply into his palms. What he wouldn't give to face Jabin and Sisera right now, blade in hand, and put an end to them both. His breath came faster, matching the pace of his feet. *Adonai, why do You allow this?* Surely these men and women had not done such evil as to deserve this punishment.

The prayer made him pause to listen, but if he expected an answer, he did not receive one.

Deborah strode back and forth over the length of her sitting room while the man from a neighboring town visibly shook in the seat they had offered him. "Tell me again," she said, though he had already recounted the unbelievable tale.

Talya offered the man a cup of cool water, and he drank greedily. He sat straighter, but his hands, held tightly between his knees, belied his attempt to keep his composure. "Prophetess, it is like I told you. Sisera came

200

to Endor. I wouldn't be here to tell you if I hadn't been away trying to sell my wares to a passing caravan." He cleared his throat. "While I was gone, Sisera charged through the gates in the short amount of time they are open, rounded up all the men and all the virgin maids. He killed the elders and took the virgins into his custody. The men he left are barely men, not yet twenty years old. Some might be strong enough to fight, but with their fathers dead and their sisters taken, they've no strength within them."

"Young men should be hot-blooded and angry, ready to fight Sisera." Deborah could not believe such a horrific story could end with men losing heart. Unless . . . "Did Sisera harm the young men in any way?"

The man started shaking again. This part he had obviously left out in the first telling, and Deborah only now thought to ask the question. "Some of them, yes."

Deborah did not need to know how. "That explains it then." If Sisera had maimed some of the lads, the others would fear he would come back and do the same to them if they ever crossed him, even to rescue their sisters. They would be of no use to Barak in his army, strengthening Sisera's hold on Israel.

Deborah sank onto a cushion and leaned

against the limestone wall. Lappidoth spoke to the man for more details, but she had heard enough. She blinked back tears, as a mother would for her children. *Oh Adonai, Adonai, how long? Will You forget us forever?*

Sisera was using every tactic he could to destroy them from the inside. He was cutting to the heart of their morale. He was making them weak.

She stood and left the house, walking in the cool night air toward her palm tree, grateful for the breeze that tugged at her headscarf. How long until Sisera found their little village and came to pillage them? Would he kill Lappidoth and their sons, take Talya and the other virgins? Who would stop him? They had so little defense.

She looked up at the night sky now dotted with stars, a fresh reminder of her Creator. Had not God promised Abraham, "Your descendants will be as the stars in the sky"? And yet they were being systematically decimated by a tyrannical murderer and his ruthless king.

Even if Barak went to war against them, who was left among the clans of Israel to join him? She lifted her gaze to take in the whole of the sky. *Are there any left who have not worshiped Anat or Baal or Asherah or Molech or others I can't even name? Am I and*

*my family the only few who would tear down
such altars and idols and banish or destroy
those who worship them?*

Memories of Shet's wife surfaced. Talya
had destroyed the idol, but not everyone in
their village truly obeyed Yahweh. Deborah
sensed it in her heart. At least for Shet's
sake his wife had not enticed others to worship the idol she sought in secret. She had
acted alone. But her husband had still sent
her away for a time until she could return
fully repentant. Deborah wondered if the
woman would ever come home — or would
she maintain her defiant attitude against
Yahweh and run off to Canaan?

The skin prickled along Deborah's arms
as the dusk deepened. The very thought of
Yiskah in Canaan chilled her. What happened to the women Sisera kidnapped and
used for pleasure? Did they die giving birth
to illegitimate children? Did he toss them
aside and enslave them after he stole the
one precious thing they owned? Did God
not care for the souls of Israel's daughters?

If God were a Canaanite goddess, Deborah would have her answer. Anat the warrior goddess stood behind Sisera's success.
Asherah stood behind Canaan's fertility.
Baal stood behind Canaan's king.

You are greater, Adonai Elohim. You can

defeat them with a word. She paused and tilted her head, listening for some sound, some word from him. *If You but ask, I will obey.*

A stirring grew within her, a certainty that had not been there during the nightmares of late. Sisera may have conquered Endor, but he had not conquered all. God would answer soon. There was still hope.

14

Barak made his way slowly down the hill as the moon lit the field below but kept him in shadow. Five men followed him, Keshet among them. He questioned his own good sense about trusting his friend's idea, but in the end he knew that Keshet was strong and smart and quick. They would do their best or die trying.

When his feet touched the valley floor, he signaled for his men to go in opposite directions and meet at the spring behind the city. If one group was noticed by the guards, they could alert the other with signals they had planned months before on previous raids. One hoot of the owl meant danger lurked. Two and it was imminent.

But as they neared the spring and nothing unusual happened, Barak glanced heavenward and thanked God for blinding the eyes of the guards. Reaching the spring and then moving the stones without notice, however, was another matter.

Laughter and singing spilled from the city at their approach.

"They must be celebrating. They will be more easily distracted if they are," Keshet said.

Barak nodded but held his peace. When they reached the spot he and Keshet had found earlier that day, the strongest men used every tool they carried to dig out the pitch and mortar from between the stones attached to the wall above the river and loosen the rocks below. Hours passed and the moon went in and out of the clouds.

"How much longer? Can anyone fit through and swim to the surface?" Barak glanced toward the wall, but no guards seemed interested in this part of city.

"We're through," a man whispered.

Barak came to the opening. "The prisoners are held to the right?" He pointed a little northwest of where they stood.

One of the spies spoke. "Yes. But the servants are there too. It is too dark to tell, but there is a small gate that separates the two. I expect that is because servants aren't much different than prisoners, but for the humiliation and public torture."

Barak stared at the slowly moving water and the narrow opening the men had dug.

The water came waist deep to the man standing there.

Keshet touched his shoulder. "I will go," he whispered. But he could not swim.

Barak shook his head. "No. I'll go." He looked to his small band of men. "Who will go with me?"

Keshet stayed behind to stand guard while Barak led the other men into the icy water, dunked beneath the surface, and slowly waded toward the opening in the city. They came to a wide cistern the height of at least two men rising out of the water, with walls that would be difficult to scale. Probably a place where the women came to draw water, but no rope hung low to grab, no steps to climb. When Barak placed a hand against the surface of one wall, he winced and pulled back, stifling the urge to cry out. Barbs of sharp metal and rock and thorns from thistle branches had been imbedded into the cistern walls.

"No wonder the guards pay so little attention to this part of the city," whispered the man closest to him, who had also cut his hand on the wall. "They know once an enemy breaches the passage, the cistern will stop them."

Barak lifted his gaze, searching for some place, *something.* But there was no obvious area visible in the darkness that would allow a man to climb. The icy waters of the spring seeped deeper into his bones with every passing moment.

There would be no rescuing prisoners tonight.

"Retreat," Barak whispered, praying their voices would not be heard in the cavernous room. After each man had ducked beneath the water and swam back toward the opening, Barak followed, feeling more defeated than he had ever felt in his life.

Two days away from Hazor, near the shores of Kinneret, Barak spied Heber the Kenite and his sons heading north. He stopped and waited as they approached.

"What brings you to this part of Naphtali?" Barak asked, taking note of the donkeys heavy laden with sacks. He glanced beyond them for some sign of the rest of the family. Were they trying to escape Canaan's territory? But they wouldn't be headed toward Hazor if they were.

"We have an order of weapons for King Jabin," Heber said. By the look on his face and his clenched jaw, he was not happy to divulge this information to Barak.

"*More* weapons?" Barak walked to the donkey and peered into the sacks on its sides. Daggers filled one, shields the other.

"I am following orders from Sisera," Heber said, his tone defensive. The man glanced at Barak's one hundred followers. Barak's men could easily take what Heber had made and leave him empty-handed. But to do so would surely mean Heber's death, and the death of all he owned.

"Is Sisera holding something against you to expect you to do this thing?" Barak moved to face Heber, his men grumbling behind him. They would overpower Heber's men if Barak did not stop them. He turned and held up his hand for silence. "You will stay as you are."

He faced Heber again. "I have no reason to harm you, my friend. It does not please me that you make weapons for my enemies, but you are not of Israel. I cannot force your loyalties."

Heber did not speak for a moment. "Sisera enters our camp, and he makes advances at my wife, my daughter. When I was off gathering his weapons, he nearly forced himself upon my wife, and his guards are armed, keeping my own guards from defending what is mine." Defeat filled his voice. "Until I can find a way to escape, I have no choice."

"How do you know Sisera won't attack

your women while you are here?" Barak crossed his arms over his chest, sizing up the man.

"Sisera does not know the timing of our mission. He thinks I am coming to Hazor next week. I decided it was best to come early, to keep him off guard."

Barak did not comment that Sisera could be angry that Heber did not obey his commands to the exact letter. Perhaps Heber's metalworking was too important to Sisera to risk truly harming the man's family.

"Please, is there something I can do for you? We must be on our way." A note of anxiety entered Heber's voice.

Barak relaxed his stance. "We mean you no harm, but I have one request of you." Perhaps Heber could succeed where Barak had failed. *If* the man was willing to take the risk.

"How can I help you?" He seemed uncertain and was probably unwilling.

Barak studied him but a moment. "We just came from Hazor, though the king does not know it." He rubbed his beard, weighing his words. "My men did some spying on the town and found men and women of Israel who are kept there as slaves. I cannot repeat to you the things done to them, but you will notice them when you enter the

210

market square."

Heber waited, saying nothing.

"I want you to buy back at least one of them, more if you can afford Jabin's prices."

Heber's mouth dropped, but he quickly closed it. "Are you mad? To even ask the king such a question could cost us our lives."

"Not if he is pleased with your workmanship. Tell him the slave is to help you in the ovens or in the making of molds. Or if it is a woman, tell them your wife has need of a slave, and could he spare one? He need not know you intend to free them." Barak paced the short space between them. "Once you understand what that man is doing to our people . . ." He stopped, arms outstretched, imploring. "We tried to enter the city by night to rescue as many as we could, but the way is blocked by sharp rocks and barbs and a steep climb. I will try again, but I cannot do it without weapons, without further planning."

"I don't see how my purchase of one slave will help your cause, Barak," Heber said. This time his voice held disappointment, perhaps in himself. "There are so many who have been taken. What is one among so many?"

Barak shrugged. "I don't know. Hope, perhaps. I need to know it can be done, that we can rescue those who have been taken."

Heber studied his feet, then met Barak's steady gaze. "It is a hard thing you ask, my friend."

"We live in an impossible situation."

"I promise nothing," Heber said.

"I expect nothing. I only ask you to try." Barak nodded to his men to continue on down the path. "When you return, stop in Kedesh-naphtali and tell me what became of your visit."

"I promise nothing," he said again. He paused. "I will send word when your weapons are ready."

With that the men parted ways. Barak's sense of failure grew stronger with every step homeward.

15

Jael looked over the dark camp and glanced once more at the heavens. The moon had not moved since the last time she checked its place. Still there was no sign of Heber or her sons. She shivered, and with the chill came the fear she could not shake.

"It's been nearly a week," Nadia said, wrapping her cloak tightly about her. "Do you think they came upon robbers?" Her whispered words held the same thread of fear that was in Jael's heart.

Jael reminded herself that she was the older, wiser one here. It was up to her to comfort. "I'm sure they are fine. They must have been delayed in Hazor. Perhaps the king invited them to a banquet." Or imprisoned them for some ridiculous reason. But if Sisera had sent them to King Jabin, he would know what had become of her husband and sons. And if something bad had happened, his chariots would be on the door of her camp. Even now she and her girls would be in Canaanite hands.

"If they don't come soon," Nadia said, pacing with her words, "what will we do?"

Jael glanced at the tents where Raja and Daniyah had bedded down for the night. Pray God they slept, for Raja with her swelling belly needed her rest. Worry would not help her, might in fact cause harm to the child. And Daniyah's fears were evident with every waking moment. "Where is Abba?" she had asked over and over. "They should be home by now."

It had taken all of Jael's self-control not to rebuke the girl for her repeated worries. To do so would only reveal her own.

"You have a plan, don't you?" Nadia's soft voice brought Jael's thoughts around to her again.

"Not a good one." She fiddled with the scarf at her neck, repositioning it over her hair. She should go into the tent and let down her hair and sleep as one who expects pleasant dreams. But she had kept her hair up and her staff and cloak at the ready. Just in case.

She looked at Nadia and touched the girl's slight shoulder. "If they do not return in two more days, we will pack everything up and move south, back to our people. It is

214

the only place where we might find safety."
How they would get there unnoticed, she
did not know. They would have to keep to
the paths in the hills, off the main roads.

"It is what I would do," Nadia said, her
voice catching on a sob.

Jael took the girl into her arms and patted
her back. "Mahir will be fine. They are just
delayed. I'm sure it is nothing."

Nadia nodded and clung to Jael for a
suspended moment, then pulled away. "I
best get some sleep."

"Yes, as will I." Though Jael knew sleep
would come fitfully, if at all, for another
night. For despite the guards Heber had left
to watch over them, Jael would not feel truly
safe until her men rested near her again.

The slow clomping of donkeys' hooves woke
Jael the next morning. She jumped up,
smoothed her rumpled clothing, which she
had not bothered to set aside the night
before, and peered through the door of her
tent. Daniyah rose to look out as well, but
when she saw Heber, she burst from Jael's
tent and ran straight into her father's waiting arms.

"Daniyah, my sweet." He kissed each of
her cheeks, held her close, then looked her
over again. "How tall you have grown in

just a few days."

Daniyah laughed. "You make fun, Abba. I am the same as I was when you left."

Jael hurried from the tent, taking turns hugging each one of her sons, clinging to them as though her very life resided in theirs.

And then everyone was talking at once. Her daughters-in-law claimed her two married sons, and Daniyah moved to talk to her brother Ghalib. Jael walked to Heber's side, but one glance behind him made her stop and stare.

A young woman sat huddled on a donkey, covered from head to foot in a filthy, torn robe and headscarf.

"Who is this?" Jael met her husband's gaze, searching.

"She was a slave to Jabin. I purchased her freedom." Heber pulled Jael into his arms and bent low to her ear. "It is a long story, and I am too weary to tell it more than once. I will explain everything over the evening meal." He kissed her forehead. "She is not a concubine to me or any of our sons. She was kidnapped and abused. She is a Hebrew. I will tell you the rest later."

He turned then to extend a hand toward the frightened girl. "This is Yiskah. Please treat her kindly and make her presentable."

His look toward Jael held apology. "Her clothes . . . it was the best we could do."

Jael nodded. "No apology needed, my lord. We will take care of her." She lifted a quizzical brow at Heber to let him know she did not intend to be left without knowing all. Then she turned toward the girl with a smile and led her to her tent.

"Where are you from, Yiskah?" Jael searched through a basket of clean tunics for an appropriate one for the girl, who stood shivering near the tent wall, unwilling to sit or even speak.

Daniyah stood at Jael's side and pointed to a pale yellow tunic near the bottom. "That one should fit." She bent close to Jael's ear. "She won't answer you, Ima. She's afraid."

Jael pulled out the tunic and found a matching belt and a spare robe, then turned to face the girl. "Here, give me the veil."

The girl clung to it as though the flimsy material would protect her.

"I'm not going to hurt you," Jael soothed, her voice soft, as though speaking to one of her children when they were small. "Please, let me see your hair."

The girl stared, wide-eyed, her gaze shrunken, her eyes deep wells of anguish and sorrow. At last she let the veil fall from hair that was matted and filthy and . . . short. Someone had cropped it closer than a man's hair. No wonder the girl was ashamed.

"There, now," Jael said as tears filled the girl's dark gaze. "Come. We will take you to the spring and wash the dirt from you first." She grabbed the soap and hyssop and a thick woven blanket and motioned both Yiskah and Daniyah through the tent.

They made their way through the trees to a spring that ran behind the campsite. Daniyah held the blanket for the girl's privacy while Jael helped her bathe. "There, there, it's okay to weep." She could not miss the deep welts along her back or the bruises on her arms and legs, not to mention the mark of shackles or ropes at her wrists. How much abuse had she suffered?

Yiskah's tears fell in silence, mixing with the water Jael poured over her head. On the third rinsing, Jael declared her clean and quickly helped her dry off and dress.

"Why, you are beautiful, dear girl." With a new veil covering her short-cropped hair, she was pretty. But who was she? From where had the Canaanites taken her?

Yiskah shook her head but still said nothing. Jael shrugged, then sighed. She couldn't make her talk. She had done what she could.

"Come. You will eat something and then sleep. We can talk in the morning."

The girl followed Jael and Daniyah back to the camp, accepted cheese and dates in silence, eating them as one savors a last meal, then lowered her body with great care onto the mat Jael provided. Jael watched, her heart squeezing tight at such a broken creature.

She left a lamp burning in the tent, then went outside to prepare food for the men, wondering at how easy it was to fix the outside of a person. But the inner Yiskah might never be healed.

Later that evening, after the men were fed and had gone to their tents, Jael slipped into Heber's tent and lowered the flap. He rose up on one elbow to look at her.

"Good, you are still awake."

He rolled onto his back and placed one arm over his eyes. "I wasn't until you walked in. What do you want, woman?"

Jael lay at his side and snuggled beneath his arm, resting her head on his shoulder. "Tell me what you know of this girl."

"I already told you at the mealtime."

"You told me what you wanted our daughters to hear. But you know more than you told them. Who is she?"

Heber's chest lifted and fell in a defeated sigh. "You push too much, Jael."

"It is a wife's job to do so, my lord." She placed one arm across his chest, waiting.

"I told you what Barak's men found when they entered Hazor."

"Yes." She shuddered to imagine such a gruesome sight.

"Well, it was worse than I said. Jabin had certain slaves standing, never allowed to sit, on either side of his throne." He sighed again. "They were not clothed."

Heat filled Jael's cheeks at the image in her mind's eye. "How awful for them."

"Yes," he said softly, as though it pained him to say even that one word. "Barak, when I'd met him along the way, had pleaded with me to save even one of them, to purchase one of the men or women from Jabin. He did not know about the girls in Jabin's audience chamber."

Jael shifted, clinging to him for his comforting presence.

"I knew I could not help the men and women in the market square, nor the ones in the ring meant to die. But apparently Jabin displays these few for his courtiers and visitors. They were . . . for sale." Heber turned to face her. "He is despicable."

"Yes. As is his commander," Jael whispered, shivering again at the way Sisera had touched her.

"I only had enough gold to buy the one, or you would have two servants to care for."

"You did what you could." She stroked his arm, his bearded cheek. "You are a good man."

"She is related to the prophetess."

Jael sucked in a breath. "The one in Israel? The one who judges those who come to her?"

"The same." His gaze held hers. "That meant her cost was greater. I ended up trading all of the weapons for her."

"It is of no consequence. We will get by." Related to the prophetess. Jael's thoughts whirled. "They must be frantic, wondering what has happened to her."

"Perhaps." Heber yawned, and Jael knew he would say little more.

"Would you think otherwise?" She had to know his thoughts.

"It is strange that no one has come searching for her. That the prophetess wouldn't have known where to find her. Perhaps the girl lied about the connection. There is only one way to know for sure." Heber stroked her cheek, placed a finger on her lips. "You must take her to Deborah."

"Me?" She stared at him, dumbstruck. "Not alone, surely."

"Of course not. I would send Ghalib and Fareed with you. You will stay to the side roads and hill country. The journey is not very far." He lifted her chin with a gentle touch. "And you might consider leaving Daniyah with her. I think she would be safer with the prophetess than here where Sisera . . ." He did not finish the thought, but he did not need to.

Obviously, her husband had thought about this, and not for a little time. "But if the prophetess's village is so safe, how did Jabin's men get Yiskah?"

Heber shrugged. "I do not know. Ask Deborah. If her answer pleases you, leave Daniyah in her care. If it does not, bring her home. I will find a way to send you all back to my brother, though it troubles me to even suggest it."

She kissed him, recognizing the struggle of such a statement. He would forgo his pride to save his women. "Kiss me now and we will talk of this later." She ruffled his hair and drew him to her. His slow smile warmed her, and she gladly welcomed him into her arms.

16

Barak moved into the courtyard of his empty house, his steps tentative. He had stayed away so long. Even when he had returned to Kedesh-naphtali and stayed with his parents instead of his own house, he had been unable to bear being so near the memories of this place. Perhaps this determination to face them now was foolish.

He glanced about the decaying court. The clay bowl Nessa had placed his feet in to wash after his work in the fields lay covered in dust, and a nest of cobwebs filled the dry hole now. The stones of the court held a thick layer of road dust as well, and Nessa's broom stood silent, as forgotten as all that used to be normal about his life. All that used to give his life meaning.

A weary sigh escaped. Three years. How was it possible? Only yesterday she stood laughing as he twirled her in his arms and kissed her in the center of this court. Only yesterday she had stroked his beard and whispered sweet words in his ear. But now, all that remained of this place was dry earth and stale memories.

He swallowed. Hard. There was so little hope left — especially after the news of Endor's shame and decimation had reached them. Sisera had killed Endor's men and maimed their youths, and eventually he would find and destroy Kedesh-naphtali, the prophetess's village, and every other small town left standing in Israel.

The defeat should have sparked greater determination, but Barak had lost the strength for the fight. He'd had no choice but to send his men home — even Keshet — for there was nothing more to do. Before long Barak would lie in Sheol with Nessa.

He raked a hand through his hair.

His grip tightened on a lamp he had borrowed from his mother, and he walked about the rooms, trying to see them without imagining Nessa weaving in one corner or spinning in another. He closed his eyes and took in a long, slow breath. *Nessa.* His throat thickened. He moved to another room. Their bedchamber.

He stopped, staring into the semi-darkness. The room was musty from disuse, the mats in dire need of beating, which his mother would have done if he had allowed it. He couldn't bear to change a thing even now. A painful ache filled his chest. He took one step. Another. Stopped again and looked slowly from one edge of the room to another. He had laid her here when the women of the village tried to save her. The scent of her blood and the foreign smells that had clung to her were gone now. Nothing but dust remained.

For you are dust, and to dust you shall return. The Creator's words to his ancestor Adam on that long-ago day when beauty was broken.

Nessa had been beautiful. So beautiful.

He set the lamp on a low table and knelt beside the mat. She was there again in his mind's eye, her eyes closed . . . peaceful.

"Please, Nessa . . ." His voice had cracked, and he wasn't sure he could say more. But he must. He must convince her to stay. "Don't leave me." He gripped her pale, lifeless hand, and her strength ebbed even as he held tighter.

Her eyes fluttered open for the briefest moment. "Barak."

She attempted to lift her hand to touch his cheek, but she could not raise it high enough to reach him. Just as he could not reach her now.

Memories of that day blurred — shouts to the women to *do* something! Curses at Sisera as Barak had stomped the fields near the burial cave. And tears. They came in the wilds where he had wandered for weeks once darkness fell, and outside the tomb where Nessa's bones lay. She had gone to a place he could not follow, and he needed her. Desperately.

How could he live without her? Even now the question brought pain, and yet somehow he had managed to still breathe. His own body had betrayed him and refused to follow her to the nether world, despite his constant prayers to do so. Revenge and hatred had grown strong, pushed him forward. He *would* avenge her death. He would live long enough to destroy the man who had done this to his only love. Then he would stop caring what happened to him.

And yet, he had made no dent in Sisera's terror and was no closer to catching and killing the man. He had only proved his own failure by watching Sisera grow stronger with each passing year. And Israel grow weaker.

He sank to his knees, his thoughts as deflated as his anger, like a cloud dissipating into air too thin to hold it. How bitter the taste of defeat.

I wish these days had never come. Hadn't he walked with God? While his neighbors and fellow Israelites had followed other gods, hadn't he clung to his faith? Hadn't he done all he could?

His self-defense did not comfort.

The fronds of the palm branches swayed above Deborah's head as afternoon waned. The line of people who had come seeking her judgment had at last dwindled. She shaded her eyes against the sun's slight glare and drank greedily from the flask of water at her side. In the distance, she caught sight of two men and three women coming from the city gates, walking along the main street as though looking for something.

Looking for her, no doubt.

She sighed, suddenly weary of the weight she carried. *Why, Lord?* Why her? If she hadn't been so outspoken, if she hadn't listened to Lappidoth's coaxing when he insisted God intended her to lead, if she hadn't been called by the visions and dreams . . . *Why, Adonai?* If she could have chosen, she would have picked a different way of life.

As the group drew closer, one woman older than the rest hurried forward. She was not of Israel, Deborah immediately noted. She sat straighter. Not Canaanite either. She tilted her head, studying the unusual markings on the woman's robe. Kenite. Deborah breathed easier.

"Are you Deborah, the prophetess of Israel?" the woman asked, coming to kneel before her.

"I am Deborah. And you are of the Kenite clan." She glanced at the rest of the people in the small group.

The woman looked at her strangely for a moment, her eyes wide with a hint of wonder.

"The markings on your robe give you away," Deborah said, pointing to a small emblem of something metal, a dagger or a tent peg perhaps.

"Ah yes," the woman said, smiling. "My husband is a metalworker. I am Jael, wife of Heber the Kenite."

Deborah gave a slight nod. "What do you seek?" She should offer the woman hospitality, but she waited, wanting first to hear why they had come.

The woman backed slightly away and motioned for another, younger woman to come forward. "My husband had dealings with Jabin, king of the Canaanites. While he was in Hazor, he saw that they had female

228

slaves . . . for sale." She halted briefly as though choosing her words. "This woman was among them." She glanced from the woman to Deborah. "She claims she is related to you."

Deborah squinted, searching the other woman's face, trying to deny the recognition that had pierced her heart the moment she drew close. It couldn't be. But her heart told her otherwise.

"Yiskah," she said, her voice a gentle command, "look at me."

The woman seemed to find fascination with her sandals, but at last she lifted her head. "It is I, Prophetess." She lowered her gaze again, no longer the defiant woman who had cast a rebellious eye toward her when confronted with her false gods.

"What happened to you after Shet sent you away?" Months had passed since that long-ago moment, and there had been no word. More troubling to Deborah was Shet's lack of concern or any obvious desire to seek out his lost wife.

Yiskah did not respond for many breaths. "I went to Hazor. I thought I could find refuge there." The girl would not meet Deborah's gaze, and her cheeks grew pink beneath Deborah's lengthy stare.

"And did you?" Deborah asked. "Find

refuge?"

Yiskah slowly shook her head. "No, Prophetess."

Deborah shifted in her seat, praying for wisdom. She looked at Jael. "Why have you brought her to me?"

Jael took a step back, one brow lifted in surprise. "I thought . . . that is, my husband thought that if she belonged to your family, it would be best to return her to you." She lifted her chin, but no defiance warmed her gaze. "If she is not pleasing to you, Prophetess, I will keep her as my servant."

Deborah clasped her hands in front of her. She looked beyond Jael. "These people belong to you. Your guards?"

"My sons. And my daughter."

Deborah nodded and rose slowly. "This situation is not entirely mine to decide," she said, holding Jael's gaze. "Yiskah's husband sent her away for worshiping Asherah. She was to stay in the hills seven days to pray and repent of her sin. Since she had not attempted to cause others to follow her rebellious ways, her husband thought it the prudent thing to do. Had she caused others to follow Asherah, he would have been forced by law to stone her."

Deborah stepped from beneath the palm and pointed to the grassy knoll around it.

"Wait for me here. Since Yiskah did not return to Shet as she was supposed to do, it is up to her husband to decide what to do with her now." She walked off, but Jael's words stopped her.

"If her husband would put her to death, I will not wait for him. I will take her back with me at once." Her tone held a fierce edge.

Deborah turned to face her. "He will not seek her death," she said quietly. "But he may not wish to keep her." She motioned again to the grasses. "Wait here."

She walked to the city gate, her mind whirling. Shet's response was not one she could foresee. But Yiskah's return had also been hidden from her, as were so many things. The dreams came often, but they normally hinted of war. What had happened to Yiskah during her stay at Hazor? Deborah was not sure she wanted to know.

She climbed the steps of the gate where Shet's grandfather sat with the elders. She came and knelt before him. "Uncle Chayim, I need you, Amichai, and Shet to come to my house when they return from the fields."

Her uncle squeezed her hands. "Ah, my Deborah. But of course we will come." He looked deeply into her eyes. "Something troubles you, my daughter."

231

She leaned forward and kissed his cheek. "Visitors have come bringing Yiskah. I will not send her away until I know what Shet would do. Will he cover her shame and embrace her once more, or write her a writ of divorcement? She has abandoned him, and he must decide."

Her uncle sat up straight, his eyes wide. "Yiskah has returned?"

"Yes, Uncle." Deborah waited, patient while the shocking news took hold.

"Shet will accept her, of course. He must." He still seemed taken aback, but his eyes lit with a determined gleam she had not seen in him since Yiskah was sent away. Yiskah was her uncle's only granddaughter-in-law, as Shet was his only grandson. Her loss had been a blow to the entire family.

"I will send someone to find him now. There is no sense in keeping your guests waiting."

"Thank you, Uncle." Deborah rose and hurried down the steps.

The courtyard buzzed with the usual pleasantries and an underlying awkwardness. Deborah's aunt and uncle and Ilana had come to welcome the Kenite clan before Amichai, Shet, and the rest of the men returned from the fields. The women offered almonds and cheeses and watered wine to the guests, but Deborah could not eat. She glanced continually toward the street that led to the city gate for her men.

At last she spotted them. She jumped up and hurried out to meet them, accepting Lappidoth's kiss on her cheek. "Your grandfather is here," she said to Shet, waiting until he fully met her gaze. "I asked him to come."

"I am sure he was pleased to visit," Shet said, his bearing stiff. "But what purpose is this that needs both me and my father to come home before the day's work is over?"

Deborah studied him, then glanced at his father Amichai. "Your wife has returned," she said. "There is no sense entering our courtyard until you tell me what you will do with her."

Shet's surprise surpassed that of his father's. He rubbed a hand along his bearded jaw, his dark eyes rimmed with sleepless shadows. Yiskah's disappearance had not been handled well by any in Chayim's household. "At last she returns? Where has she been these many months?"

Deborah touched his arm and gentled her tone. "She did not stay in the hills. She followed the roads until she came to Hazor. She sought refuge with the Canaanites."

Shet reeled back. "She what?"

"They did not treat her well," Deborah said, trying to appease the heat of anger in his eyes.

"She deserved whatever she got." He cursed and spat in the dirt. "Let her rot in Sheol." He turned on his heel and stalked off.

"Do not leave yet, cousin." Deborah's tone halted him, and she knew he would listen out of respect. "Your grandfather is waiting for your decision. You know they love Yiskah. You owe it to him, to them, to hear your wife's tale. Before you would cast her out, hear what she has to say."

Shet's back remained to her, but he slowly turned to his father, who simply shrugged. How could he act so indifferently? Deborah realized yet again how glad she was that she had never married the man.

"I do not wish to hear her tale," Shet said. "She betrayed me with other gods. She betrayed our marriage and my trust."

"You have every right to think so, Shet," Deborah said softly. "She is as guilty as you say."

"Then why do you care what becomes of her?"

Deborah sighed deeply and glanced quickly at Lappidoth and each of her sons before facing her young cousin once more. "She was brought here by Kenites who purchased her freedom from Jabin. When they learned she was related to me, they brought her here."

"Then forgive me, cousin Deborah, but you keep her."

"I will decide her fate, but only after you have heard all. Then if you would still cast her aside, you must give her a writ of divorcement so that she will be free."

"No other man would have her."

"Probably not." Deborah looked beyond him a moment, and in a flash she saw a vision of what Yiskah had endured. Energy seeped from her, causing her to stumble.

"What is it?" Lappidoth caught her arm. He knew the look that took her away to places she did not want to visit.

"She has endured much." She took a steadying breath. "Come," she commanded Shet, turning to walk back to the house.

Shet obeyed, though he was the last to enter the courtyard.

"Yiskah," Deborah said sharply, bringing silence to the gathering. "Come here."

The girl stood and came trembling, hands clasped tightly in front of her, head bowed.

"Tell your husband what was done to you in Hazor." Deborah paused a moment. "In

235

private," she amended, the vision still too vivid in her mind. She pointed beyond them. "Take her to the palm tree, Shet. I will come in a few moments. Then you can give me your decision."

Shet stared at his wife. His dark eyes held no warmth.

"Be merciful, son," his grandfather said, pleading.

Shet glanced up but did not reply. He whirled about and walked quickly toward the palm. Yiskah hurried to catch up.

Deborah looked the group over. "The images are not seemly to repeat to you." She caught Jael's gaze. The woman nodded. She knew. "I will give you Shet's decision in a few moments. For now, rest and eat. You are welcome to stay with us as long as you are able."

"We will be leaving at dawn," Jael said.

17

Jael accepted a clay plate of flatbread and a dipper of stew from Deborah's daughter, but she could not eat. She watched the prophetess, saw the uneasy exchanges with her daughter and the way the men obeyed her word. Deborah held power here, though Jael did not see arrogance in the woman's gaze. The men obeyed her because of the visions, they said. And since Jael had not told Deborah what Yiskah had lived through, nor had Yiskah been alone with her to tell her so, the woman's visions must be true.

The thought comforted Jael, and yet . . . this village even with its hidden walls and barred gates could be easily scaled by Sisera's men. Daniyah would be safer in Judah with her uncle Alim, even if it meant wounding Heber's pride to return home. None of them would live long with Sisera so easily invading their camp.

Jael glanced at her daughter eating in silence, then looked at her two sons. Uneasiness crept into Fareed's gaze. Did he sense something she did not? But a moment later one of Deborah's sons engaged him in conversation, and he seemed to relax. She nibbled the end of the bread, listening as Deborah's daughter spoke to Daniyah.

"Did you travel far?" Talya asked as she sat near, holding a clay cup of water.

Daniyah looked at her mother as though she was not sure whether to respond.

"A few days' walk," Ghalib answered in Daniyah's place. "We kept to the side roads, so the trip took longer than it would have if the highways were safe to use." He gave Talya that crooked grin Jael had always loved. He scooted closer to his sister, which put him closer to Talya.

"Did you take the path through the woods?" Talya's interest seemed piqued as she looked at first him, then his sister, and Jael leaned slightly forward to better hear the answer. "Sometimes Sisera's men hide in the woods," she said.

"We stayed clear of them," Ghalib said, straightening, his bearing one of a man of confidence. "Fareed and I felt it would be too easy to get lost there, as we are not familiar with these lands."

Talya nodded and took a sip from her cup before she spoke again. "Tell me about the place you are from. I have never been far from these hills."

Jael glanced at Daniyah, who seemed to have been excluded from the conversation, as Talya's gaze now met only Ghalib's. Conversations of the other men came in low waves around her. Her stomach knotted each time she glanced toward the palm tree. How long would it take Yiskah to tell all to her husband? Would he forgive her?

"We come from the Negev of Judah, but in recent months we moved to the oak in Zaanannim. Our families still live in Judah's desert." Ghalib's tone held its usual longing and hint of scorn, and Jael did not miss Talya's questioning brow.

"You are not happy with the move?"

Jael watched her son's narrowed gaze, wishing he could adjust and get past the hurts he still clung to, but also knowing he was more right than she gave him credit for. They had been foolish to leave, and she would do all in her power to remedy that if she could. But how to save Heber's pride in the process?

"I would not have left," Ghalib said, pulling Jael from her musings, "if the decision had been mine to make."

"He misses our cousin Parisa," Daniyah said.

Ghalib cast his sister a withering look. "Mind your own business, little one."

Talya stiffened and her dark eyes narrowed. She looked Daniyah's way, seemed to assess her, then faced Ghalib. "It is rude to call a woman 'little one.' Anyone can tell your sister is not a child."

Ghalib glanced from his sister to Talya. At last he shrugged. "It matters little now. A cousin was nearly promised to me in marriage, but we left before the betrothal could be pursued."

"I'm sorry to hear it," Talya said, her gaze suddenly drifting beyond Ghalib. "Good men and women are hard to come by in these difficult days." She faced Daniyah and Jael, her expression suddenly awkward. "Forgive me. I did not mean to pry into your personal affairs. If you will excuse me."

She stood and walked into the house.

Jael watched the girl go, puzzled by her sudden change in tone and interest. Was there someone she also pined for who had been lost to her?

She turned at the sound of voices and squinted to better see into the gathering dusk. Deborah emerged from the shadows alone. Jael released a relieved sigh, but a moment later Yiskah came behind, her feet dragging in the dust. Her husband did not follow. Yiskah staggered, then righted herself. Jael jumped up, then sat back down as she realized it was not her place to interfere.

Yiskah came into better view, tears falling freely from her dark, sunken eyes.

"He refuses to give her a writ, but he will not accept her return." Deborah looked at an older man whom Jael had learned was Shet's grandfather. "She will stay with us in the meantime."

"I thought you said he had to give her a writ," Shet's grandfather said, slowly standing. "He must either take her back or let her go. He cannot just turn her out."

"And he will not, Uncle," Deborah said, taking the girl's arm. "I promised to give him time."

"How much time?" Her uncle came close to the girl, and Jael sensed he wanted to pull her into his embrace. There was still love in this place, in the girl's home.

"Enough to accept what has befallen her, what her choices have caused." Deborah's tone said the matter was finished. "She will stay with me until next week. Then if Shet will not take her back, you must decide whether to stand by this woman" — she pointed to Yiskah — "or your grandson."

She ushered Yiskah into the house, where the girl's weeping grew louder, though muffled. Deborah's uncle looked at his wife as though someone had pierced him with an arrow. The men crowded around them both, taking his arms and that of his wife's and seeing them safely home. Another woman, probably Shet's mother, walked in silence behind them.

"We should leave first thing, before dawn," Fareed whispered close to Jael's ear.

"Yes, I agree." Jael handed her uneaten food to Talya, who had returned to see if she could offer them anything else. She left just as quickly with no further comment to Daniyah or Ghalib. Jael studied Ghalib's expression as the girl walked into the house.

"So soon?" Ghalib said once Talya was out of earshot. "But . . ." He met Jael's gaze and did not finish his sentence.

"Your brother is right. The prophetess will handle the matter. It is why we came. We leave in the morning."

Daniyah would not be staying.

The following morning, Jael stood at the courtyard gate with Deborah. She caught Ghalib talking quietly with Talya, and Fareed standing nearby tapping his foot. Daniyah stood at Jael's side, silent, watching.

"Thank you for bringing Yiskah back to us," Deborah said, her smile genuine. But her gaze held a hint of regret. "I wish you could stay longer."

"My husband will worry if we don't quickly return." Jael put her arm around Daniyah and bowed toward Deborah. "I am grateful that you will see to Yiskah's safe-keeping."

Deborah studied Jael a moment, but Jael did not flinch. "Your husband paid money to retrieve her, yes?"

Jael nodded. "In a manner of speaking. He took her in trade." It would do no good to tell the prophetess exactly what Heber had traded for the girl. Better the Israelites not know of her husband's dealings with Canaan.

Deborah pulled small silver nuggets from a pouch at her side and placed them in Jael's hand. "This is to cover some of what was lost on her account. I am sure it is not sufficient, but I hope it pays at least part of what we owe."

"You owe us nothing." Jael glanced at the silver and nearly returned it, then thought how pleased Heber would be to regain some of his earnings. She hesitated.

"Keep it," Deborah said. She offered Jael a knowing smile. "I will not ask why your husband has business with Jabin, and you will not refuse me to offer you payment in kind."

Jael flushed, certain the woman could read her very thoughts! "Thank you, Prophetess." She glanced again at her sons. "We should go."

Deborah bid them farewell, and Jael turned to her sons. "Come," she said, despite Ghalib's pleading look to stay a moment more.

"Perhaps we will meet another time," Ghalib said to Talya as he hurried after Jael.

When they passed through the gates of Deborah's village, Ghalib fell into step with his mother. "Ima, what would have been so wrong with getting to know the prophetess and her family? Father would not have minded if we had stayed another day or two."

"You were too taken with the girl," Fareed said, jumping in before Jael could speak.

"And what is wrong with that?" Ghalib's voice rose, and he took a step closer to Fareed. "She is beautiful."

Fareed chuckled, further incensing Ghalib. Jael moved between them. "Enough. You are acting like children." She stopped and faced Ghalib. "I am not sure you would be happy married to an Israelite." She glanced back at the village gates, now small in the distance. "Besides, I doubt very much that such a woman, a prophetess who hears from their God, would allow her daughter to marry outside of her tribe." She touched his cheek. "Just as we do not marry outside of our clan." She clucked her tongue and sighed. "What am I to do with you? We should have married you off before we left your uncle's home."

"Yes, you should have." Again scorn riddled his words.

Jael looked into his hardened eyes. "Your father will find a wife for you. We will send to Judah for Parisa if you still want her. Are not your sisters-in-law of our own family?" She huffed and continued walking. "Come now. We will go home and I will speak to your father. But you must forget the prophetess's daughter. Beautiful or not, she is not Kenite, and that is more important."

Barak startled at the sound of scraping in the courtyard and struggled to pull himself from the sleepy haze he had wrapped himself in since the day he had sent his men home. How long had it been? A week? A month? Time seemed to meld one day into the next.

He dragged himself up and considered

splashing the brackish water over his face and scrubbing the sleep from his eyes, but changed his mind. Ignoring the water, he moved through the semi-dark house to the door, then blinked and squinted in the bright sunlight that met his gaze as he opened it. A man stood before him, one who looked vaguely familiar.

"Barak, son of Abinoam?" The man looked him up and down, then smiled. "I am Fareed, son of Heber. My father sends word to tell you that what you have ordered is now ready." He glanced behind him as though he feared the shadows.

Barak opened the door wider and bid him enter. "Let me light a lamp."

"If you open the shutters there is no need," Fareed said.

Barak nodded and walked to the window, blinking hard to clear his head, then turned to face his guest. "The weapons are ready, you say?"

Fareed nodded, "Yes, my lord." He glanced about the sparsely furnished home. Barak did not even have a cushion to offer the man a place to sit.

"Forgive my lack, Fareed. I fear the place has been without a woman's touch since my wife died." Saying the words disturbed him, but he was surprised that the pain had dulled in the weeks since he had returned to this place. Perhaps he was finally adjusting to Nessa's loss. Or perhaps he had drunk too much wine the night before. He cared little why.

"I would have brought the weapons with me," Fareed said, "but Sisera's troops are too unpredictable. My father would not allow me to risk it." He pulled a dagger from the sheath at his waist. "This is one of them." He extended it to Barak.

Barak took it and examined the blade. "This is good work."

"Thank you, my lord. My father made as many as the ore would allow. I am afraid Sisera brought another load of fine ore just days after you did, so we have been busy trying to finish both orders. I do not know when Sisera will return to claim his. I suggest you bring your men with you as protection when you come." Fareed gave Barak an uncomfortable nod and backed toward the door. "I should get back while it is light."

"I would offer you food and drink, but I fear even that has been depleted here in recent days." When was the last time he had eaten? His stomach rumbled at the very thought.

"It is no trouble, my lord." Fareed tapped a sack at his side. "I have plenty of provisions. But I must go. Sisera's men hide in the most unlikely places, and I must take great care returning."

"Let me go with you. Two are better than one." Barak's sudden desire to do so surprised him. He had given up all hope of overcoming Sisera. Why should he care about weapons now?

Fareed shook his head. "Do not trouble yourself, my lord. You must gather your men and come. One man cannot carry all of the weapons alone." He gave Barak a sidelong glance.

Barak ran a hand over his beard. "You are right, of course. Tell your father we will come very soon."

Jael looked up from her grinding and glanced across the circle of tents at Daniyah talking with Raja, Fareed's wife. The girl's curves could be seen beneath her robe and tunic, something the guards had surely noticed. Uneasiness crept into Jael's heart. The girl needed a husband to keep her safe.

Safe. Did such a thing exist in this land? As long as men like Sisera roamed the earth, there was no place that would ever feel truly safe. Sisera could kill any husband they might find for Daniyah and take her from him. Even Alim's tents were not free of his reach, though the distance made it seem so. But Heber's attempts to send for his niece Parisa, daughter of his younger brother, for Ghalib, and safe passage home for Daniyah had met with scorn once Alim got word of it.

She tsked her tongue, aggravated with herself. She should have pushed Heber to make peace with Alim from the moment the fight ensued rather than allow pride to send them away. They should have humbled themselves, submitted to Alim's leadership, however hotheaded and foolish the man was. She released a pent-up breath. It was too late now. They were truly alone in a sea of peoples they did not know.

The women departed into Raja's tent, and Jael returned to her grinding, wishing the constant motion would take her thoughts with them. She stopped to rest and rubbed the crick in her back. Men's voices came from a distance.

She stood, cautious. *Please don't come out of the tent,* she silently begged Raja and Daniyah. They knew to stay hidden if male voices they did not recognize were heard in the camp. Jael alone would face any intruders, though her heart skipped a beat with every memory of Sisera's bold touch.

She fingered the small dagger strapped to

her side. Heber had insisted she carry the thing, but she had never used it for anything but cutting meat from the bone to put into a stew. She walked slowly toward the coming men, whose voices quieted as they approached. And then Barak's face appeared as he emerged from the trees.

"Barak," she said loud enough for the girls to hear. "You have come." She noted Keshet at his right hand and several men behind them.

"Jael." Barak greeted her with a smile, and Daniyah chose that moment to rush from Raja's tent to join her mother. "Daniyah," the man said, his voice kind. But Jael did not miss the way his eyes quickly caught her frame. He too had noticed the changes in Daniyah. Jael searched his face for some hint of interest, but he turned back to Jael as though Daniyah were a sister or friend, nothing more.

"Is Heber working?" Barak glanced toward Heber's tent, which showed no sign of her husband or sons.

"Yes, my lord. He is preparing an order for Sisera," Jael said.

Barak nodded. He knew. Of course Fareed had told him. "Has Sisera given a time when he will come for it?"

Jael studied him a moment. If he knew

when Sisera would come, he could lie in wait.

"He has not." Jael gave him a look that said she knew his thoughts. "If he had, I would surely tell you. But he comes at will, and we must always be on guard because we do not know when."

Barak nodded. "Exactly as he does so with every attack, every ride through Israelite villages and cities." He glanced at Keshet. "We must gather what we came for." He nodded again to Jael and walked off.

"You must stay for the evening meal," Jael called after him. "You and your men."

Barak turned slightly. "Thank you. We would be most grateful."

She silently counted the number of men who followed and wondered how many stayed back near the road guarding the way in case Sisera should come calling. She turned to Nadia, who had awakened from a nap and now knelt in the dirt, sifting the grain. "We must kill a goat for the stew." She looked at Daniyah. "Go find Ghalib and tell him to do so at once, then return and gather more vegetables. We have many mouths to feed this night."

18

Deborah entered the courtyard of her home when the sun was at its highest point, a time she had learned she must rest. There were so many cases. Too many. And each year the people seeking answers increased. She drew a deep breath and released it, her heart wearied. So much pain lined the faces of her people. So many hurts she could not fix.

"Come, Ima, let me get you something to eat and drink." Libi stood and retrieved a cool dipper of water before Deborah could refuse.

"Thank you," Deborah said, drinking deeply. "It is warm today." She fanned her face and glanced back toward the village square, where some people waited on the knoll.

"You must tell them to come another day, Ima." Libi grasped her upper arm and gently guided her into the house. "You do not sleep well. I hear you walking in the courtyard when the moon is still high."

Deborah met her daughter-in-law's gaze. "If you hear me, then you do not sleep well either, my daughter." She smiled at Libi's nod of amused acceptance.

"Except I have Elisheva as my excuse. She still wakes in the night to feed." Libi had birthed the girl only a few months before, and while Sheva was a quiet babe, she had yet to sleep through the night.

Deborah looked fondly at her daughter-in-law as she took a seat among the cushions in the sitting room. "How well I remember those days." How long ago they seemed now, though Deborah was still considered young by many. She had married at only fifteen and had her children quickly. Except for Talya, who came as a surprise a little later.

"Where is Talya?" The memory brought the typical concern she always felt for her only daughter.

"I think she is below in the cave, practicing with her bow."

Deborah nodded and closed her eyes. Libi's footsteps receded as Deborah pondered the thought of confronting Talya. She had been moody and quiet for weeks now, and her eyes flashed fire whenever Deborah caught her looking at Yiskah. Was Yiskah the only one of their village to worship false gods? How many more men and women had caused their families such pain?

Shet's angry voice filled her memory, and the image of him standing in their courtyard the week after he had heard Yiskah's tale still rang in Deborah's mind.

"I will not give her a writ of divorcement, Deborah. I cannot give her such freedom to do as she pleases. But I also will not cover her shame. How can you even ask it of me after what she has done?" The vehemence in his tone did not surprise her, but the bitterness troubled her.

"Are we not all sinners in God's sight?" she asked him. "Can you look at me and tell me that you have not coveted in your heart? For though you may have kept the whole law, you and I both know that no one can keep the law of the heart. All of us want what we should not have or long for what belongs to our neighbor. If you try to tell me otherwise, I will know you are not telling me the truth." She had held his gaze, unflinching, until his face flushed pink and he broke eye contact.

"Even if I have coveted," Shet finally said, his voice tight with anger, "I have not worshiped other gods, nor thrown myself into the arms of other women." He set his jaw and crossed both arms over his chest.

"No, you have not," Deborah conceded, hiding the sense of defeat she felt. "But even the least of sins needs to be atoned for, my son. Even those of which we are unaware will separate us from Adonai. Do not harbor such bitterness in your heart that you end up with the greater sin."

Shet's eyes grew wide, his look askance. "*Mine* is not the greater sin, nor could it ever be."

"Be careful of where pride will lead you." But her words had fallen on deaf ears, for Shet had blocked them as certainly as the village gates were blocked each day and night.

Deborah sighed. She opened her eyes and shifted on the cushions, startled to see Yiskah nearby, refilling the lamps with oil. She sat up and studied the girl.

"Yiskah, come sit with me."

Yiskah turned and did as Deborah asked without question, her dull eyes as lifeless as a goat recently sacrificed.

"My child," Deborah said, taking the girl's hand. She masked her startled feeling at Yiskah's cold fingers and rubbed them between both of her hands. "I must ask you something, and I want the truth."

Yiskah looked down at their joined hands and simply nodded.

"Do you want to return to Shet? If he were to ever forgive you, would you return as wife to him? Would you treat him kindly, with respect?"

Yiskah looked up, but her gaze moved beyond Deborah's. "He will never want me. Not after what I have done."

"I am not asking you to decide whether you think Shet will forgive. I am asking if you will willingly return as wife to him." Deborah squeezed the girl's fingers and smiled when their gazes met. "It is not so hard a question, is it?"

"I love his grandparents and his mother," she said softly. "I do not know what I feel for Shet."

"Feelings matter little, my child. Commitment is a choice. Will you give it? Will you respect his wishes in running his household?" There was no sense wishing Shet would cover her shame if Yiskah still harbored rebellion in her heart.

"I would not worship other gods again," she said at last. "I would do as the law commands." She lowered her head again, but Deborah saw color heighten her cheeks and understood the embarrassment she felt. "I only wanted a child, Deborah. I thought

256

Asherah could give us that." Her voice fell to a whisper.

Deborah released her hands but rested one on the girl's knee. "Is our God your God now, my daughter? Or do you still pine after Asherah in your heart?" She coaxed Yiskah to meet her gaze.

Yiskah looked away, but Deborah did not miss the tear that slipped down her cheek. "How can I call Him my God when I have broken the very first of His commands? I am no use to Him now."

Was this how the men and women of Israel felt, those who had played adultery with Canaan's gods, when Israel's God had clearly said, "You shall have no other gods before me"?

"Oh, my child," Deborah said, and this time Yiskah looked up and held her gaze. "Our God is a forgiving God, a merciful God. He gave us the law to show us that we cannot keep it. He gave it to guide us, but also to make us realize that His law is perfect, He is perfect, but we are not. It is why He allows us to repent and sacrifice. A broken and contrite heart our God will not despise, Yiskah."

"I am broken," Yiskah whispered, clasping her hands in her lap and wringing them as one would a wet garment. "But even if God forgives, Shet does not."

"Perhaps Shet will . . . in time."

Silence fell between them until at last Deborah spoke once more. "You will stay with us until Shet comes to a better decision." With that she stood. "It is time that I return. Send Talya to meet me as the sun begins to set."

"Yes, mistress." Yiskah stood and hurried from the room as though the demons of her past still chased her.

The day waned as Deborah heard a case involving two men from the same tribe, one in service to the other. "You cannot keep a man longer than six years. You must release him in the seventh year. His debt to you is paid."

"But he still owes me far more than his work has covered," the owner protested.

"Nevertheless, you must release him. And in addition, you must give to him liberally from your flock, your threshing floor, and your winepress. Give to your servants as the Lord your God has blessed you." She studied the man until he acknowledged her with a look and nodded, though he said nothing.

Deborah watched them go, glad they were the last of the day. She rose, took her flask of water, and headed for home. Talya met her partway as requested.

"You needed me, Ima?" Talya's dark eyes did not hold their familiar spark, nor did they seem displeased. Yet something was not quite the same.

"Yes," Deborah said, falling into step with her. "I want to know what troubles you." She paused. "I am asking as your mother, not a judge. You do not have to tell me, but I would like to know if I can help."

Talya kicked a stone along the path and stopped. Their courtyard was some distance ahead, but they would soon reach it. "Many things trouble me, Ima." She glanced toward the house. "I don't like having her there." She met Deborah's gaze. "How long must she stay?"

"Until Shet is willing to take her back." Deborah wondered how wise that answer truly was. She could not force a man to forgo his pride. She could only suggest, especially where a man was in the right to refuse.

"He never will, you know." Talya's certainty caused her to look up.

She lifted a brow. "You know this how?"

"I've heard him talk. She should have been stoned." Talya's bitterness nearly matched Shet's.

259

Deborah's shoulders drooped, defeat settling within her. "What else troubles you, my daughter? For the frown you wear and the silence you carry cannot be for Yiskah alone."

Talya kicked another stone and slowly began walking again. "Why is it so hard to convince a man of your worth?"

This time it was Deborah who stopped to face her daughter. "Are you speaking of someone in particular?"

"Barak, Ghalib, how many do you want? Even Shet before he met Yiskah. But I was probably too young then for him to notice me." Talya's voice wavered slightly, and Deborah scrutinized her daughter, searching her face.

"Barak, I understand. He is not ready to care for any woman, and you did not make things easy for him."

Talya nodded and looked away. "You don't have to remind me."

Deborah shifted from one foot to the other. "You barely met Ghalib, yet you hold interest in him?"

Talya shrugged. "He seemed kind, and I thought he liked me, though perhaps it is a cousin he longs after, and I was just a distraction for him." She looked up the street toward the homes of the other villagers. Toward Shet's home.

"Tell me you are not thinking you could replace Yiskah." The realization struck Deborah like a blow. Surely not. Talya was many things, and she and Shet had been friends for years, but . . . Deborah could not possibly allow such a thing. Not now. Not while Yiskah lived.

Talya shrugged as if she had, in fact, entertained the possibility. But a moment later she shook her head. "No, Ima. I would not interfere in my cousin's marriage. I could not marry a man who harbors such bitterness." She met Deborah's gaze, and in that moment Deborah glimpsed the change in Talya, one she had somehow missed earlier. "I could not wed Barak either. Not as long as Nessa is still wed to his heart."

Talya's chest lifted in a deep sigh, and she continued slowly walking toward their home. "The Kenite seemed to like me," she said softly. "But I don't think his mother did."

"His mother probably thought her son should marry within their clan." She did not add that Talya should do the same. What good would it do to completely dash the girl's hopes? There were so few men from which to choose.

"Then what do I do? Find some random

Israelite and beg him to marry me?" Talya gave a mirthless laugh.

"Of course not."

Talya pulled her sling from the pocket of her robe. "Let me kill Sisera. Then the men will be less afraid to seek wives, and the voice of the bridegroom will fill our streets once more."

The girl's fixation with killing Sisera could have matched Barak's.

"Give it time, Talya," Deborah said. The courtyard stood a stone's throw from them now, and the noise of the women and children carried to them. "Perhaps the next time Barak visits he will see how you have changed."

Talya glanced at her, but her look held disbelief. "If Barak ever returns to us, I doubt he will even notice me." She walked ahead and entered the house, leaving Deborah staring after her.

Barak entered the courtyard of his neglected home with his men in tow. Keshet moved about the sitting room while some of the men went into the village to purchase food and others went to draw water.

"This place needs a woman's touch, my friend," Keshet said, shaking his head as he opened blinds and picked up the flax broom that had seen better days. "Did you notice Heber's daughter? That girl is ready for marriage if ever I saw one so ready . . . and so fair," he added, giving Barak a wink. "You should consider her."

Barak turned his back on his friend and bent to pick up an old wine flask now shriveled and useless. "Methinks it is not I who should consider the girl, since you are the one who noticed that she is . . . fair." He mimicked Keshet's tone and laughed.

"Perhaps," Keshet said, his voice suddenly carrying a serious edge. "I was just giving you the option first."

Barak turned to face Keshet. "She is not of Israel."

"If she believes in Yahweh, it matters little to me. The Kenites have married into Israel in times past, given Moses's history with them." Keshet smiled and straightened. He seemed much too pleased with himself.

Barak threatened to toss the wineskin at him, but refrained when he heard the slightest sloshing in the bottom. No need to make a greater mess of the place. "I will not stand in your way."

He was saved further discussion by some of his men entering the courtyard. He walked out of the room to join them. "You found bread and cheese? Good. I could eat

263

an entire goat."

Keshet joined them, and as dusk settled, the men began to strategize and plan the next best way to attack Sisera. The weapons they had gathered from Heber were now distributed among them, with more in the saddlebags waiting for a greater army.

If an army could be had in Israel. Who would come? Barak's thoughts grew troubled as his mind listed the cities that had lost men or women to Sisera's attacks. Endor was the most recent, but even Shechem had not held its defenses, and since the loss of its daughters, the elders had grown fearful. Could they be persuaded to rise up to attack?

That Deborah's village and his own had remained untouched could only mean they were hidden enough or God's hand had hidden them. He couldn't discount that thought. A miracle it would be, but God had performed plenty of those in years past. When had so many men and women in Israel stopped believing miracles could happen in their day? A deep sigh lifted his chest. When they had stopped worshiping Adonai Elohim and replaced Him with the gods of Canaan. Anat, the fertility, hunter, and war goddess, and Baal her consort brother. And Asherah. He spat into the dirt. The goddess whose fertility rites could make a man blush.

Repent. Pray. Deborah's constant plea turned over in his thoughts.

Had he done both?

The men's conversation went on around him, but he could not concentrate on their words. He had prayed, surely. In his hurt and anger he had lamented and cried out to God for relief, for understanding, for something. For he had no strength in himself to replace the grief he bore.

And yet, as he searched his heart for the briefest moment, he realized that the grief was not quite so sharp, the memory of Nessa not quite as painful. Perhaps his prayers had been heard to some measure.

As for repentance, he could think of nothing for which to repent. He had not followed the Baals or Anat or Asherah or other Canaanite gods. He had obeyed and done all he could to please Adonai. What reason was left for him to repent?

The question would not leave, not even as the men bedded down for the night. Not as he listened to Keshet's soft snores across the room he had once shared with Nessa. Perhaps there was something he had missed. But despite his best efforts, he could not find it.

19

Deborah returned late from judging the people a few weeks later to find Lappidoth in the sitting room with Talya. She paused in the arch of the door, listening.

"I don't want her here, Abba." Talya glanced toward the side room where Yiskah had been staying. "She doesn't belong with us."

Lappidoth nodded as though he would appease the girl, causing the familiar frustration to rise within Deborah's chest. "Your mother thinks she does, Talya."

"Must everything always be as my mother wants it to be?" Talya's anger caused Deborah to take a step back. The sound of the grindstone in the courtyard nearly drowned out this conversation, and suddenly Deborah wished she had not heard as much as she had.

"Your mother hears the voice of God, my daughter. We must listen to her." Lappidoth's voice held the slightest hint of doubt, despite his words.

"She does not always hear His voice. And if Shet will not have his own wife, why is she allowed to stay in this village? Send her away. Let the Kenites have her."

"Talya, Talya, why does this upset you so? Yiskah is no trouble to us here." Lappidoth's tone had shifted to the one that always gave in to Talya's wishes.

"Abba, please," Talya said. "Just looking at her reminds me of the woods, of the man who attacked me . . ." Her voice trailed off. Deborah glanced into the room but could not read the expression in Talya's eyes.

"Yiskah is no threat to you, my daughter." But Lappidoth had stood and wrapped Talya in his arms, patting her back as he did when she was troubled, ever since the first time she had run to him from Deborah's sharp commands.

Why could he never back her up, take a stand against this girl?

"If it worries you that much, I will speak with your mother."

Of course he would. Deborah clenched her jaw.

"Even she admits she is wrong sometimes, Abba." Talya's voice carried a thread of emotion, but Deborah could not tell whether the emotions were true or manipulative.

"She does hear God's voice though, my daughter. We cannot discount that." Was that a lack of conviction in his tone? Surely she heard it this time.

She turned and went around the back of the house to the small room where Lappidoth had so often taken the time to teach her to read and write. Away from the strife she would surely create should she enter their sitting room.

She sank onto the wooden stool and rested her elbows on the bench. Where was the man who had convinced her this was the path she should take? Where was the man who had urged the men of the village to follow her lead? Had his daughter reduced him to doubt even in the wife he claimed to love? Her heart twisted with an almost physical pain. She had worked so hard to care for this man. But ever since Talya's birth . . .

She leaned forward, careful not to brush against his stylus and carving tools that lay neatly to the side. Stacks of clay pieces stood on a shelf beside the table against one wall. Light angled inward, the setting sun's glow sending the world its last bit of warmth.

Oh Adonai, what am I to do?

A shadow fell across the door. Deborah glanced up to find Lappidoth looking down at her.

She searched his face but could find no words.

"Deborah." His voice sounded strained, as though he too were at a loss of what to say. Had their marriage come to this?

"Perhaps you are right," she said at last. "Talya too. I don't always hear from God. I have not heard from Him in too long, and I do not have what it takes to be your deliverer. So that doubt you have in me is well placed."

He stared at her as though he thought her foolish. "Deborah," he said again, stepping into the room. He came to kneel at her side and placed his large hand over hers. "I do not doubt you."

"Your tone said otherwise."

"My tone?"

"When you spoke to Talya. You always take her side, and your tone mimicked her doubt." She pulled her hand from his and crossed her arms.

He leaned back and looked at her, his eyes squinting in the dim light, a frown creasing his brow. "If you heard doubt in my tone, you did not hear correctly."

"I know what I heard."

"And now you can assume my motives? You did not hear the entire conversation, my love."

"So what else did you talk about? Are you going to cast Yiskah out because Talya is too immature to accept her?"

He shook his head, the frown deepening. "How you twist things."

Anger flared, and she abruptly stood. "You said you would speak to me. What else could that possibly mean other than you hope to convince me to give in to our daughter?"

He drew himself up to his full height. "I said I would talk with you to appease her. She is distraught over many things. Yiskah is only one of them."

Deborah drew a breath. "A daughter should not share her troubles with her father but with her mother."

"Not when her mother makes her feel as though she does not listen."

"I listen."

"Of course you do, my love."

"Don't."

He tilted his head and looked at her strangely. "Don't . . . what?"

"Don't call me 'my love' as though you can make everything right with a few words."

She pushed past him and stomped off. How foolish she was to think he would follow as he always did, but when she reached her palm tree and looked back, she felt a kick in her middle that he had not done so. Had she pushed him too far?

Oh Adonai, what have I done? Lately it seemed she could do nothing as well as she wished, and Yiskah had added more strain between her family members than already existed. And yet Deborah felt at a loss as to what to do with the girl.

She sank to the ground and pulled her knees beneath her skirt, her back against the tree's bark. Eyes closed, she longed for escape. Suddenly she was no longer sitting beneath the palm tree but standing on a ridge of Mount Tabor, looking down at the Jezreel Valley. Barak stood beside her and Sisera's chariots gathered below. Ten thousand men of Ephraim and other tribes stood at her back, armed, ready. Clouds billowed overhead and thunder clapped, jolting her. Lightning flashed straight at Sisera, whose body disappeared from where he stood in his chariot.

Deborah blinked and the vision faded.

Shaken, she looked about her, saw Lappidoth standing within arm's length, his wide eyes telling her he had witnessed something she did not.

He came to her, and she placed her hand in his. He pulled her up. "The fire swirled about you again," he said, his voice wavering in awe. "What did you see?"

She swallowed, met his piercing gaze. "I saw war. It is time to send for Barak."

Barak pulled an arrow from its quiver and aimed at the target in the field just outside of his village. Keshet had already beaten him in a practice round where they attempted to shoot broken pottery that rested atop the stump of a felled tree. He could not afford to let the man gloat, nor win again next time. Barak glanced at his friend, who was returning with more pieces of pottery that had been thrown outside the village wall. Some created a sharp detour to anyone trying to scale the walls, but these few pieces for practice with the bow and sling would not be missed.

"Think you'll beat me next time?" Keshet said, laughing. "You know I'm a better shot than you are, so why fight it?" He stood at Barak's side and watched him. Barak ignored him as he sighted another arrow and let it fly.

The pottery shattered and Barak whooped. "Ha! Top that if you can." He slapped Keshet on the back, surprised to find himself capable of laughter. He reached for the water flask and drank deeply, wiping the droplets from his beard. "Any news from the message we sent to Ephraim?"

Keshet shook his head. "None yet."

Barak had sent a runner to some of the cities in neighboring tribes, hoping more men would join him. But so far there had been no response.

"Hopefully soon," Keshet said as he walked to the tree stump and added more pottery pieces.

Barak followed his friend to retrieve his arrows from where they had landed. The sound of running feet made him turn. One of his men, with two young men at his heels, raced toward him.

"Barak," the man called. "A messenger from Deborah has come."

The first man came into view and Barak recognized him as one of Deborah's sons. He strode closer. "Lavi? Is it you?"

The man nodded. "Yes, my lord. It is I, Lavi, son of Lappidoth." He put both hands on his knees and drew a breath as though he had run the whole way.

Barak glanced at the other man but didn't recognize him. "Your servant?" he asked.

"A cousin from the village," he said,

straightening. "We did not think it wise to travel alone."

"Not in times like these. No. Now tell me, what is wrong? Why have you come?" Barak stiffened, half afraid of the man's news, half anxious to hear it.

"My mother bids you come at once," Lavi said. "It is time for war."

Deborah walked from the palm tree toward the city gates. *Please, Adonai, let them make haste.* And let Barak listen to her. But of course he would. Why did she suddenly feel so uncertain? She had commanded men and women to obey the law for years. But Barak, the man who had rejected her daughter, she held with different regard. Respect, perhaps? Something she struggled to muster for her own husband. Would she feel differently if Lappidoth were a warrior like Barak?

The thought settled within her as though God had spoken it aloud. She had been trying to force Lappidoth to carry the mind and attitude of a warrior, a stronger man like his sons Lavi and Elior had become. But he would not change. She had always known her attempts were futile. And now was not the time to think on it.

Nor was it the time to worry. Lavi and

Barak could be another day in coming, and wasting time watching for them was also futile. She must prepare her girls for what was to come.

Talya met her as she crossed the threshold to their sitting room. "You are early," she said, taking Deborah's cloak from her. "You are exhausted, Ima. Come and rest."

Deborah looked at her sharply. After that last overheard conversation, she did not thoroughly trust this child. It was unlike her to be so caring or to notice Deborah's needs. "I am fine."

Talya ignored Deborah's comment, another sign of her strange behavior. "Come, Ima, sit." She retrieved a cup of water and handed it to Deborah.

Deborah sipped, then set the cup aside. "What do you want, Talya? I will not argue with you or appease you as your father does."

Talya's dark eyes grew wide, but a moment later understanding dawned. "You heard me speak with Abba."

Deborah nodded. "I heard enough. But we have no time to discuss this now. War is coming." She met Talya's gaze, not truly surprised when the girl seemed to have already heard this information.

"Lavi went to fetch Barak," Talya said.

"When you did not send a simple messenger but your own son, I knew." She sat beside her mother. "I want to go to war with them." She held up a hand as though staving off Deborah's protest. "You know I can handle a bow as easily as any man. I can help. I can kill Sisera."

Deborah released a deep sigh, studying her only daughter. "I take it you already tried and failed to convince your father. Or do you plan to seek him next when I refuse you?" How harsh she sounded. "War is no place for a woman."

Talya clasped her hands in her lap, but she did not pout as she might have done a few months or even a few days before. Barak was coming. Perhaps that was the reason for the change in the girl.

"Barak would not wish you to be part of a war camp. Surely you do not think you will impress him with military prowess."

Talya shook her head, but when she looked into Deborah's eyes, her gaze held a fierce light. "Ima." She paused as if searching for the exact words. "When I found Yiskah worshiping Asherah, I knew why she did so."

Deborah waited, lifting a brow. "What does that have to do with war?"

"Everything," Talya said, glancing about

the room.

Deborah followed her gaze. There was no sign of Yiskah. "She has gone to the fields with your father. To work in Lavi's place," Deborah said.

Talya nodded.

"So tell me what is going through that head of yours." Her heart beat steady, if not anxiously.

Talya retrieved more water and drank, leaving the flask between them. "Canaanites worship Anat and Asherah. Asherah is a goddess of fertility. Yiskah had no child, so it made sense to her to pray for one." Talya paused. "But Anat is also Canaan's god and a goddess of war. And when I smashed Asherah's image, I wanted desperately to destroy both Anat and Asherah — utterly." Her eyes blazed as though she saw a vision of herself doing that very thing.

Did she?

"You think you can destroy Canaan's gods by killing Sisera or his men?" How innocent her daughter's thoughts, but Deborah did not say so. "However God destroys Sisera matters little. Our men can accomplish as much without you." She would not, could not, allow Talya to consider her desire even one moment longer. "You and I will be staying right here with the rest of the women.

They need us to keep them safe while the men fight the battle."

"Ima," Talya said, her voice holding the slightest hint of impatience, "Anat and Asherah are goddesses. What better person to destroy a female god than a woman?"

Deborah's eyes narrowed. "One does not destroy a goddess by killing evil men. The object worshiped will be found by others sometime in the future."

Talya paced the room, fully spirited now. "Yes, but do you not remember the gods of Egypt? Did not Adonai Elohim destroy them all to show His power over them?" She stopped, facing Deborah.

Deborah released a soft breath. Adonai did have power over evil, even through one as weak as a woman. Hadn't He been using her to give His word to Israel's leaders all these years? Surely if He could use one such as she, He could do as Talya suggested.

But in the next moment she recoiled at the thought of that woman being her daughter. She stood and faced Talya, arms crossed. Then slowly the anger she'd been carrying toward the girl dissipated. How could a mother remain angry at her own child? She opened her arms, drawing Talya to her. "You are wise, my girl," she said, holding Talya close.

"Then you will let me fight, Ima?" Talya pulled back so that Deborah held her at arm's length. "If Lavi goes, he will watch over me."

Deborah shook her head, fighting the onset of a sudden headache, and a sinking realization that life was about to change utterly. "I cannot." She released Talya and turned. "Please, Talya, I cannot lose you. And though I know you are strong and capable, I cannot send one woman into a camp with ten thousand men!"

Silence fell between them. Deborah expected Talya to stomp off, but instead she felt the girl's arms come around her from behind. "It's all right, Ima. If you do not have approval from God, I will not disobey you."

Deborah turned. Her tears fell as she cupped Talya's cheeks. She swiped them away.

"I want to help, Ima. I want to help Barak and you. But I won't fight you anymore."

Deborah pulled Talya close once more and kissed her cheek. "Thank you, daughter. I do not have approval from God to let you go."

But where Talya was concerned, she later realized, she was not so sure that she could hear God apart from her own choices.

279

20

Barak shed his outer cloak and the quiver strapped to his back and carried them over his arm. The narrow passage between the rocks that led to Deborah's village forced him to walk sideways for many cubits, and the less bulk the better. Sweat beaded his brow as he turned to take a tight turn at an angle between the rocks. He did not care for closed-in spaces, but this was the best way to reach Deborah's village from this direction and avoid Sisera's chariots along the main roads. He squeezed through, glancing back to make sure Keshet and Lavi followed.

Two hundred had joined them from several cities along the way, with more giving promise to do so. Men were anxious for war, ready to do whatever it took to rid the land of their Canaanite nemesis. But they needed thousands, not hundreds.

His heartbeat quickened as he emerged at

last near a copse of trees and wiped the sweat away with the back of his hand. He breathed deeply of the pine-scented air and surveyed the area before him as he donned his cloak.

"Just through these trees and over the next rise," Lavi said, coming to stand beside him. "My mother will be waiting."

"She is no doubt anxious for your return," Barak said, sizing the man up once more. He'd grown into a strong ox of a man, one Deborah was sure to trust well. But what mother wished to send her sons to war?

"She is anxious to give you the word from the Lord," Lavi said, his voice confident.

"Let us not keep her waiting then." Barak strode off, his mind filled with questions. Was God finally going to destroy Sisera? Would their land finally know peace?

He could not recall a time of peace in his life. Too many years had passed since the days of Ehud or the brief victory Shamgar had garnered over the Philistines. It had not always been this way. Under Joshua's leadership Israel had conquered kingdoms and taken possession of much of the land God had given to Abraham, Isaac, and Jacob. But not all. And his people seemed powerless to oust those left living among them.

Barak sent a twig flying and picked up his

pace. Perhaps now things would be different. If men and women had listened to Deborah's call to repent and pray . . . But he would not allow himself to dwell on the wherefores until he heard Deborah's words.

The village gate appeared before them moments later, shut to them as dusk had now fallen. Lavi strode close to the guard standing watch and called for him to open. The leather hinges creaked against the wood as the gates swung open just enough to let the men through.

Barak followed Lavi, though he knew the way in his sleep.

"She will be waiting at the palm tree," Lavi said when Barak turned to take the street to Deborah's home.

"But it is late." Barak tilted his head, hesitant.

"She will be expecting us at the center of town." Lavi headed straight toward the middle of the square. Barak followed in silence, surprised to see a gathering of the town's men holding torches, standing near Deborah's palm.

Deborah stood at their approach and embraced her son, kissing each cheek. She smiled into his eyes, then faced Barak. "Welcome, my friend."

He nodded his assent, glancing at the men

around her. Their expressions told him they did not yet know why she had summoned them, but eagerness shone in the eyes of the younger men. He looked at Deborah as she took her seat beneath the palm.

"Has not the Lord, the God of Israel, commanded you," Deborah said, her voice calm and sure, " 'Go, gather your men at Mount Tabor, taking ten thousand from the people of Naphtali and the people of Zebulun. And I will draw out Sisera, the general of Jabin's army, to meet you by the river Kishon with his chariots and his troops, and I will give him into your hand.' "

Barak swallowed. So this was it. The time truly had come. "You've had a vision then?"

Deborah nodded. "God has clearly shown me that the time is now. You are ready?" The light in her eyes drew him, and her steady look made him feel as though she could see into his soul.

He blanched at that thought and looked away. He glimpsed Talya standing near, bow at her side and a fierce light in her eyes. Why was it these women seemed more prepared to fight than some of the men in his own band? But they had not seen what his eyes had seen. They had not witnessed what Sisera could do.

"How does God plan for us to destroy

Sisera's chariots? We are few in number." It wasn't an excuse, but he needed to know, to understand how he would accomplish this task. Surely God would fight for him, but how would he hear God's voice or know that He was the one leading? Barak had no powers of insight as Deborah did. He did not hear God's voice or see visions.

"Is it not enough to know that God will deliver Sisera into your hands? He will reveal Himself to you once you are there. You must leave at first light to draw the men to Mount Tabor."

Deborah crossed her arms in that commanding way she had, and Barak knew he would get no more information from her. Perhaps she had no more information to give. And yet . . . something in him hesitated. He studied her, glanced about at his men, saw the uncertainty. Would God go with him as she had said? How would he know?

He cleared his throat, rubbed a hand along his bearded jaw. "If you will go with me, I will go, but if you will not go with me, I will not go." He planted one foot on the grass nearest her seat and crossed his arms in a stance of equality. He would not put the lives of his men at risk without knowing God was truly with him, and only Deborah had God's ear.

Deborah seemed to consider his words. Talya stepped closer and placed a hand on her mother's shoulder, and in that moment Barak caught an exchange between mother and daughter he had not seen before.

"I will surely go with you," Deborah said at last. "Nevertheless, the road on which you are going will not lead to your glory, for the Lord will sell Sisera into the hand of a woman."

A knot formed as though a man had punched him in the gut, but Barak did not move, trying to keep his expression neutral, certain he was failing miserably. The words were a blow, especially when he saw the look of triumph in Talya's dark eyes. Did she intend to go with them? Would God give Sisera to this slight of a girl when he, Barak, had spent the last many years of his life going after the man? To have a woman win the battle for a man would be humiliation.

"To be struck dead by a woman's arrow will be the ultimate defeat for a Canaanite worshiper of Anat and Asherah," Talya said, stepping closer to Barak. Her gaze held that alluring fire, the desire for vengeance that he had seen only in men.

Barak ran a hand over his beard, still masking his expression and the shock Talya's and Deborah's words had evoked. He needed to sit, to drink wine and fill his belly and forget these women who had just upended his world.

But one was standing a mere handbreadth from him, and the other watched him from her seat of judgment, waiting for his response.

"Very well," he said, dragging the words from some place beyond his conscious thought. "We will go and fight Sisera. May it be as you have said."

He would never live down the disgrace or the ribbing he would take from his men if Talya's arrow pierced Sisera's armor. He glanced at her as the men started talking in excited voices and dispersed to their homes, taking some of his men with them for the night. Deborah led the way to her home, and Barak fell into step with Lavi on one side and Talya on the other.

"You can't possibly have convinced Ima to let you go to war with all of those men." Lavi looked at his sister but did not sound convinced or pleased. Good. How could they possibly keep such a beautiful girl safe in such surroundings?

"I can only assume by her comments that she means just that," Talya said, giving her brother a knowing smirk.

"I do not like it," Barak said, glancing over Talya's head at Lavi. "How will you protect her?"

"I can protect myself." Talya held the bow high and pretended to reach for an arrow in the quiver at her back.

Barak held up a hand to stay her actions. "As you did in the forest when one of Sisera's men nearly killed you?" He studied her out of the corner of his eye as they walked. The air seemed sweeter in her presence, and he suddenly realized that she truly was beautiful.

"That was then," she said, lifting her chin in that defiant way of hers. "This is now." She gripped the bow. "I am ready."

Barak shook his head but said nothing. What point was there in arguing with the girl?

They reached the courtyard of Deborah's home, greeted by her daughters-in-law and a young woman he did not recognize, whom they introduced as Yiskah. Lavi's quick explanation told him that this was Deborah's cousin, the Israelite Heber had rescued, as Barak had asked of him. Respect for the Kenite filled him.

He accepted food and drink from the women and watched as Deborah and Talya slipped into the house, no doubt to talk about the coming battle. Lappidoth sat with his sons and Barak, but said little as evening waned.

At last Barak had a moment alone with the man when most of the household headed to their mats. "Are you truly going to allow your daughter to go to war, my lord?"

Lappidoth studied Barak a moment in silence. "I know God has given my wife a gift I do not possess, my son. And if God has told her it is right to go to war with you, as you seemed most certain my wife must do, and if God has given my wife direction to take our daughter with her . . ." He shrugged. "Who am I to argue with God, let alone two women?"

Barak smiled at the mirth in his eyes. "I imagine they are equally difficult to win an argument against." He could not recall ever arguing with Nessa. But Nessa was nothing like Talya.

Footsteps made him turn. "Abba, Ima is asking for you." Talya stood in the doorway, her arms wrapped about her in a protective gesture. As Lappidoth slipped past her into the house, she said, "Sleep well, Abba."

Barak would bed in the courtyard with some of his men, who had taken a short walk beyond the house. "If I stay here tonight, can I trust that you will remain on your own mat? Or should we seek refuge in the cave below?" He watched her expression, saw the way her gaze flicked beyond him.

"You have nothing to fear from me," she said, keeping her distance. "I will not interrupt your dreams."

Barak did not know how to respond to that, so he simply nodded. "But you have convinced your mother to allow you to travel with ten thousand men." The idea still galled him. Deborah was different. She was like a mother to them all. But Talya . . . Talya would be a difficult distraction.

"I want to kill Sisera," she said, interrupting his thoughts. "He deserves to die a humiliating death."

Barak studied her. "That he does." But in that moment he realized that he did not want her to be the one to kill him.

Dawn's first light sprinkled faded pinks across Talya's mat, as though the color alone could draw her to rise. She sat up, immediately awake, heart pounding, the sense of adventure filling her. She donned a plain brown robe over a tan tunic, strapped a pouch with ten smooth stones to her side, tied the sling to her wrist, and pulled a brown veil over her dark hair. The earthen colors blended well with the forests and fields, and she determined to keep as hidden as possible on this mostly male adventure.

A small goatskin bag hung by a peg on the wall in her chambers. She snatched a fresh tunic and an extra veil to tie her hair up out of the way and stuffed them into the bag. When the time came to run as the men did, she would tuck her tunic and robe into her belt as had become her practice. By then no one in the camp would care what she looked like.

She stepped from the room she now shared reluctantly with Yiskah, glancing back once to see that the girl had already risen from bed, no doubt to draw water for their trip. A twinge of guilt nudged her that she had blamed this woman for fears she had overcome long ago in an excuse to support Shet, and for thinking Yiskah the same woman she had been that day when Talya caught her in the olive grove. But since her return by the Kenite woman and her rescue from Jabin's clutches, she had not been the same. Though Shet could not see it, nor did he attempt to try, Talya noticed. Yiskah walked stoop-shouldered, her head bowed, and rarely looked a person in the eye, face-to-face. Her shame seeped from her, her wounds deep like one caught in a hunter's snare.

Talya walked to the sitting room, pushing thoughts of Yiskah aside. Later, when Sisera was dead, she would confront Shet, see what she could do to convince him to give the woman another chance. Or a writ of divorcement so she could be free again. His indecision and bitterness had hardened in recent weeks, and the change was not becoming.

She spotted her father strapping provisions to his belt, loins girded, ready for travel. "You are going too, Abba?"

"You thought I would let your mother go to war while I stayed behind to guard the house? What is there left to guard if not her?" His tone held an edge, and Talya sensed he was also going as her own protection.

"Elior and Lavi?"

"Are both coming," her mother said as she entered the room. She gathered a spindle and ball of wool and tucked them into a sack she would carry across her back.

"But who will watch over Libi and Ahava and the children?" Her great-uncle Chayim?

"Do not fear, my child," Deborah said as they all headed to the courtyard. "The women will head to the caves until our return. God is giving Sisera into our hands, remember? We have nothing to fear." She accepted flatbread from Libi, who passed some along to each of them, then handed them baskets of food to tie to the sides of one of the few donkeys they would take for provisions.

Talya nodded and accepted the food in silence, then hugged each of the children and the women and fell into step with her mother as the men made their way toward the city gate. She glanced back once, catching sight of Yiskah slipping into the house out of sight.

"What is to become of her, Ima?" She should have said something to the girl before they left, but there was no going back now. "She is broken and so wounded. I did not see it before, but I see it every time I look at her now. And though she thinks I'm sleeping, I often hear her weeping in the night."

Her mother also glanced behind, following Talya's gaze, but said nothing. There was no sign of Yiskah now. Shet marched somewhere behind them in the throng leaving the village. But when she finally caught a glimpse of him, he was engaged in conversation with Elior, seemingly oblivious to the woman he still legally called wife.

Talya's jaw clenched at the thought.

The gates opened and the men surged forward. Talya was caught up in the throng, and they split up in different directions. She stood near her mother, listening as Barak spoke to the leaders he had appointed.

He pointed to one group and motioned for them to head out. "You will go to Beth-shan, then travel on to Jezreel. Meet us in Kedesh in Naphtali in three days."

As the men set out, Barak gave commands to others, sending them to Shimron, Rehob, Beth-anoth, Shechem, Tirzah, Dothan, Taanach, and Megiddo. Elior and Lavi split up to take commands, though Shet remained with Barak and Deborah and Lappidoth. Even Barak's right-hand man Keshet took a troop to gather more men, reaching every northern tribe in Israel.

There was little time to talk after that until they had made camp for the night in the caves surrounding Shiloh. The men secured the area and were now making plans for the battle in the deeper recesses of the cave. Talya settled near the fire, warming her hands, then set to work mixing water and the grain she had quickly ground between two stones.

"You mentioned Yiskah earlier today," her

mother said, taking some of the ground grain and pouring it onto the three-pronged griddle over the fire. "Is there something more you want to tell me?"

Talya looked at her mother. "You refer to my conversation with Abba asking him to send her away."

Deborah nodded. "Your attitude is not as it was those few days ago."

Talya felt her cheeks heat. "I was wrong," she said, glancing toward the cave. "But how can Shet be so indifferent to Yiskah's needs? What is to become of them? How can they be wed but not be wed?" She stirred the grains, tossing in a few spices, then added more water for the griddle cakes.

"Shet was wronged," Deborah said softly. "Sometimes marriage is complicated when one person hurts the other so deeply."

Talya took the bread into the cave and handed it to her father, wondering if her mother spoke of more than Shet's relationship with Yiskah. What could be so complicated about love?

21

The thunder of chariot wheels rushed past on the road below the berm that hemmed in Heber's encampment. Jael's heart skipped a beat as she peered around the trunk of a large oak tree, watching for Sisera's insignia on his gilded chariot. He would come. Surely. He had promised Heber he would come soon for the last shipment of his weapons. Heber had worked long into the night, and when he wasn't working, he'd paced the tent.

Jael swallowed the fear, feeling the unease from her husband seeping into her heart, encasing it with dread too great to bear. The memory of Sisera's stench, his probing, the way he touched Daniyah . . . She shuddered, her fear growing, a living thing, only heightened by what Heber had not said, what she knew he had seen in Hazor.

She closed her eyes, blinking away the thoughts, the images. For now, her girls would be safe in the cave Ghalib had found nearby. Especially with him standing guard. Had they reached the spot by now? She glanced at Heber, who would have sent her with the girls, but she could not, would not, leave him. He gave her a troubled look. Chariots whizzed past with no sign of slowing. Why in such a hurry? She strained and squinted her eyes, certain there must be something wrong with her eyesight, but despite her searching, there was no sign of Sisera's chariot or his arrogant face.

The last chariot disappeared from sight, and Jael backed slowly away from the tree, looking in every direction. Quiet descended with the dust the chariot wheels had kicked up, until the only sounds she heard were the sudden chirping of birds in the branches high above. Even they had seemed to hold their breath in the wake of Canaan's iron beasts.

She drew a breath, then another. When at last she felt her heart slowing to a normal rhythm, she stepped down from her perch along the base of the berm and met Heber walking toward her with their sons.

"He didn't stop for his weapons." Jael looked directly into Heber's pinched face, as though the tension had caused him a massive headache.

"No, he didn't."

"More men are coming." Fareed stepped closer. "One walks like Barak of Naphtali."

Voices grew louder as men approached, and the company of them was not small. Jael glanced at Heber, a question in her eyes. But he only shrugged and motioned her to return to her tent. She thought to resist him, but when he handed her a knife larger than the normal dagger she carried, she did not argue.

Had Barak summoned an army?

She moved to the awning of her tent, waiting. She stiffened, listening intently to see if Barak's voice was among the throng.

But it was a woman's voice she heard, one she immediately recognized.

"It is the prophetess, Deborah," Jael said, moving out from the tent's protection to the center of the camp, where Heber and her sons now stood. "We can trust her."

"Can we?" Heber raked a hand over his beard, the gesture born of weariness. "You did not seem so sure when you returned without the maid. You said Deborah seemed unable to make a decision and had no power to restore the woman to her home."

"Yes, but Deborah took her in to protect her. She is not one who intends our harm." She slipped her arm through Heber's. "Let us meet them."

And in the next few moments, she did see Deborah climbing over the rise with Barak at her side. The woman's hand shaded her eyes as if she were searching to find where they were hidden in the trees. At last both Barak and Deborah climbed down the berm, followed by another woman and a few men. Was that Talya, the woman Ghalib could not stop talking about?

For the briefest moment Jael wondered if God had brought the girl here to fulfill Ghalib's dreams, ridiculous as they were. But when she saw the weapons hanging from the Israelites' shoulders and strapped to their sides, she knew they had not come for a marriage alliance.

"Heber, my friend," Barak said, stepping from the group to greet her husband. "Jael." He nodded at her, then at Mahir and Fareed. "Forgive our intrusion so unexpectedly. We are headed to Kedesh-naphtali." He motioned to Deborah and those with them. "God has called us to war against Sisera. I came seeking weapons. Deborah said you have many that will go unused, and that you would be willing to give them to us."

Jael lifted a brow and looked at her husband, then glanced at Deborah. How did she know this? Even Jael did not know it for sure. She had only sensed it in her husband's expressions, in the change in him since Hazor. She did not think him capable of deceiving Sisera and giving the general's weapons to his enemy.

"Your prophetess knows much," Heber said, his voice kind. "Please, won't you join us for a meal while my sons gather what you seek?" He motioned to the hearth outside of his tent, then spoke to Mahir and Fareed to gather Ghalib and donkeys and fill baskets with the weapons planned for Sisera. "You are fortunate to come at such a time. I have just finished the largest order I have yet made for Canaan's forces. Sisera's men just flew past our camp and did not stop to retrieve them."

"Sisera's days are few," Deborah said, taking a seat on one of the stones lining the hearth. "We thank you for entrusting us with this gift."

Heber sat opposite her, while her husband and daughter sat at her sides. Barak leaned closest to Heber, and Jael hurried to her tent to retrieve grain and a large jug of water to make a quick porridge. By the look of her guests, they were hungry but anxious to be off, and she knew her sons would work quickly to gather the weapons that were already waiting for Sisera's men.

When Jael returned a short time later with porridge and clay bowls to pass to each one and flatbread to dip into the spicy grain, the men were discussing war plans.

"I will go with you," Heber said quietly.

Jael startled, nearly dropping the bowl. Deborah caught her arm, steadying her. She glanced at the prophetess but spoke to her husband. "You can't. Who will protect us?"

Heber studied her a moment. "You have the cave. And the guards." He did not say, "And our sons."

"You plan to take our sons with you?" The shock of his decision made her knees weak. She looked around and found a place to sit before they completely gave way. "You can't," she said again, but her voice carried no strength.

"Your sons and your husband will be safe, Jael." Deborah's words broke the sudden silence that had fallen over the group. "Trust Adonai. Soon we will rid the land of the Canaanite tyrant. No more will our women and children or our men live in fear of him. We will worship Adonai in freedom, no longer in hidden caves and villages carved out of the rock." She paused, looking over the men and women gathered there. Her daughter's eyes gleamed, and

Ghalib's shone the moment he stepped into the camp and saw the girl sitting there.

"You are allowing your daughter to go to war?" Jael struggled to comprehend why two women would follow thousands of men into battle.

"Their gods are women. A woman will kill Sisera." Talya spoke before her mother could, and the confidence in her eyes told Jael that Talya had full intention of being that woman.

"Your God is powerful if He can defeat the Canaanite goddess of war," Jael said, rubbing her hands up and down her arms to warm them from a sudden chill.

"He is," Deborah agreed, her smile reassuring. And suddenly Jael's fear vanished in the presence of the prophetess. "Our God is a consuming fire."

Deborah's words crackled with the fire coming from the pit, and each man and woman glanced as one at the flames sparking upward. Sisera did not stand a chance against a God like that. And yet . . . why had it taken Israel's God so long to destroy the man?

The question would not leave as Jael accepted the help of her daughter and daughters-in-law to feed the crowd and then help their men gather all they needed to head off with Israel to war. Neither did it leave as she lay alone in her bed that night, listening to Daniyah's soft breathing, wondering how the girl could relax when the threat of Sisera loomed larger than the shadows of the trees overhead.

Jael's fear came and fled with the dawn as she awoke to a quiet camp, as she went about her morning tasks, and as she prayed to the Unseen One words she could not even form to fully express. *Keep them safe* seemed so simple. *Destroy Sisera,* too bold.

As dawn turned to day and the girls quietly spun or ground a far less amount of grain, keeping to the door of her tent, Jael's only heart cry turned to a single, hopeless word.

Help.

22

Kedesh-naphtali's streets overflowed with men too numerous to count. Barak climbed the steps to the city gate and stood near the parapet looking down on the throng.

"Men have come from Zebulun, Issachar, and Naphtali, as well as a few other tribes. No more will come." Deborah stood at his side, her bearing serene, confident.

"There are thousands, but not nearly as many as I had expected or hoped for." Barak tamped down his disappointment with a smile. "But if you say we are enough, then we will go."

"Arrange them into groups of a thousand and appoint leaders over each," she said.

He resisted the urge to tell her he had already considered that very thing. "Yes, Prophetess." He surveyed the crowd, catching sight of Keshet weaving his way through the wall of men to reach him. Deborah's sons and a few of Barak's other leaders were with him.

"Of course you had already planned this, no doubt." Her quiet comment made him turn to face her.

"But you suggested it regardless."

She shrugged. "I was simply affirming your thoughts. They are given to you from above, Barak. It is God who trains our hands for war."

He considered her a moment before the noise of his men clamoring up the stairs drew their attention.

"We have counted the last of them, my lord," Keshet said, giving a slight bow. "There are ten thousand of us. Not many carry shield or sword, but every man has a sling and many wield the bow."

"We have divided them by clans and tribes," Lavi said, glancing at his mother. "They are eager to leave for Mount Tabor."

Deborah clasped her hands together, and Barak noticed Lappidoth and Talya appear at the top of the stairs to join her. "We will leave at dawn," she said. "Give the leaders your instructions this night and make sure all is packed. We will need tents to shield us on the mountain, for I sense a great storm coming."

Barak looked at her, studied her certain gaze. "The winter rains are still months away." He pointed overhead. "The sky is clear of even a single cloud, and yet you say a storm is coming? How can we fight the enemy in a downpour?" By her expression he did not doubt her words. Had they gathered men just to sit in tents while the rains turned the roads into rivers?

"God will fight the battle for us, my son." Deborah raised her hands high. "The Kishon will aid our fight, the moon and stars will shine in our defense." She lowered her arms and faced the leaders. "Be strong and have great courage. Tomorrow we travel to Tabor. Let us not lose heart along the way."

Barak puzzled over her comments as he watched her retreat to the street below, her family following behind her. Had Deborah's presence here given her the right to lead the warrior's charge, to shout the battle cry?

"You gave her the right to lead when you asked her to come, you know." Keshet stood close to his ear, his words meant for Barak alone. "In case it troubles you to have a woman — two women — in the camp now. Just remember why that is."

Barak scowled at his friend, ran a hand over his beard. "If I wanted your opinion, I would have asked for it." Sometimes a friend could be more trouble than a brother. But one glance into his friend's dark eyes told him that Keshet knew him better than he cared to admit. "Never mind. You are right. I asked for a woman's help. It is fitting that the men will follow her lead, not mine." He didn't care about the glory of winning regardless.

But as he walked to his home to face Deborah and her family already waiting for him, he was not so sure he had spoken the truth.

The sound of the shofar filled the streets the following morning. Deborah tucked the last of the unleavened bread into a pouch as stuffed full as the skin would allow, tied another skin of water to the belt at her waist, and walked to the courtyard of Barak's home. Talya was already waiting, her bearing proud. Deborah looked at her daughter, her heart searching for some confirmation, some truth, that Talya did indeed belong here. *Is she the woman who will kill Sisera as she so desires?* But her prayers drifted on the winds of thought, and no peace followed.

Barak's command to move out drew her attention, and she fell into step behind him and Keshet as they marched. What if she had made a grave mistake allowing Talya to join them here? If a Canaanite arrow pierced her daughter's heart, if a Canaanite captured her as a trophy of war . . .

"Are you all right, Ima?" Lavi's touch and his gentle tone roused her to her surroundings. The men were long past the village now, headed to the base of the mount near the Jezreel Valley.

Deborah glanced before and behind her, but Talya was several paces ahead, speaking with her father. "I am not sure she should have come." She angled her head in the direction of Lavi's sister.

Lavi stopped, letting the men continue around him, and faced his mother. "Is there some word of the Lord you fear, Ima? Has God told you Talya does not belong here? Because if you say the word, I will take her now and return her to our village out of harm's way." He did not say, "Where she should have stayed," though Deborah knew the thought had crossed his mind.

Deborah shook her head. "No, my son." She touched his arm, meeting his earnest gaze. "It is only I, your mother, who fears for her daughter. I have had no word from the Lord in this."

Lavi tilted his head, then glanced quickly around them. He leaned closer and lowered his voice. "Are you suggesting it is not my sister who will kill Sisera? I thought Adonai had given you this word."

Deborah drew a breath, wishing she could retract those words, but in an instant she knew they were still true. "The Lord clearly said that a woman will kill Sisera. Only, I do not know whether that woman will be Talya. That is Talya's desire, so it may be that our God will use her to fulfill His plan. I do not know every detail of His plan until He reveals it."

Lavi studied her, his broad shoulders flexing as though trying to relieve a kink in his neck. "Do you think that woman will be you, Ima?" His heavy brows knit beneath the turban that covered his dark hair. "You have no weapon, nor training in war."

Deborah felt the sling tied to her wrist. "No, but every woman knows how to wield a stone against wild animals, my son. Sisera can be caught as easily by a sling as by a bow or sword." She touched the pouch with the stones at her side. "If God should will it, I would use whatever skill I possess to kill the man." She held his gaze, unwavering.

Lavi tucked his hands into the belt at his waist, and she didn't miss the soft smile at the corners of his mouth. "I have no doubt you would do just that, Ima. I wish neither one of you had come, though." He glanced once more at his sister. "I wish war had not come to either of you."

"War has come to all Israel, my son, because we fashioned the gods of Canaan to be true gods. Israel caused her own testing by putting the Lord our God to the test. Sisera is evil, but he would hold no power if we had fully trusted our God." Deborah released a breath.

"It is because of Yiskah and others like her," Lavi said, spitting in the dust. "Weak women and faithless men have caused this." His large face grew hard, and she did not like the glint of hatred she saw in his eyes.

Deborah touched his forearm. Men continued to pass them as they stood near the trees, and she knew they could not stand here much longer. "My son, listen to me."

He met her gaze, waiting.

"When we worshiped other gods, war came to our gates, this is true. But none of us can say that we serve and obey our God with perfect hearts. Is there one among us who has not coveted? Is there even one who has kept the commands of our God without blemish, like a pure, perfect lamb? If we had, the sacrifices would no longer be necessary." She brushed strands of hair that the breeze had blown across her face and tucked them under her scarf.

"But we don't worship other gods, Ima.

Not everyone disobeys." Lavi's protest gave her pause, but she sensed that he had softened as his thoughts turned to truly consider the matter.

"Our forefathers did not drive out our enemies as our God commanded, my son. Yahweh commanded this to protect us from the worship that drove those people to evil, to abandon their Creator. As Sisera has done. As Jabin has done. And so many nations and peoples before them. So Adonai allowed them to live among us to test us and see if we could resist the temptation to follow after their gods. We failed His test. And so we have come to face war." She looped her arm through his. "But come. We will fall too far behind, and we must stay close to Barak."

Lavi nodded, saying nothing, but Deborah knew her son would think long about her words.

Quiet murmurs and the consistent shuffling of men bedding down for the night mingled with the sounds of winged creatures overhead. No one slept as well as they would have liked with war so imminent. Barak strode through the sea of black goat-hair tents, heard the hushed conversations. Anxious excitement moved like ripples of water upon the sand, and Barak could not shake the feeling of justice the coming day evoked.

He walked the length and breadth of the camp, his mind whirling with plans. There were simply not enough swords among them, so they would have to rely on some distance for the use of bow and sling. The image of Talya with her bow slung over her back made him pause. He would keep her on the mountain unless her mother objected. If the girl was truly to kill Sisera, God would make a way.

He came to the central fire, where the embers had nearly died out to keep their presence less conspicuous. Deborah sat before the pit, her head bowed as if in prayer.

He sat opposite her, keeping his peace, but she looked up at his approach. "Is everything secure?" She looked at him, and it seemed to him the fire had moved from the pit to her brilliant gaze.

He nodded, staring. "You have been praying. Have you seen another vision?" He had never been near her at such a time. "Your eyes are aglow."

She blinked, and the light in them slowly dimmed. "I did not realize," she said softly. "Sometimes Lappidoth tells me my face is like the sun when I awake from one of the dreams. And twice he has seen fire surround me." She released a deep sigh. "All I see is a warm light, like a swirling blanket." She clasped her hands in her lap. "And my dreams are always of danger and war."

He studied her, this woman whose hair shone dark as night, with the slightest tips of bright white along her temples as though she had been scorched by God's flames. Though she was not a warrior, she had the look of unbending strength.

"I would that your dreams be peaceful, your life surrounded by good, Deborah." He rubbed a hand over his beard, at a loss for more to say.

Her smile held distance, but a moment later she looked at him full on. "You are called to destroy our enemies, those who have plotted our harm for these past twenty years. God has put you in this place for this time, and the faith you carry now is that which will win the day. Forget any doubt you faced until this moment, my son. Forget your past failures. You can trust Adonai to keep His word."

Barak studied his hands now in his lap, then rested them on his knees. "I know that. I know that what you have said is true. But can I request one thing of you?" He held her steady gaze.

Silence followed his remark, as though she was not sure whether to allow him to question her, but after a moment she nodded. "What do you request?"

He glanced beyond her to the tent she would share with Talya. "I want you to keep Talya in the camp on the mountain when we go after Sisera. If she is to kill the man, God will make a way for her to do so. But if she runs down the hill with those men" — he gestured to the surrounding tents — "when she is not accustomed to battle, she will be hurt, perhaps killed. And the injury may not even come at the hands of Canaan."

"She is capable of using her weapons," Deborah said slowly, assessing him. "But I share your concerns. My daughter has lived a protected life in our village. Except for that one time when she was lost in the woods, she has never been alone. I, too, fear for her safety."

Barak lifted a brow. "But you allowed her to come. And you yourself said that Sisera will die at the hand of a woman."

"I do not know whether that woman is Talya." Deborah's matter-of-fact tone caught him up short.

"I thought that was why she came." His

pulse quickened as the realization dawned that the girl had probably persuaded her mother and father, rather than God Himself doing the sending.

"I thought so too, my son." Deborah's voice held sorrow. "I fear I do not always discern the voice of the Lord from my own thoughts. But this I know. God did not give me a vision of Talya killing Sisera. Perhaps I will be the one to do so. Perhaps she will have the honor. Perhaps another woman entirely will pierce Sisera's armor with a final blow." She twisted the belt at her waist. "I fear I do not know."

"Then Talya should stay behind until you do." All she had to do was walk among his men, passing out bread, and they couldn't take their eyes from her. No. She was better to stay.

"I will tell her, but she will not obey me," Deborah said, suddenly sounding like a defeated mother rather than Israel's judge and prophetess.

"Then I will tell her," Barak said, straightening. "She is a distraction to my men. She will be a hindrance to the battle. I should have insisted before, but I thought . . ." He paused.

"You thought God was sending her to join us."

"Yes." He stood, and Deborah did the same. "I will tell her in the morning."

He bid Deborah good night, then went to his tent, all the while wondering if Talya was a distraction more to his men or to him.

23

Dark, ripe clouds rose in great stacks, churning what little was left of the morning's blue. Dampness clung to Barak's skin, and his hair stood on end. Rain would come, as Deborah had predicted. They had little time to climb the mountain and pitch their tents before the onslaught.

"Wouldn't we be better off waiting in the valley or hiding in caves until the storm has passed?" Keshet glanced at Barak out of the corner of his eye. "The tents on the mountain will be fully exposed. There is no reason not to wait it out."

Barak trudged on, one weighted foot in front of the other. "Deborah said to meet on Mount Tabor by this day. We will do as she says." Yet even now he questioned the wisdom in bringing her. Keshet was right. They would be drenched and their tents blown apart by nightfall if they were caught in this storm on the mountain's peak.

"You know I'm right though." Keshet raised his voice above the rising wind. "This is madness."

Barak paused in his climb, glancing back at Deborah and her men not far behind. Where was Talya? He needed to speak to that girl. Deborah looked up at that moment and caught his attention. She motioned him to wait for her.

"Perhaps she has changed her mind," Keshet offered, stepping aside to allow Deborah and her family room on the narrow mountain road.

"Do me a favor and go find her daughter." Barak spoke without meeting his friend's gaze, then offered Deborah a hand to help her up the incline.

"She is walking with Ghalib the Kenite and her brother Lavi." Keshet's words caused Barak to face him.

"Get her for me."

The man walked off without a word.

"I heard Keshet's comments," Deborah said without preamble. She glanced at the sky, then into Barak's eyes. "He is right . . . if this was a normal storm. But we have nothing to fear. Do not stop."

Barak studied the prophetess's earnest gaze. "We will do as you say," he said, then turned to continue taking the road that zigzagged upward. Lightning sparked in the distance, not overhead, but no furious thunderclap followed. Perhaps they would arrive at the summit in time to seek shelter. He found himself questioning yet again.

Why is it so hard to trust her, Lord? Was it because she was a woman, one whose husband was too passive to take charge of his own village? Lavi and Elior could handle themselves, of that he had no doubt. Even Talya could probably take down a warrior or two. But Lappidoth seemed more interested in penning Deborah's words or working the fields than in fighting this war. He should have left the man in the village, but he couldn't go that far to show such disrespect. The man had come to protect his family, whether he was capable of doing so or not.

A kink settled in Barak's shoulder, and he rubbed it a moment as he walked. Keshet found him as he was taking a bend in the road, Talya in tow. Ghalib was nowhere in sight.

"Here she is, my lord." Keshet bowed in uncharacteristic respect, then strode on ahead to join his other men.

Talya looked at him, then beyond him. He followed her gaze. Her mother and father and brothers were several paces behind. Barak started to walk once more and Talya did the same.

"You had need of me, my lord?" Talya said at last, breaking the silence.

Suddenly, seeing her like this, dressed for battle, he doubted the wisdom of telling her to stay with her mother. Hadn't God said a woman would kill Sisera? Perhaps she was strong enough to outshoot Canaan's warriors.

But as quickly as that thought entered his mind, he banished it. "Yes," he said, glancing her way, increasing his pace. "When we reach the summit and set up the tents, I want you to stay with your mother."

"Of course I will stay with my mother. Who else's tent did you think I would share?"

Her ire made him feel like a fool. He shook his head. "No, no. You misinterpret my meaning." He stopped abruptly, facing her. "I don't want you going with the men into battle. It may be that God will bring Sisera to you and you will have the chance to pierce his heart with your arrows. But you are a distraction to my men, and I will not have you cause us defeat because they are more worried about protecting you than fighting the enemy." He heaved a sigh. There. He'd said it.

319

But by the storm brewing in her gaze, he knew he had not said it well.

"You think I cannot handle myself. You think I need protecting like a child." Her voice rose, and color heightened her cheeks.

"Not like a child. How you twist my words." He raised both hands in a defeated gesture. "Like a woman." He ground the words out between clenched teeth.

"And a woman is too weak to defend herself, is that it?" She stomped off, and he shook his head. This was harder than he expected.

He jogged after her. "I have no doubt you can wield a bow, Talya. I have no doubt you can use a sling and never miss." How it irked him to admit such truth! "But I see the way my men look at you every time you pass them a plate of bread or walk through the camp. Women do not belong in war!" He heard the edge to his voice and cringed, for he feared by the shock in her eyes that she would cry. What on earth would he do with her then?

"You would not even go to war without my mother." She lowered her voice and leaned close. The scent of her skin brushed his nostrils, and one look into those large round eyes was nearly his undoing. "Who is the coward now?"

His jaw clenched and he gripped her shoulders, gently but firmly pushing her back from him. "Your tongue has the sting of a viper, woman. You would be wise to learn to curb it."

Anger flared as he met her defiant look. How was he supposed to get her to listen? If she wouldn't obey her mother or him, she would risk her life just to prove a point.

It was his turn to walk off, fully determined to keep his distance until he could gain the backing of her brothers at nightfall. He did not like the confusion she stirred in him. Confounded woman!

"I am sorry, my lord." Her voice sounded close at his heels.

He whirled to face her. "Don't sneak up on me like that!" How had he managed not to hear her footfalls? He looked down at her feet. Her slight build would not weight the earth. She did have stealth on her side.

"You are by no means a coward, Barak. I spoke out of turn." Her use of his name caused an uneasy feeling in his middle.

"Forget about it," he said, perturbed with himself. He drew another breath. "But listen to me, Talya. You should not have come. It has nothing to do with your ability. It has everything to do with the way the men see you. I can't change the hearts of ten thousand men on the eve of war. And I can't have them looking over their shoulders worrying about you, the daughter of our prophetess. How would they live with themselves if you were killed? How would I face your mother and father?" His chest heaved as though he had run to the summit and back again.

Thunder clapped nearby, making them both jump. Talya looked heavenward, and Barak followed her gaze, though he allowed himself a slow glimpse of her as he did so. With that rich dark hair peeking beneath the tan scarf she wore, the wide dark eyes a man could lose himself in, and the determined flaring of her nostrils set among flushed pink cheeks, the girl was too beautiful for her own good. No woman should be so sharp tongued and pleasing to the eye at the same time. No man could live with such a woman!

"I will not promise to obey you," Talya said, drawing his attention to their conversation once more.

His eyes narrowed to slits. Stubborn, willful child.

"But I will give it consideration," she said, as though she had a right to do so.

His hands clenched in and out. If he had married her, she would have no choice but to obey him. But then he would have to deal with her confounded stubbornness every single day.

"I do not wish to cause you worry," she continued, pulling him from his thoughts, "nor do I wish to distract your men, my lord." Her tone suddenly sounded humble, submissive even.

Barak lifted a brow, searching her wide eyes for some sign of guile or misleading. "I hope you understand," he said, giving his tone a commanding edge, "that it is within my right to command my troops. You came under that command the moment you joined this band. It is not your right to question my judgment, Talya, prophetess's daughter or not." He could not tamp down the lingering anger her challenge had evoked. He needed time to put it aside, and with her standing here looking at him, he found the ability to do so extremely difficult.

Talya bowed her head a moment and twirled one sandaled foot in the dirt. The voices of her family drew closer and still she did not speak.

"I expect an answer from you," he said, taking her arm and leading her forward. He did not want this conversation to carry to the rest of the men. Not when his heart was pounding with anger . . . and a feeling he did not wish to explore.

She shook his hand off and crossed her arms over her chest, as though she would protect herself from him, from everyone.

"You can desire an answer from me all you want, my lord, but I am not ready to give it." She gave him a sidelong glance. "I am not my mother. I do not hear God's voice or see His visions. But I know His passion in my heart, and I have wanted to destroy Sisera since the day I found my cousin caught in the lies of Asherah, worshiping her. As I destroyed that idol of clay that day, so I will destroy Sisera tomorrow, should God allow." She hurried ahead. "But I will not obey you like one of your men. I am not a man for you to command."

Barak watched her stalk off. She had rattled him, frustrated him, and he did not know what to do with her. But she also posed a good argument, one he found difficult to refute. At least for now, while his anger, his fear of what foolish thing she might do next, warred with feelings for her that he should not possess.

He raked a hand along his neck, aware of the stiffness in his shoulders from clenching so hard so as not to lash out at her. Or to do something even more foolish such as to strike her, which he would never ever do. No. It was not his wrath he feared, but his attraction and the overwhelming desire he'd just avoided by a hair — to pull her close and kiss all sense from her.

Deborah stood hours later on the summit of Mount Tabor, near the edge that overlooked the Jezreel Valley. The sun remained hidden behind clouds that darkened with each passing hour, their ominous black billows stretching fingers of whirling grays to dip and touch the earth. Sisera's chariots stood in rows so numerous they seemed like fields of grains standing tall in the wind.

Deborah shaded her eyes, squinting into the darkness. Men too numerous to count or see clearly at night seemed to fill the valley, in addition to those who manned the chariots. They were seriously outnumbered here.

She glanced heavenward, but the sky held no comfort, only the dread of an overwhelming storm. *Did You lead us here to slaughter, Lord? What can we do against so many?*

She looked back again at the valley, the men below bathed in darkness. But as she stood watching, praying, the sudden familiar light of vision encompassed her, its warmth both frightening and comforting.

Her heartbeat quickened as she gazed on the valley now teeming with men and horses far greater than Sisera's numbers. Lightning flashed in terrifying brightness, and thunder, powerful and deep, rumbled from one end of the sky to the other. Her knees buckled beneath her, but before she could plant her face to the earth, the heavens split as one rolls back a scroll.

Her breath held, frozen. Lightning flashed again and again, as though in a continuous arc over the skies. The blast of a shofar sounded, its sound unending. And then it stopped as a white winged horse burst upon the clouds, its rider tall, his eyes flames, his head burnished gold. A horde, an army clothed in blinding white robes, followed. A sword flashed from the mouth of the blazing man, and in an instant the men on the valley floor fell where they stood, their blood rising, a rushing current beneath them. Carrion birds whooshed in to gorge on their flesh.

"Deborah." Lappidoth's voice resounded in her ear, and suddenly the vision vanished. She blinked, heart pounding, unable to rise. She sank to the earth, hands outstretched, breathing shallow. She had not witnessed Sisera's destruction. These were not Canaanite or Philistine or any army she had seen in her lifetime.

What is it, Lord? Who was the rider upon the white horse?

But she knew the answer would not be given her. The battle she had witnessed was for another time, another place. And yet, the Lord was in both battles, and He would win them. A sense of peace filled her.

"Deborah," Lappidoth said again as he slowly approached. He offered his hand, and she allowed him to help her up, though she barely looked at him. She turned instead to gaze once more on the valley below. All light had disappeared from view, the men in Sisera's camp cloaked in shadow.

"What did you see, beloved?" Lappidoth's voice drew her to face him.

"A vision of war, as always." Somehow she could not tell him the truth, and she resented his intrusion into what she had seen. Might God have shown her more if he had not come upon her and spoken?

Lightning flashed above them, its fingers pointing downward, illuminating her husband. She noted the bow still slung at his back, and he stood before her a warrior.

"So you truly plan to join them?" She could not bring herself to imagine him capable of battle.

"Did you expect me to stay behind?" He tilted his head in that curious way he had, his gaze kind. He touched her cheek as the first pelts of rain hit them.

"I don't know what I expected," she admitted, wishing she had always seen him as courageous, the kind of man who would follow the rider on the white horse.

"I will do my part, Deborah." His tone held an edge, and she knew in that moment that whatever he did, he did for her, to gain the respect she seemed incapable of giving to him freely.

Rain came heavier now, and he took her hand and ran toward the tents. He paused in the awning of the place she would stay with Talya and cupped her cheek. "I love you, Deborah."

He rushed off to join their sons before she could respond. Her heart tripped. "God go with you, my husband," she called after him, but the winds whisked her words away.

Talya paced her mother's small goat-hair tent, watching through a slit in the opening as the rain came in sheets, coating the grassy mountaintop. "How long is it going to do that?" She pointed to the door, feeling like a bird caught in a snare. If she had brought a change of clothes besides a tunic, she would brave the storm just to escape the confines of the tent with only her mother for company.

"As long as God allows," Deborah said, pulling her spindle and wool from a goatskin sack she'd carried on her back. "Sit down and help me untangle these threads. You will wear me out just watching you."

"I am weary of sitting." Talya frowned, then peeked around the opening, only to be met with misty air. She whirled about and released a sigh. "We should have stayed in caves along the side of the mount."

"The rain will not hurt us, nor get through these tents." Her mother's calm voice only irritated Talya's mood.

"At least in a cave we could have talked to Father and Lavi and Elior." And Barak, though she did not say so. She was not sure she wanted to speak to the man again anyway.

"And Ghalib?" Deborah asked quietly. "And Barak?" She lifted her gaze and gave Talya a knowing smile. "You did not resolve the argument you had with Barak, did you?"

Talya sank onto the mat and took up the wool her mother handed to her, roping one end around her palm and turning the rest to create a ball. "The man is impossible, Ima." She leaned closer to be heard above the pounding rain. "Why does he suddenly seem so squeamish about allowing me to go to war?" She continued with the yarn but gave her mother an imploring look. "He knows I am as capable as any man. And if the men find me distracting, then they are thinking thoughts they ought not to!" She huffed and mumbled words she did not care to say aloud.

Her mother ignored her outburst, but a humorous smile lit her eyes. "Dear child. If you have no idea how easily men are taken with women, then it is truly time your father and I seek a husband for you." She took one end of the wool Talya had wound and fastened it to the spindle.

Talya sat in silence, watching. "I want to marry," she said softly. "But I did not come here to seek a husband. I came to kill Sisera."

Deborah's brows lifted, and Talya knew by that look that she understood more than Talya wished her to. "I sincerely doubt that your motives were purely military, my daughter. Look at me and tell me truthfully that you did not hope to impress Barak with your skills."

Talya looked away, toward the tent door. At last she shrugged, then sighed. "I do want to kill Sisera."

"I know you do. And perhaps you will."

"But you know Barak was of interest to me once." She picked up another mound of tangled wool and began to turn it into a ball.

"But no longer?" Her mother's spindle did not stop with the question. "Is it Ghalib you have now set your heart upon?" She moved the distaff in time with the spindle.

Talya stopped winding the thread and shrugged. The raindrops had slowed in their drumbeat upon the tent's roof. "Ghalib is a kind man," she said, lowering the pitch of her voice, "but I think he pines after a cousin in Judah."

Her mother's gaze searched hers. "Perhaps that is best."

"It is better if he marries within his clan, and I wed within my tribe." It wasn't a question, but Talya waited for her mother's response just the same.

Deborah angled her head to better meet her gaze. "Yes."

Silence fell between them for several moments. "Then who? If I am so beautiful as you say, if I'm such a 'distraction' as Barak says, then any man should want to wed me." The words came out more petulant than she'd intended. "Let's just not talk about it anymore." She was weary of men, but worse, she was confounded by that last conversation with Barak. If she didn't know better . . . She had sensed a change in him. But perhaps it was simply his anger at her for "distracting" everyone.

She tossed the wool into the bag, frustrated with the work, with the waiting, with the rain, with the men who had tents spread around hers in a circle of protection. She wanted to step onto the mountain's grasses, run the length of its summit and back again, do something to quell her leashed energy.

She peered into the night again, feeling the mist of the rain still dampen her cheeks. Behind her, she heard her mother pack away her tools and unroll her mat.

"Come, daughter, get some rest. It is too wet to light a fire, and the dates and nuts we ate will have to suffice for the meal for all of us. Dawn will come soon enough, and the rain will stop by then."

She turned to see her mother roll onto her side, her back to the tent's wall, sling at her side. Talya heaved a sigh, discontent still raging through her. But her mother was right. It was too wet and too dark to make a daring move like climb down the mount and infiltrate the enemy camp. If Sisera didn't capture and kill her for such a bold act, Barak would surely confine her to her mother's tent and set a guard over her.

She picked up her own mat and rolled it out onto the hard ground. But as she lay there trying to sleep, her mind would not rest. Barak's commands and authoritarian tone grated her every nerve. Whether he found her interesting or just a nuisance, she did not know, and she did not care. She had come here for one purpose. To kill Sisera. Tomorrow she would find a way to do just that, whether Barak liked it or not.

24

Jael felt Daniyah move imperceptibly closer in the dark tent while thunder clapped its mighty hands overhead. Nadia and Raja had also taken to sleeping with Jael, but no one slept this night, with the storm flashing bright behind the dark goat-hair coverings and the voice of God booming with the light.

"How long will it last?" Daniyah's whine reminded Jael of the girl's childhood, and the times when her daughter used to wiggle beneath Jael's wool blanket during a storm.

"As long as it does," Nadia said, placing a hand on Daniyah's arm. "There is no sense in fearing something we can't control."

"But what about what we can control?" Raja stroked her belly in a protective gesture and spoke softly, though even with the rain her words were heard. "What if Sisera returns while our men are away? If he comes with a troop, it would not take long for them to search the area and find the cave." She shivered, though the air was hot and sticky.

Jael looked from one woman to the next, pulling Daniyah closer into her embrace. "Raja is right," she said, her mind whirling with the thoughts she'd had since Heber took her sons to war. "While we can fight back, we are not trained to attack as warriors. Heber left me this" — she lifted the dagger and held it out — "but I cannot fling it at a man and hope to hit him. I have practiced with the trees, and the blade bounces to the ground every time." She shrugged one shoulder. "I think we need another plan."

"What plan?" Raja rubbed her middle again, and Jael wondered how well the girl could travel in her condition.

"We should have left weeks ago if we thought to return to my father's tribe in the Negev," Nadia added.

She was right, but Jael refused to admit it. "If we keep to the byways and avoid the main roads, we could arrive there in a week or so. We could leave after the rains stop."

"Would the guards go with us?" Daniyah poked her head up from beneath her mother's arm.

Jael gazed down at her daughter, glanced at each beloved daughter-in-law, and looked toward the tent's door. The rains still pummeled the ground outside the flaps, and before long she feared the roads would be flooded.

"We couldn't very well leave without telling them. They would notice we were gone and come looking for us." She looked around the tent. They could travel light. The guards would allow them safe passage.

"Will Uncle Alim welcome us in?" Raja asked.

"He is family," Jael said firmly. "He will do right by family when we are in such need no matter what trouble there was between us." Though the memory of Alim's anger brought with it a palpable sense of doubt. If Alim would choose to disavow his brother over an enemy slave, what proof did she have that he would protect her girls from such enemies now?

"Why has your sister no husband?" Ghalib's question to Lavi caught Barak's ear as he stood near Mount Tabor's ridge. He didn't mean to listen where the subject did not concern him, but just the mention of Talya made him pause.

"Talya? She is young yet." Lavi brushed Ghalib's question aside as though waving at a fly. "My parents will seek a match soon, I am sure."

Ghalib said nothing, and it took all of Barak's strength not to turn around and watch his expression. He looked to the left, scanning the valley below, but perked up when at last Ghalib spoke again. "Would your father entertain your sister's marriage to a foreigner? We are not of Israel, but we are related in a sense through your ancestor Moses."

Barak felt a swift kick to his gut, the question more than jarring him.

"I do not know the mind of my mother and father, Ghalib. But I do think they hope she would wed someone from our tribe. It is the way we do things in Israel." Lavi's words only partly appeased Barak. He was not of Deborah's tribe, but neither were Lappidoth and Deborah of the same tribe — Lappidoth coming from Zebulun and Deborah from Ephraim. Barak himself was from Naphtali. And yet Deborah had offered a match had he been ready to accept one.

He turned slowly in an arc, searching the area below. The rains had created a valley of slick mud, and though the chariots were not yet in battle array or heading closer to the mountain's base, the men were struggling to slosh through the black tar-like muck.

Fighting them and avoiding the valley floor would be tricky. Hand-to-hand combat would be impossible.

Perhaps Talya with her bow could be of use to them after all. But he squelched the thought as he turned toward Lavi and Ghalib and casually walked closer. "Is all in readiness?" He looked at Lavi, his gaze glancing off Ghalib's. Good. The man did not suspect his purposeful listening.

"All is ready, my lord," Lavi said. "My mother said to meet her here."

Barak nodded, resisting the urge to run a hand over the back of his neck. He looked out over the camp instead. Men stood in groups broken by the divisions Barak had given them three days before. He squinted against the bright rays of dawn's glow, searching. No sign of Talya . . . There. She emerged from the tent with Deborah, and the two moved toward him with determined strides.

Deborah reached him first, as Talya held back. He glanced at her, but she would not meet his gaze. The girl belonged in her mother's tent, not here.

Deborah seemed oblivious to Barak's frustration. She walked to the edge of the summit, to an outcropping of rock that hid her from the men below. Barak walked toward her, holding back a moment while Deborah studied what lay before them. Time stilled, and he wondered if she was seeing more than Sisera's men. She tilted her head as though listening but said nothing. At last she turned to face him, fire in her dark eyes.

"Go!" she commanded. "This is the day the Lord has given Sisera into your hands. Has not the Lord gone ahead of you?" She straightened her back, the wind whipping the scarf from her face.

Into his hands? Had the Lord changed His mind? Would Sisera be given into his hands after all? Bolstered by the thought, Barak gripped the sword at his waist. The belt held secure. He reached instead for his bow and pulled an arrow from its quiver. He turned to the men behind him and shouted, "For the Lord and for Israel! To victory!"

"For the Lord and for Israel!" Ten thousand men repeated the words down through the ranks until the mountain shook with the sound.

Talya watched Barak lead the charge while her mother stood to the side. This was a man's fight, she had said again that morning. There had been no more discussion. Talya was not to descend into the valley.

She was not to bring her bow or nock an arrow aimed at a Canaanite's heart.

She caught the look on Ghalib's face as he raced after Lavi. He wanted to speak to her, wanted her to promise him that she would wait for his return. She knew it without him uttering a word. She prayed for his safety, but she was glad he had not voiced his thoughts. She did not want him to beg a promise from her that she was not prepared to give.

A sigh escaped as each troop rushed past first her, then her mother. She slowly moved backward, easing her way toward her mother's tent, not wishing to distract them as Barak had so insisted she was capable of doing. She slipped into the dark tent and rummaged through her sack. She quickly placed the dark veil over her head, twined the ends into a rope, and wound them around her head like a turban. Satisfied, she pulled her robe and tunic between her legs and secured them into her belt. She glanced down at her chest, readjusting the robe to completely conceal her breasts. If a Canaanite caught her and discovered her secret . . . She shuddered. She dare not risk it.

Her heart thumped hard as she double-checked the pouch with the stones and secured the sling to her wrist. Her quiver was slung over one shoulder and the bow over the other. She must sneak down another way, not past her mother, or she would be caught. But not so far as to be completely away from the battle.

Her breath quickened as she peered out of the tent. Her mother still stood near the edge of the ridge watching the men, no doubt praying for their success. Guilt filled her at that thought. Had she prayed over what she was about to do, she probably would not be doing it. She would obey her mother and Barak instead and sit quietly in the tent spinning wool while the world fought the fiercest war of her lifetime all around her.

Pray God forgive and protect her, for she could not sit idle. Not when she had trained for this. Not when she knew she could shoot the bow as well as any man and better than most. And not when she despised Sisera for all the horror he had caused Israel with such fierce hatred that it took her breath. She could not live with herself if she let the day go without acting.

She went around the back of the tent out of sight of her mother, bent to the earth, and rubbed her legs with mud left from the rains the night before, then edged her way toward the side of the mountain where her mother's back was turned. Shouts of angry men met her ear, but she did not turn to look until she had dipped below her mother's line of vision. At last she faced the south side of the fray, saw the men slipping in the muck, heard the war cries, and smelled the heavy metal scent of blood the closer she drew.

Chariot wheels stuck fast, and horses whinnied and struggled in a pathetic vain attempt to free themselves. Talya's heart raced to the beat of the distant war drum as men abandoned their chariots in frustration.

She crouched low, seeking her bearings. Barak's men were within an arrow's shot, and some had made their way closer to the valley floor. Canaanites shouted words she could not understand. She darted a look here and there, using the scrub as cover.

She paused for breath. Peeked her head around a tall pine. Braver now, she moved stealthily down the mountainside, keeping Israel in front of her and Canaan beneath. She could do this.

Her breath grew even, more confident now. Even her mother would be proud of her once she proved herself, once she took down a few Canaanite men.

An arrow whizzed past her head.

She hit the ground on hands and knees and looked quickly in every direction. Her heart thumped hard. She blinked, catching the scent of smoke. The Israelite men were shooting flaming arrows at the captive chariots.

She slowly rose, pulled an arrow from her quiver, and caught sight of Ghalib looking in her direction. Disbelief and . . . was that anger? . . . filled his gaze. He turned to his companion — Lavi, whose sudden recognition made her pause.

"Talya!"

Barak turned at Lavi's shout. Her disguise had not fooled them.

She turned away. She had little time to prove herself now. The arrow nocked, she shot at a fleeing Canaanite. He fell, lifeless.

She pulled another arrow, repeated the same, then another, until her arrows were spent. She dared a look toward Lavi but saw no sign of him. Good. Padding quietly toward the fallen men, she yanked the arrows she could retrieve and headed closer to the lines where the men were flailing in the mud. Where was Sisera?

Barak appeared at her shoulder. He touched her arm but said nothing, simply nodded toward a Canaanite, then hurried off in another direction. She shot her arrow and hit the mark, only slightly relieved at Barak's apparent acceptance.

25

The leftover raindrops encased Jael's sandals like dew the following morning, and sunlight caused a mist to rise from the forest floor. The earth smelled sweet, refreshed, and suddenly the fears of the night before faded. She looked around at the trees, the tents, the quiet of dawn, knowing her girls would soon rise to begin preparations for their trek to the Negev.

But as Jael neared the base of the berm, she paused. Water covered the grasses ankle deep and rolled from the road over the small hill. To step further would soak her sandals and ruin the leather, or at least make the walk uncomfortable. She moved away and sought another path to the road, but everywhere she looked she found that the rains had hemmed them in.

She returned to her tent just as Daniyah and Nadia emerged. "Raja is just waking," Nadia said, jug in hand. "Daniyah and I

345

thought we would let her rest while we filled the jugs from the barrels of rain."

Jael nodded and glanced toward Raja's tent, where the barrels stood. "The ground is soggy, so take care that you don't slip."

The girls walked off and Jael ducked into her tent. Raja was sitting on her mat combing her hair. "You are up."

Raja stifled a yawn. "I could have kept sleeping. The rain was soothing."

"And everything is wet and mucky now that it has ended. I fear we will not be able to travel like this." She knelt at Raja's side. "It could be several days before the waters settle upon the earth. The downpour last night will have made the roads, especially the byways, nearly impassable. We dare not risk it."

"But what if Sisera . . ." Raja's words broke off, but Jael did not miss the gleam of fear in her gaze. "The cave will be flooded. We will have no place to go."

"We will hide you girls in Heber's tent. If Sisera comes to call, I will draw him out, away from you." The words surprised her. She only wished bravery accompanied the bold statement. For if Raja's gaze could see into Jael's heart, she would see that Jael's fear matched her own. Possibly more so.

Jael wanted nothing more than to run

away, far from Sisera's clutches, far from anything to do with the people of Canaan. But the God of rain had hemmed them in just as effectively as if a man had barred their camp with ropes and briars. They were stuck. With only a few guards and four women to defend themselves.

Deborah watched the carnage below her with a heavy heart. Blood mixed with the thick tar-like mud of the valley, and the cries of Canaanite men mingled with the shouts of pursuing Israelite warriors. She drew in a weighted breath. She had prayed for this day. Longed to see Sisera's hold on her people destroyed. And yet . . . so much suffering had led to this.

Why, Adonai? Why had it taken twenty years for God to hear their prayers? But she already knew the answer. They had left Adonai and true worship of Him for the gods of these nations they now battled to overcome. This was not a war of peoples but of the rights of gods to rule. Whose god held the power of life and death? Whose god could destroy both soul and body in Hades? Asherah and Baal? Or Adonai Elohim, the Lord God Almighty?

Deborah closed her eyes, imagining Sisera's end, but she could see no clear picture as to how that would take place. She looked out over the warriors once more and walked the length of the ridge, surveying the war from every angle. Why had not more men come to help Barak? Reuben, Dan, and Asher had received the summons the same as Ephraim, Zebulun, and Issachar, and yet no sign of their men had appeared in the camp. They were too busy pondering, trying to decide what to do while they sat lazily and watched their sheep or their ships.

Frustration tightened her jaw. God would deal with the faithless who remained in Israel. She sent a prayer of thanks heavenward for those who had come at all. For after the terror Sisera had inflicted upon the families, upon the towns and villages of northern Israel, she had actually been surprised that any men had come at Barak's summons.

She glanced again at the men below, catching sight of Barak leading the charge westward toward Harosheth-hagoyim, Sisera's headquarters, with ten thousand men behind. Was Lappidoth still in the group? Her heart quickened. He had gone off to war to please her, and here she stood thinking of everything and everyone but him.

I love you, Deborah. How often had he said

such words? How often had she simply nodded, unable to say them in return? She had
appreciated him, been grateful for the sons
and daughter he had given her, the protection he had offered when her father and
brothers were slain. Why could she not share
the love he craved?

The thought beat deep within her breast
as she turned to walk back to her tent. At
least Talya had not gone with them. Talya
was safe in the tent, unless somehow she
had convinced her father, behind her mother's and Barak's back, to allow her to come
along.

She shook her head at the thought. Lappidoth would not go against both of them,
even for Talya. Not if he truly loved Deborah. Of course not.

But doubt lingered.

Talya fitted a stone into her sling and
ducked behind an overturned chariot. Barak had disappeared into the fray, and his
men had run after him in pursuit of the fleeing Canaanites. She squinted, shading her
eyes against the sun's angled glare, catching
sight of her father several paces from her.
His arm moved with practiced rhythm, and
in the next moment she watched the stone

fly and hit its mark. Another Canaanite down.

Talya silently cheered, her respect for her father's ability heightened. How had he kept such skill secret from her? Did her mother know he possessed such courage, such ability? She rose to her full height, seeking the best place to go next, when out of the corner of her eye she saw her father once more, this time with the enemy close on his heels.

"Father!" She shouted his name, but he did not hear her. "Father!" Her heart hammered as she ran. If she could get within shooting range, she could take out his pursuer with one arrow.

"Father!" Lavi's voice called to him this time, and at much closer range. Talya stopped, watching in horror as the Canaanite brandished his spear and flung it toward her father.

"No!" Talya screamed as her father dropped to his knees.

Deborah lifted the tent flap and peered into the darkened interior. The empty dark interior. No sign of Talya. But there were definite signs that she had been here. Heart pounding now, Deborah walked to the girl's mat and riffled through the leather satchel she had brought with a few personal items, some of which had obviously been disturbed. What had the girl done?

But Deborah knew. If her father had stood up to her more often . . . *Had* he allowed this? Anger flared, and her temples began their telltale throb.

Emotion rose. *I love you, Deborah.* If he loved her, he would have forced Talya to stay home. He would never have given in to her childish whims. He would have taught his sons to teach their sister to act like a woman should.

Deborah staggered, seeking her footing. *Like you do?* She breathed in and out. That wasn't the same. Her life and her daughter's could not be compared in that way. She didn't ask to see visions, to judge Israel, to lead men to war. *But how do you know that Talya is not also called in a different way?*

Talya had obviously entered the battle. But she had done it under the cloak of secrecy. Perhaps she would not be so foolish as to engage the horde of Canaanite warriors. Perhaps she would shoot at them with her bow from a distance. Hidden.

But Deborah's heart did not beat with that certainty.

Talya stared, her feet unwilling to obey her

commands to move, to run to help her father. The least she could do was to shoot the Canaanite. Kill the beast for what he had done. The thought spurred her, and she at last forced her legs to carry her closer.

But before she could reach him, another Canaanite appeared, then another, nearly surrounding her father, Lavi . . . and was that Ghalib?

She nocked an arrow even as she ran and sent it flying, taking down one Canaanite. Still her father did not rise, had in fact rolled to the side as though truly dead. Lavi flung a stone, hitting another of the enemy in the forehead, piercing through the leather helmet. Ghalib shot at another, one closest to her father.

The immediate threat having passed, Talya rushed to her father's side, met by Lavi, who raised a curious brow at sight of her but said nothing.

"Is he dead then?" Talya could barely speak the words as Lavi touched their father's shoulder.

Lappidoth rolled to face them and lifted his head. Talya breathed at last. He was alive. *Praise be to You, Adonai!*

"They are gone?" He aimed the question at Lavi, but in one glimpse of Talya, his eyes registered disbelief.

"Those who were after you, yes." Lavi glanced around. "The majority of the men have run after Barak toward Harosheth-hagoyim. We should catch up with them."

Her father stood. His gaze cut through Talya, his tone a sharp blade. "You will not go with us." She staggered back, struck by the unfamiliar look of anger in his eyes. "I have not gone against your wishes often, Talya," he said, every word punctuated with urgency and displeasure as he motioned Lavi and Ghalib to run on ahead of him. "But this time, you *will* obey me. I will not allow you to worry your mother, who waits for us all to safely return."

Talya lowered her head, her face flaming as though he had slapped her. Never had he spoken to her thus. If he cared so much, why did he wait until now to reprimand her? But she did not ask the question. "Yes, Abba."

She could disobey her mother so easily. But not her father.

She turned then, not waiting for further rebuke, and hurried up the hill, while her men took off in the opposite direction.

"Talya!" Deborah's voice had grown hoarse shouting her daughter's name, every beat of her heart heavy with dread. "Talya!" Where was that girl? But if she had run off with Barak's men, she could be halfway to Harosheth-hagoyim by now. She was in the thick of the battle, and only by God's grace would she come out of it alive.

Deborah lifted her gaze heavenward. They needed God's grace if they were to win this war. The battle was the Lord's, not theirs. She hurried closer to the ridge, panting as though she had climbed its summit in a single bound. She stopped, placed both hands on her knees, and heaved. She was going to be sick. She was sure of it. But she dragged for breath and slowly released it. No. She could not allow fear to destroy her. Talya would be fine. Lappidoth and Lavi and Elior would all return to her unharmed. *Oh Adonai, why is it so hard to trust in times like these?*

She straightened and searched the valley. There was no longer any sign of the men. But there, not far from the edge now, a lone figure climbed the mount, sure-footed but slow. Unharmed, or they would stagger. Deborah studied the figure, slight of build, turban askew. Certainly the person was no man, for none of the men in the camp had been so built. Though the tunic and robe were girded as a man's, and the legs showed a smearing of mud as though the person had attempted to keep the men from guessing her true identity, Deborah would know her daughter anywhere.

"Talya?" Deborah called down to her, her heart rate slowing as hope filled her.

Talya raised her head. "I'm coming, Ima." But she did not look happy.

Deborah ignored the reasons the girl might feel as she did. Perhaps Barak had spotted her and told her to return. Though she had already argued with Barak and disobeyed his earlier command. Had she been injured?

Deborah tried to see more clearly, but the distance was too great. By the way she trudged uphill, Deborah deduced nothing wrong, simply a purposefully slow climb. She would find out soon enough. And she would make her daughter tell her everything.

Barak studied the gates of Harosheth-hagoyim and paced the ridge overlooking the thick, impenetrable walls of the city. "How are we supposed to get through that?" He pointed at the massive fortress that mirrored Hazor and glanced at Keshet.

"Deborah said our God would make a way." Keshet shrugged, then headed down the embankment. "You coming?" he called over his shoulder.

Fleeing Canaanites passed them on the road below, and before Barak's eyes they coaxed the guards to open the gates. Keshet glanced back, his grin wide. Barak's men rushed after them, cutting down Canaanites left and right.

Barak caught up with Keshet. "Didn't I tell you?" the man said, grinning.

"I'm going up into the gate. I'll meet you outside the walls." He would never live down his brief attack of doubt, but he would deal with his annoying compatriot later.

He pulled his sword from the sheath at his side and worked his way up the stairs, Lavi at his heels. Quick glances into the side rooms told them they were deserted. The guard post at the top stood empty. Barak walked to the parapet and looked down. In the distance, a palace-like structure stood, no doubt Sisera's living quarters.

"Give orders to have that place searched for our women and children. Men too," Barak told Lavi. "It is time to set them free."

"I will run and catch up with Keshet to tell him," Lavi said, turning to go.

Barak touched his shoulder, staying him a moment. "Give orders to another. I want you and Ghalib to come with me. Lappidoth too."

"Where are we going?" Lavi's dark, heavy brows lifted in question.

"To search for Sisera."

"You do not think he is here?" Lavi glanced over the city. "We have not even begun to search every house or room."

"He is not here." Barak was not sure how he knew it to be true, but for the first time in his life he sensed that God was the one directing him, truly showing him something he could not see with human eyes.

"How do you know? Surely we should look first." Lavi's protest was nearly drowned out by the shouts and agonizing cries of warriors falling at the hands of Barak's men in the streets below.

"Because Sisera is smart and self-preserving. If he saw that the war was taking a turn against him, he would run from the pursuit." The man was a coward despite all his posturing.

Barak leaned on the parapet and looked over the carnage. No, Sisera was not here. Not even to protect his home, his family. If he had one. He would care only for himself, and in the end he would do whatever it took to protect his skin.

Barak set his jaw and headed down the stairs. This time Sisera's skin would not be saved.

26

Deborah studied her only daughter for a lengthy moment. She touched the girl's cheek. "Why did you return after you had gone with the men? Did Barak grow angry with you?"

Talya looked beyond her and did not speak for many breaths, but at last, after the release of a deep sigh, she shook her head. "Barak seemed grateful for my skill, for the Canaanites I killed." Awe tinged her voice. "I think he realized I could do as I said I could."

Deborah lifted a brow. "Then why did you return?"

Talya looked toward her feet. "I saw the Canaanites go after Abba. I thought he had fallen. The shock of it . . ."

Deborah stilled. *Lappidoth . . . Please, Adonai.* She could not lose him.

Talya drew a sharp breath. "I saw they were still coming. I ran and shot at them. It turned out that Abba had merely played as though he were dead to avoid their arrows."

Deborah's heart raced like a skittish horse, but she could not speak.

"Abba was not pleased to see me. He did not want you to worry over me, so he sent me back." She still could not meet Deborah's gaze.

"He spoke harshly with you." She knew it deep within her. Though Lappidoth had never once spoken in such a way with Talya, this time he did. Because of her. Because of the many arguments they had had over the girl. Because he loved Deborah more.

Shame crept up her neck, heated her face. She had driven him, had put a wedge between his favorite child and herself. "Did he . . . did he embarrass you — in front of others?"

Talya shook her head, but her lower lip trembled. "No. He sent them on ahead." Tears caused her voice to rise in pitch, and she stopped short. Talya was not used to her father's commands.

"Come," Deborah said, motioning Talya to follow her back to their tent. She grabbed the lamp from just outside the door and lifted the flap. "We must find food and busy ourselves with other things."

"Shouldn't we watch from the cliff and pray?"

"We can pray here as well as there." Deborah did not need the reminder or the scent of carnage that had begun to drift toward them from below. "Keep your weapons close. In case."

"Bring the ropes and help me tie them to the beam," Jael told Daniyah, her voice tight like the muscles along her jaw. She had not relaxed a moment since Deborah and Barak had come and taken her men away. Why did they listen to Barak when they could have been halfway to the Negev by now? It was not like Heber to take such a risk or fight in a war that was not his own.

But for Hazor . . . What he had seen there had changed him — added to what Yiskah had described. Jael felt sudden nausea churn in her middle. She stopped, forced a deep breath.

"Are you all right, Ima?" Daniyah's concern brought Jael's thoughts up short. She had to be strong for her girls. If she showed her fear, they would panic. If they spoke too loudly, Sisera could hear. The birds might speak of it, fly away, and tell the man they were alone . . .

She shook herself. She was becoming

fanciful now, foolish in her imaginings. "I am fine," she assured Daniyah. "We must hurry to secure this wall and then set it up so the three of you can hide here without giving yourselves away. We must store food and water in case we come under siege."

Daniyah's dark eyes grew wider, and Jael silently berated herself for sounding so harsh. She must not frighten the girl, who was already skittish. "Do not fear, my daughter. Fear will only lead to trouble."

"But will you not hide with us? What if Sisera tries to kidnap you?" Daniyah's voice rose in pitch, and she cupped her mouth to suppress a sob.

"I will be fine, my daughter. Trust me. I can handle Sisera." She stifled the shudder that came with every thought of the man, of what he had already done . . . She had no real faith in her own proclamation. But better her daughter believe the lie than fear the truth.

Nadia entered the tent carrying a jar of water and a sack strapped to her back. Raja came behind with spindles and distaffs and a sack of wool. They would need something to keep their hands busy if they were forced to wait any length of time.

"There," Jael said when the last of the rugs was secured near the wall of Heber's tent.

"You will be close by for me to warn you, and your father will not mind if you sleep in the larger section until such a warning comes. But I want you all to stay here. If my guess is correct, Sisera will attack the women's tents first. The proper thing to do, should he come, would be to visit your father's tent to seek hospitality. But Sisera is not proper, nor does he care what men think. He will take advantage of our weakness. It is his practice."

"He thinks it is his strength," Nadia said, giving a disgusted grunt. "He is a fool."

"Yes, but let us not dwell on that now. We will hide and we will pray and we will wait. Barak and his men will kill Sisera, and they will tell us all is well soon enough."

Daniyah seemed only partially appeased by Jael's words. She had not forgotten the way Sisera had touched her in the presence of her own family, nor the fear that rippled throughout the camp whenever he approached.

Hatred for the man surfaced, and with it heat curled inside Jael, rising until her face flamed. He would pay for what he had done. The men would make sure of it. Deborah had promised it. Surely, surely, they would be rid of him soon.

■ ■ ■ ■

Barak kept up a steady jog from Sisera's city around the muddy Jezreel Valley and circled toward Heber's tents and his own home of Kedesh-naphtali, zeal flowing through his veins. They would pass each village on their way toward Hazor, where Sisera was no doubt headed.

He turned to glance behind him just as Lavi drew close, huffing next to him. Ghalib and Keshet and his men were swift on their heels. "Word has come from the ranks, my lord," Lavi said as he caught up to Barak. "Not a man of Canaan is left of those who joined Sisera." He slowed his pace, and Barak did the same.

"Any sign of Sisera?" He asked because he had to, but deep down he knew the answer.

Lavi shook his head. "No sign. They say even his house was empty of all but the slaves. We rescued all those of Israel and took the others until we can decide what to do with them."

Barak nodded and scratched at his beard, continuing at a fast-paced walk. "They say he has a mother somewhere. If his mother was not at his house, then he must have hidden her safely away in another city." Barak tilted his head, listening. Was that rushing water in the distance?

"If Sisera's mother is hidden, no doubt she is somewhere in Canaan. Perhaps she is at the palace in Hazor." This from Keshet.

"Hazor is well fortified," Barak agreed. If he were Sisera, he might put his parents in such a city.

"The sooner we get to Hazor the better," Ghalib said, his tone sharp. "The place is evil. Their king is evil. And if Sisera is there, he will be well protected."

They drew closer to the sound of a river, and Barak stopped to look around. "We will find Sisera before he gets to Hazor." He spoke the words to make them true, but he said a silent prayer for success just the same.

"If Sisera is on foot, which way would he have gone?" Keshet met Barak's gaze as they reached the river's edge. Vines hung low from overhanging trees. If they would hold, a man could use his weight as leverage and let the vine carry him to the opposite bank, or at least give him something to hold on to as he managed the protruding rocks.

"My guess is he would first head south, away from the battle to throw us off, then turn north to Hazor. If he crossed this river, he could be far ahead of us. If he avoided it, we will have a better chance to get ahead of him." Barak grabbed one of the vines, pulling hard. It held. He looked up. The tree above them was old, sturdy, with deep roots. He took a running leap and swung, jumped down, and landed on his feet on the other side.

Jael woke with a start, sweat drawing twin lines down her brow. The dream. It was a dream, wasn't it? She cocked her head, straining for some sound. Nothing. Not even the birds had begun their morning calls.

She rose from the mat she often shared with Heber and glanced about the dark tent. They had made a practice of allowing the lamps to go out once the flap to the tent was drawn closed. Now, as she fumbled to feel about her, she questioned that wisdom. Surely one lamp would not pierce the black goat hair of the tent. Their snores would give them away faster than the light would. Jael had taken to sleeping on her side to avoid making noise. Though she wondered how often she truly slept.

She crept along the outer wall farthest from the girls, her eyes adjusting to the darkness. She had heard something, surely.

For if it had been a dream, she would remember some detail of it. Yet her mind replayed nothing other than the blank bliss of sleep.

She felt the door to the tent at last beneath her fingers. She fiddled with the rope that held it fast, untied it, and slowly lifted the flap. She glanced back at the sleeping girls, then slipped outside. Moonlight bathed the path before her, and she took it slowly toward her own tent. She paused, peering through the trees to glimpse the sky. A pattern of zigzag wisps of clouds crossed the heavens, and stars filtered through the trees like tiny lanterns hanging low. The crescent moon shone bright, like the tip of God's fingernail. Was God so big that He could hold the moon in His hand?

She shivered, grateful she had remembered her cloak, and pulled it close to her neck. Even the crickets had gone to bed for the night, with only the wind rustling the leaves in the trees above. *Are You there, God of Israel?* She felt the prickle of gooseflesh along her arms at the mere thought of Him, and of her standing here alone in the camp, known only to the trees and the breath of the wind.

And to your Creator.

She gripped both of her arms, the chill

seeping deeper, though no dew had yet settled to cause her bare toes to feel cold. This cold was not coming from the ground nor the air around her. Did God walk among the trees at night when no man was looking?

The thunder two evenings before had seemed like the voice of a god, though she could not have named one with such power other than the God of the Hebrews. Was He truly the only God? Or did the gods of Canaan share space in the skies with Him? Her ancestors had worshiped the God of Moses, and tradition passed down through the ages had carried many of the Hebrew stories and interconnected them with the Kenites' own.

Jael looked heavenward again, awed by the way the clouds sent silver streaks like glowing arms, almost low enough to touch her. *Are You there?* she asked again. But only the breeze responded, its touch as gentle as a kiss.

She stood listening, lingering, unaware at first that tears wet her cheeks. Had He touched her through the whisper of the breeze? Her thoughts were surely the makings of a woman who had gone too long without sleep, whose fear for the safety of her loved ones had taken too great a hold over her mind. How silly to think the simple breeze could be the breath or whisper of God. She was not Hebrew, nor chosen. She carried no special purpose like Deborah the prophetess. She was a simple metalworker's wife who lived in tents, one who did not even own a business of her own, who could not contribute much to their household for fear of Sisera's men. How could she weave or spin or make goods to sell when merchants avoided the highways and women who plied similar trades were of no use to any but their own households? Heber would be better off if she could help him more.

But she had her family. She brushed a stray tear and offered a tentative smile at the heavens. *I am not worthy of Your notice, but You have given me a family to love. For that I am grateful.*

She wanted to add, "Please, keep them safe and bring them back to me; please keep my girls from Sisera's notice," but she held her tongue. Somehow she sensed a change in her spirit. She had no right to ask such things, to beg mercies from the Unseen One. She was not foolish enough to think she had really felt His touch, nor sensed His . . . love.

She shook herself. No. Her thoughts were the rumination of an overwrought mind.

She turned away from the moonlight and slipped into her own tent.

Later that morning, as dawn made its way toward the midpoint of the sky, Jael stood at the door to Heber's tent, speaking to the girls inside. "Let us leave off grinding the grain today. We will soak it and make porridge instead of bread."

Daniyah pouted. "But I'm sick of porridge. We have it nearly every day."

"Be glad you have food to eat at all," Raja said, her tone sharp. She rubbed her back, obviously uncomfortable. "I need to walk, but where can we go that we are safe anymore?"

"Now look who is grumbling." Daniyah's whiny tone had turned to anger. She crossed her arms and planted her feet near the grinding stone. "How long are we to be cooped up in here, Ima? You don't even know if Sisera will come. If he is at war with Israel in the Jezreel Valley, he could be dead by now."

Jael looked from Daniyah to Nadia and Raja, reading weariness in each of their gazes. "All right, fine then. All of you take a walk to the cave to see if the water has receded. But be warned, take care when you return. Do not allow yourself to be seen or heard in case . . ."

Daniyah jumped up and down like a child before realizing how immature she must look to her sisters-in-law. She ran to embrace Jael, and nearly collided with Raja in her attempt to reach the tent door and slip past Jael first.

But the whistle of the guard halted their movement.

"Someone is coming," Jael whispered. She glanced around. "You must stay in the tent. Hide quickly." The girls obeyed in silence, without question.

Jael turned and met the guard in his haste to find her. "There is a man, alone. He is on foot and appears to have come a great distance." The guard's eyes grew wide at this point, and he leaned close to Jael's ear. "I think it is Sisera, my lady."

Jael's heart leapt at the man's name, her whole body going rigid, her mind whirling. "He is headed this way?"

The guard nodded. "Do you want me to shoot him? He appears unarmed."

Jael stared at the guard, no more than a boy, really. Had her men truly left such young men to watch over them? The boy was not even old enough to sprout a beard. Could he aim straight? Would Sisera overpower him if he missed?

She thought of the other guard near the fire pits, but he was an old man, and not nearly as steady as he used to be. The two stronger guards strode the perimeter of the camp, and they had gone in different directions some time ago. She was alone with her girls and a boy barely able to help them.

"No," she said at last. "Do not shoot him. If you miss —"

"I will not miss."

"Nevertheless, if you do" — Jael held his gaze with an unbending look — "Sisera will know he has the upper hand, and he will not spare you."

The boy looked uncertain, but his chin lifted in defiance. "I've practiced long. I can take him."

Jael shook her head. "I know you can." *Or you think you can.* "But let us first see what else we can do. Perhaps he comes seeking sanctuary. Perhaps we can hold him here until Barak and his men catch up to him."

The boy looked at her, his light eyes dubious. But he did not argue as he slowly stepped back and hid out of sight.

Jael drew a breath and felt for her sling, but realized she had taken it off her wrist the night before. She had also left Heber's knife in his tent by her side as she'd attempted sleep. At least the girls would have another weapon if it got that far.

She straightened her back, willing resolve into her heart. *Help me, God of Israel.* Whether she deserved His help or not, it could not hurt to ask for it. She walked slowly past her own tent and out to the berm. With weighted steps she climbed the berm and stood near the edge of the road. The guard had not been mistaken. Sisera was stumbling straight toward her.

Jael clenched her fists, trying to instill strength into her limbs, and felt fear and fury mingling equally within her. She stepped farther onto the road so he could see her.

"Come, my lord, come right in. Don't be afraid," she called, extending a hand and motioning toward the camp.

Sisera stopped and stared at her, his glazed look slowly clearing to recognition. "Heber's wife. I have made it to Heber's camp." His chest heaved, and she realized he was caked in mud from foot to knee, his normally regal robe soaked from a wadi or river, his hair matted, his turban askew. He looked like one who had lost all strength, not at all like the evil warrior she knew him to be.

"Come," she said again. "Don't be afraid." She would offer him shelter, and once he slept, she would bind him with ropes until Barak arrived. The plan had formed the moment she saw him, and she thanked the God of heaven for such clear direction.

She allowed him to precede her, never taking her gaze from him. He stopped at the opening to her tent and looked around, seeming to suddenly realize she was behind him. He turned.

"You first." His dark eyes narrowed a bit, but weariness still edged them.

She bowed to show respect she didn't feel and walked, back straight, into her tent. She turned to face him. "There is nothing to fear, my lord. Come."

He looked the room over, blinking at the darkened interior. She moved to retrieve a lamp from behind a clay cup that hid most of its light.

"Don't," he said, coming closer. "Keep it dark."

She left the lamp where it stood. "You look exhausted, my lord. Would you like to lie down?" She motioned to her mat, though she took a step back from him, hoping he would not think she was offering him more than a mat.

His look grew wary, and for a moment it held a glint she recognized. "When I awaken . . ." He left the sentence unfinished, but by his look she did not miss his meaning. "You know you want me." She barely heard his whispered words as he stretched out on the ground, and she absently covered him with a blanket. But she had heard enough.

Her heart pounded in response, her fear rising. How long would he sleep? Would Barak get here in time? Once Sisera awoke refreshed, she would never be able to stop him from searching the camp, from taking her, from hurting Daniyah . . .

"I'm thirsty," he said, jarring her thoughts. "Please give me some water."

He rested his head on the mat as though he had no strength to keep it upright. A thousand thoughts filled her head as she moved toward the tent's opening where the water jar stood. She stopped midway. Water might refresh him. But milk . . . She glanced at the skin she had filled from the goat Daniyah had milked that morning. It still felt warm to her touch. Warm milk would aid his sleep.

Out of the corner of her eye she saw him rise up on one elbow, watching her. She moved quickly to the skin, poured milk into a clay cup, and took it to him.

"Here, my lord. This will calm you." Their fingers brushed as he took it from her, and she fought the need to recoil.

He took it and drank greedily, then tossed the cup from him. She heard it crack as it landed in the corner, but she didn't care. No one would drink from the cup of Sisera, and she would smash what was left with her foot once he was gone.

Gone. Would he be gone? What would Barak do but kill him?

She watched the man closely, his eyes heavy with sleep. He relaxed and turned to lie on his side. She adjusted the blanket, covering him like a mother would a child.

She stepped back, staring, but his words caught her up short.

"Stand in the doorway of the tent," he said. "If someone comes by and asks you, 'Is anyone in there?' say, 'No.'"

Even in his exhaustion the man had the gall to tell her what to do. But then he assumed he was safe here. Hadn't she invited him in? Hadn't Heber acted the part of host when Sisera demanded the weapons from him? Heber's tentative alliance with Jabin gave Sisera too much confidence.

"Yes, my lord," she whispered. But he had already succumbed to sleep, his soft snores growing louder as she walked away from him.

She stood at the tent door, watching the

road. No sign of Barak or any of his men. Had Sisera gotten free of the entire army and fled with no one's notice?

Surely they would come for him. They would think he was headed to Hazor and would come this direction to get there. She hoped. But there were other ways to reach Hazor from Mount Tabor, and Jael had no certainty that Barak would take the one that would lead him to her tent. Her pulse quickened as she looked from one edge of the camp to the other. The girls had made no sound from Heber's tent, and there was no sign of any of the guards. Had they all deserted her? Or were they planning something, some way to surround Sisera?

She released a slow, pent-up sigh, as though her breath could not fully come until something was done about that man. One glance told her he still slept deeply, his snores attesting to his exhaustion.

She stepped quietly under the flap. Glanced down at the ground and caught sight of the peg holding the ropes taut. Extra rope lay in her tent. If she could somehow manage to get Sisera's arms behind him and tie his feet together . . . But the movement, the time it would take to tie a knot tightly enough, would surely wake him.

She shook her head. No. Rope was not the answer she'd first thought it to be.

She could hurry to Heber's tent to retrieve the knife . . .

A tent peg was sharp.

She moved as one in a dream back into her tent to the basket that held her wooden hammer and a few extra metal tent pegs that Heber had especially designed for her. Thank the heavens she kept the extra pegs close. If she tried to pull one from holding the tent in place, the sound and movement could awaken the man.

The hammer felt comfortable in her right hand, as it did every time she set up camp. One blow would put the peg into the ground unless the ground was hard as stone. She looked at Sisera, his chest lifting and falling in shallow breaths. He lay still on his side, the turban missing from his dark mop of hair. She could not take the risk of brushing the hair aside. She must find the perfect spot on his temple, away from the protruding bone . . .

She longed to draw a deep breath but feared the noise would wake him. *Calm, even movements. Don't rush.* The words repeated in her mind as she moved with a snake's stealth toward the man who bore that very emblem on his arms and around his neck. Anat and Asherah were goddesses, not snakes. Sisera obviously liked the reptile or somehow thought he needed protection from both the goddesses and the serpent.

She drew alongside his head, looking down at him, forcing every thought in her mind to flee except the one that mattered most. Place the peg at his temple and slam the hammer down hard. One blow. She needed to do this in one blow, or she would weaken and fail and everything she loved would be lost.

She steadied the peg in her left hand and bent slowly to her knees. *Help me.* She could not consider the words a prayer, lest she anger Adonai by such a request. *Keep my hand steady.* Her heart said the words just the same.

She held the peg a hairbreadth from Sisera's temple and lifted the hammer. *This is your last breath, Sisera.*

One blow.

His chest stopped moving, his snoring ceased.

27

Barak paused for breath, bracing both hands on his thighs. The jog since they crossed the swollen wadi had winded him, but he dare not stop. Sisera was out there somewhere.

"He had to have stopped to rest," Keshet said, breathing heavily beside him, his chest heaving from their rapid pace. "We've been running and fighting for a day and a half, and look at us." He pointed to himself, but his look told Barak he was also noticing the disheveled and exhausted mess he had become.

"If he's alone, he could get farther than we can trying to keep the group together." Barak raked a hand along the back of his neck, brushing away the sweat that had gathered there.

"He could have holed up in a cave to sleep."

Barak thought a moment on that, but shook his head, scowling. "We checked every cave we passed. There was no sign of him." He blew out a breath. "No. I think he went on to Hazor."

"He could have stopped in one of our villages along the way."

Barak's thoughts moved to Kedesh-naphtali. "If Sisera wanted to taunt me, he would head to our home." His gut clenched with a pain akin to fear. "We have to reach it before he does."

He took off at a run again, ignoring the ache in his side. If that man had laid one finger on his parents, his friends, or his relatives still living in that town, he would wish he had never been born.

Jael stared down at the blood pooling on the mat beneath Sisera's head. Her right hand still clutched the hammer so tight the muscles begged release. Her breath came in spurts, and a sense of shock rushed through her. Sisera was dead. Truly. Dead.

She dragged in air, but it was tainted with the sickening smell of fresh blood. She forced first one foot, then the other, to move away from the man. Slowly, methodically, she trudged to the tent's opening and dropped the hammer in the dirt. She inhaled the scent of oak and pine and air so fresh it nearly burned her lungs.

Chest heaving with the weight of what she had just done, she bent forward, pressed her hands to her middle. Tears filled her eyes, and she could not stop them from running into her mouth, then dripping into the dirt.

She had killed a man. She had only meant to detain him until Barak came, but in her fear, she killed him.

Oh Adonai, help me. The prayer felt real this time, for it accompanied a deep ache for God's forgiveness. She knew this was not murder, for it was an act of war. But she could not bring herself to feel anything but pain. How did one recover after watching the lifeblood seep from a person, enemy or not?

She breathed again, her heart rate slowing with each intended breath. And as she breathed, truth dawned. She breathed. And her girls still breathed. Sisera, who could have done more than kill them all, was gone. Forever.

"Daniyah, Nadia, Raja!" She shouted their names, suddenly needing to hold them, to see them, to kiss their cheeks. She faced Heber's tent, waiting. And then there they were, running, tentative at first, glancing this way and that.

She waved her arms, and they saw her,

ran toward her.

"Ima!" Daniyah was first to reach her and fell into her embrace. Jael wept, kissing her daughter, holding her close. "Is it over?"

Jael nodded, pulling each girl into a tight hug that encased them all. "Sisera lies dead in my tent." She angled her head to indicate through the opening. "Do not look."

Nadia stepped back and examined Jael. "Blood has spattered on your robe, Ima Jael. I will soak it and scrub it out for you."

Jael glanced down at her clothing, startled that she had not noticed the mess Sisera's blood had made. She darted quick glances at each of her girls. "Have I spread it to you?" But no, the blood had remained on Jael's clothing alone. "We will not wash it," she declared, ripping the garment from her. "We will burn every piece of clothing that carries his blood. He does not deserve to live even in our memories." She would have to wear an older robe and tunic until they could afford to weave more, but it mattered little.

"Wait here while I fetch clean ones." She held her breath and stepped into the tent, avoiding even one glimpse in the direction of her mat where Sisera lay. She quickly changed to clean clothes, then carried the bloodied ones outside, tossed them into the pit in front of her tent, and used her lamp to light them on fire.

Barak turned a corner in the road, at last headed north toward the sea, where Kedesh-naphtali stood on the south end near the shore. Heber's campsite lay an arrow's shot from where his men were congregating before they took the last trek toward home and then on to Hazor.

Weariness crept over Barak as he took a long drink from the sagging goatskin at his side. They needed to refill the skins, but it would have to wait until they reached the sea.

Ghalib sidled up next to him and nodded toward the oaks ahead of them. "It would do us good to stop for a moment and let my mother and sisters refresh us with food and water, my lord. We would not stay long."

Barak pinched the bridge of his nose to forestall a headache, to no avail. "We cannot take the time, Ghalib. If you wish to go home, I cannot stop you. Your father and brothers aren't far behind, and we do not expect any of you to continue on to Hazor. But we do thank you for your service to Israel."

Ghalib straightened, his look offended. "I was not suggesting we stay, my lord. I just know the men are weary. A short stop might help us all."

Barak studied him, wondering if it was his own jealousy of Ghalib's interest in Talya that made him keep the man at arm's length, made him question his motives and almost want to be rid of his presence. Almost. He couldn't deny that Heber's family had been an asset to them in every way during this fight, not just in providing the weapons but in wielding them.

"We move on," he said to Ghalib. He turned to do just that, when a woman appeared in the distance waving a scarf and calling out something he could not quite hear.

"That's Ima!" Ghalib took off at a run, and Barak hurried to follow.

It was indeed Jael, standing in the road, composed and jubilant. "Come," she said, smiling at Ghalib, but her gaze focused on Barak. "I will show you the man you're looking for."

Barak's heart quickened at her words. He glanced at Keshet, who had joined them. Could it be? But he did not speak, simply followed her as she had asked.

They climbed down the berm and made their way through the trees until they came to Jael's tent. Jael's daughter and daughters-in-law stood to the side of the tent, and the guards Heber had left to watch over them circled behind them, looking chagrined.

Barak pondered why they did not look as triumphant as Jael did, but still he said nothing. Jael lifted the tent flap and beckoned Barak to enter. The scent of blood hit him like a wave. Jael had rolled up the sides, but still the smell was strong.

Barak entered, cautiously at first.

"He's on the mat in the corner," Jael said from where she had stayed outside in the courtyard area.

Barak moved closer, Keshet at his side. And there he lay. Sisera. Lifeless. A tent peg holding his head fast to the earth, his blood spilled and now dried to his hair and the mat beneath him.

Barak glanced at Keshet, who simply nodded. They both left the tent together. Outside, Barak approached Jael, who was now surrounded by Heber, Mahir, Fareed, and Ghalib, along with her girls.

"You did this?" he asked, unable to keep the awe from his voice. Hadn't Deborah said Sisera would fall by the hand of a woman? Hadn't Talya agreed that God would show His might over Canaan's goddesses through the weakness of a woman who relied upon Him?

"By your God's help, I did, yes," Jael said, her gaze glancing off him to study her feet. But a moment later she lifted her eyes and shrugged. "I cannot say I find it pleasing to kill a man. But I knew once he had rested, my girls would suffer at his hands. So I made sure his rest never ended."

"I am certain he does not rest even now," Barak said, wondering what Adonai Elohim did with the souls of men like Sisera. Surely the Judge of all the earth would do right and make sure Sisera paid for all the evil he had done.

"But he can no longer hurt us," Jael said, her eyes searching his for some kind of affirmation.

"He can no longer hurt us," Barak agreed. "And you are blessed of Adonai, for He gave you the privilege of ridding us of such an enemy. And his humiliation is complete at having died at the hand of a woman."

"Talya wanted to be that woman," Ghalib said, coming up and putting his arm around his mother. "But I'm glad it was you, Ima." He kissed her cheek, and Barak felt a sense of kindness toward the man for caring so about his mother.

He turned to the men behind him. "Gather up Sisera's body and cleanse Jael's tent," he said to the troop under Keshet's leadership. "The rest of you, replenish your skins of water, and if they can spare it, take some nuts for your journey and head north to Hazor. This war is not over until Jabin's soul joins Sisera's."

After bidding Heber and his sons to stay and rest a bit, then meet up with them again on Mount Tabor in three days, Barak took Lappidoth and Lavi and Elior and Deborah's cousin Shet and continued north with the rest of the men.

28

Deborah stood again at the edge on Mount Tabor, shading her eyes against the last bits of color that filled the sky before the world became engulfed in blackness. Surely Israel had seen a great victory here. Surely they had. But the troops had yet to return. Barak was still out there searching for Sisera, and her sons, her husband, were with him.

Please, Adonai, keep them safe. Why had Lappidoth seemed so insistent, so willing to fight? He was a farmer, a scribe. Could he even wield a bow or a sword?

"I did not realize a war could take so long." She startled at the sound of Talya's voice, her nerves frayed, her trust waning.

"Men grow weary in battle. They must stop to rest now and then." *Please, Adonai, let that be the only reason they grow weary. From fighting. Not from burying our dead.*

"You are worried." Talya nodded in the direction of the valley. "Do you think Sisera lies among the horde of men down there?"

Deborah's gaze swept the area once more, then she shook her head. "If Sisera had been slain there, the men would have sent someone to tell us. No. I think he ran when he saw the battle turn against him." She wrapped both arms about her waist and shivered. The uncertainty of waiting mingled with the surety of God's words to her. He had never let her down in the past. She had no reason to doubt Him now.

"The commanders of Israel offered themselves willingly among the people," she said, noting Talya's furrowed brow. "They had no shields or spears to guard them, only simple weapons of the shepherd or farmer." She saw Lappidoth's sure stride in her mind's eye. "And yet they came at our summons. They obeyed the Lord." She moved her arm in an arc over the swollen, bloody land, willing herself to believe her husband had been just as strong as the rest of the shepherds and farmers among them. "Look what God has done for us."

Talya followed where Deborah pointed, but Deborah did not miss the hint of sadness shadowing her gaze. "I could have helped them."

"You are more help to me here." Though she knew her reasons for wanting Talya near were protective motherly instincts mingled with fear.

"Abba seemed to think so."

Deborah looked from the valley to Talya, awed yet again that her father had stood up to the girl, had commanded her out of harm's way for Deborah's sake. *I love you, Deborah.*

Guilt filled her. Why hadn't she repeated the words back to him that night? What if she lost him and he never returned — like her father and brothers that long-ago day?

Her stomach tightened in that dread feeling between fear and terror, and she felt suddenly faint. Her knees weakened. Blood drained from her face.

"Ima, are you all right?" Talya gripped her arm, holding her steady.

"I . . . yes, I think so." *Awake, Deborah, awake!* She must pull herself out of this longing stupor. Lappidoth, Elior, and Lavi would surely come away unharmed, while the kings of Canaan, the rulers and leaders of their enemies, would rue the day they exalted themselves against the people whom Adonai Elohim had chosen.

"I still hope it is I who kills Sisera," Talya said, dragging Deborah's thoughts from her musings. "If he comes up this mount, I shall not hesitate." She held her bow in one fist and clutched it to her side.

"I am certain you will." Deborah touched her daughter's cheek, suddenly grateful for this child's obedience to her father. She could have defied him as she had defied Barak. "But I am glad you are here."

She turned away from the ridge to spend another night with only her daughter on the mountain's heights. Talya's quiet footfalls touched the earth as they walked side by side. Deborah entered the tent and Talya followed, but she did not remove her robe or weapons. She paced the floor as Deborah pulled nuts and dates from a sack and poured watered wine into cups.

"Sit, my daughter. There is no reason to stand at the ready all night." She held the cup out to Talya, waiting.

Talya took it at last and sat cross-legged on the ground. "Why do some men exasperate us so?"

Deborah sat on the floor and parceled out the nuts and dates. "Do you speak of your father or some other man?" How ironic to have such a conversation when war raged around them.

"Barak exasperates me more than Abba does. Despite his nod of approval for my skill, I could tell he was not pleased with me. I cannot say a right thing to him, Ima.

391

He feels the need to either reprove me or command me. He does not speak to me as an equal."

"When a man exasperates you, perhaps it is because he brings out both the best and worst in you. That can be a good thing, Talya. It makes you weed out the things that need to change and keep the things that don't." Deborah chewed on a date, her thoughts carrying to her own marriage, wondering how she could possibly change things with Lappidoth at this late hour of their lives. He had proven his love for her — more often than she had realized — but how was she to prove her love for him? She did love him. The thought turned over in her mind. It was not a perfect love, but surely the spark of it nestled within her.

"Your thoughts are far away, Ima." Talya reached for a handful of nuts but did not eat. "I know we do not always get along . . ."

Deborah shook her head. "It is not that." She looked into Talya's innocent eyes. She could not share that she had not loved Talya's father when they wed. That she still struggled to respect the man. "I fear I am not a very good judge of relationships, my daughter. It is easy to judge cases of the law for people I do not know. It is far harder to judge my own heart or to advise the people

I love the most." She sighed, knowing in her heart that she had much to ponder before this war was over.

"I think you do an admirable job of showing the people you love the best way to live." Talya lifted her chin and smiled. "Do not fret so, Ima. When the war is over, much will change. Sisera's hold over our nation has changed us all, and not for the good."

"And yet there is much good," Deborah said, realizing it was true. "Men have come willingly to fight. God has sent even the stars and rains to aid our victory. We have much in which to rejoice."

"Then we should set to doing so, to welcome our men home." Talya chomped on the almonds in her hand.

"A victory song," Deborah said. In neighboring kingdoms it was customary for the women to welcome the returning warriors with songs of victory. Even Moses and his sister Miriam had sung a song of praise to Adonai after He got them safely across the Red Sea. Surely Sisera's defeat deserved such a song.

Once she was certain Sisera was truly dead.

"You should write the song even before we hear the news, Ima." Talya's comment caused Deborah to meet her gaze. "It shows our faith in Adonai, that He will do this."

Of course it did. When had her daughter grown such faith?

"You are right, Talya. He will do this. For our God is true." Deborah rose to search for a small stick to write in the dirt the song that only God knew if she would ever get the chance to sing.

Jael shivered and pulled her cloak tighter at the neck. Despite the men's efforts in removing Sisera's body and destroying by fire everything that he had come into contact with, the air still carried the pungent odors of smoke, of death. She swayed, her heart beating sluggish strokes.

"It's all right, Ima." Ghalib's arm came around her, and she fell into his strength. When had this boy become so much a man? "I'm proud of you," he whispered against her ear.

She nodded, unable to speak. A lump formed in her throat, and she feared she would break down in front of her men and weep. She glanced up, catching Heber watching her. Ghalib released his hold as Heber opened his arms wide. She stumbled toward him, grateful for his strong embrace. He said nothing as he rubbed her back. She breathed in the smell of him and fought the urge to give in to emotion. She gulped on a sob, then another.

"It's all right, Jael. It's over." Heber's quiet words were a soothing balm.

She hiccuped another sob. "I can't enter that tent again," she said against his thick chest.

He continued to draw awkward circles along her back, then patted her head, her hair. "We will burn it as well and make you another."

Jael blinked hard against the threat of more tears. "I will have no place to sleep, to work, and such a thing would be too costly."

"You will stay in my tent. The cost is minimal." He said nothing more, and she knew by his deep sigh that he would hear no argument. He turned to the guards and commanded Jael's tent to be disassembled and taken outside the camp and burned.

The women seemed to awaken from a stupor once the offending tent was gone.

"Come, let us fix something to eat," Raja said, aiming a look Nadia's way.

Nadia complied without comment, and Daniyah moved to help them. "Where will I sleep?" Daniyah said loud enough for Jael to hear.

"You will stay with us," Nadia told her, taking the girl's arm. The three of them moved to work in front of Raja's tent, while Fareed and Mahir approached their father.

"We want to go with Barak," Fareed said.

Jael pulled away from Heber's embrace to face her sons. Ghalib had joined them now, his dark eyes bright, anxious.

"Fareed is right," Mahir said. "We have not finished what we started. It would be wrong to let Barak and his men continue without us."

"We are not cowards." This from Ghalib, who stood tall as though he had suddenly grown another hand span.

"Of course you are not cowards." Heber's words were measured as he looked from one son to another. He placed an arm around Jael's shoulders. She was not used to such open affection from the man, but she sensed he needed to prove she still breathed — especially after what he had witnessed in her tent. "But Barak gave his orders to meet him in three days. We will take your mother and sisters with us. Do you not think your mother deserves to be protected now, after all she has done for us, for Israel?" His tone held a sharp edge, and Jael looked into his face, searching his expression.

She courted a soft smile. "Thank you, my lord. I am honored to go with you all to celebrate Israel's victory on Mount Tabor."

She looked at her sons. "Perhaps instead of disobeying Barak's orders, you could send messengers throughout the nearby cities to join in the celebration as well. Word will spread quickly now that Sisera is dead. All Israel should come and join in this victory." She glanced at Heber for his approval, pleased with his nod and the slight lifting of the corners of his mouth.

"Can we send a message as far south as the Negev, Father?" Ghalib held his father's gaze, his look pleading. "Could we not at least let Uncle Alim know the land has been rid of the threat to us all?"

"And get word to a certain cousin?" Jael asked, though she wondered if Talya had replaced Parisa in Ghalib's thoughts.

Ghalib shrugged. "It would not hurt to try to make amends."

"Ever the peacemaker, my son?" Heber's voice held a hint of iron, and he stiffened beside her. "You know we cannot go back there."

Ghalib did not waver. "I did not ask that, Father. I only wish . . ." He did not finish his thought but turned away instead. He walked off alone, leaving Mahir and Fareed still standing there.

"The boy does not understand," Heber said, his gaze fixed on some point beyond

397

the trees.

"He is a boy no longer, Father," Fareed said. "Forgive me, but I think Ghalib is right."

Jael looked in the direction her youngest son had gone. "Your father tried to make amends." She looked at her two oldest sons. "Your uncle would have none of it."

Heber gently tightened his grip on her arm. "Alim is the one who turned a peaceful confrontation into a war of words." Hurt laced his tone. "I should not have fought his rule. Our leaving jeopardized your safety."

"You did all you could, Father," Mahir said. "We do not blame you."

"Alim believes I am responsible for some vast crime against him. All because I favored the decent treatment of his slave."

"Ghalib did not understand the implications," Fareed said. "If we had been able to bring our cousin with us for him to wife, he would not be so anxious to return."

"Ghalib longs for peace, with or without Parisa. Could we not at least send a servant with word of the victory?" Jael studied her men, her heart aching with the loss of family. "I understand we cannot hope to mend the estrangement, but could we not make one last attempt to show kindness before they hear it from another?"

Heber looked at her then at their sons, sorrow in his gaze, saying nothing. At last he nodded. "It would not hurt to send a servant. But do not expect a response. I will not have my family raise their hopes only to see my brother dash them once more." He gave her a knowing look. "Do not even think of sending for Parisa. Not unless Alim changes his thinking."

Jael smiled into his eyes, knowing the blow to his pride such words evoked. In time, he would change his thinking about Parisa if she had any hand in it — if Ghalib was still interested. But not today.

Today she needed rest. And time.

Sisera is dead.

And in time her family would be whole again, with or without a reconnection with Alim. And who knew but that the God of Israel might not even heal that as well?

Despite Heber's failures to make amends in the past, there was still the hope for second chances. She had to believe that. Love for family just didn't dissipate, despite anger's force.

Barak stood at the gates of Hazor, now breached, its guards toppled from the walls, its women and children running from his men and screaming in the streets. The few Canaanite warriors left to guard the city lay in pools of blood.

Keshet approached Barak as he headed toward Jabin's palace. "The king is dead, my lord, and the men are searching for the Hebrew captives as we speak." Blood coated Keshet's legs to his thighs and spattered his girded robe and tunic. He still clutched a sword in his right hand, clenched in a grip that turned his knuckles white.

"The city is secure then?" Barak looked from side to side but saw no sign of a threat.

"Yes, my lord. The king's wives, along with Sisera's mother, were in their living quarters behind their latticed walls. They did not expect us, nor apparently did King Jabin, who was feeding his overstuffed face when our men stormed the palace." Keshet moved his shoulders as if to release the tension.

"So you found Sisera's mother." Barak ran a hand along the back of his neck, wondering just what type of mother such a man would have had.

"Yes, my lord. They found her staring out the window, asking why it was taking so long for Sisera to return to her. She uttered all manner of nonsense, then turned and cursed the guards before they killed her." Keshet stopped when they reached the square.

Israelite guards surrounded the group of Hebrew slaves, some of whom were barely dressed, their tunics torn, feet bare, skin blistered from long hours in the sun. Every one of them needed to be washed clean in a river to remove the vermin from their hair, and given new clothing and sandals for their feet.

Barak's stomach twisted as he saw Nessa in the look of each broken woman, saw the fear even now in their shaking limbs, in the timid way they wrapped their arms about themselves and stared at their feet.

"Gather the spoils from every house. Find fresh clothing for these people." He raked a hand through his unkempt hair and drew a breath. *Nessa.* What he would not give to

401

have her standing with him here. "Take them to the Jordan to wash. We will not take them to Mount Tabor dressed in rags."

Keshet moved to do his bidding as Lappidoth drew up beside him and placed a hand on his arm. "God has set the captives free," he said softly. "You have done well, my son."

He nodded, grateful for the affirmation, but somehow feeling that for some of these he had been too late.

"There are no survivors, my lord," Keshet said, joining them a short time later, followed by Lavi, Elior, and Shet. "The city is ours."

Barak looked about at the carnage, the stench turning his stomach. "After the spoils have been gathered and our people are a safe distance away, burn the city."

"I wonder how many of these people knew Yiskah, how many men?" Shet's comment carried the hostility he'd shown since the day they left Deborah's village.

"Don't trouble yourself with such thoughts, my son," Lappidoth said, resting a hand on Shet's arm. "It only feeds your own hatred. The best thing you can do is forgive Yiskah and put the past behind you."

Shet looked away, but Barak understood the anger simmering in his gaze. Still, Yiskah could not change what had been.

He moved to Shet's side and drew him away as the rest of the men set out to do as he had commanded. "Your cousin is right," he said as they walked toward the broken-down gate. "I know you are angry, as I was angry when Sisera killed my wife. At least your wife still lives." Barak swallowed. It was the most he had ever said to a man he barely knew. He had rarely shared such thoughts even with Keshet.

"My wife betrayed me with Asherah. Was your wife unfaithful to our God?" Shet met his gaze, his dark eyes filled with familiar pain.

"No," he said softly. "No. She was not." Nessa's beauty had gone deeper than physical features. She had carried the joy of Adonai and a faith far greater than his.

"Then you have no idea how such a thing feels." Shet gave Barak an anguished look and stomped off.

Deborah looked down on the bones of the dead men, picked clean by God's carrion birds. Another good rainfall would likely bury the bones beneath the muck. Relief filled her. Their enemies would no longer hold sway over the land, and her people would soon know peace.

Voices of men grew loud behind her as

403

dawn broke through a sea of clouds. Deborah turned at the excitement and hurried to her tent as Talya emerged to see the commotion.

"They are back!" Talya came alongside Deborah.

"Yes." Deborah motioned for Talya to follow, and the two of them walked among the men toward the other side of the mount. And there came her men, Barak at the head, leading Lappidoth, Lavi, Elior, Shet, Keshet, and more. Deborah caught Lappidoth's eye and smiled wide at the sight of him. She rushed forward and he encased her in his arms.

"You are back." She cupped his face, seeing the longing in his gaze.

"Yes." He gripped her hands and leaned closer, smelling of sweat and earth. One glance told her he had taken the time to wash the blood and mud from himself before climbing the mount.

"I am glad." Her heart skipped a beat at his possessive look. How long had it been since he had made her feel thus? Had she ever felt such emotion for him? Surely . . . But she was not as sure as she wished to be.

"I have missed you," she whispered, resting her head on his shoulder. "I'm so glad you returned unharmed."

He bent close then and kissed her, tentative at first, then as a man who knows what and who it is he loves. When at last their lips parted, he traced a line along her jaw, his smile gentle, like the man she had always known him to be. "We have much to discuss in days to come."

Words failed her as she stared into his determined gaze. At last she nodded, wondering just what thoughts were going through his head.

"Come," he said as they turned to the commotion around them.

She hugged each of her boys and glimpsed Talya standing near them, watching Barak move among his men. "Did he speak of her while you were away?" Deborah whispered in Lappidoth's ear.

He frowned and rubbed a hand along his bearded jaw. "He did not speak of her to me, though Ghalib the Kenite spoke of her often." He looked down at her. "She told you my words?"

Deborah nodded. "I do not think she expected such a reprimand from her father. But I am glad you gave it."

He dipped his head in silent acknowledgment. "You did not need another person to give you cause to fear." He took her hand in his as Barak approached.

"The victory is complete, Prophetess. Sisera is dead at the hand of Jael, wife of Heber the Kenite. Hazor is secure, and its king is dead."

Deborah searched Barak's gaze. "God has given a great victory."

Barak nodded. "Yes, He has." He glanced beyond her. "Has Heber arrived yet? I told the Kenites to meet us here in three days. They should arrive soon."

"I have not yet seen them." No doubt Ghalib would seek out Talya if he were here. "Jael is coming with them?"

Barak's smile reached his eyes for the first time in more months or years than she could remember. "Yes. And she has quite the story to tell you."

"I shall be pleased to hear it." Some of the men had spoken of Jael and her tent peg, but Deborah wanted to hear the full tale from Jael's own mouth.

Barak stood a moment more, then quietly excused himself.

"When everyone arrives, we will celebrate," Deborah said to Lappidoth. "I have composed a victory song." She searched his gaze, looking for, hoping for, affirmation of her efforts. She had done so little to help in this fight except to pray. And to keep Talya from running off after the men again.

"I cannot wait to hear it, my love." Lappidoth took her elbow and led her toward her tent, away from the throng. "For now, let us gather food and wine and set out to feed these men."

She looked at him, raised a curious brow.

"You don't expect me to allow you and Talya, the only two women in the camp, to serve us all, do you?" He smiled, and Deborah thought it the most perfect smile she had ever seen.

When had she started to love him so? Had she missed something precious in him in years past when she wished he had been something he was not? Or had he been what she wanted all along but she could not see it?

She pondered the thoughts on the way to her tent, her heart light and full of joy.

Talya took a step away from her brothers as they grew immersed in back-slapping and laughter with the returning warriors. She glimpsed her parents heading toward her mother's tent, knowing she should follow to help gather food for the men, but still she hesitated. Emotions of joy and apprehension mingled within her — joy over the victory, apprehension over her future. What was to become of her now?

She would wed, of course. Her parents would find a suitable husband somewhere among the clans represented here, for they would not seek one whose tribe had failed to join the fight. Likely they would want a man from Ephraim or Zebulun or perhaps Naphtali. She searched the sea of men milling about for some sign of Barak. She spotted him speaking to his friend Keshet, surrounded by men from his tribe. He would have no reason to seek her out here. Perhaps he never would.

She shouldn't care. But her mind whirled with confusion, her heart twisting this way and that. She moved away from the gathered men and walked toward the edge of the mountain, the place her mother had often stood these past few days when she looked over the valley to gauge the pace of the war. A shadow passed near and she startled, whirling about, hand on her bow.

"There is no need to fear your cousin, Talya." Shet appeared from behind a tree and stood near her, his gaze fixed on the carnage below. "So the war is over." His words did not sound nearly as jubilant as the rest of the men.

"Yes," Talya said, giving him a sidelong glance. "And yet you do not seem glad of it."

He looked at her, his dark eyes carrying that same pain she had seen in him since the day they discovered Yiskah's betrayal. How would she feel if a husband played the adulterer, as Yiskah had essentially done with her false gods?

"I fear I understand something I do not wish to," he said, raking a hand through unkempt hair.

"And that is?" She knew him well enough to know that he often needed prompting to reveal his thoughts.

His chest lifted and fell in a deep sigh. "Why have we suffered all these years under Sisera and Jabin?" He held her gaze, waiting.

"Ima would say it is because Israel had turned away from the true worship of Adonai Elohim. We became a nation that allowed other gods into our camps, our villages, our hearts." Her mother had been proclaiming a need to repent for many years, though few had listened to her words, and even those who came to her for judgment did not always leave their divided ways.

"And so Adonai sold us into Jabin's hands to test our hearts, to draw us back to Him alone." Shet's words echoed her mother's.

"Until we cried out to Him for relief."

"And yet we cried out for twenty years." Shet's voice held a mix of anger and frustration.

"Perhaps only some of us were ready for redemption," Talya said, suddenly uncertain. Why had it taken so long for Adonai to send relief? The answers did not seem as simple as she once thought.

"How do you think God feels when we betray Him?" Shet's words caught her off guard.

She faced him. "I have never given thought to God's feelings." She could not deny it. How did one equate human feelings with the Almighty? Did God feel as men and women did?

"Well, I have given it much thought. And if we are made to be like Him, if we are His image bearers, then it stands to reason we hurt Him by our unfaithfulness with other gods. Just as Yiskah hurt me when she went off to Canaan to seek refuge rather than return to me and repent." He looked away, the lines of his face drawn as though he had aged as he stood talking with her.

"She felt betrayed when you did not immediately accept her back. You sent her outside the camp for seven days." Talya did not want to defend the woman, and yet she wanted to see Shet free of his grief.

"Did not God send Miriam outside the camp for her harsh words against Moses? Does not a husband have a right to make sure his wife still wants him? Still worships as he does?" He nearly choked on the words, and his voice dropped in pitch. "Still loves him?" He covered his face with both hands and looked away, and Talya knew she was witness to something he could not share with anyone else. But they had grown up together, been friends since childhood.

She touched his shoulder. He shook himself as though ashamed of his display of rare emotion. "Forgive me," he said. "It is not your concern."

"But it is my concern," Talya said, stepping in front of him to force him to look at her once more. "Yiskah has come under my father's care at the direction of my mother. She works in our home as a servant, longing for you to reclaim her." She took his hand in hers. "Shet, I would not say this to you if I had not seen it, but I think Yiskah has changed. I do not think she is the woman who betrayed you, yet she has no words left to make you see it. She is ashamed of what she did and was humbled by the Canaanites. They used her and threw her away. Those she sought refuge with became her enslavers."

The glint of anger in his eyes softened the slightest bit, and Talya squeezed his fingers then released them. "When Israel cried out for mercy, our God delivered us from Sisera, from Jabin. Does that not show us that our God is a God of forgiveness? He wanted to restore us. He wants you to restore your wife and take her to yourself once more." She leaned forward and planted a kiss on his cheek. "Think on what I have said, cousin. To harbor your anger will only destroy you."

She turned and left him, realizing how often her own anger toward her mother had caused rifts and struggles in her life, in her father's house. The thoughts turned over in her mind as she headed to her mother's tent to help with the gathering of food, and she nearly bumped into Ghalib as she neared the tent.

"There you are." He seemed much too pleased to see her, his wide grin filling his round face.

"You are here," she said, smiling in return. "Did you just arrive?" She glanced beyond him for some sign of his family.

He nodded eagerly. "My mother and sisters have come as well. Ima is with your mother now." He angled his head toward Deborah's tent.

She looked in the direction and spotted Ghalib's sister and sisters-in-law. "I should join them. We must find a way to feed all of these men." She moved her arm in an arc over the crowd.

"Who were you talking to just now?" Ghalib's change of subject also came with a change in his tone.

She looked into his eyes, seeing the slightest hint of . . . jealousy? She looked back to where she had come from talking to Shet, but he no longer stood overlooking the valley. She briefly wondered where he had gone, but knew he had probably gone off to think alone.

"I saw you with another man, alone . . ." Ghalib's words trailed off, but his expression looked troubled.

Talya smiled, understanding dawning. "I was speaking to my cousin Shet. We have been friends since childhood. He is the husband of the woman you brought to our camp, whom your father rescued from Jabin. Did you not recognize him?"

Ghalib sighed as if in relief. "I could not tell. His back was to me, and I did not wish to interrupt. You looked as though you were having a serious conversation."

Talya nodded. "We were." She looked into Ghalib's gentle dark eyes, wondering if he would be the type of man who would question her often. "I should really go and help the women." She did not wish to reveal what she had said to Shet. It was not Ghalib's business to know.

He nodded. "Of course."

She turned to walk away, but his touch on her arm made her turn back. "Yes?"

"Later, when you have time, can we talk?" He seemed so eager she could not refuse him.

"Certainly." But she was not sure she wanted to have that conversation. "We have a celebration to attend first," she reminded him. "My mother has written a celebration song." She glanced behind her. "I really must help them."

He nodded, and she hurried off.

"Until later then," he called after her.

She quickened her pace and did not acknowledge that she had heard him.

30

The top of Mount Tabor buzzed with voices as more men, women, and children — many of those who had been rescued from Sisera's and Jabin's enslavement — stood dressed and washed clean in new white linen tunics and fine robes, spoils from their enemies. Barak looked on, searching the faces of the battered, abused women, wishing he could wipe the hollow expressions from their sunken gazes. It would take time, he told himself, for the women Sisera had used for his sexual pleasures to heal, to feel deep down that they were finally safe.

He sighed, the weight still heavy in his chest. This was not a day to mourn, and yet . . . how he wished he could have stopped Sisera even once before this day. For all his efforts, the best he and his men had been able to do had not been enough. A few arrows had been shot against a handful of charioteers, but where one enemy fell, another had arisen. Sisera had laughed at them behind his shield, while two helpless virgins cowered, tied together at the back of his chariot.

Barak shuddered at the memory.

"Strong thoughts trouble you, my lord." Talya's voice jolted him.

He spun to face her and searched her gaze, her dark eyes probing back at him. "Yes," he said, recalling how relieved Deborah and Lappidoth had been the day he had seen the girl safely home to them. She could have been like one of the victims standing in the group, clean yet broken, wondering what life held for her now.

"I did not expect to find you at such a loss for words, my lord." Talya glanced beyond him to the freed captives. "Ah, I see," she said, her gaze too observant.

They shared a look. "What becomes of them?" she asked. The very question he struggled to answer.

"I don't know." He glanced toward the rescued slaves once more, then turned to walk Talya away from the group. "I suppose they will return to their families. Those whose families are gone will live with their closest relations. If there are any truly destitute among them, they will become the servants of the wealthiest in the communities." They strode slowly toward Deborah's tent, where a large crowd had begun to gather.

"Will none of them marry then?" Sadness tinged her voice, and he tilted his head to better look into her eyes.

"This worries you?" He hadn't expected so much compassion to fill those large round eyes.

She nodded. "For all they have endured . . . they should be allowed to live in homes as the happy mother of children." Her declaration made him look at her more closely.

"It will take a strong man to accept a blemished bride." Barak swallowed. Could he do such a thing? When an unblemished one stood before him now, her gaze so earnest, so innocent?

"Are we not all blemished in God's sight?" She tucked a strand of wayward dark hair beneath her headscarf, the very hair that had caused him to declare her a distraction to his men. To him. Though he could not tell her so.

"Yes," he said softly. "Of course. But God is more forgiving than most men." It would take a feat of giants to overcome the images he would see every time he held a woman whom Sisera had used. A better man might not think so, but he knew his own weakness.

Talya lowered her eyes, an action that nearly caused him to gently grip her chin and draw her face close to his. But he stopped himself before making such a grave mistake. She did not belong to him, and he had no promise that she had not already been given to Ghalib or some other man since he had refused her. He groaned inwardly as the dusk cast her form in soft shadows. They were only a short distance now from the milling crowd, and Deborah had emerged from her tent.

He glanced toward her, saw her searching, most likely for him. "I must go," he said abruptly. "Your mother is looking for me."

Talya lifted her gaze to him at that moment, and he nearly stumbled at the look of openness in her eyes. But she said nothing, merely nodded.

He tried once, twice, to pull away from all that he read in that one look, finding it nearly impossible, but at last he mumbled something inane about talking later, and hurried off to meet Deborah. The girl would surely be his undoing.

"There you are," Deborah said, catching sight of Barak at last. "It was hard to find you among so many."

"I was speaking to Talya," he said, his tone curt and irritated.

"Now what has she done?" Deborah shook her head. That girl would find a way to stir up trouble even on a day of victory. She met Barak's gaze, but the look he gave her did not match his tone. Perhaps she had not done anything. "Never mind," she said, motioning him into her tent where Lappidoth and her sons waited. She would sort out the details of Barak and her daughter on a later day.

"I have written a song you must sing with me." Deborah looked at Barak, then pointed to Lappidoth. "My husband has written the parts out for us on some of the soft clay here." She picked up a small rug that held the clay spread over it.

Barak leaned over the words while Lavi held the lamp closer for him to see.

"I have called to the trumpeters and those who have brought anything with which to make music — drums, tambourines, and there are a few reed flutes among us — to accompany us while we sing our praise and thanksgiving to El Yeshuatenu, the God of our salvation, our deliverer." Her heart filled with a sense of sheer joy at the memory of the words that had come to her during her wait with Talya. Adonai, the Lord, deserved the glory and honor for this victory, and Deborah intended to make sure the men of these tribes knew that, lest they be tempted to forsake their God again. They dare not fall into the same traps they had succumbed to before.

"I added to it after I heard Jael's story," she said at Barak's quizzical look. "You are pleased?"

"It is a good song," he said, admiration in his voice.

He stepped back and allowed her to lead them out of the tent. She moved ahead to the center of the camp, Barak on her heels. She raised her arms to quiet the crowd. Silence fell like gentle rain, each man's face eager, even humbled, to hear from their prophetess. *Oh Adonai, I am not worthy.* But the respect in their faces remained.

She cleared her throat and glanced at each one, then lifted her face to the heavens, her heart suddenly beating with the rhythm of a fresh tune. God had delivered them from Sisera! No more would the people of Israel cower behind barred doors or stay off the main roads.

"Freedom has come to Israel this day," she said, her voice carrying over the quieted crowd. "Freedom only El Elyon, the Most

420

High God, our El Echad, the only God, could give to us. He showed us His power over the gods of Canaan, as He once did over the gods of Egypt. So join me now as we worship His Name, as we sing praises to our great King."

The people cheered, and she waited for them to quiet. Barak drew closer and held the clay tablets before her, but she had already committed the words to memory. They took turns singing the verses.

"That the leaders took the lead in Israel" — her voice grew throaty with sudden emotion — "that the people offered themselves willingly, bless the Lord!"

She swallowed, catching her breath as the people shouted, "Bless the Lord!" A trumpet sounded once long and loud. Silence fell again as all looked to her.

"Hear, O kings. Give ear, O princes." Barak's baritone was both soothing and sweet. "To the Lord I will sing. I will make melody to the Lord, the God of Israel."

Deborah chose another verse and Barak followed her lead.

"In the days of Shamgar, son of Anath, in the days of Jael, the highways were abandoned, and travelers kept to the byways."

"The villagers ceased in Israel, they ceased to be until I arose — I, Deborah, arose as a mother in Israel." Deborah paused, looking out over the crowd, searching their faces, lest they think she spoke in pride. "When new gods were chosen" — her voice fell to a near whisper, holding the note long, ominous — "then war was in the gates."

Another pause. The people bowed their heads as though in shame. The flutist played a haunting, sorrowful tune. Deborah waited, letting it play out, allowing the words to sink deep into the hearts of her people. For had new gods not been chosen, they would not be here today. Ruined women would not stand frightened among them, and war would not have come to the gates of their cities.

Barak's voice, still carrying that haunting tone, continued her words. "Was shield or spear to be seen among forty thousand in Israel? My heart goes out to the commanders of Israel who offered themselves willingly among the people. Bless the Lord."

"Bless the Lord," the people said.

"Tell of it, you who ride on white donkeys, you who sit on rich carpets, and you who walk by the way." Deborah's voice rose in pitch. "To the sound of musicians at the watering places, there they repeat the righteous triumphs of the Lord, the righteous triumphs of his villagers in Israel. Then down to the gates marched the people of the Lord."

"Awake, awake, Deborah!" Barak's voice jolted her. "Awake, awake, break out in a song!"

"Arise, Barak, lead away your captives," she joined in again, "O son of Abinoam."

The sounds of trumpets and flutes filled the air, and drums beat to the harmony of the dance. Men moved their feet in time to the music, but the captive women stood still, watching.

"Zebulun is a people who risked their lives to the death," Deborah sang. "Naphtali, too, on the heights of the field. The kings came, they fought, then fought the kings of Canaan at Taanach, by the waters of Megiddo. They got no spoils of silver."

Barak took up again where she left off. "From heaven the stars fought, from their courses they fought against Sisera. The deluge of Kishon swept them away, the ancient torrent, the flood Kishon. March on, my soul, with might!"

"March on, my soul, with might!" The men shouted the response to them both.

Deborah's pulse quickened, and as she looked out over the sea of men, saw the broken women huddled together, her eyes misted. How much her people had suffered.

Please, Adonai, keep us ever faithful to You from this day forward.

She waited a breath until she was certain her voice would not waver, then glanced at Barak and Jael, who was standing not far from their inner circle.

"Most blessed of women be Jael," she said, meeting the woman's gaze, "the wife of Heber the Kenite, of tent-dwelling women most blessed. He asked for water and she gave him milk — she brought him curds in a noble's bowl. She sent her hand to the tent peg and her right hand to the workmen's mallet. She struck Sisera, she crushed his head, she shattered and pierced his temple. Between her feet he sank, he fell, he lay still. Where he sank, there he fell — dead."

A shout of victory followed that nearly shook the earth beneath Deborah's feet. She held steady, waiting for the men to quiet once more, until at last she raised a hand so they would allow her to complete the song God had given her.

"Through the window peered Sisera's mother," Deborah sang, her tone mocking now. "Behind the lattice she cried out, 'Why is his chariot so long in coming? Why is the clatter of his chariots delayed?' The wisest of her ladies answer her; indeed, she keeps

424

saying to herself, 'Are they not finding and dividing the spoils: a woman or two for each man, colorful garments as plunder for Sisera, colorful garments embroidered, highly embroidered garments for my neck — all this as plunder?' "

She looked toward the group of captive women, those whom Sisera's mother would have had no pity on. She motioned them closer, and the men parted, allowing them to come. They came slowly, timidly, and the men surrounded them as if to protect them from ever being hurt again.

"So may all Your enemies perish, O Lord! But Your friends be like the sun as he rises in his might." Deborah raised her arms overhead.

"So may all Your enemies perish, O Lord!" Both the men and some of the captive women joined in that final phrase. Musicians spontaneously continued to play, and the women were given tambourines and coaxed by Talya, who had joined their group, until even the most timid among them rejoiced in the Lord. And danced.

31

The feasting lasted long into the night, as men and women repeated Deborah's song over and over again until they had memorized parts of it. Deborah sat in the opening of her tent, her heart beating with the sense of satisfaction. Adonai had heard and answered and given them victory over their enemies, though she knew there were still men among the clans of Israel who did not follow Adonai El Yisrael, the Lord God of Israel, with a pure heart.

She shivered at the thought of what might become of their land in the future, the land her grandchildren would inherit, if the people lost faith again. Somehow she must make it clear to them even now that they dare not take lightly the mercy of their God.

She stirred at the sound of voices drawing near and looked up to see Jael and Heber with Ghalib in tow. She straightened and motioned for them to join her. "Please, sit

426

by the fire and rest yourselves."

"Thank you, Prophetess," Jael said, taking the makeshift stone seat closest to Deborah. Her husband sat at her side, looking most uncomfortable, while Ghalib remained standing behind them. "We have come to seek your blessing."

Deborah tilted her head and gave Jael a curious look. "You need not seek it, for you surely have it already."

More voices drew close, noisier than the Kenites. Deborah recognized the sound of her sons' laughter and saw Lappidoth and Barak also among them. They spoke between themselves, so Deborah turned her attention to Jael once more.

"How can I help you, Jael? After what you have done for Israel, we owe you much."

Jael glanced at her husband, then back at Deborah. Tight lines formed along her mouth, and Deborah wondered what troubled this woman who had so bravely killed Sisera. "You owe me nothing, Prophetess. I only did what anyone would do in such a circumstance."

"Not everyone would do such a thing. Whole towns were not strong enough to capture Sisera. Yet a woman alone put an end to this nemesis. So on the contrary, Israel owes you a great debt." Deborah watched Jael's face soften slightly, but her hands were clasped tightly in her lap.

"It is not Israel we petition," Jael said so softly that Deborah had to lean closer to hear her. "We have come on behalf of our son, who seeks your daughter Talya as his wife."

Deborah leaned away, studying the trio. She should not be surprised by this request. Had she not seen the way Ghalib looked at Talya? Yet what of Barak? The man had clearly been rattled by his recent discussion with the girl. If only Barak had been ready for another wife months ago when Talya had so clearly wanted him.

Her men's voices grew louder, and they entered the circle of the fire in front of her tent. "There you are, Ima," Lavi said, smiling. He glanced at Barak. "Settle a dispute for me. This man insists that he must return to his village at dawn, when I say he must come with us to our village and allow us to show him hospitality without the threat of war." Lavi crossed his arms, a self-satisfied grin on his face as though he knew Deborah would side in his favor.

She looked from her men to Barak, pausing momentarily to try to read the thoughts behind those hooded dark eyes. "Barak knows he is always welcome in our village, my son," she said, her words measured. "But Lavi is right, Commander. The humble home of Lappidoth would heartily welcome you."

Barak tipped his head in her direction. "It is kind of you, Prophetess." He glanced beyond her, and Deborah followed the direction of his gaze. Talya stood in the shadows on the side where her brothers sat, opposite Jael and her family.

She had not expected to make a decision for Talya's future for many days to come, and in truth, she was weary, too weary for such a thing so soon after the victory. But the Kenites would be returning home, so it made sense for them to want some type of answer, to know whether their request was one she and Lappidoth would welcome.

Deborah folded her hands in her lap and looked down at their callouses. A lifetime of work showed on her fingertips. A woman did not stop working in the daily tasks simply to settle one dispute or another.

"I am afraid I cannot give you an answer just now," Deborah said, looking at Jael. "I must discuss the matter with my husband and think on it. May I give you an answer in a week? I will send a messenger to you with our decision one way or the other."

Jael seemed to ponder Deborah's words a

moment before looking to her husband and son. Ghalib did not look pleased. Not a patient man? But she supposed a man in love would be anxious to know his choice was a good one.

"We will wait, Prophetess. And thank you." Jael rose gracefully, Heber with her. The three left the campsite to join the rest of their family in tents some distance away.

"What did they want, Ima?" Lavi, ever the curious one, intruded on her thoughts.

Deborah glanced at her son, this lion of a man, and could not keep the pride from her gaze. "You are a good son, Lavi." She looked to Elior. "As are you, Elior. I am most blessed to have the gift of you both. But Jael's business does not concern you right now. It is between your father and me."

"And me," Talya said, stepping closer and taking a seat beside her mother. "Whatever is decided, please consult me."

Deborah placed a hand on Talya's arm. Surely a mother's choices for her daughter were best. Her own mother might have chosen Lappidoth for her against her wishes, but she could not look upon him now with regret.

Still, she looked into Talya's pleading gaze, recalling the very feelings Talya certainly faced now. "We will discuss it with you,"

430

she promised. "Now, if you will excuse me." She rose to enter her tent with a glance back at Lappidoth, who was listening to something Barak was saying into his ear.

Did Barak know what had just transpired here? Could he see what Deborah saw in her daughter's eyes — a heart that beat with love for him? For if Deborah had to choose between the two men this moment, she knew she would choose Barak over Ghalib.

Except Barak was not the one doing the asking.

"Why did you not press the matter, Ima?" Ghalib's pout reminded Jael of the young boy he once was, and she did not like the image of a man acting like a child now.

"The timing was not right." Jael looked from her son to Heber. "We should have waited, gone to visit them after all is settled. We had no time to discuss your desire to join Israel, to show them that an alliance with us would not compromise their faith in their God. It was foolish to act so rashly, and now at a time when the whole land is concerned with celebrating their God's victory and cleaning up after such a war." She paced the tent they shared, small in comparison to the ones they left under the oak of Zaanannim.

"Your mother is right," Heber said, sinking to his mat, his whole body rigid. She sensed his unease, even the anger bubbling within him. He was not a man who easily gave in to useless pursuits, but Ghalib had cowed them both in the height of revelry. He rubbed his head, then began to untie his sandals. "I agreed to this ridiculous attempt to secure the prophetess's promise because I have failed to get you a wife from my brother's clan." He tossed his sandals into a corner and stretched out on the mat, hands behind his head. "But I am tired, Ghalib. You must learn patience, my son, if you truly hope to get what it is you want." He suddenly leaned up on one elbow and looked past Jael to meet Ghalib's bewildered gaze. "But be very sure it is Talya you want. I do not think you are her only suitor."

"Which is exactly why I wanted you to secure her for me now!" Ghalib's outburst startled Jael. She stopped her pacing and waited for Heber to respond, if he would.

"My son, you are not ready to take a wife," Heber said at last. "A man is not a man who cannot control his temper." He rolled onto his side then, away from Ghalib, indicating the conversation at an end.

"Like you controlled your temper with my uncle?" The words were sharp barbs, sinking deep into Jael's heart.

"Don't say such things, my son," she said, attempting to soothe the suddenly charged air. "The anger that sent us away from our people was your uncle's, not your father's. When you can accept that, perhaps you can also accept the fact that a woman like Talya does not need a husband who will jealously guard her every move. I have seen the way you look at her when another man speaks to her. Such jealousy might seem admirable, but it hides a lack of trust." Jael crossed her arms over her chest and stared her son down.

Ghalib looked as if he would challenge her, but one glance toward his father's back seemed to deflate his anger. Though by the spark in his eyes, she knew the anger still simmered.

She took a step closer, placed a hand on Ghalib's arm. He did not pull away when she coaxed him to meet her gaze.

"I love her, Ima," he said, his voice low, husky. "I've never met anyone like her."

"And yet you have met very few women, my son. You do not know if another might be better suited to you." She cupped his cheek, wishing she could hold him as she once did when he rocked in her arms as a small child. "I know you long for a wife, and you think Talya is that woman. But she has eyes for another. Did you not see it in the firelight tonight when she stepped into the shadows?"

Ghalib's expression moved from anger to hurt, and he suddenly pulled away and took a step back from her. "She thinks she cares for Barak," he said. "But I do not see that he cares for her in return. When they speak, they argue. And if she truly cared for him, she would obey him, but she did not even respect his role as commander and ran off to fight in the battle despite his orders."

Heber's low laughter came from the mat, and Jael could not hide a smile. "Forgive me, my son. We do not laugh at you, but at your lack of understanding. Sometimes the spark of attraction ignites arguments. It does not mean there is no love hidden beneath."

"We have spared you many an argument, my son," Heber said without rising. "You have much to learn about women."

Ghalib huffed but did not speak. He looked from his mother to his father's back, seeming as though he wanted to say something, but then shook his head and left the tent. Jael watched him go, his stride strong but his shoulders slumped. They had dealt him a blow tonight. Deborah had as well, and his pride would surely suffer for it.

The thought troubled her as she stepped into starlight and watched her son stalk off into darkness. Such a gentle and kind though sometimes frustrated soul was her Ghalib. One whose pride held too much sway over his heart.

She turned back to the tent and sank down beside Heber. "Will he be all right?" she asked, wanting desperately to run after him but knowing how foolish that action would be.

"He will recover," Heber said, grunting and repositioning himself. "Give him time." He released a deep sigh, and Jael waited for the sound of his soft snores. But a moment later his arm came around her. "I will send to my brother again, and peace or not between us, I will request Parisa as a wife for Ghalib."

It was a sacrifice for him to say so. She leaned into him, grateful for this humble gift, but worried that Ghalib might not so easily accept it.

Dawn bathed the mountain in soft pink light, and Talya stood outside her mother's tent facing the east, watching as the colors danced along the ridge. The camp was just beginning to stir, and soon the men would take down the tents and return toward their towns and villages. She moved softly on bare feet from the makeshift courtyard along the row of tents toward the ridge. The valley spread before her, the stench of death replaced by the smell of ash left from the fires the men had set to destroy what remained of Sisera's army. Only the iron chariot wheels were visible here and there, stuck to the earth as though they had grown up from the ground.

She placed a hand over her eyes to better see into the distance. She shivered, pulling her cloak closer.

"You're up early."

She turned slowly to face her cousin Shet. "As are you," she said, searching his gaze. "Have you made a decision?"

Something determined flickered in his eyes, but he glanced beyond her. He rubbed his hands together as if to warm them. "Did you see the looks on the faces of the captives we rescued?" He glanced at her then, and she was taken back to that moment, seeing it now through his eyes.

"I saw. I could have been one of them." Talya fixed the scarf that the wind wanted to snatch from her head. They stood outside of the tree line, where the windbreak would normally block the stiff breeze.

He touched her shoulder. "I am glad Barak found you." His voice cracked. "I am sorry Yiskah's behavior caused you such risk."

"It is of no consequence now," she said. "She has learned a terrible lesson for her rash acts." She searched his face, saw his jaw tighten and a muscle move over his left eyebrow, a sign of his anxiety barely held back by his self-control.

"You are going to put Yiskah out?" she asked when he did not speak. The thought pained her.

"No," he said slowly. "I am going to take her back." His breath rushed from him as though the words took all of his strength. "Mind you, it will not be easy. I do not even know if I love her still." He stroked his beard. "I know I do not trust her."

"And yet you would take her again as your wife? What if she does not wish to come? If you cannot offer her love or trust, what will you give her?" Talya straightened, a sense of protectiveness for Yiskah, for all of the women whom Sisera had taken, rising within her like a solid force.

"I will give her time," Shet said softly, pushing the anger from Talya's heart. "I will forgive what she has done and offer her a home. It is all I can do."

Talya studied her feet, suddenly ashamed

that she had judged him so. "I am sorry. I expected the worst." She met his gaze and caught him smiling down at her.

"And you would have gotten what you expected if not for the sight of those broken, innocent women." He paused. "Though Yiskah was not innocent, she did not deserve to be abused."

He looked behind them at the waking camp. The female former captives huddled around a handful of tents, busily loading their few new belongings onto white donkeys, bounty taken from Sisera.

"At least Yiskah has a husband to return to." Talya touched his arm. "You take a great risk in forgiving. Only a great man would risk his heart a second time."

"A third," he corrected. "If she had not run away . . ." He left the sentence unfinished.

"There is no sense in thinking about the past, cousin." Talya linked her arm through his. "Come, let us help the rest of the camp prepare. It is time to go home."

32

Barak tightened the last of his gear to the strap of his belt, felt the hilt of his sword out of habit more than need now, and headed toward the edge of the mountain, where his men had already begun to move toward their homes. He spotted Keshet talking to someone. One glance and he knew the object of Keshet's attention. Daniyah the Kenite. He looked away, fighting the sinking feeling in his gut. Why shouldn't his friend seek a wife now that the danger had passed? He imagined many of the men would quickly return to the lives they knew or the ones they hoped to build now that they could live in safety, even prosperity, should God allow.

He looked past Keshet for a sign of Ghalib. No doubt the boy would be hounding Talya now that Jael and Heber had asked Deborah for a marriage alliance. And why should he care? He had refused Talya's attempt to woo him and Deborah's willingness to accept him as a son. He raked a hand over his neck, nearly sending his turban to the dirt. There was no use trying to return to what had passed.

But he could not shut out that vulnerable look Talya had given him. She had revealed herself in a way she had never done before. He squinted, searching the crowd for her. Trust. That was the look she had offered freely. One of trust in him.

The sinking feeling lifted slightly. Was it possible? Perhaps it was not too late.

He moved on past several groups of men still packing or slowly making their way toward the path. Deborah's tent had come down long ago, and though her family had invited him to join them, to return to their village, he had refused Lavi's prompting. But his gut told him to speak to Lappidoth before they parted ways. Who knew when he would get the chance to see them again?

He shaded his eyes, searching. There. Lappidoth stood several paces from Deborah. Lavi and Elior and their cousin Shet led donkeys laden with supplies ahead of them, while Talya walked beside her mother. Good. Lappidoth appeared far enough apart for Barak to speak to him alone.

Barak quickened his step to catch up with

the man. Was this action foolish on his part? He found Talya annoyingly intriguing, the exact opposite of Nessa. Could he live with a woman so entirely different from his first love? He paused, uncertain again, and slowed his step.

"Barak, my friend, there you are." Keshet spoke from his right, startling him.

"You should not sneak up on your friends."

"And you should not let me." Keshet chuckled. "Obviously, some thought has taken you far away." He touched Barak's shoulder, his look too telling. "You know it is time to move on, Barak. Find another wife. Otherwise your soul will always be bound to a place you cannot go and a person you cannot hold close again."

Barak stiffened. "You know nothing of it."

"True. I don't know that kind of loss. But I hope to know that kind of love." Keshet's smile widened.

Barak stopped walking. "Daniyah?"

Keshet nodded, his dark eyes shining. "I have spoken with her and with her father. They are agreeable."

Barak took a step back, assessing. But a moment later he clapped Keshet on the back. "When we arrive home, we will gather everyone in town to celebrate with you." He smiled, hoping the gesture did not look as forced as it felt.

"Ghalib hopes to wed Talya," Keshet said, continuing to walk forward with the throng. "Daniyah told me her brother is not sure what he wants. He pines after a cousin *and* after Talya. I am going to assume he doesn't expect to have both." He glanced around and leaned closer. "I thought you should know." His look said more than his words.

Barak nodded. "They spoke to Deborah last night." The sinking feeling settled once more inside of him.

"Are you going to say nothing then?" Keshet shifted the pack on his shoulder.

Barak glanced ahead to where Lappidoth still walked one pace behind Deborah and Talya rather than ahead of them with his sons. "He carries a weight," Barak said absently, ignoring Keshet's question, inclining his head toward Lappidoth several steps away.

Keshet followed his gaze. "So you do intend to speak with him?"

Barak gave him a sidelong glance. "You don't give up, do you?"

Keshet smiled again, the smile of one who has conquered his world. "Not if I don't have to." He put one meaty arm around Barak's shoulder. "I love Daniyah, but I do not think her brother is the best person for Deborah's daughter." He released his grip and strode ahead, glancing back once to give Barak a confident look.

Barak did not respond, but his feet seemed to increase their pace of their own accord as he considered seeking an audience with Lappidoth.

"You're terribly quiet, my daughter," Deborah said as the two of them followed her sons down the winding path to the base of Mount Tabor. They'd been walking since just after sunup and were nearly halfway down the mount. "What troubles you?"

Talya took a step behind her mother as they maneuvered a narrow spot in the turn. Deborah waited as they came around the bend for her daughter to join her once more.

"I don't want to marry Ghalib," Talya said, her voice low. "I do not want to marry outside of Israel."

Deborah looked ahead, catching sight of a trio of mountain goats climbing the rock to the place they had just been. "Then you shall not marry him."

Talya looked at her, eyes slowly widening. "That's it then? You will accept my wishes without consulting my father?"

Deborah released a sigh. "I have already

discussed it with your father, Talya. It is not something we have wanted. But at the same time, Jael did a great service for Israel. To refuse them will not be easy."

Talya settled her gaze somewhere in the distance. "I still want to marry Barak."

Deborah studied her daughter, noting the bright flush to her cheeks. "And if Barak still grieves Nessa?" she asked after a lengthy pause. "Would you wait for him, even if it meant waiting many years?" She touched Talya's arm. "I would not wish that for you."

Talya dropped her gaze and kicked a stone in the dirt. "Perhaps Father could ask him just the same."

We have already been refused. But Deborah felt a check in her spirit. Now was not the time to remind Talya of her failed attempts of the past.

"I've seen the way he looks at me, Ima. Whether he is over Nessa or not, there is interest in his gaze. I've felt it." She picked up the belt of her robe and twirled it between her fingers as though the whole subject made her nervous.

"I will speak with your father again once we camp for the night," she promised. Surely Lappidoth would agree with her assessment. Just because he had refused Talya once did not mean he would do so again. But suddenly Deborah was not sure that he could be so easily controlled. A soft shiver moved through her at this new feeling toward her husband.

Talya gave Deborah an uncharacteristic hug. "Thank you, Ima."

Deborah touched her daughter's cheek. "Don't hope too quickly, my daughter. If Barak does not share your feelings, or if your father does not agree, you must accept it."

Talya released her hold, her brow furrowed. "Abba will agree. Surely he will. Has he said something?"

Deborah patted her daughter's arm. How unusual for both of them, this feeling that Lappidoth might give an opinion they would not like. "He has said nothing against Barak. But I would not proceed without his blessing." And suddenly she wanted far more than Lappidoth's blessing. She wanted him.

Talya hugged her again. "Abba will say yes, and Barak will accept me." Her grin did not waver.

Such overconfidence and naivety in the hearts of the young. But Deborah accepted this rare camaraderie as a good sign and walked along while Talya fairly skipped beside her.

Barak sat at the campfire in the midst of a sea of tents that his men had pitched for the night. Mount Tabor stood at his back, and the Jezreel Valley, where the bones of the slain were now buried in thick, drying mud, lay to their west. Keshet had left his side to sit with Heber and his family, no doubt anxious to set a time for Daniyah to become his wife. The sound of the bridegroom in the streets had not been heard during Sisera's terror. People were ready to find joy again.

He stirred the fire with a green twig, watching the flames fly upward. He never had found the courage to approach Lappidoth or speak to him of Talya. Every thought of her held confusion, though he also could not seem to put her from his mind.

He released a long-held breath as movement caught his eye from the shadows, and he glimpsed Deborah approaching.

"Come to join a lonely captain, Prophetess?" He smiled and stood, offering her his seat.

She waved off his gesture of kindness. "Don't trouble yourself. I have not come to stay."

He remained where he stood, his stomach

doing an uneasy flip at the look in her eyes. "Is something wrong?"

She studied him, her expression revealing little. "My daughter's heart is bound to you, my lord. Months ago, she expressed her desires in an immature and inappropriate way." Deborah lowered her gaze, and she seemed overly concerned with the way her belt was tied at the waist. "She does not always listen, nor did she obey your command when the time came for war." A sigh escaped, but with it her head lifted and she faced him once more. "She is still a woman to contend with at times, but I see much maturity in her in recent days." Her gaze searched his. "I have come to see if your thoughts on remarriage have changed."

His mind stirred with the memory of the awkward position Talya had placed him in should anyone but Deborah have discovered them. But in the same moment, he saw that vulnerable glimpse of Talya's trust, vivid in her bright dark eyes. He had thought of little else since.

But was he ready to admit such a thing? He swallowed as his gaze swept the area around them. No sign of the Kenites or Keshet or Deborah's family. Satisfied that they were truly alone, he took a step closer to Deborah.

"I was under the impression the offer was no longer mine to accept." He could see now that he should have followed through with the desire to speak to Lappidoth on the trek down the mount, but he could not bring himself to discover he had lost out to a boy.

"The offer, though never officially made, was also never rescinded, my friend," Deborah said quietly. "It was refused." She crossed her arms, and he could not tell by her expression whether she was angry or holding herself in a state of self-protection.

He looked at his feet and dug his toe into the ash near the edge of the fire. "If the offer still stands," he said carefully, "it would not be refused a second time."

He heard the air release from her lungs and looked up to meet her gaze.

"You have made peace with Nessa's parting then?" Her brows drew together, and he suddenly saw why the people of his nation called her a mother in Israel. Truly, she seemed to care about him as a mother would her child. Certainly she cared about her daughter's feelings, despite their differences and frequent disagreements. Why else come to him without her husband? She would not risk her husband's pride nor her daughter's heart to hear him push them away a second time.

He nodded. "As best as a man can do, I suppose. Nessa will always live here." He placed a hand on his chest where his heart beat strong beneath it, and at his middle, the seat of his emotions.

"As she should," Deborah said, her arms resting now at her sides. "I do not expect you to forget her. I only need to know whether my daughter will regret spending her life with a man who has already loved well."

He flushed hot at the sudden intimate turn of the conversation. He should be having this discussion, which would be a much less probing one, with Lappidoth. But he knew he could never get past the prophetess without her searching out the very depths of his thinking.

"Your daughter may regret wanting to be with a man like me, but it would not be for lack of love." He looked beyond her, embarrassed at his words, and yet somehow glad he had said them.

Deborah's soft chuckle made him glance at her once more. "The two of you will likely be at war over one thing or another, and I daresay I am not sure who will win." She smiled, and he returned it. "But if you will treat her kindly, our offer to you stands."

His stomach flipped over again, this time with a sense of hope, even anticipation. "What of Ghalib? They are closer in age."

"Are you looking for excuses?" Deborah searched his face, but her eyes held a hint of mischief.

He relaxed. "Not at all. But I assume Jael and Heber did not visit you yesterday, with Ghalib following like a lost sheep, for no reason."

She tilted her head and gave him a curious look. "You do not like Ghalib." A certain knowingness crept into her gaze. "That is why you keep your distance when he is near. Or try to."

"I do not dislike Ghalib," Barak said, straightening.

"I will not argue the point with you, Commander." She gave him a pointed look. "If you are agreeable, I will ask Lappidoth to speak with you to settle the terms of the marriage."

He nodded once. Whatever Deborah and Lappidoth had decided regarding Ghalib, it did not concern him now.

She turned and left him alone, and he stood still, facing the fire. His heart quickened as he allowed his mind to recall Talya's trusting gaze.

So she would be his after all. The thought made him smile.

33

Deborah's mind soared and her feet hurried as she returned to her tent where Lappidoth waited. Her heart sang with the new remarkable thought — Barak wanted to marry Talya. And Talya wanted him — so foreign to what Deborah had known in her quickly forced marriage. How often had she wished she had been allowed a choice. But now . . .

She paused at the tent's door to catch her breath. So much had happened in only a week's time. And yet she could not deny the way her thoughts had changed toward the man she called husband. Her heart beat in an unexpected rhythm, one of need, of deep longing, for him alone. He stepped out of the tent at that moment, a twig he used to draw letters in his hand.

"Can we take a walk?" she asked when she drew close to him. "I know we have walked all day, but I must speak with you and I cannot sit still."

His warm yet quizzical smile filled her with a sense of rightness. He left the stick beside the tent and took her hand, intertwining their fingers. Dusk had long since turned to blackness, but when she reached to take a torch, he said, "Leave it. There are plenty of fires about the camp. We will be guided by them and by the glow of the moon."

She squeezed his hand and fell into step with him, allowing him to guide her among the rows of tents. When they had passed those closest to them and stepped into a clearing away from the crowd of men, he stopped and gently turned her to face him.

"You are troubled, my love. Or you have news. Tell me." He stroked her cheek, sending soft tingles through her. How long had it been since he had attempted to love her like this, slowly wooing her? Their relationship had become stale, one of duty more than desire. What was this new feeling stirring inside of her?

"I . . ." She stopped, suddenly too aware of him. "I am not troubled. I simply wanted to tell you . . ." She paused as his finger traced a line up her arm, then along her jaw.

"Tell me what, my love?" He cupped both

hands along the sides of her face and bent his lips to lightly brush the edges of hers.

"Why do you love me?" Her voice was husky, and she feared she would weep if she did not force her emotions in check.

He pulled her close, his mouth bent over hers. "Ah, Deborah . . ." He kissed her again, possessive, determined, yet in his familiar, gentle way. "I have never been bold, never had the courage to even speak to you when I first came to live with my uncle after I lost my family." He stroked her cheek again, trailed his fingers through her hair. "The first time I glimpsed you at the well, the first time I saw you dance at a wine treading, I knew I had lost my heart to you."

Moisture filled her eyes, and he brushed an errant tear away with his thumb. "What is this about, beloved? Why the questions here, now?"

"Barak is willing to marry Talya." She swallowed hard. "In all of the talk of which man was right for her . . . and when you said you loved me . . . and then you stood up to our daughter." She stopped, touched her burning cheeks. "I have asked myself why I could not love you all these years. I fear I have failed you." She looked at her feet, unable to meet his tender gaze.

"I have always known of your feelings,

Deborah." Lappidoth spoke so softly she nearly did not hear him past the thoughts whirring in her head. He cupped her face once more and leaned so close she could feel his warm breath. "You were young and fearful, and I daresay you longed for another when my uncle came calling on your father's door." He tipped her chin upward. "I believe Amichai held your heart then." A shadow crossed his fine features, but he did not ask what she sensed was on the tip of his tongue.

"Amichai lost my respect long ago," she assured him. She gave him an awkward smile. "But you, my husband, have earned it."

He took her hand and kissed her fingers. "I'm glad of it." He intertwined their hands again, his strong, solid fingers holding hers in a bold, possessive grip.

She squeezed his hand. "But I would not disrespect you now, my husband, and fail to seek your blessing. Shall we offer Barak Talya's hand in marriage?"

"Barak will make a fine husband for her," he said, his smile warm in the moon's soft glow. "You were right to seek him out and ask him a second time. If I had spoken to him, his refusal would have been a dishonor to us both." He drew her alongside him. "Thank you, my love, for sparing this blow to my pride."

She nodded, wondering at this new heightened feeling she felt in his presence. Was this what young lovers were meant to feel? She blushed at the thought.

"So you will speak to him and to Heber? I do not think I have the strength to face Jael and tell her no." Though she could not recall ever claiming such weakness in times past, she truly did not have the strength just now.

"I will speak to both men before we break camp at dawn."

"Perhaps you should speak to Barak tonight, if he is still at the campfire." She fell into step with him as they wove their way back through the sea of tents.

"I have better plans for tonight." He slanted his gaze at her and winked.

She quickened her pace to keep up with him.

Jael looked up from removing a peg from the ground to dismantle her tent. Heber's voice drew her attention, and she glimpsed Lappidoth striding toward them. Alone. She glanced about for signs of her family. The girls moved back and forth, busily packing the few belongings on the backs of donkeys, while Mahir and Fareed spoke with Keshet.

No sign of Ghalib.

She straightened, unable to keep the foreboding from her heart at Lappidoth's expression. He would not be here unless they had already come to a decision about Talya's future. She moved away from the work she was doing to join Heber at Lappidoth's approach.

"Greetings," Heber said, his arms open in a welcoming embrace. Each man kissed the other's cheeks, then stepped back, keeping an arm's length between them. Lappidoth acknowledged Jael with a nod. "I assume you have come to a decision?"

Lappidoth held her husband's gaze. "Yes." He looked from one to the other, his expression holding a hint of sadness.

Jael held her breath, waiting, though she knew the words he would say.

"I must explain to you that before your son met our daughter, we had already offered her to another man. That man was still grieving his first wife and needed time." Lappidoth clasped his hands, but no sign of nervousness entered his dark eyes. "I am sorry we could not tell you this at the time of your request. Please forgive us for not giving you an immediate answer."

"It was not an answer you could give straightaway," Heber said, his tone reasonable. "My wife made the request of your wife. It was meant to see the possibility. Obviously your wife needed to seek your word in the matter."

Lappidoth gave a nod of agreement. "I only hope your son does not see this as a slight against him. Ghalib is a good man — one any woman would be proud to wed." He straightened and glanced over the area as if searching for the object of their discussion.

"We will tell him you said so," Jael said, crossing both arms, realizing she felt suddenly cold. Daniyah would wed before Ghalib? She was younger and a woman! Unheard of. But unless Heber sent quickly to his brother, Ghalib had no other prospects.

"Thank you for telling us so quickly, my lord," Heber said, bowing to the man. "You do us a kindness not to make us wait. But please, do not let this come between our families. The household of Heber will remain allied with Israel from this day forward." He smiled and tilted his head toward the area where Fareed and Mahir laughed freely with Keshet. "As you can see, my new son-in-law will make sure of that."

Lappidoth followed Heber's gaze and smiled in return. "Keshet is to marry your daughter then?"

"Yes," Heber said, a hint of pride in his voice. "And by the sound of things, he wants her very soon."

Lappidoth chuckled, a pleasant sound, and Jael found that despite the news he had brought, she couldn't fault the man. He was a likable man and one whom Ghalib admired.

"I wish your daughter great happiness with the man you have chosen," Jael said, surprised to realize that she truly was happy for the girl. "May I ask who?"

Lappidoth looked at Heber when he spoke. "Barak, son of Abinoam."

"The commander of Israel's armies. A good choice, my lord," Heber said, grasping the man's hand and shaking it. He laughed, though Jael did not find the matter all that humorous. "Ghalib will not mind losing out to such a man. It would be wrong for the commander to lose the woman he loves to a man not of your people."

"Thank you, my lord," Lappidoth said, bowing graciously toward Heber.

More words were said, but Jael tuned them out. So Barak would marry the daughter of the prophetess. She smiled, glad of it, for Barak had been kind to them. But when she turned to disassemble the rest of her tent, she saw Ghalib standing nearby. One look told her he had heard. She went to him, but he turned abruptly and walked away.

Jael caught up with Ghalib several hours after they had departed the Israelite campsite. Keshet had left them to return home to set things in order. He promised a quick return for Daniyah, who could not stop talking about her betrothed. Jael had listened to her, glad in her joy, but her mother's heart ached for the son who walked dejectedly ahead of her now.

She quickened her pace until she fell into step beside him. "You will wear me out walking so fast, my son." She spoke lightly, hoping to keep him from tromping off again.

To her surprise, he slowed to match her stride. "I'm sorry, Ima. I needed time alone."

"I know." She touched his arm, glad when he did not pull away. "I know you cared for the girl."

"They should have told us she was promised to another. Why did they let me think I had a chance?" Anger seeped into his tone, and Jael lifted a silent gaze heavenward, praying for understanding.

"I do not think they knew for sure themselves, Ghalib. Barak was still grieving his

460

first wife. They were giving him time." She sighed when he simply huffed and remained silent.

They walked without speaking for many moments, until Jael wondered if the boy would say any more. When he spoke, his words were softer, filled with less anger. "I hope she is happy with him. I think I always knew she loved someone else." He looked away as though the admission embarrassed him. "Besides, I knew they didn't want her to marry outside of Israel. It was a risk to ask."

"But a risk worth taking," Jael said. "For now you know the direction you must take."

He nodded, but his expression was distracted, as though his thoughts were far off. "Perhaps I will never marry."

"What?" Her heart thumped hard at the unexpected words. "Every man marries. Why would you say such a thing?"

"Not every man," he said, his voice holding challenge. "Perhaps God has other plans for me."

"Perhaps God has saved Parisa for you, you mean."

He shrugged.

"Enough of this talk of nonsense. Your father has agreed to send to your uncle. If not Parisa, another woman will come from our family." Heber could not act soon enough as far as Jael was concerned.

"If Abba would send someone to fetch me a wife, I will go with him and do so myself." Ghalib stopped walking to face her. "I am no longer a child, Ima. And I do not trust my uncle to send me a wife who is fair to look upon or one who will find me pleasing. If Parisa is no longer free, I must know. I have many cousins and not all are acceptable. I will go."

Jael shook her head. Since when had this son grown so bold? Even daughters offered opinions they were not entitled to these days. She raised her hands in a gesture of defeat. "Ach! You will send me to my grave with worry, you hear me?"

He laughed, a sound she had not heard in many weeks. Good. Let him laugh, even if it must be at her expense.

"You laugh at my worry? And what makes you think this is humorous?" She crossed her arms, pretending to be offended. "You will not go alone, my son."

"I will take a servant or two."

"Your brother or father will go as well. I do not trust your uncle to be fair." What did the boy know about marriage contracts or the struggles of Heber's family? He was too young to understand, even now at mar-

462

riageable age.

Ghalib smiled. "As you wish, Ima. I cannot have you fussing over me or blaming me for sending you to your grave, now can I? You will come back and give me no peace whatsoever."

She chucked him on the shoulder and linked her arm through his. "You are a good son, you know that?"

He sighed, and she knew that despite his agreement to marry a girl from their tribe, he would take many months to forget Talya. Sometimes a man did not always get to marry the woman he longed for. Memories of another time, a cousin Heber had favored, popped into her mind. He would have married another if he could have had his way, and yet he had never made her feel as though she were his second choice. Ghalib would do well to treat his future wife the same.

"Trust me, son. I know of what I speak." He gave her a quizzical look, for she knew he could not read her thoughts, but he did not push for an explanation. She walked on with him, relieved when the familiar oaks of Zaanannim came into sight.

Barak settled the lone pack on his back and looked around at his men. Most of the tents had come down at the break of dawn, and over half of the men had dispersed, back to their towns and villages in the tribal lands. Barak stood at the banked fire, weighing what to do next. Go home to Kedesh-naphtali or follow Lappidoth's family to their village and wed Talya now?

His heart quickened at the thought. He had not spoken to Talya since Deborah's visit last night or Lappidoth's visit early this morning, something he must soon bring himself to do. But should he take her back with him to the house he had shared with Nessa? Or stay with Deborah and Lappidoth, becoming part of their larger clan?

Voices drew his attention, and he recognized Talya's among them. He turned to see her deep in conversation with her cousin Shet.

"You have no need to be nervous, cousin," Talya said, her head tipped back, her pose confident. "Yiskah will welcome you. But you must be patient with her. You do not know how she feels over what she has endured."

Barak tilted his head to better hear. He knew Talya was close to her cousin, but their interchange intrigued him.

"I will be kind to her. Do not fear." Shet ran a hand over his beard — a beard that by the looks of it was in need of a long wash in the river. Had the man poured ashes in his hair?

Talya placed a hand on his shoulder. "You have mourned her," she said simply, observing what Barak had noticed.

"I have mourned her unfaithfulness, her purity, and all that we once shared," he admitted, his expression still showing his grief. "I thought it fitting to grieve before I see her again."

"Our God is not far from the broken-hearted." Talya removed her arm, then bent to kiss his cheek.

Shet took her hand in both of his. "I am grateful to you, cousin. My family will appreciate your visiting when you can. And Yiskah and I would welcome you as well."

Talya said something more, but her voice had dropped low enough that Barak could no longer hear her. Shet left her then and headed toward the river, while Talya turned in the direction of her parents' tent.

"Talya," Barak called to her as he walked quickly closer. "Wait."

She stopped to face him. "Barak."

He smiled. "That is my name, yes."

A slow smile tipped the corners of her mouth. "A name I find easy to speak."

"A pleasing name, I hope." He bent close

to better see her eyes.

She seemed concerned with her feet, for she would not meet his gaze. "Yes," she said. "A well-pleasing name."

"Then you will not mind saying it often in years to come?" He lifted her chin with a finger.

She cleared her throat and then slowly nodded. "As long as I can say it to summon you to a meal or to ask you a question or to . . ." She let the words hang in the air between them, but he read desire in her eyes.

"Whisper it in my ear?" he finished for her.

She nodded, even as her cheeks flushed. He cupped her face, longing to pull the veil from her head and loose the strands of her dark hair in his rough hands. The urge to kiss her suddenly overpowered him, but he forced himself to take a step back.

"Your father has offered me your hand in marriage. I accepted." He waited, watching her.

A sigh escaped her, along with a look of contentment. She smiled, a smile of innocence and longing. "I am glad," she said, searching his face. "Will you come for me soon then? Will we live in Kedesh-naphtali?"

He suddenly was not certain he could

answer, nor wanted to answer without seeking her opinion. "Would you like that?" He reached for her hand, then kissed and held it.

Her breath hitched, and the sound delighted him. She loved him. He sensed it in every look, in every vulnerable glimpse.

"I would like to wed soon," she said. "If we must wait a year, I think I will go mad with longing." She gave a nervous laugh. "I should probably not admit such things, should I?"

He chuckled. "It only endears you to me more." He bent closer until his breath fanned her face. He touched her lips, the briefest of kisses. Best to savor, to wait until the moment was right. "I must return to Kedesh-naphtali to set my house in order. Then I will come for you." He straightened. "That is, if Kedesh is where you wish us to live. I have a house there, but it is the place I shared with Nessa." He searched her eyes for some reaction to his first love's name, but she showed no hint of anger or jealousy.

"I would live with you anywhere," she said, smiling. "But I would make your house my own, if you do not mind." She grew bolder then, placed a hand on his chest, and leaned close. "If it is I you are to marry, then it will become your home and mine.

We will lay Nessa's memories to rest, yes?"

He nodded, for he was not sure he could even speak in that moment. And for another, heady moment, she looked as though she would meld into him, forcing him to kiss her. But she stepped back, giving him space to breathe again.

"If you would rather we live in your parents' village . . ." he began, but stopped at her upraised hand.

"I would rather follow where you lead, Barak. A woman goes to the home of her husband. Your home is in Kedesh-naphtali, unless you want to live elsewhere. I will go where you go." She squeezed their fingers in a comfortable bond and looked into his eyes.

The longing to take her with him grew, though he knew things must be done in order and he must prepare the house to receive her. "The sound of the bridegroom will soon ring in the streets for you, my love," he said, his voice wavering with emotion. He swallowed. "Go home with your mother and prepare for my coming."

Talya's eyes gleamed with unshed tears, and a wide smile lit her beautiful face. "I will be waiting, my lord."

He released her then, despite his desire to pull her close and kiss her soundly. They must wait until the proper time. And suddenly that time could not come soon enough.

EPILOGUE

Lappidoth rang the bell from the tower in the city gate, then took the steps two at a time and ran all the way home. "He is coming!" he called to merchants and neighbors he passed along the way. "The bridegroom is coming for my daughter!"

He reached the courtyard of his home, his breath coming fast. "Deborah! Talya!" His daughters-in-law emerged from the house to the courtyard, scrambling after his grandchildren.

"She is sitting on the dais in the house," Libi said, smiling into his eyes. Such beautiful girls were his daughters-in-law, but none could match the beauty of his little girl. A catch in his spirit brought a sudden lump to his throat. Talya. She no longer belonged to him but to Barak, whose entourage of men and singing women could be heard even now coming from the direction of the city gate.

470

"Deborah!" He hurried into the house, searching, but it took only a moment for his eyes to grow wide at the splendor his sitting room had become. Talya sat decked in a striped, multicolored robe, her hair covered in a filmy veil bordered about her head with a garland of fragrant rose of Sharon. Ten maids and cousins, including Yiskah, stood around her all chattering and laughing.

Deborah appeared at his side. "He is coming?"

Lappidoth looked into his wife's dark, anxious eyes. "Yes. Can you not hear him?"

The chatter ceased, and all of the girls seemed to lean toward the door as one.

Talya gasped and raised a hand to her throat. "He is truly coming for me?"

Lappidoth looked at his daughter, his own voice catching in that moment. How could he let her go, this child who had eased so much of the burden he felt when he seemed incapable of pleasing Deborah? And yet, he saw the moisture, the wild excitement, bubbling just beneath the surface. She loved Barak, and she could not wait for the moment of his knock upon their door.

He felt Deborah's touch on his arm. "It is a good match," she said, smiling at him.

He nodded. Of course it was. "Yes."

The sound of the bridegroom drew closer,

the songs louder. The maids surrounding Talya started to flutter like the wings of a butterfly, releasing anxious giggles here and there. And then, all at once, sound ceased. Barak knocked on the outer door.

Lappidoth's palms grew damp as he turned to open the door to this man, his new son-in-law. The man who would take his daughter away to be with him where he lived. Away from the home he and Deborah had built for her all of her life. The home where he had watched her grow from infant to mature woman. What would he do without her?

He sensed Deborah's presence beside him as he opened the door to Barak. "I have come to claim my bride," Barak said, his voice booming in the small sitting room.

Lappidoth stepped aside to let him pass, watching as he walked to the dais where Talya waited and knelt at her feet. Barak took Talya's hand and kissed it. At that same moment, Deborah slipped her hand in his.

"I love you, Lappidoth," she said softly, leaning close to his ear, while Barak spoke words of promise to Talya and laid gifts at her feet.

Lappidoth turned, facing her, the words heady and unfamiliar in the same moment. He touched her cheek. "What did you say?"

Surely his mind was playing tricks on him on this day of such monumental change for them all.

She stood on tiptoe, for he had always towered over her, and kissed him lightly on the lips, her touch lingering longer than he expected. "I love you," she whispered. She placed her free hand on his chest and leaned closer. "On this day of all days, and from this day forward, I wanted you to know."

He looked at her, unable to pull his gaze away from the vulnerable warmth in her eyes. Voices erupted around them, the men and women surrounding Barak filled the room, and singing ensued. Talya and Barak sat side by side on the dais while neighbors and family members, well-wishers, came to present them with gifts to start their new life.

But Lappidoth suddenly had eyes for only one woman. The woman who had captured his imagination from that first day he had seen her at the well and watched her at the village wine treadings. The woman who had given birth to his three children and held his heart captive for as long as he could remember. The woman he had always known was chosen of God to do great things — things he was meant to help her do well by teaching her the law and all he knew.

The woman whom he would love with all of his heart and would live with the rest of his life.

Deborah.

NOTE TO THE READER

Thank you for taking the time to read Deborah's story. I know I say this often, but in this case it is truer than most — this was a book I did not think I could write, one I actually turned in early and took back because it just wasn't working. A book I dreaded.

Why? In Scripture, Deborah seemed too perfect. We know so little about her other than she judged Israel and wrote a victory song. Oh, and a brief mention that she was the wife of Lappidoth. (Though some interpret that to mean other than a literal wife, I chose to believe Lappidoth was a real man and her real husband.) Still, how does one come up with a story with so little information?

While much of the story did come from imagination, this is where research and attention to detail come in. For instance, Sisera and his mother are mentioned in

Deborah's victory song, which gave a springboard to imagine what kind of woman is mother to a terrorist. This is not to place blame on parents for the choices of their children, but in Sisera's case, based on Deborah's song, we get a glimpse of a woman who probably fed her son's rage and savagery.

In stories like this, it also helps to bounce ideas off a friend or critique partner. The idea for Talya came from such a discussion, and now I can't imagine the story without her in it.

Another clear picture that emerged had to do with what it might be like to live with terrorism. With the constant barrage of militant extremists attacking innocent people all across the Middle East and beyond — even on our own shores — it was not hard to imagine. Terror is very real and has been for millennia. Deborah and Barak lived in such a time as this. And suddenly her story didn't seem so impossible, nor she so perfect. Undoubtedly, Deborah felt anxiety, even fear, over Sisera's advances, and concern for her family, her clan, and her country.

The final help came from two friends who came to my rescue when I knew the story wasn't working. They helped me see that I had to address how Deborah came to be the only female judge mentioned in Scripture, and to give more detail in her relationship to her husband. I could not have finished the book without their input.

As with every biblical novel I write, I do hope you will turn to Scripture and read Deborah's story there for yourself in Judges 4 and 5. As God had mercy on Israel when they cried out to Him for help and relief from the terror, may we also cry out to the Almighty One in our own time of need.

Until He Comes,
Jill Eileen Smith

ACKNOWLEDGMENTS

"Thank you" always seems like an understatement when it comes to writing a book, but here is my humble attempt to give credit to those who were such help and inspiration to me along the way.

Thank you to all of the people at Revell, particularly to my editors, Lonnie Hull DuPont and Jessica English; my marketing manager, Michele Misiak; and my publicist, Claudia Marsh. Also to Twila Bennett and Cheryl Van Andel, who do more than I can imagine — and Cheryl, your covers are always phenomenal! Thanks always to my agent, Wendy Lawton, who loved Deborah before I did, and who prays for clients and makes them feel like friends.

Super thanks go to Jill Stengl, Kathy Fuller, and India Edghill for help with this story. I can't even find words! This story needed you. I needed you! Thank you for reading early drafts and later editions and helping me find the problems I couldn't see.

Thank you to my readers who patiently wait while I plug away at these stories, who pray for me, because I honestly don't know where I would be without the Lord's guidance every step of the way. My prayer team — you know who you are — I really appreciate you.

To my friends who are there when I need coffee or lunch or just long to "phone a friend" — you are some of the most precious gifts God has put into my life. Thank you for being there.

To my family, immediate and extended, who willingly share their lives with me. I don't take you for granted for a single moment. Randy, Jeff, Chris and Molly, Ryan and Carissa — you are my heart and soul.

Adonai Elohim, my Lord, my God, my Creator, the giver of creativity, the one who inspires us to dream — I don't know if my version of Deborah's story comes close to Yours, but I'm grateful You shared her life with us in Scripture. For however little there is recorded, there is surely something she can teach us — things she has already taught me of Your holiness and grace. And her song of victory, of thanksgiving, of joy, is one that isn't necessarily easy to understand in every detail, but it is one of the few

You have chosen to record in history. Songs of thanksgiving after a great victory are a wise way to share in Your glory. And after completing this difficult story, I share in her song.

Thank You.

ABOUT THE AUTHOR

Jill Eileen Smith is the author of the bestselling Wives of King David series and *The Crimson Cord,* as well as the Wives of the Patriarchs and the Loves of King Solomon series. Her research has taken her from the Bible to Israel, and she particularly enjoys learning how women lived in Old Testament times.

When she isn't writing, she loves to spend time with her family and friends, read stories that take her away, ride her bike to the park, snag date nights with her hubby, try out new restaurants, or play with her lovable, "helpful" cat Tiger. Jill lives with her family in southeast Michigan.

Contact Jill through email (jill@jilleileen smith.com), her website (http://www.jill eileensmith.com), Facebook (https://www.facebook.com/jilleileensmith), or Twitter (https://twitter.com/JillEileenSmith). She loves to hear from her readers.

The employees of Thorndike Press hope you have enjoyed this Large Print book. All our Thorndike, Wheeler, and Kennebec Large Print titles are designed for easy reading, and all our books are made to last. Other Thorndike Press Large Print books are available at your library, through selected bookstores, or directly from us.

For information about titles, please call:
  (800) 223-1244

or visit our Web site at:
  http://gale.cengage.com/thorndike

To share your comments, please write:
  Publisher
  Thorndike Press
  10 Water St., Suite 310
  Waterville, ME 04901